SUSPENDED
IN DUSK

EDITED BY SIMON DEWAR

BOOKS OF THE DEAD

"CHANGE, LIKE SUNSHINE,
CAN BE A FRIEND OR FOE,
A BLESSING OR A CURSE,
A DAWN OR A DUSK."

WILLIAM ARTHUR WARD,
1921-1994

Book & Cover Design by James Roy Daley
Edited by Simon Dewar

SUSPENDED IN DUSK

BOOKS of the DEAD

Collection Copyright 2014 by Simon Dewar

For more information, contact: Besthorror@gmail.com
Visit us at: Booksofthedeadpress.com

Table of Contents

Introduction
Jack Ketchum

News of your first published novel is a hell of a moment for any writer. Of course it is. Simple reason. What it means is that you've established beachhead on one of the most sought-after, disputed, out-of-the-way islands in the creative world. To a lesser degree, so's your first published story. It means you've gotten off a very crowded boat. And you're headed toward shore.

Whether you're in the business of writing or not—but especially if you are—you know this. *A First means something. A First is to begin to unravel promise, trajectory, maybe even a future.* It's time to throw your hat in the air, kiddo. You've done something.

It seems to escape most of us that the same is true of editing your first anthology. It doesn't seem to be quite as big an accomplishment somehow, does it. We seem almost to think anybody could do it. All you need is the publishing connection and a bunch of good stories, right? You pick the best of them. So what's the big deal?

Ask any good writer who's been at it for a while now, who's appeared in more than just a few anthologies in his day.

The big deal is the company.

Not the corporate company, for god's sake. The *people*. The other writers you're surrounded with.

And there's only one way to get really good company.

Your editor. Who elicits and then selects the company. His or her intelligence, sensitivity, and taste. His or her determination that this is going to be special, as special as that novel you know you'll remember for years to come. *That* good. That strong. That extraordinary.

There are editors working today who have been devoted to digging out the extraordinary for years now—and among those of us who write horror and suspense, their names are practically legendary. Ellen Datlow, Richard Chizmar, Tom Monteleone, Stephen Jones, Peter Crowther, to name a few. Then there are younger, newer editors planting their own solid flag on the beach. I'm thinking of guys like K. Allen Wood, who edits SHOCK TO-TEM, Michael Bailey, editor for CHIRAL MAD and Richard Thomas, editor of THE NEW BLACK.

If really powerful, really imaginative short horror fiction is thriving these days—and it is, friends, amazingly so over the past few years—I hold editors like these largely responsible. They're favored with great good taste. They're not throwing together the biggest names or the theme antho *du jour* and calling it a good day in publishing. They're working to find the best. There's a real devotion, a hunger in the blood, to show us how really good it can be.

SUSPENDED IN DUSK is Simon Dewar's first anthology and as such, should be celebrated—because I'm scenting that same fine hunger to deliver up the best and brightest in this one. It's an auspicious debut.

Many of the writers in this book—in fact, most of them—are pretty new to me. In and of itself cause for personal celebration on my part, because I love being surprised by the new guys. I welcome them into the fold. The more the merrier.

Back in 2003 I wrote an introduction to Tim Lebbon's WHITE AND OTHER TALES OF RUIN, in which I mentioned an evening a few years back sitting around at the bar of some convention or other, with a bunch of us old-fart writers bemoaning the shallow, derivative, by-the-book junk we'd been seeing lately and wondering where the hell the new blood was.

At the time it seemed a serious question. We were all of us somewhere in our fifties. Stephen King, Richard Laymon, Thomas Tessier and T. M. Wright were all born in 1947. F. Paul Wilson, Tom Monteleone and I were born in '46. Peter Straub and David Morrell were three years older than us. And Charlie Grant, *four* years older still.

We were getting up there.

So where was the new generation? Where were the torch-bearers? Where were *the kids?*

We named names and couldn't come up with many. Edward Lee. Graham Joyce. John Skipp. John Shirley. A couple of others.

We grumbled into our beer.

And then, not much later, that quiet, exuberant explosion of writers born in the 1960's and '70's occurred. Tom Piccirilli, Neil Gaiman, Brian Keene, Christopher Golden, Tim Lebbon, Gary Braunbeck, Bentley Little, Sarah Langan, and Joe Hill among others. Inventive, serious writers who knew how to scare you and have fun with you, challenge your mind and engage and break your heart.

Since then they've spawned enough healthy offspring to fill the pages of the books and magazines mentioned above and quite a few others. SUSPENDED IN DUSK sits squarely within those healthy parameters.

You're in good hands here.

* * *

Over the span of years I'm talking about, another important expansion has taken place. We horror readers in the U.S. have finally gotten our short-form British Invasion.

Twenty years ago I dare you to have found a new U.K. horror novel published here in the States that wasn't written by James Herbert, Graham Masterton, Ramsey Campbell—whose story included here is a dilly, by the way—Clive Barker, or Brian Lumley. I dare you to have found any *anthologies* whatsoever.

SUSPENDED IN DUSK is proof positive that those days of want are over. Of the nineteen stories Dewar has collected here only five come from American writers. Four are by Australians, three are South African, and seven from writers in the U.K.

One of the reasons I've always enjoyed Martin Cruz Smith's Arkady Renko novels—GORKY PARK, POLAR STAR etc.—is that while as a reader I'm perched on the tried-and-true ground of the hard-boiled detective novel, I'm also a total stranger in a strange land, culturally speaking. Smith's Moscow is as unfamiliar to me as the moon. And much more interesting. Likewise Stieg Larsson's Sweden or Rogert Smith's Cape Town. If you're at all like me, in these books, unfamiliarity enriches the experience of reading them. As it does in so many of the stories, ahem, *SUSPENDED* here.

So let's see what we've got.

Some fine, all-new stories—*did I mention that they're creepy as hell? They are.*

Fresh voices speaking from fresh locations.

And a brand new editor in town staking his claim on the territory.

Me, I'm good with that.

Congrats on your First, Mr. Dewar. Here's to many more.

Jack Ketchum is the author of over thirty books -- novels, novellas, story collections, essays, poems, reviews and plays. He is translated in twelve languages, is the four-time winner of the Bram Stoker Award and a Shirley Jackson Award nominee. Five of his novels have been made into feature films—THE LOST, THE GIRL NEXT DOOR, RED, OFFSPRING and THE WOMAN, the last of which was written with film maker Lucky McKee and which earned him and McKee the Best Screenplay Award at the Sitges Film Festival in Spain. His novella THE CROSSINGS was cited by Stephen King in his 2003 speech at the National Book Awards. In 2011 he was chosen Grand Master by the World Horror Convention.

A NOTE FROM THE EDITOR SIMON DEWAR

After such a fantastic introduction from Jack, I'll keep this short and sweet. I was very honoured to work with a fantastic bunch of writers on this project. Check out their other works, you won't be disappointed.

When I began the SUSPENDED IN DUSK project, I sorted through the stories, reading and pondering—wondering how they'd coalesce together into something more. It wasn't long before the stories themselves told me what the anthology was to be about.

When I looked at the diverse collection of stories, many of which were about dusk or were set at the time of dusk, something else occurred to me. As much as they were about a change in the time of day—they were about change itself.

In some cases the stories collected here were about a character's experience through a period of great change. Or about a person—or even a society—that is trapped on the brink of change. Trapped in the dying days of something—like dusk is the dying light of day. Like dusk is the time between the light and the dark. A time between times.

Some of the stories are about people who trap or collect things. Others are about people who trap themselves.

Some of these stories are very literal interpretations of the title theme; some are metaphorical. Some are obvious, and others are little more obscure. Keep an eye peeled and see if you can spot the connections I made, or perhaps see what connections you can draw yourself.

But more importantly, dim the lights, get comfy and enjoy the ride.

* * *

Thanks to Amenah and Habibah for their love and support. Without you none of the good things are possible. Nerine Dorman for her patience in teaching me the basics, and for setting me on a good path. The Canberra Speculative Fiction Guild peeps (and extended family), for all their encouragement and support. Roy for giving me a shot. Dallas, Kaaron and Jonathan for your time and kind words.

Shadows of the Lonely Dead
Alan Baxter

His eyes are tight with pain as he turns away from me, buries his frustration in the pillow.

"Something I said?" I ask nervously. "Or did?"

He shakes his head, rustling against the duvet pulled up tight under his chin. "I'm sorry. It's not you... I can't... This has happened before, I... I don't know why."

"It's okay. We don't have to. No pressure, you know."

He sniffs, turns it into a humourless laugh. "Sorry. I'm damaged goods."

I put a hand on his shoulder, remove it quickly as he stiffens. "Oh, Jake, don't say that, it's okay. It happens to loads of guys, but no one ever admits it. Stay here, just sleep, you know."

He nods. "Maybe in the morning?"

"Sure."

* * *

I don't push for anything in the morning. Something difficult is happening and I like him too much to scare him off. I make coffee and bring it to the bedroom. He's beautiful, a wave of dark hair half obscuring his face, cheeks dusted with two day's growth. He smiles softly as I creep up to the bed.

"I'm awake."

"Hi there."

We stare at each other for a moment, still getting used to how the other looks, everything so new.

"Sorry about last night," he says. "First time I stay and I can't..."

I hold up one hand, pass the coffee with the other. "Doesn't matter. We've got plenty of time, right?"

His smile comes back. There's an edge of melancholy that seems to live behind his eyes, but that smile pushes it away like a breeze behind clouds. "I guess so. Thanks."

"Take your time getting up, have a shower and stuff if you want. I need to get ready for work. I start at ten."

* * *

The hospice is quiet as I enter. Mary offers me a subtle nod from the reception desk and I push through double doors into the smell of carpets, disinfectant and death. Claire Moyer catches my attention, coming the other way.

"Mr Peters last night," she says. "About three."

I nod. "Thought so. His family there?"

"No. No one."

I shrug and walk on, drop my coat and bag in the nurse's station. Poor old Mr Peters. His daughters stopped visiting about two weeks ago, when he started to spend more time asleep than awake. It doesn't really matter. We all die alone.

Even people surrounded by loved ones are utterly alone as they slip away, the sea of grief around them unnoticed. Death is the only truly personal thing there is. No one can ever understand it, even someone like me. I've seen death take people hundreds of times, held their skeletal hands as the darkness closes in and their breaths stretch further and further apart until they don't breathe again. But I have no idea what it's like.

I check the roster, see who needs medication, bathing, feeding, simple company. I knew Peters was leaving last night. I hope he didn't realise his daughters had stopped coming, but it's surprising what gets through the haze of terminal illness. Even as their minds go and they forget the faces of people they've known their whole lives, moments of clarity spike through the deterioration like lighthouses sweeping the night and they ask, "Where's my wife?" "Where's my son?" And they know they're alone whether those people are there or not and the last of their resolve crumbles as they slide into that stygian unknown.

Edie Sutton is on my list. She needs a wash, and a feed if she's up for it. Doubtful she'll eat, she hasn't managed more than a couple of teaspoons of jelly a day for almost a week now.

I'm surprised to see her awake as I enter, eyes wet and frightened in the glare of spring through thin cotton drapes. I take a sponge lollipop, dip it in the glass of water beside her bed and gently press moisture to her cracked lips. Her chin quivers as the liquid rolls over her desiccated tongue. "That taste good?" I ask quietly.

Her eyebrows rise, the almost translucent skin stretched tight across her skull wrinkling like tissue paper. "Tired." Her voice is barely audible, but you get used to listening for their words, every syllable a struggle.

"Had enough, huh?"

Tears breach her red, sagging eyelids and she nods ever so slightly.

"You can go whenever you like, love," I whisper.

A moment of softening around her eyes. "Can I?"

"Of course you can. You've seen everyone you were waiting to see."

"My Damon?"

"He'll be here at lunchtime." Her son. Visits regularly as he works nearby, sits with her every evening for hours. "Another couple of hours."

She closes her eyes and her exhalation is slow and weak, like heat escaping a long summer day. *She'll be gone soon, I'll have to keep a close check.* I lift her hand, a collection of brittle sticks loosely attached to an arm like old bamboo wrapped in papyrus, check her radial pulse. *Barely there and so slow.* I let my mind pass through my touch, search out the decay and failing organs, take the shadows of her dying softly into myself. *I can't cure her, but I can collect the scourge, its malice.*

A dark stain spreads into me and I store it away.

* * *

The day goes slowly and quietly. It's usually quiet here, except those moments when someone cries out, sudden terror giving voice to weakened lungs as they momentarily face their mortality without the softening armour of fatigue or drugs. Or the howls of grief, sometimes from friends and family, sometimes from the sick themselves. Sometimes both.

I clean up Kathy Parsons, who's been uncontrollably shitting viscous blood onto plastic sheets for more than a week now, check her meds. She exudes the sickly sweet, cloying odour of death. She's terrified. Only forty-eight years old, eyes always wide in child-like fear, but she's got a little while to go yet. A little while to reach some kind of acceptance, though not all of them do. Some are gasping in disbelieving horror, even with their last breath. Almost everyone dies scared, especially the young ones. Some people are calm and accepting, content as they drift away, but they're rare, usually very old. Everyone has time to think as they lie here, suspended in the last darkening hours of their life. It's good that some find peace in that mortal dusk.

I reassure Kathy as much as possible, sit with her as a sedative soaks through her struggling veins.

Edie's pulse is almost gone when I check her again an hour later, breaths so far apart every one seems certain to be her last. I call her son to tell him he needs to get here, but his phone goes to voicemail. I leave a message imploring him to hurry if he can.

I pull the chair up beside her bed and take her fingers in my palms, rest my forehead against the back of her hand. Her frailty wafts into me and I soak it up, gather that insipid, creeping death into my cells. *It can't hurt me. I don't know why, but it can't. So I collect it. I don't know why I do that either. Because I can.* It doesn't heal them or ease their suffering, but at some level I like to think they know I share their pain and that offers some subconscious solace.

Edie's pulse weakens until I can't feel it any more. Her breaths are tiny, sharp intakes, almost imperceptible, more than ten seconds apart. Her exhalations are silent, air leaking from lungs little more than deflated sacks of inert offal.

Fifteen seconds apart. She's going.

Her life leaks into the air and the shadow of her sickness, her fear and loneliness, washes through me and she's gone. I shudder with the gift she's given me. My hands tremble as I stand and move away to mark her chart, dimness swimming behind my eyes.

Her son is hurrying along the hallway to her room as I emerge and his face falls when he sees me.

"I missed her?"

"I'm sorry. Only just. She passed moments ago. But she didn't wake again since this morning."

He barks an uncontrollable sob and tears tumble over his cheeks. We're all five years old when our mothers die. "I can see her?"

"Of course."

I'll send the counsellor down with the relevant pamphlets after he's had some time alone with her.

* * *

Not much else happens through the day, which pleases me. It's terrible when more than one patient dies in a day, as the first one feels somehow cheated of their time in my mind.

Jake is parked outside when I get home, an embarrassed smile twitching his lips. "Hi."

I'm so pleased he's there. "Hi." I had wondered if I might not see him again. Our few faltering dates that led to our first night together had been cautious but full of hope. When something got in his way last night, I worried it would frighten him off.

"Try again?" he says, holding up a bottle of red.

"I'd really like that. I have some steaks in the fridge and wait till you try my potato rosti."

* * *

We gently fumble at each other's clothes, clumsy with nerves and the dull edge of the wine. Edie's death still floats around me, within me, but that helps. I embrace it. Nothing makes me hornier than death. Something about mortality reminds us at a level beyond thought of the importance of contact, of touch, of the life within lovemaking.

I'm not too proud to admit I usually masturbate a lot in the privacy of my home after we lose someone. It's unavoidable, the desperation to feel alive—to feel *life*—especially when I've absorbed the death into my marrow like I do. I hope Jake can see it through this time.

14

I'm as gentle as I can be, as caring as I know how. He shivers and stiffens with nerves as I run my hands across his shoulders. He looks into my eyes, a nervous smile. "It's okay, I'm sorry. I want to." He reaches back and unclips my bra, lets it drop beside the bed.

"You are so lovely," he whispers.

There's tension, fear, but he keeps assuring me I should continue and so I do and he eventually performs. It's soft and urgent, but electric. Afterwards he grabs hold of me and hugs me against his chest so hard I have to gently force a breath into my constricted lungs.

"That was wonderful," he whispers, his hot breath tickling my ear.

"It was," I say. "I'm glad."

He holds me tight and his breathing changes. He turns his face away. I push away to look at him and tears stand in his eyes.

"I'm sorry," he whispers.

"Are you okay?"

"Yes, really. It's hard to... this is difficult for me. But please, don't feel bad. I just can't help it."

"Anything I can do?"

He smiles, leans down to kiss me. "Just keep being so nice to me."

"That's easy."

I settle beside him and turn to let him spoon me, push myself back into the curve of his body. He's so warm and strong and vibrant—the opposite of poor Edie's hard, cool, frailty, all jutting bones and oxygen tubes.

"Was someone less than nice to you?" I ask, biting my lip the moment it's out. Probably not the thing to say.

"Something like that."

I stroke his hand, not game to risk saying anything else, ask for any more of his secrets.

"I'll tell you one day," he says, voice thin with pain.

He holds me tight until we fall asleep. It's good to have someone so alive to hold on to, a beacon against the shadow of all the death in me.

* * *

The days at work pass slowly and my hours rotate to nights. I prefer the solitude and peace of the night shift, and most deaths happen then. It's strange how people who have been unconscious for days or weeks almost always seem to slip away in the depths of the night, like they know somehow that leaving while the sun shines is unusual. I remember Edie dying in the middle of the morning; her shadow still drifts through me, the echo of her disease. It's all that's left behind, her life and body far away now.

We haven't lost anyone for nearly a week. The orderlies are taking bets on how much longer it'll be. Sam's aiming high, reckoning another few days. Marek is less confident, thinking Mr Patel will die tomorrow. They're both wrong. Jack Oswald will die tonight, maybe in the next two hours, three at the most. I can *feel* it. I've always been drawn to death, always offended by the hopeless indignity of it. And I've always sought to care for the dying, take into myself something of their pain, a memory of their suffering. I was destined for this career.

I pad into Oswald's room, put a hand against his cheek. It's very cool, his eyes flickering gently behind thin, pale lids. I was wrong—it's happening already. No one to ring for old Jack; he has no one to come. "Last of a line and good riddance," he said to me when he arrived three weeks ago.

"You can't be all bad," I'd said, and he laughed.

"Not bad, really. Just not much good either. Never had kids, wife died twelve year ago. Worked fifty years for fuck all and here I am being tucked away in a corner to die alone."

"We all die alone, Jack," I said, an attempt to soften his hurt.

"Yeah, but there's alone and alone, ent there."

Darkness swells up in him. He hasn't woken in five days. He had a drip in his arm feeding him a bare minimum of hydration, anti-nausea medication and painkillers—a poor simulation of normal life while he dies—but we took that out a few days ago. He's a skeleton under linen stamped with the name of the hospice.

He'd asked me the week before to speed it up for him. "Can't you jab me wiv somefing, make it happen? What's the fucking point in hanging on?"

I'd told him I wished I could, and I meant it.

We wouldn't let our dogs and cats suffer like this but we'll happily put our own parents away to wither and waste into ignominy and despair. They deteriorate to frightened babes again as everything they've ever been deserts them, and we think it's the humane, moral thing to do, to let that happen. To watch it happen while we tell them everything will be okay. Which is the worst line of bullshit we ever try to sell in a world powered by lies and deception.

Jack's eyes pop open, a flood of panic blanching his already ivory face. After a moment he focuses on me and nods, a tiny movement of understanding and he's gone. His darkness swells into me, the entropy of his illness drawn up through my hands where I hold his. It adds itself to the blackness I carry inside, that I've carried for so long. Will I fill up one day, no room for any more, and then what?

With trembling fingers I close Jack's eyes and fill out the paperwork. Marek will win the bet. His guess was closer even though they were both wrong.

* * *

"I want to tell you why sex is so difficult for me." Jake's face is creased with what looks to me like grief.

"You don't have to."

"I know, but I want to. We've been together a couple of months now and it feels serious. It is, isn't it?"

I nod vigorously. "Oh, I hope so." I really do hope so.

Jake draws a deep breath that shudders on the way down. "I never knew my real dad. He left when I was too little to remember."

I open my mouth to say something, I'm not really sure what, and Jake holds up a hand.

"Let me get this out in one, or I may not make it."

I nod and he smiles, squeezes my hand across the table.

"I don't mind not knowing him. My mum was young and irresponsible. She's always been fucking useless, so I can hardly blame my dad for leaving. It's what I did, first chance I got. She should have protected me, but she couldn't even protect herself." He draws another breath, sips wine. "My mum shacked up with Vic when I was about six years old. She'd knocked around with guys before then but never for long. She did her best by me, even though her best was bloody rubbish. But when Vic came along, every-thing changed.

"He drank heaps, was always on the edge of violence. Mum told me how much she loved him, but it was clear she was terrified of him too. She said how we needed him to pay the bills and he wasn't such a bad guy. Even with two black eyes and a split lip she'd tell me how he wasn't such a bad guy."

Rage flares in me and Jake can see it in my face.

"Let me finish." He reaches out, strokes my cheek. "You're such a good and decent person, the way you care for the dying. You're so good to me. You couldn't be less like Vic *fucking* Creswell." He drinks more wine, his hand shaking. "Anyway, it wasn't long before Vic started… touching me."

I let out a soft sound, part growl, part moan of dismay.

A tear breaches Jake's lashes. "I'm sorry, I need you to know this."

My knuckles creak as my fists clench in my lap. "I want to hear. You shouldn't carry this alone."

Jake nods, sips. "Anyway, he went from fondling and making me do things to him to raping me in very little time."

"You were six?"

"I was probably eight by the time he started that."

He says it like that makes it somehow better than if he were six. "What a fucking…"

"He ruled my mum and me, did what he liked to us. My mum should have protected me, but she was trapped too. He would beat her if she tried to intervene. Beat me if I threatened to tell. We lived in terror. When I was fourteen I told mum we had to go, we had to run away. She said we had no money, where would we go?"

"There are shelters," I start to say and Jake nods again.

"Of course, but that wasn't the point. You know what she said to me, after years of beatings and sexual assaults?"

I sigh and shake my head. "She told you she loved him."

"Yep. So I ran away. I have no idea what they're doing now. He could have killed her for all I know. I haven't spoken a word to her since I left. I was on the street at first, then in shelters and care. A foster home took me in when I was sixteen and I was a bastard, doing all the things my mum did and worse, acting like her boyfriends, thinking I was different."

"You're nothing like that," I say. "You're amazing."

He smiles, but it's not enough to chase away the melancholy this time. "My foster mother is a lady called Glenda Armstrong and she fixed me up. Wouldn't take my shit, made me finish school. I was lucky. She gave me direction. I got a job, turned myself around. Twenty-five now, finally feeling like I've got it somewhere near together. And then I met you. For the first time I feel something real, instead of just angry fucking because I thought that's all I deserved." His tears have stopped and there's anger in his eyes.

"You should be so proud of where you've come, given where you started," I tell him.

"But I'm scared and you mean a lot to me and that's why it's so hard for me to be intimate, emotional. It's always been an act before, an act of defiance more than anything else, a show of power. But with you, I have no guard and it's terrifying."

I stand, move around to hug him and kiss his hair. "I'm honoured," I whisper. "I'll never hurt you."

"I know."

The shadows of all the people who have died with me mask my vision, make Jake a distant blur. "So many wonderful people die every day, struck down by disease or age," I say. "And yet fuckers like that Vic get to live."

Jake nods against my chest. "There's no justice in the world. We have to hang on to our luck when we find it, because that's all there is."

* * *

After nearly a week of no deaths we get two in a day. The darkness wells inside me, that delicious blackness I can't help but gather. Sometimes I think it's going to overwhelm me, but there's always room for more. The journey home is muffled by the circling presence of their passing.

Jake comes around not long after I get home, bag of shopping in hand. "I'm going to make us a great dinner tonight. Special recipe! Something Glenda taught me."

"Great! I'm glad we're having a good dinner. I have to go away for a couple of days."

"That's sudden." His brow is creased in concern and it breaks my heart a little.

"There's a two-day course Claire Moyer was supposed to go on, but she's come down with something. Someone needs to go. It's about a new drug administration practice, and they asked if I'd step in. I head off early in the morning to Newcastle. I'll be away overnight, back by dinnertime the next day. Sorry."

He smiles. "Don't apologise. Work is work. Let's enjoy tonight then, eh? Maybe you can lend me your key when you leave and I can get my own cut? Then I can have something ready for when you get back on Thursday?"

I raise my eyebrows, give him a crooked smile. "Your own key?"

"If you think…"

I sweep him into a hug. "Of course I think. I'd love that."

* * *

It took a lot of searching to find this place, but hours of free time in a palliative care hospice can be put to good use with a search engine and access to hospital records. Hints from Jake about where he grew up and a keen eye. Plus friends in social services to join the dots. The idea, the realisation, hit me like lightning when Jake told me his story.

There's a broken down car on the front lawn, leaking oil across the dirt like black blood. The house is peeling. The paint reminds me of the skin of a dying woman's lips. I knock on the door, heart hammering against my ribs.

A large figure shimmers through the frosted glass panel and the door swings open. A man stands there in shorts and a stained shirt. He's a tall bastard, muscular, but a beer gut mars anything close to a good physique. He has muddled tattoos on his arms and legs, grey and black stubble across his face like a TV tuned to static. His eyes are dark and mean. "Well, hello, darlin'."

"Victor Cresswell?" I ask.

His eyes narrow. "What?" He glances to my hands, probably checking for a summons.

"*Vic* Cresswell," I ask.

"Yeah."

I hold out my hand. "It's nice to meet you."

His lip curls in a sneer and he takes my hand, squeezing too hard to assert his dominance as he puffs his chest out. "Nice to meet you too, sweetheart. What the fuck is this?"

And I let my darkness out. It rushes through my palm, desperate to escape, and races into him. I feel it gust up his arm, into his chest to nestle in his lungs. It wraps shadowy arms around his liver and coats his gallbladder in an inky embrace. It snakes through his intestines, finds his prostate and slips down into his balls.

A shudder ripples through him as I break our grip and smile, turn away.

"What the fuck was that all about?" he yells as I make my way back to the waiting taxi, a tremor in his voice.

As I tell the taxi to head back to the station Vic stands in the doorway, one hand rubbing absently at his throat. There's a patina of fear across his face. How much does he suspect? I give him a month at most before the decay begins to set in. Before the tumours start to blossom through his organs. Black, flowering death.

I'm empty inside, somehow hollow but with whiteness swelling into the places where I've collected all that dark over the years. Perhaps I shouldn't have let it all go, should make it last. It's disconcerting. I'm a little lost without the shadows of the lonely dead inside me. I'll have to start collecting again. No matter, at least three at work have less than a week left.

I knew I gathered it for a reason. A shame it took me this long to realise what my purpose is. I have a mission now, giving this unfair blackness to bastards truly deserving of it.

I'm going to be busy.

* * *

Jake is watching television and looks up in surprise as I enter the house. I'm glad he decided to stay at my place, not his. When the moment's right I'm going to ask him to move in.

"I thought you weren't back until tomorrow," he says, smiling. It's genuine happiness on his face and that warms me.

"We got through the training in one day and finished up in time for me to get the last train back. So here I am." I had taken into account that Vic might be harder to find, maybe not home. It had all been much easier than I anticipated.

"Well, that's a lovely surprise," Jake says, gathering me into a hug.

I breathe deeply of the clean smell of his skin. "Yeah," I say. "Maybe there is some justice in this world, after all."

Taming the Stars
Anna Reith

Michele

There was never a good reason to get in a car with Antoine. I should have known better. Perhaps the heat had fried my brain, turned it to a loose mush that filled my head like cotton wool. Of course, that would have made no difference. I was twenty. Whatever my head was or was not filled with, I still did my thinking with my cock.

* * *

It was so hot that summer that the tarmac melted and over a hundred old people died in Paris, while their relatives escaped into the lavender-scented countryside. If I'd had money I would have done the same. Unfortunately for me, I was too poor for vacations. I lived hand to mouth then—*tirer le diable par la queue*, as my grandmother used to say. Pulling the devil by the tail. I didn't think I'd ever see the day he'd turn around and bite me.

Antoine found me in a bar on Rue Saint-Denis, a narrow little building chipped out of the dirty limestone that faced much of the third arrondissement. It perched uneasily among the grim, tight-drawn shutters and whitewashed windows of the shops that surrounded it: seedy places that sold porno movies and dirty magazines, and had hookers' cards wedged under the cash register like so many pieces of forgotten chewing gum.

It was a cheap local workers' tavern, untouched by pretension or the march of modernity, and neither the old men nor the migrant Arab boys cared about the greasy pinkish reflections the red light district cast over their beer glasses.

I didn't notice Antoine come in at first. I was drinking a cold beer and thinking sour thoughts about the girl I'd intended to marry, who had been inconsiderate enough to fuck my brother and callous enough not to regret it.

"Michele!" Antoine clapped me between the shoulder blades with his wide, soft hand. He never had done a day's hard work in his life. "I've been looking everywhere for you, *mec*."

Antoine rarely wasted time looking for anyone who didn't owe him money, so I doubted that. More likely, he was here for the little blonde *morue* who could sometimes be found on the corner, and who—as Antoine put it—not only knew how to enjoy a good cigar, but also swallowed the smoke.

I squinted up at him, my lips still wet from the beer. The place his hand had touched felt sweaty and sticky, and the shirt clung to my back.

"What do you want, Antoine?"

He smiled broadly, but the expression hung off his mouth like a wet, greasy rag. One thing about Antoine: he never saw the point in pretending he wasn't full of shit. I almost liked that about him.

"I was looking for you," he repeated, sliding onto the stool beside me and still smiling that flimsy lie of a smile. "I want you to drive a car."

"A car?" I grimaced as I drew the cool beer bottle from my lips, watching the condensation slide down the dark glass neck, mostly so I wouldn't have to look at him. "What do you need me to drive a car for, *mec*? I'm no chauffeur."

Antoine caught the bartender's attention with a wave of his thick fingers. They always reminded me of andouillettes fresh from the barbecue, brown and blunt-ended, but tipped with rounded, pink nails glimmered as if he'd oiled them. Like me, Antoine's family had made the trip from North Africa a couple of generations ago—mine from Morocco, his from Algeria—making us both *petits beurs*. French-born melons, instead of the kind grown in the swelter of the Maghreb.

"It's just a little trip," he said, shaking his head from side to side as he smiled at me—a snake dancing its death-trance before it readied to strike. "What, you don't want to get the fuck out of this heat? Just a little trip to the countryside, *mec*. That's all it is."

The bartender brought Antoine a beer as I sucked the last life out of mine. I said nothing, and just watched our reflections in the mirrored cabinet behind the bar. Past my shoulder, the grimy window looked out onto the street and little fragments of the world beyond it seemed caught in the mirror the way a puddle nets broken pieces of the sky.

On the other side of the street, in the lee of a boarded-up tobacconist, two women were walking the awkward, peg-legged, hip-swinging hobble of girls in bad shoes. Dusk had settled over everything, blurring the edges of the buildings; the sun had sunk from the sky, and the city was finally losing the last of its second-hand daylight, those dregs of gold it clung to like a miser. I watched those girls, and imagined the sound of their heels on the sidewalk, the smells of their bodies… the taste of their sweat. I was sweaty. I stank like a butcher and, whether I trusted him or not, Antoine was right. I did want to get out of Paris, and out of this sick, festering heat.

"How far into the country are you going?" I asked, seeking out Antoine's reflection in the mirror's fractured gaze. "I can't take time off work."

"Bullshit, Michele!" He laughed companionably at me. "That old fuck you work for at the warehouse? He's so ancient he's probably too blind to know whether you're there or not. Get someone to cover for you, *med*! Or does he watch you so closely, eh? Staring at your ass all day, just waiting for a bite?"

Antoine's elbow dug into my ribs, and I winced.

"*Va t'faire!*"

He grinned all the wider and, despite every sensible thought I had left in my head, I said, "Well, maybe I could take a day."

"That's the spirit, Michele!" Antoine beamed. "It's only as far as Nantes. A bit farther, perhaps. A nice little gîte, belongs to the father of a friend of mine. *Tres bon chic, bon genre.* You know the type."

I nodded slowly. I did. Yuppies with cellular phones and gold watches. Who knew what they did with their spare time. I didn't ask why Antoine needed someone to drive him to Nantes. Not right away, at least. He bought me another beer, and asked about my girl, and agreed with me when I called her a bitch.

"There's a lot of pussy in Nantes," Antoine said as we watched one of the old men totter out of the bar and off down the darkened street, pausing only to glance furtively around him before he darted into the doorway of the porno store beside the old tobacconist. "The guy whose place it is? Always got plenty of pussy on tap, you know? Black, brown, white, yellow… you ever fuck an Asian chick, Michele?"

I shrugged again. "They're all pink inside, no?"

He laughed at that, and clapped me on the back with that soft hand of his. The air felt grainy, as if the heat had made it swollen and stale, and it was an effort to force it into my lungs.

"All I'm saying," Antoine said, very deliberately uncurling a finger from the neck of his beer and pointing it at me, "is we take a day, drive out there, I see Radouane, we get laid, we come home. You try to tell me that doesn't sound good."

It did. I swallowed the last of my beer and wrinkled my nose.

"I still don't know why you need a chauffeur," I said, a trifle petulantly.

Antoine smiled his sad rag of a smile… the one I should have known better than to trust. "The fuck do you think, *branleur*? I don't want to be bored on the drive. Besides, I want you to watch my back. You can do that, can't you, Michele? You know I'll make it worth your while. I've always been good to you, no?"

I nodded reluctantly. True, I could do what he asked, though I didn't see *why* he'd asked me. I guessed it was about drugs—it often was, with Antoine—but it puzzled me why he should need to go all the way to

23

Nantes for blow and pussy. Then again, if I was getting a little holiday out of it and all I had to do was drive, what the fuck did I care?

"All right," I said. "You got a deal, *mec.*"

Antoine grinned and—somewhere, somehow, at the very back of my mind—I would like to say I had a bad feeling.

Unfortunately, I was an idiot when I was twenty.

* * *

Esther

She straightened up, wiping the back of her hand across her mouth. Under the streetlamp's thin, ravaged glow, the last smear of red lipstick looked like black oil, and the faint orange light painted an eerie, ashy tone over her skin. There was no moon to speak of tonight, just a slender gold-stained echo of its edge suspended between clouds that tore across the sky like black rags. No stars. The so-called city of light all but blotted them out, numbed them, bathed the whole of the heavens in the reflection of its polluted glory.

In the pretty, touristy parts—the Bois, the Champs-Élysées, the *fin de siècle* facades and trendy nightclubs—everything was different. There, light pooled on the cobbles and the pavements, and the night made paintings of it, daubing impressionistic swathes of colour that outdid nature and decried the daylight.

Here, Paris slept. Here, the multi-storey car parks and the hypermarkets were square concrete carbuncles amid desolate streets, and the glamour was tucked away in boxes, kept for dreams and holidays. The lights still played against the sky—the Tower, with its blinking crown and coruscating scaffold, could be seen from certain attic windows—but, here, she saw them from the city's shadow. Apart, away… standing just beyond the glass, as she had always done. It was the same everywhere. It had been for as long as she remembered. Every place, every name, every time. Always the same. All of them.

Esther ran her tongue along the back of her teeth, hating the stale, salty taste. She pulled her cigarettes from the pocket of her pink leather jacket, patting herself down as she searched for her lighter.

Shit.

She didn't swear in French yet. Not in her head. Didn't think in the language at all, though she could speak enough to get by for daily living. *Donnez-moi le fric* was a good start. Her fingers brushed the greasy crumple of notes in the pocket of her skirt—purple, with Debussy's face on them, because even the damn money was fruity in this country—and finally closed on the lighter. Sparks burst in the darkness; a scatter of fire in the night, morsels of it coalescing into one sharp gout.

She lit her cigarette, pulled deep on the burn of ash against the cold air, and glanced dispassionately down at the mess she'd made. He was still crumpled against the wall, leaning like a half-crushed soda can, his unbuttoned pants and untucked shirt resembling ridges of creased metal, all careless folds and torn paper labels. She didn't know his name. Hadn't asked, didn't care. He had offered a nervous little cough of laughter along with the handful of banknotes that made her think of *Clair de Lune*, and she had rolled her eyes at the whole "I don't really do this" pose.

It was always the same. Different faces, different names, but the same old shit every time. Months, no, years now... she'd lost track of the time, just like she'd lost count of *them* and their stupid faces.

She'd thought it would be easier here. She'd come because she believed in new opportunities, and believed in the man who'd brought her. Paris was supposed to be special; the city of a million blinking stars, even if she *was* looking at them from the gutter. She had believed the press of the place crowding in would lend her some kind of anonymity, shield her silence with its noise. Plenty of those like her—the monsters in the shadows, those who embraced the bloody night—took that graceless abandon of big-city living as a gift. In places where buildings bit the sky like uneven teeth, everyone was always staring up, and no one noticed the meat go missing.

It was just the same as anywhere else, though. She couldn't breathe here, couldn't see... couldn't get past the choking sensation of so many minds, so many voices, so many people pushing on in their seamless desperation to exist. And the rot wasn't dry. There was a wetness to it that seeped under her skin until it met her own corruption, and it called to her irresistibly. It twisted her, swelled her up like a void and a beacon, made her one shrieking, dark flame that burned in the night and itched in the day, and she wasn't sure how much longer she could hold it back.

There was no way to calm it. Nowhere to run except back into the shadows, and not even the shadows were helping any more. The man at her feet had been the first in a long time. She knew he wouldn't be the last. It wouldn't even matter if she fled. Sure, she could hide away from herself—hide away from this life—but, in the dark, Esther was afraid she would become nothing but a relic, a shard of a creature split away, split open and devoid of what little humanity she had left. She would become a ghost whispering in the ruins, kissed by the moon and desiccated by the sun, part of nothing but her own amorphous madness.

She didn't want that. Didn't want to sink below the surface and leave no trace of herself. She wanted change.

Plenty of people—plenty of girls like her—believed in new starts. She heard those whispers time and again from the desperate and the optimistic. Dreams of cleanliness, rightness. New beginnings. Maybe it could happen for them—she doubted it, but maybe it could—if they could leave the taint and the rot behind. Most of them couldn't. Once the darkness bloomed in a person, its petals opened out like a great lotus, cupping souls like raindrops, swallowing them whole.

It wasn't fair, of course. It was always the same, everywhere, every*when*. There was never going to be anything different, anything easier, or anything better. Anyone who thought different was a fool. People like her—those rare, infrequent few, fashioned from another flesh—were not given the same grace. For monsters like her, there was no acceptance, no tolerance. No entitlement to the riches of normalcy. Believing anything else was just clinging to a fairy tale.

Esther sucked in her cheeks, sucked on her cigarette and let the gritty burn of it fill her up, drawing in the smoke just as she drew in the beast, remaking her body in a shell of innocence. She hadn't intended to kill him. This crumpled remnant of a man with his clothes awry and his limp dick hanging like a sad, lost sock… she'd only meant to take his money. One brief suck, one fleeting business transaction, and that would have been everything she needed. Even the dead had to pay rent, after all, unless they were prepared to waste away in the shit-stained, cardboard-walled hellholes that offered sanctuary for the penniless whores and crackheads. Men like Radouane kept their acquisitions in line by those methods: powdered white lies and cheap backhand blows, a dozen girls to one flat, hot-bunking or sharing space on the floor. You let him do you one favour and then you owed him, and he would never allow you to forget.

She supposed she should have known better. Perhaps she had. Perhaps she'd never trusted him in the first place. Perhaps all of this had simply been a choice. And this life did serve its purpose. It gave her the things she needed, the pretence at functioning within a part of the world, but it should never have lasted.

Now, she looked down at the body, and wiped the last flecks of blood from her cheek. Her time of penance was over. If it wasn't enough anymore, what was the point? Why keep pretending to be his pet, if he didn't keep her safe from herself?

No. It was over. Radouane Sehere could go and get fucked. Esther was leaving, and he could not stop her. He *would* not stop her, whatever she had to do to get away. She owed him nothing. Not anymore.

The light still painted her grimly, though now the shallow glow of the streetlamp outlined a face more human than not, the twisted shapes of hunger and need hidden beneath dull skin and an empty gaze. She put the cigarette to her lips again, tasting tar instead of blood, and she gave one more glance to the dead man by the wall, his throat ragged red lace and his left eye gnawed away.

Perhaps she should have felt guilty. Perhaps, once, she might have been able to, but there was nothing left in her now. No guilt, no shame. Just the dull ache at her centre, punctuated with the screaming pain of need. It filled her, gave her life where life had once been, and it drove her onward.

Esther zipped up her jacket, despite the night's warmth, and began to walk home. A few cars drifted past—one or two drivers sounded their horns for her attention, or called from their open windows—but she ignored them. She only needed a few hundred francs more, and she could go. Fuck Radouane. Fuck this city. She didn't know why she'd ever thought it was a good idea. There was no point in trying to hold onto the past, no point in trying to find something new. There was no secret paradise out there, no sudden key to unlock a perfect life, and she was as stupid as the rest of them for ever thinking it could happen.

She walked on, the cigarette smoke a dirty halo around her head, and the clouds continued to streak across the starless sky.

* * *

Michele

I met up with Antoine two days later, outside the pool hall that he liked to call his base of operations. He'd found a car: an ugly grey Citroën Visa with rust in the wheel arches and only one working headlight.

"The fuck is this?" I asked as I surveyed the wreck. "This thing is *foutue* before we start!"

Antoine just shrugged and smiled his unsmiling smile, so I got in and hoped the engine held out until Nantes, or wherever the damn place was supposed to be. We drove for almost four hours. The air in the car was stifling, hot metal and plastic stinking of rubber and staleness. Sweat ran down my back and the waistband of my jeans grew damp, my seat on the worn upholstery becoming a boggy swamp. Antoine rolled two joints and put a cassette on, blasting IAM through the open windows as we ripped along the autoroute. I enjoyed that early part of the journey—rap music and weed and one giant "fuck you" to the blue-haired little biddies and wrinkled old men we passed in the suburbs—but, as we neared the toll roads, Antoine broke out the whisky and attitude.

He started to talk, to complain and bitch about this guy, Radouane, and what a dummy he was. Antoine knew better, Antoine was going to run rings around him… all of that shit. He sat there, sprawled in the passenger seat, one foot up on the dashboard, smoking and swigging the booze, and I started to think that maybe I wasn't going to get a nice holiday. I started to feel afraid, and the pounding of the music against the beat of the sun and the road grit that blew in through the open windows began to give me a headache.

I couldn't complain, of course. You didn't complain to Antoine, because he would only respond by laughing at you.

When we were about half an hour from Nantes, he pulled out a gun.

27

"Fuck, *mec!*" I was so busy gawping at Antoine and his piece, I nearly plowed into a cyclist, and I had to swerve hard. "What the fuck?"

He just laughed at me, although for once at least it reached his eyes.

"C'mon, Michele. Don't pussy out, hey? I told you, we go there, I see Radouane… we get laid and, once all the business is done, we'll go home. Back in Paris by tonight, huh? All easy. Easy like slow dance, huh?"

Antoine held the gun up to his cheek, making kissy lips and swaying his head from side to side as the side of the flattish black muzzle pressed into his skin. If I hadn't been so freaked out, I'd have rolled my eyes and called him an asshole.

"You know what this is?" he asked, bringing the gun around in front of him, pointing it up at the roof. "You know what's special about it?"

I shook my head and kept myself focused on the road. It was coming up to lunchtime, but my whole day had already gone to shit. "No. No, I don't know."

"Glock 20," Antoine said proudly. "American. I look like Dirty Harry, eh?"

He laughed again, the fat end of the joint drooping from the corner of his mouth. I didn't want to say that Dirty Harry carried a Magnum, so I took the bottle of whisky he passed to me and buried my mouth in a big gulp. It burned the taste of the weed away and mixed the stale, hot air into something sour and acrid that coated my tongue. We weren't far from Nantes. I had been there once before, on holiday when I was a child. I didn't remember much about it, except that there had been a carnival: lights and music, all twisted together in one warped reality.

"Take a right," he told me, gesturing impatiently at the windshield, although at least he had put the gun down. "I know where I'm going, *mec.* Quickly!"

I shook my head, but followed his directions. There wasn't really much else I could do, although I was beginning to feel afraid, like maybe this was a holiday from which I would not return. Antoine had me skirt the main routes, driving way out past Nantes, toward the coast and, finally, the neat roads fringed with green grass and tidy, white little houses. The midday sun hid its face behind grey clouds, as if it was ashamed to watch us, and rain began to fall as Antoine piloted me toward a speck of nowhere just down the coast from Pornic. Everything was fields and trees, and we no longer played loud rap as we drove. Antoine called it "silent running", and held the Glock tenderly in his lap. He told me the place was quiet, set back up a long driveway with no near neighbours. I was to come in with him, but I better be ready to run back to the car and drive like a fucking madman. I started to think he might not be intending for both of us to get back to Paris… that maybe I was only ever supposed to go far enough to get him out clean.

Sweat pricked my palms as I nosed the Visa into the bare, gravelled approach that led up to the gîte. With nothing around but trees and swells of green—the last signpost I'd seen was for Monval—I could hear the echo of the sea beneath bird cries, though I couldn't see it. I was glad of that. I was a city boy; I wanted no part of any great, wide emptiness... no threatening void that only held horizons.

"Stop here," Antoine said, his face so very still and sullen.

Usually there was some hint of movement about him, some glance or glimmer of impatience that whispered of his dangers, but he was quiet now. Drawn in on himself.

I stopped the car on the grey driveway, within sight of the long, low house ahead. It seemed to cling to the ground like a limpet, hiding amongst the flourishing shrubs and borders; the kind of place that must once have been expensive, with a backyard the size of a field, and maybe a swimming pool. Now, though, it looked unkempt, uncared for... as forgotten as the memories of a dozen childhood summers. Lots of windows, but each and every one shuttered with blinds. I could see why Radouane had picked this place. It was private, remote... the kind of bashed-up, out-of-the-way old house that no one ever bothered to look at twice these days. No sign of anyone. Not even a dog barked. It was the kind of place no one would hear a damn thing, and my heart trilled behind my ribs, my palms wet against the wheel.

Antoine had tucked the gun into his jeans. He motioned me to follow him as he got out of the car and we began to walk toward the house, rain spotting against my face—cool and calm, like a benediction. Humidity purred in the air, and it seemed as if the rain should have smoked, each drop sizzling as it slipped through the heat.

I glanced at the gite, and thought I saw a face in the farthest window: a girl, dark-skinned and wide-eyed, yet unafraid. When I looked back, blinking through the thickening rain, she had disappeared behind the blinds once more.

Beside me, Antoine's lips curled into that snake-sway smile of his.

* * *

Esther

Radouane called it a party: his terminology for getting a bunch of girls together and shipping them off to take care of clients for a weekend. Any big deal, any major score he wanted in on—or anybody he'd managed to piss off, with his winning charm and top-drawer personality—and he applied them like bandages or buttercream, either patching up problems or sweetening the pot.

She had agreed to go, which was more than the other girls had. Two Macedonians, a Bosnian, and a couple of French junkies from the Loire... out of the six of them, Esther was the only one who spoke coherent

English. The Bosnian was almost as high as the French girls, and the Macedonians only spoke to each other—they seemed to have some intense and dubious bond going, given the way they clung to each other in the back of the van—so, especially considering her poor French, communication was limited. It didn't really matter.

Do a favour for me, Radouane had said when she returned. Back to roost, he called it. His blackbird. Like that shit was cute. *Go to Pornic and wait for me. I'll meet you there. It won't take long.*

She'd nodded, let him believe she still liked it when he touched her. Maybe he didn't see through it. Maybe he thought he was still playing her— that he'd played her in Illinois, when he offered to get her into France, offered her the new life she'd never have gotten any other way.

Esther didn't know much about his plan. Just that there was a deal worth a lot of money going on, and that some kid who hustled dime bags thought he could cut in. Radouane wanted to play the brat off against the big boys; scare him a little, perhaps. Maybe he planned to kill him. Maybe he planned to throw the deal in the first place and screw over the Slavs, or Germans, or whoever the hell was making the score this time. She didn't need to know, and didn't care to.

Dusk was drawing in when they arrived at the house, and Esther blinked as she stumbled from the van, staring up at the mingled hues of blue, purple, and red mixing like spilled paint or vivid bruises across the sky. Although it was undeniably beautiful, the echo of the daylight raised shivers on her skin. Esther belonged to the night, her darkness wrapped in its embrace, where no one could see the terrible things she did. As the shadows came for her—skimming across the flat, boundless fields, where the wind swallowed up sound—she feared them, and the things they would give her the freedom to do.

The boys who did Radouane's dirty work and cleaned up his messes, hung around on the house's grey gravel driveway; the red stars of cigarettes being lit, one by one, pricked the dimness.

She went inside with the others, and the feel of the place closed over her like a dark pond, damp-smelling and clammy. The heat outside seemed to have perfumed the air within, lending it a flavour, a texture... something that spoke of the summer's corruption. It made the beast stir within her, the flesh-print of a memory that rippled beneath her skin, stretching out in luxurious remembrance of the way it felt to feed. Tonight would be as good a night as any, she supposed. Like gutting fish in a barrel... but it would be better to wait a short while. Better to play along for now, to choose her moment. She'd been hiding in plain sight for so long that one more night shouldn't matter. Just one more, and then she would creep away.

This place was isolated. Quiet. Radouane's father owned several of them; holiday chalets, cottages, and villas rented out to *rosbifs* and other tourists. Esther doubted he knew what happened here in the fallow seasons... unless he was complicit in his son's schemes. Did he know? Did he sanction these empty times, allowing Radouane to fill the slow weeks with these jokes of human beings? Radouane arrived around ten that night, and the Slavs, or Germans, or whoever the fuck they were appeared less than an hour later. The entire place changed its face in a moment. Music, champagne... all the trappings of the party he'd promised them. Two of the men—shaven-headed white guys with heavy gold rings on their hands— had the Bosnian girl on one of the pale cream couches. She didn't seem to notice it much.

Esther was given one of the older men for a while. Back bedroom with a window that looked out across the fields, sky falling like a curtain over the spines of hedgerows and fluffed-up summer trees. On her back, upside down through the glass, the world beyond was an edgeless dark that grew thicker as she watched it. Thickened like cooling blood, like mud, like water freezing over. By the time he was done, it had grown impenetrable, impassable, pierced only by the tiny fires of stars lit within the cold. They winked at her, calling down to her and the beast she hid inside.

She dressed, went back to the room that held the booze, coke, and assholes, and Radouane greeted her with a smile and a joint. She was exotic tonight. *Américain*, they all insisted, and Esther didn't bother to correct them. She was the import, along with the whisky and the guns. The temptation to let her mask slip had rarely been stronger; her fingers itched for the feel of skin tearing beneath them, and the hunger for blood-salt made a home in her mouth. She wondered, as she often did, what they'd think if they knew what she was. Men like these did not believe in monsters. They always thought they were the scariest thing in the world—the biggest, the toughest, the meanest—as if their violence made them narrow, hemmed them in on all sides by its hardness.

The thought amused Esther. It almost made her want to hold out against temptation, to do all the things Radouane wanted tonight, and then to leave under the shadow of the next darkness... a quiet darkness, instead of one raging with blood.

For a while, she tried. She held onto the thought of the money and let the smoke curl around her, hoping it would numb the beast without gnawing away at her resolutions. Even monsters had to know restraint, and she wanted to believe she was capable of that.

After all, if a shadow is only given definition by the light, then a monster must find its shape outside the darkness.

She put the joint to her lips, and watched the dance the humans made, each one of them so convinced of his own superiority, as if they weren't all so fucking transparent. Radouane smiled, the sleeve of his black leather jacket skimming his chunky gold watch as he reclined back against the couch, his other hand a possessive weight on her thigh. Esther looked down at it as if his flesh was an improbability, a nothing blown against her like a fallen leaf caught in the breeze. Perhaps she should never have tried to believe that she could be a part of their world. No matter how secret she kept herself, how tightly she locked her hunger away, she was not of their kind.

She had no place among them. Perhaps the time to pretend anything different was past.

* * *

Michele

There was blood everywhere. I couldn't get past that. So much of it, smeared across the windows from the inside... and not just blood. Flesh, bone, maybe brain matter? I didn't know. I was no doctor, no mortician, no fucking psychopath who looked at the carnage we saw in there and thought it could have been wrought by human hands. Bodies lay on the beige carpet, the pale couches spattered red and the faded wallpaper redesigned with arcing spots and streaks of blood.

"Fuck, *mec*..." Antoine shook his head as we surveyed the mess inside.

The front door was unlocked, and nothing halted our progress as we moved through the gîte, encountering corpse after corpse. Men in black leather and gold, women with their bare breasts bloodied. It was a mess, a degeneration of flesh torn apart, laid out wet and glistening, and the stultifying air was thick with the smell of meat and copper.

Shots had been fired. At least three of the men in the main room still held their guns—Glocks, like Antoine's, and he laughed at that, motherfucking *laughed*—but no bullets could do the extent of what had been done here. I wanted to puke, to get out, to run away, but Antoine gravitated to the low coffee table in the centre of the room, smiling at the plastic-wrapped kilos streaked with red and brown. His head moved from side to side—that snake-strike dance—and he laughed to himself as he looked down at the body of the man slumped against the couch.

"Ah, Radouane," he murmured, unclasping the watch from the dead man's wrist. "I always said you'd get yourself in trouble, *mec*. Too much for you, the big boys' game, no?"

"Antoine, are you crazy? Whoever did this—"

"Relax, Michele." He turned to me with his false smile and his dead, dangerous eyes, the Glock held in one hand and the watch dangling from his fingers. "They just fucked each other over before we got here. It's fate, *mec*. Providence. Life is making it easy for me, huh?"

It was then that I saw how crazy Antoine really was. In my sweat-stained panic, my fear that made that hot, stinking room feel cold, I could see the edges of his madness, and the bare, hard face of the monster staring back at me.

A movement near one of the bedroom doors caught my eye, and we turned. I thought at once of the girl at the window and, at first glance, it could have been her. She was young, her black hair pinned back high and tight, but her pink leather jacket was riddled with bullet holes, and she was misshapen, miscast; a creature made to look human but wrought from different proportions.

Oddly elongated wrists forced her hands into a loose-jointed pose, blood-dipped fingers splayed and reaching out. Hips, back, neck… everything seemed shifted somehow, angled wrongly, and her chin, cheeks, forehead, and nose all hung crooked, swelling and moving beneath the skin. Lips peeled back from a raw, red mouth, that whole inhuman face rippling like water breaking beneath a stone.

Only her eyes seemed real: dark and wide, but more full of life than any I had ever seen. Unafraid, yet not brave through anger or blind fury. The stare that met mine was that of another creature entirely, and with it she looked straight into my soul.

I heard Antoine speak as he raised the gun. He called her a stupid whore, and I barely saw my hand move. I struck him, pushed him as hard as I could, sending the shot off-balance and him stumbling to the floor, falling among the dead.

He rose angry, angry like a wild dog, and yet his eyes still held that same dullness, that lie of life. I saw the Glock's flat muzzle swing toward me, heard the noise and saw the flash, but felt only the concussive force of the blow. No pain. I was aware of falling, of the preternatural movement of the girl as she sprang at Antoine and split his throat apart. His blood spattered my face with wet heat.

I tasted salt. How strange that she seemed more real than him… more honest, if not more human. Antoine gave one last gurgle, and the soft growl of the girl's breath scraped the air as she left him and moved closer to me. It brought with it the scent of blood, a heat that washed over me in bitter sourness.

Her teeth closed on my throat, and I knew nothing more.

* * *

Esther

She didn't know why she did it. She didn't know why *he* had done it, come to that. What human was moved to save a monster? But he had. He

33

had walked into that theatre of death—the scene of all that rage and mistrust—and he had tried to save her... and now he was dying on the threadbare carpet.

Radouane had shot first, killing one of the Slavs. That had been his plan from the start, though he'd over-reached himself, as usual. Always thinking he could have it all: keep the product, knock out the competition, kill the dime-bag boy—when he arrived—and be the big man left holding all the goodies. He always had been an idiot. Of course, it had ended poorly, ended in a firestorm that grew frenzied after the first bullets passed harmlessly through her. Suddenly, it had stopped being about the men, their money, and their macho pissing contest... it was almost funny to watch the ones who hadn't already shot each other come together in panic, firing blindly at the monster.

Silly, silly boys. Esther was not sure which she had killed and which were down to the number of bullets flying. After a while, between the feeding and chaos, it grew hard to tell which bits belonged to which body anyway. Perhaps it didn't matter. She ate herself sluggish, resting in the sunlit hours until the sound of tyres on gravel woke her.

She had been foolish, perhaps. She had certainly surprised herself.

Perhaps it had been something in his face, in his eyes... that moment of complete serenity as he turned on his companion, pushing the gun aside. He wasn't to know bullets couldn't hurt the dead. He had made a choice, allied himself with her against the other, even though she was clearly not his kind.

Esther hadn't expected that. Hadn't believed it was possible.

It had happened all the same, and she had seen the shadow-petals inside the other: dark flames that had long since burned out his core. She had seen it in the way he smiled as he'd fought back, raising the gun and then blowing a hole through her would-be saviour's chest. A callous, easy cruelty; a pleasure found in blood that was familiar to her, and yet which she wanted nothing more than to deny him.

He'd tasted rotten when she bit him. No sweetness in his blood, his life a bitter thing that had corroded within him. His death hung on her mouth like a mirror of her future, and it revolted Esther.

Perhaps that was why she spared his friend.

She knelt over the brown-skinned boy bleeding from the chest, and watched the ragged little gulps he made as his life edged away.

What did she hope to gain? She wondered at her reasoning, even as her fingers traced the contours of his clammy face. Perhaps she was just tired of being alone, being adrift... being the outsider. Perhaps she simply wanted to return the favour. He'd tried to save her and, though the gift of life was beyond her, maybe this was enough.

She leaned in and bit his throat with tenderness. The reasons no longer mattered once the act was done. It was irreversible, irreparable: her unliving life, halved and shared with him.

Esther bit him, and laid his head gently down among the corpses, sitting cross-legged in her bullet-pocked jacket to watch as he died, and woke from death. He cried, panicked, ranted. His fear was oddly soothing, because it gave her both time and reason to talk.

For the first time in so long, she poured out words. She told him her tale—her life, her death, and the undying, unliving existence that had followed—and for the first time the words didn't weigh heavy on her tongue.

He asked why, of course, just as she once had. She told him she didn't know.

She never had. There were no easy answers, no simple explanations. What was she? What was this body that bent itself around nightmares and became the horror of untold tales? All she could tell him was that it didn't matter. The words made up to match the monsters were fantasies, fairytales… they were inaccurate, untrue. Who knew how many monsters were out there, or how far they each differed from the other?

The boy—he said his name was Michele, and he was surprisingly cordial for someone in his current circumstances—glanced at the torn body of the man with whom he'd arrived. He rubbed at the bloodstained bullet hole on his T-shirt, and said something about how monsters all wore different faces.

Esther smiled. Perhaps she had been selfish. What did she think she had done here? Created herself a friend, a mate? Perhaps it was simply another form of the drive to feed that swelled within her in the night, or perhaps it was something unseen within *him*, something that had called to her and reached out a dark tendril of shadow, begging to be roused and made anew. Perhaps he was as terrible a creature as she was; perhaps worse. Only time would tell.

They talked out the long hours, furnishing them with questions he wanted to ask, and answers he was ill equipped to receive. Esther talked until the second night she had spent in that house fell, and Michele began to calm.

"Where do we go from here?" he asked her, as they sat among the stiff, ripe bodies, the smell of blood and copper still rich and sickly in the air.

Esther shrugged. There were no rules, no precedents. For all she knew, she had made a terrible mistake and, between them, they would either burn the world down and piss it all to ashes, or tear each other to pieces trying. Or, perhaps she had done him a favour, and bought herself the first slice of peace she had ever known. Perhaps, together, they would found a new world, a refuge for the beasts and the outcasts.

"I don't know," she said.

Michele nodded slowly, as if he hadn't expected anything else.

Outside, the dusk swelled into darkness, and Esther knew that—as it did—he would find his own beast blossoming. The seed that had been there all along would start to grow, and she would nurture it. After all, everyone has something monstrous inside them... and perhaps their kind were not destined to hide away, but to live alongside the world. In every shadow, in every corner, unafraid of the reflections of themselves they found in the eyes of their prey.

Esther looked up, and stared into the dizzying spin of a thousand stars, each one bright against the sky, an untamed jewel in the night.

AT DUSK THEY COME
ARMAND ROSAMILIA

They came at dusk the first night, silently from the woods surrounding the trailer park, half a dozen black shapes with glowing yellow eyes and sharp claws, like little dark children. They weren't trying to be stealthy. It was just natural for them. They'd been doing it for centuries, it seemed.

They came to me as I smoked from my old pipe, sitting in my rocking chair that no longer rocked. I leaned onto the side with the brick tucked underneath when I noticed the shadows parting from the other shadows, and they swarmed at me like bees that'd lost their buzz.

They talked to me that first night without moving their mouths, if they even had any. They were kinda in my head, if that makes any sense. It still doesn't to me.

They wanted to take someone back into the woods with them… they needed someone each night at dusk, and (just my bad luck) they found me first. Only, they didn't attack me…

They swore they would let me and my family live as long as I could offer up alternatives in the trailer park. I remember thinking about Becky Palmer at that moment, the bitch two trailers down who let her damn kids run wild while she watched her stories on the boob tube.

They nodded and walked off down the road, leaving me and my pipe to the silence of the night as darkness began to fall.

They never made a sound.

* * *

"Heard about Heffer Palmer?" Chuck Gill asked me the next morning before I'd even sat down in my usual spot at the counter. Boyette's Diner was only a short drive from the trailer park overlooking the drying river.

"How about a 'Hello, how's it going? Where ya been? How's the family?' once in a while? If I want to hear the local news I'll buy a fancy television box," I said. I waved for Mabel to bring me my coffee but she'd seen me traipsing through the parking lot and was already pouring it.

Chuck waved his hand at me with a smirk. "Man, you are so cranky before coffee. I just wanted to know if you heard anything."

"If you thought I did you would have come to me last night," I said.

Chuck was the sheriff, inheriting the job from his old man and his old man before. He was a smart guy and nothing got past him. "Last night? Who said anything about last night?"

I shrugged and sipped my coffee. "I saw the ambulance and one of your cars out there when I rolled out of bed at five. I imagine something happened over night. Am I right?"

"Yep."

I fixed him with the evilest eye I could muster before a full cup of coffee. "Then get off my back with this stuff so early. If you got something let me know and be done with it."

"You're even more ornery than usual this morning." He scooped up some of his runny eggs with a piece of dry toast and shoved it into his mouth.

Mabel put a plate of grits and scrambled eggs in front of me. I'd been getting the same thing for breakfast in this diner for over twenty years and had stopped actually looking at a menu or even telling them an order in half that time. Even though I retired two years ago from the paper mill I still came here and eat. Boyette's Diner is the center of our universe, it would seem. Nothing ever happens without the news starting here. Especially with the big mouth of Chuck.

"Craziest thing I ever did see," he was saying through a mouthful of egg. "She was opened up."

"Huh?" I asked, my bent fork dangling over my food. "Did you say opened up?"

"Yep." Chuck grinned but it wasn't happy. The man was unnerved and trying to make light of it for his own sake. He'd said it loud enough most everyone in the place had heard him. There was the old adage if you wanted the world to know a secret tell it to a Gill with a badge, because every one of them through the years had been itching to tell everything they could find out. Now that something real was happening Chuck was about bursting at the seams. "She'd been gutted like a fish. From her eyeballs to her privates."

"Chuck, people are trying to eat," Mabel admonished.

"Sorry. Anyway, there wasn't much left of her except some broken bones and a few scraps of clothing. Looked like a pack of wild coyotes had taken her apart."

"In her trailer?" I asked. "Or in the woods?"

"Right in her living room whiles the Carson show was on."

"What about her brats?" I didn't need to mince words because everyone in town and the trailer park knew what monsters they were and they'd all end up in juvie and then jail before long. "Didn't they see anything, or are they dead, too?"

Chuck shook his head and sat up on the counter now that he had everyone's attention. He was still smiling but his hands were shaking. "Her kids swear they didn't hear a thing. The littlest one, the girl, woke early to pee and saw Heffer on the couch. Or what was left of her. Since they didn't have a phone she ran next door to the Colby's and used their phone to call me."

Mabel shook her head. "You mean to tell me a pack of coyotes waltzed into a trailer, ate her but didn't eat her kids? Was the trailer ripped apart? Any animal hair or droppings? Cabinets emptied and food on the floor?"

Chuck pushed his sheriff hat further up his forehead and squinted his eyes. "Nope. The kids said the door was closed but unlocked and only she had been touched."

"Coyotes don't close the door once they leave," Mabel said and several patrons nodded in agreement. "If it was coyotes or wild animals they would have stayed and tore up the place and definitely eaten them kids."

"I saw a coyote on my way over," I blurted without thinking. I guess because I knew who killed Heffer Becky. Maybe Chuck could arrest me for being an accomplice. I was the one who gave her up, after all. I didn't care for her but it was still no excuse.

As everyone peppered Chuck with questions and made him feel important I finished my breakfast and hurried home.

* * *

Winter was still a few weeks away but there was a chill in the air as the sun began to drop. I told my wife and son to stay inside because of the coyote attack. I fumbled with my pipe, my hands and nerves fighting to keep it steady, and scanned the woods with my bad eyes.

I'd spent the day tinkering around the old John Deere, taking the engine apart and cleaning it up. I wouldn't need to use it but maybe once or twice all season now but it was good to have it in tiptop shape. Besides, I needed something to keep my mind off of what had happened last night. Maybe it was a dream. Maybe I had fallen asleep on my rocking chair and heard the sirens and pieced it together in my subconscious? The Heffer's trailer wasn't too far away and definitely in earshot, even for these bad ears of mine. That made more sense than monsters coming out of the woods and asking for a sacrifice. It did to me right now as I stuffed my pipe.

But there they were, just as plain as day: a slew of them hanging at the edge of the trees. Two of them approached, one I kinda recognized from the night before and the other one fatter than the rest. They were so black it was painful to look at them.

"You are real," I mumbled and almost dropped my pipe from my mouth. "I want no part in this."

His voice came to me inside my head, only it wasn't really a voice… it was just there again. I still didn't like it, but I could understand him well enough. It was either pick another person or it was my turn. Simple as that.

"The two brats of Heffer. They'll be raised by wolves at this point. Ain't no one wants them."

I felt awful for saying it, especially out loud, but it was not a lie. The kids had been left alone all day, running around the trailer park without a care in the world. My wife wanted to take them in but I told her in no uncertain terms them brats would never set foot on my property. I wanted no part of them, and she should feel the same way. They were nothing but trouble, and if Chuck and his Keystone Cop buddies weren't so busy gossiping they'd have called Child Services to come collect 'em.

"Who you talking to, old man?" my wife, Sandra, asked me. I hadn't noticed her join me outside the trailer.

I nearly jumped out of my skin at her words. "You scared the Dickens outta me," I yelled, looking around at the woods. If those creatures were still here... but the trees were quiet.

She laughed and patted my back as I sat back down gingerly on the broken rocker. "What's gotten into you today? You've been keeping to yourself and nearly missed dinner. Your boy called to talk with you but you were in a daze today. You barely ate your dinner and now I hear you talking to yourself. You alright?" She put a hand on my forehead. "No fever."

"I'm fine. Just a little quiet today. A man in my advanced age can be silent for a time if he wants. I earned it."

"Don't you go raising your voice with me or I'll slap it outta you. Mind your manners," my wife said but she said it sweetly like she's been doing since I've known her. Sandra always had a way with words.

"I'm forgettin' who I married, dear. My fault, surely." I held my pipe against my side because my hand was still shaky. "We got any coffee?"

"We got plenty of coffee but you ain't getting' any. Not this late in the evening. You'll be up all night."

I watched her go back inside. I figured I was going to be up all night anyway.

* * *

"We got another murder," Chuck said with more than a hint of fear in his voice. "Both of Becky's kids last night." His excitement from yesterday was firmly replaced now that another murder had occurred.

Mabel made the Sign of the Cross. "That is just god-awful. Those poor little babies."

I looked at her cross-eyed but didn't say a word. Them brats were anything but poor little babies. Good riddance. But both of them dead was troubling. "They both got ripped apart?" I asked.

Chuck stared at me. "Who said anything about being ripped apart?"

I shrugged and turned back to my coffee, trying to remain calm and act casual. "I just assumed."

Chuck smiled crookedly and leaned across the counter and into my line of sight. "You know what happens when you assume?" I hated when Chuck thought he had me and I knew he was going to pounce and make me look foolish in front of everyone in the diner this morning.

"I'm sure you'll tell us all the details of why those two small children were left unattended all night in the trailer their mama had just been killed in," I said and took another sip, satisfied it would shut him up. It did the trick.

"Hey, yeah… why didn't you take them to a relative or drop them off with a neighbor? I only live seven double-wides down from them. I woulda taken them for the night," Mabel said. "Any of us would have."

I knew that was a lie. I didn't need to look at anyone else in the place to know they were glancing away from Mabel now. And she was one to talk. She'd be the first to come up with an excuse not to take them brats in. OK, maybe the second here to do it.

Chuck scooped his scrambled eggs into his mouth and shrugged before walking out. We all watched him as he sped away in the police cruiser, lights and sirens blazing as if he had just gotten a call.

But I knew there would be hell to pay soon enough. Chuck was going to hold a grudge like his daddy and his daddy before had, and I decided I might skip the diner tomorrow morning.

* * *

I decided to stay inside tonight and maybe they'd find someone else to do their dirty work. I was done and frankly I was exhausted. After the altercation with Chuck I got nothing done all day except kick around the trailer and watch the woods.

The missus didn't never miss a thing with me and she glanced at the screen door and frowned. "You feeling alright?"

"Yep." I sat in my worn armchair in the living room and stared out the window. "I'm fine. You?"

"Why ain't you on the porch? Your hand is shaking. You forgot to buy tobacco? I can go next door to Clint's and see if he has a pinch for ya."

"That won't be necessary. I'm just not really in the mood tonight is all." I wasn't, true enough. I'd barely eaten my supper and she'd made pork chops, which is my favorite. Besides, about two hours ago, I'd already gone over to Clint and bummed some from his stash. Clint and I rarely talked but we did share the common love of pipes.

"Suit yourself. If you're not going outside to smoke, you can help me with the dishes."

"Ahh, woman, can't you see I'm not up to anything tonight?" I asked a bit forcefully, even for me. I knew immediately I'd hurt her feelings. "Now,

now, don't go tearing up on me. I'm sorry. I don't know what's gotten into me."

I stood on my shaky legs and went to her as fast as my old body would take me.

"I was joshing, you know," Sandra said quietly. I hugged her. Even after all these years I can still manage to say something boneheaded and asinine to my wife. I guess some things will never change. "You going to call your boy?"

"I will when I get time," I told Sandra. I was trying to keep Junior out of my thoughts as much as possible. I didn't want to accidentally have a loved one in my head in case them things went looking inside my skull for a name.

"What's the matter?" she asked, feeling me stiffen as I had my arms wrapped around her.

"Nothing," I mumbled and pushed away from her. "I... nothing..."

They were right on the porch now. I could feel them. There were at least four of them in my head, asking me for names, asking me to give up my neighbors so they could go about their business.

"No," I whispered. "I can't."

"Are you alright?" my wife asked me, putting a hand on my face.

I couldn't put her into my head like I'd done them kids or their mama. I wouldn't let them take her in the night. "Clint," I said loudly.

"What about him?"

I know my eyes got wide then. "He's next. He's going to die tonight."

But they weren't done. No. They demanded more.

Last night I'd inadvertently given them those two brats. Now that was the new deal. Now they were expecting two.

"What are you talking about?" my wife asked. "Clint?"

I nodded. "And his wife Susie."

* * *

"You need to go talk to the sheriff," she said to me. She'd wanted to warn Clint and Susie but I told her it was too late. These creatures don't mess around. I knew she didn't believe me.

"Look what happened to Heffer and her brats," I said. "And they're going to ask me for two more names tomorrow night."

"Not if you stop them. Go to Chuck and tell him."

"Tell him what? Monsters from the woods are to blame for these murders? Creatures that talk to me without moving their mouths, getting inside my head. He'll lock me up after he charges me for the killings. No thank you, God. I'll figure this out on my own. I'm going to stay away from the diner, too."

"And draw suspicion?" she said, folding her arms. "You just sit right here with me tonight and don't leave my side. If those two are really dead come morning I'll know it wasn't you."

I felt like I'd been slapped. "What do you mean? You think I'm killing them?"

Sandra shrugged. "Maybe you snapped and are hearing Satan in your head telling you to kill, kill, kill. I'm just saying… have a seat on the couch with me and we'll get to the bottom of this." She fixed me with a hard look and stuck her finger in the air. "But, as God is my witness, if you try to kill me in my sleep I'll be pissed."

"You're making a joke out of this?"

"After all these years and all these hardships we've been through, why shouldn't I? It gets you nowhere fast by worrying. If you don't know me by now…"

"I'm not comfortable joking about this. I'm helping to kill people."

She led me to the couch, where we snuggled into each other like we'd done more nights than I could remember. The old couch knew our bodies and we slipped right into our grooves. "Shh. No more talking about it. We'll figure something out in the morning. But you need to go to the diner and act like nothing is out of sorts with you."

"Yes, ma'am."

* * *

Mabel dropped my food in front of me, her makeup streaked down her face from the tears.

"You heard?"

"Heard what?"

"Clint and Susie. Dead," she said before pouring coffee for those crowded around the counter. The diner was packed this morning.

"Same as Heffer and the brats?" I asked, already knowing the answer. I needed to show just enough interest to get me through breakfast.

"Yep. Such a tragedy. Who knows what's going on?" Mabel babbled as she kept serving.

"I'll tell you what's going on," Chuck said from where he now stood inside the open doorway, one hand on his holstered gun and the other flicking his sheriff hat back a tad, sunglasses still on even though he was inside and it was overcast today. He dangled a toothpick from his lips. All eyes went to him and I could see his mouth turned up slightly at the edges like he wanted to give a big grin. He was pausing for effect and had all of our attention.

"You gonna tell us already?" someone said from a back table.

Chuck looked annoyed as he took off his sunglasses and looked right at me, but I hadn't said a word. "We have a serial killer in our midst."

"In the diner?" Mabel asked and laughed. She looked around, damp eyes lingering on me for a second. I think. Maybe I was getting paranoid. "This motley crew can barely count out change when it comes to a tip."

"If we even make the mistake of tipping," John Murphy, a retired heavy machine operator, said next to me. We all laughed.

"It's all a joke until two more dead bodies show up, isn't that always the case? The Lynchs were killed last night," Chuck said and slapped a hand on the counter. Everyone went quiet.

"Who are the Lynchs?" Mabel asked. I already knew.

"Clint and his wife, of course." Chuck came and stood right next to me, his sunglasses dangling in my face. "They're your neighbors, ain't that right? So was Heffer and her brats. Pretty coincidental, eh?"

I shrugged and looked around. "There's at least five people in this diner this morning who live around me and Clint. Are we all suspects?" I asked. I wanted to remain calm but my nerves were shot. "I was home last night. You can ask my beautiful wife." I smiled. "Or, better yet, ask the one I'm married to now."

Everyone burst into laughing, and even Chuck smiled.

* * *

"Come inside and stop beating yourself up," Sandra finally said in that scolding manner I'd grown to love and hate over the years. "There's a solution and I figured it out."

"I doubt it," I said and squeezed my unlit pipe until I thought either it or my brittle fingers would break. "I'm cursed to keep killing off my neighbors."

"Shh, don't speak like that out here. You know everyone is a Nosy Nelly. Get your bony butt in here. I'm going to give you some of my pills."

"Your heart medicine?"

She laughed. "No, you dang fool. My sleepers. It will put you right out."

"I can't take that stuff. It will knock me out til Tuesday. Maybe if I just don't give them a name. Clear my head and smoke my pipe and stare them down?"

"You can try it, or you can do it the sensible way and go to sleep. You said they come at dusk. All you need to do is be sleeping at that time."

"What if they find someone else to do their dirty work?"

"If they find someone, it will then be on their shoulders and you'll be off the hook. But who are they going to get? Everyone is hiding in their houses after supper. People are scared and they should be. Ain't no one but you going to be sitting out on their porch tonight or any night. Now get moving before the sun drops anymore."

I went inside. What did I really have to lose?

44

I took two of her pills and she pulled down the sheets, closing the windows and blinds and turning up the fan on the desk and pointing it at me.

"Is this Christmas?" I asked, since she never angled the fan directly at me at night. She liked it blowing right in her face.

"Shut yer trap and lie down. Here, put my mask on so it's dark."

"I'm not going to wear that stupid girlie thing," I said. To be honest, I'd worn it once when she was visiting her sister last summer and I slept nicely, but I wasn't going to let her know it.

"I'm not asking. I'm telling," Sandra said.

"Yes, ma'am." I put it on and snuggled in for what I hoped was a cozy sleep without nightmares.

* * *

"Good morning," I said to Sandra, who was scrambling some eggs.

"How'd you sleep?"

"Like a log." I stretched and sat down at the table.

"I'm making lunch."

"Lunch? I'll be heading to the diner in a second," I said.

She turned and smiled at me. "It's after two. You slept about twenty hours."

"You lie," I said slowly. *How was that even possible?* "I haven't slept more than eight since before my stint in the Navy. Why'd you let me sleep so much?"

"Because you needed it. The stress over the last few days was killing you. Chuck is sniffing around, too. He was here this morning looking for you. Even peeked in and remarked how loud you snored."

"Why was he here?"

Sandra smiled and dropped fresh bacon into another pan. "He thinks you know something you're not telling him about these incidents. He thinks you might be involved somehow and it's eating him alive. I told him you were sick, you've been sick since after dinner last night and slept through. I gave you a real alibi."

I poured myself a cup of coffee. "Anything happen last night?"

She smiled as she tended to the bacon. "Not a thing. It was a nice and quiet evening, but I'd stick around inside today. If Chuck comes back over he'll want to talk with you. I think we let it go for a couple more nights and then he'll go find someone else to bother."

"But if the… incidents stopped, he'll really think it was me."

"Nope. I made it perfectly clear I was with you those nights and you and I were in the living room until bedtime. You never even stepped outside to smoke your pipe because you haven't been feeling well. But you're a stubborn old man and refused to take medicine until last night. I got it all covered. Go get me a plate. I know you're hungry and since you missed breakfast I made some for you."

I smiled. She always took care of me. "A man could get used to this."

* * *

For four days I puttered around the house, taking the sleeping pills and wearing my mask and wondering how I'd ever slept without them before. I was refreshed and felt like I was ten years younger. I finally got around to fixing the motor on the John Deere and getting the slats in the back fence nailed back up. When I announced I was going into town to get gasoline she frowned.

"I'll go get it. You stay here and relax."

"Honey, as much as I love being around you all day and working on some projects that have sat, I need to go into town and stretch my legs. I'm getting antsy. I've never been away from the action for this long."

"What action? You aren't missing anything. Besides, I like having you all to myself," she said. "These last few days have been nice, haven't they? I like us just spending time together like we did when we first met."

"Who can remember that far ago? Heck, I can't remember what I had for breakfast," I said but I had to smile. These last few days had been great. We'd spend time in the late afternoon in the living room, her reading a book and me finally finishing the lighthouse carving I'd started years ago. My fingers made it slow going but I had all the time in the world. "We could go into town together."

Sandra shook her head. "Or we can stay right here and enjoy another peaceful day."

I was mad and I didn't really know why. "What's going on? I'm starting to feel like something is afoot. You're hiding something from me, aren't you?"

"What could I possibly hide?"

I rubbed at my stubbly chin and sighed. "I'm sorry. I'm just getting antsy is all."

"You said that already. You want pork chops for dinner tonight?"

"Yeah, that sounds fine. I'll be back in a bit," I said.

She turned to me and pursed her lips like she did when she was really mad. Then she dropped her look and gave me a fake smile. I'd seen it a million times and I knew what was going to come out of her mouth. "Fine. Have fun. Don't say I didn't warn you. You never listen. And you better be home before dusk."

* * *

Boyette's Diner was closed, even though they shoulda been open for business. I peeked through the dusty windows. Nothing. I decided to take a walk down Main Street but after four steps my knee was acting up so I climbed back into my pickup truck and took it for a ride.

I stopped at the intersection in the middle of town and looked around. There was no one in sight. I laid on the horn, the blast echoing up and down the streets, bouncing off the shuttered stores. What was going on?

As I went past the police station I saw Chuck's patrol car parked outside. The windows were rolled down and it was still running. I pulled up next to it and could smell something rotting. I didn't need to look to know what I was gonna find.

I drove back to the trailer park, not passing or seeing another soul as I did twenty miles over the speed limit. It wasn't like Chuck was gonna pull me over.

When I got into the park I slowed down. There were always kids running around and it was habit to do no more than ten miles an hour. Only, right now I didn't see or hear any kids. Or anyone for that matter. Every trailer looked quiet, like the dead staring back at me.

I was just getting around the turn to my own trailer when Mabel stepped out onto the road with a wild look in her eyes. I pulled up next to her but kept it in drive. The woman was scared but scary-looking, too. "Hey," I managed.

"You're alive?"

"I guess for now," I said, trying to make her relax. I really didn't know her except from the diner. Heck, I didn't even know she lived in the trailer park until the other morning. "What's going on?"

Mabel threw her hands in the air. I could see by the mascara streaks on her face she'd been crying. "Everyone is dead. I thought you were dead, too."

"What do you mean by everyone?"

"Look around. Open your ears, old man! No one is alive. The town is empty. Bodies everywhere you look. You can't smell it?"

"My nose ain't what it used to be," I said quietly but I could detect something spoiled. "I saw Chuck in his cruiser. Or, rather, I smelled what was left of him."

"I need to leave but I'm scared," Mabel said. "I have nowhere to go."

"You can come and stay with us if you want."

Without another word she climbed into the passenger side of the pickup and we drove to my place.

* * *

My wife sat in silence while I told her what I'd seen and Mabel filled in the blanks.

"Then we need to leave," Sandra finally said. "But we can't go tonight. Mabel can stay here, with us, and we'll barricade the doors and windows. In the morning we can head to my sister's and get some help."

"We should leave now," Mabel yelled. "Before it gets dark."

I looked outside. We were only about an hour away from dusk. I didn't want to be driving when the sun dropped and those things came out to hunt. "I guess they found someone else to do the picking," I said.

"What?" Mabel asked. I felt responsible but I wasn't going to get her panicked. More than she was. But I knew I would turn myself in when we got to safety tomorrow.

"You are both going to take sleeping pills and get to bed now. We'll get up before dawn and head out. I'll pack a few things and get the house in order."

"I won't be able to sleep," Mabel said.

"You look like heck, girl," my wife said. "You need your rest. If you're tossing and turning and up all night you won't be much help come daylight. Trust me on this."

I couldn't argue with the logic. I'd felt great after a good night's sleep. And running at night would be suicide.

We set up Mabel in the unused bedroom I stored stuff in, but the bed was still good enough for one night once I got my boxes of lawn mower parts off of it.

"Isn't it odd she's the only one still alive?" my wife asked me after Mabel took her pills and settled in. "She's the only one. I think they found someone else to answer their summons, and Mabel did it. We're the only two left and now she knows it."

"Then we both need to stand guard," I said.

My wife kissed my cheek and handed me my sleeping pills. "Go to bed."

* * *

Through hazy eyes I saw the creatures in the room, dark and filled with teeth and claws, yellow irises seeming to float at me. Inside they were even scarier, a blob of darkness against the backdrop of the faded walls.

I saw my wife, standing in the doorway, hall light behind her.

"What are you doing?" I mumbled through a drugged haze.

"I had to give them five names. You never told me how this worked. Never told me if I give 'em more names each night they demand that many the next night. And the next. I ran out of people, honey. Mabel was a gift from God, though. Because if I don't give them five by dusk, we're next. Don't you see? I had no choice. I wish I knew more people, though. My sister is going to be found in the morning, and they've promised me they will move onto another town as long as I help them. But I need to keep helping. They've been asleep in the woods for so long and now they're so hungry."

She held up a yellow phone book. I noticed Sandra had been crying. "I just need to do some research every afternoon. But I'm sorry… I panicked tonight and thought of Junior."

A WOMAN OF DISREPUTE
ICY SEDGWICK

I always made a point to never visit artists while they were working on a painting but, given the chosen profession of a large number of my friends, it often happened that I had no choice in the matter if I wanted to see them. That desire for companionship in the face of tedium explained why I found myself standing in the doorway of Henry Woollenby's workshop, waiting for an invitation to sit. No invite was forthcoming, nor did I feel it would be in the immediate future, so I hung my hat and coat on a stand by the door.

"So this is what you called me to see? What is it?"

I walked across the room to view the vast canvas that dominated the narrow end of the wedge-shaped workshop. The painting depicted a misty scene on the banks of the Thames, and globules of fog clung to the lamp-posts in the distance. The black waters of the river lapped at the edge of the beach, low tide having deposited the body of a young woman on the dirty sand. Blackfriars Bridge loomed to the west. Henry darted about in front of the painting, dabbing a spot of paint here, or a streak of oil there. I wrinkled my nose.

"Henry, why must you persist in painting such morbid subjects?"

"I believe it to be reality. I seek only to paint the truth." Henry did not look up from his work, but I considered myself fortunate to have received a reply at all.

"The truth? What is true about what you've produced?"

"Isn't it obvious?" Henry paused, and turned away from the painting. I should have been repulsed, but I could not avert my eyes from the pale, outstretched arm of the fallen woman, her fingers curled as if to beckon me closer. I wanted to know her plight, what sorry state of affairs could have drawn her to such an ignominious end.

"No."

"This is a regular occurrence, my friend. These women do not fall from grace, they are pushed! What happy ending can they possibly hope for in such a world? Their only salvation lies in the Thames."

"I could not agree more, but do you have to paint pictures of it?"

"Is that not the duty of art? To 'make glorious' that which the greater public would rather ignore?"

"The duty of art is to bring beauty into the world. It is simple decoration, and nothing more—you cannot pretend that art's function should be that of moral instruction. No, you should leave such lofty ambitions to writers and orators," I said.

"Writers like yourself, I suppose?"

"Indeed, writers like myself! We may use language to communicate, and narrative should be our preserve, not yours."

Henry snorted and returned to his work. I peered over his shoulder, examining the background as his brush flickered in and out of my field of vision. A dark stain within the shadow of the bridge caught my eye, some sort of hooded figure with its head bowed, facing toward the dead prostitute. A shiver ran down my spine.

"Who is that?"

Henry stopped and followed my pointing finger. He frowned as he bent closer.

"I have no idea."

"Did you not paint it?"

"I don't know. I don't exactly remember. Perhaps I did so late one evening as my senses departed for the night. Yes, that must be it. That may be the personification of guilt, or shame, felt by the women themselves."

Henry nodded and, apparently satisfied by his own explanation, resumed painting once more. I raised an eyebrow, my gaze fixed upon the hooded figure.

"Did you actually see such a thing when you were there?"

"When I was where?"

"Down by the river. At low tide?"

Henry's ears flushed red, and he refused to turn around. He bowed his head, his brush sagging in his hand.

"You didn't go down to the river, did you?"

Henry shook his head. I raised my eyebrow.

"And this is not a scene you painted as you found it, is it?"

Henry shook his head again. The red flush crept down the back of his neck and disappeared beneath the collar of his paint-stained shirt. He'd protested so often about the veracity of art. It simply confirmed my assertions that truth is the preserve of the writer.

"Don't tell anyone, but I've never even spoken to an unfortunate. They terrify me. I'd heard the stories, and seen what the other chaps were painting, so I had the daughter of my charwoman pose for the woman."

I snorted. "It hardly makes this a painting of truth, does it?"

Henry said nothing. He resumed painting, his brush slower and more lacklustre than before. He continued in this fashion for several minutes, until it became clear that conversation would be strained at best. I shook my head, and stood.

"I can see that you are busy, so I shall leave you in peace. I assume we will all see you at Dawkins's supper on Friday?"

"That you will, Edward."

"Excellent. Until then, goodbye, my friend."

I closed the door behind me and descended the three flights of stairs to the front door. I exchanged pleasantries with the charwoman as she washed the front steps, and made my way into the thick fog of the London night.

* * *

The image of Henry's painting remained in my thoughts as I walked, and I compared it to the works I had seen at the Academy, reminding me of a discussion with that infernal Dante Rossetti about fallen women. Snippets of prose tugged at my attention, and my senses tingled with the promise of a new story. I snorted again at Henry's belief in the moral obligation of art. No, if anyone were to expose the public to the horrors of street life, it should be me.

My feet took me in the direction of Southwark. My publisher's brother-in-law had told me of a less-than-reputable club in the area, and advised that I 'sample the wares' if I wanted a higher standard of female company. I had no intention of doing such a thing, but the idea of a new muse loomed large in my mind. My last had left London two weeks ago to marry an industrialist in Birmingham, and we had all heard tales of Rossetti's circle finding their muses in the most unlikely of places. Why might I not find a new one in the bowels of the Virginia Club?

Red lamps adorned the club's tables, and corseted waitresses served drinks to men hidden in shadow. I took up a seat near the door, reluctant to venture too far inside lest I find it difficult to find my way back out, and ordered a glass of sherry. Within moments, a blond beauty appeared at my side.

"Is this seat taken?" She gestured to the empty seat.

"Not at all." She sat down and I admired her graceful poise. A pile of golden curls sat on her head, although several ringlets had escaped their pins, and lay against the girl's pale neck. I tried to picture her standing alone on Blackfriars Bridge, contemplating her fate as she stared into the churning black water below. Yes, she would do.

"I'm Ellen," she said.

"Edward Bonneville. Pleased to make your acquaintance."

She smiled and leaned forward. I tried to guess her age, which I placed at between seventeen and twenty-three. God alone knew what she'd done for employment at this establishment.

"I shall be honest with you, Ellen, I am not looking for the sort of companionship one might find in a place such as this."

"Oh." Ellen's smile evaporated and her gaze began to wander the room.

"No, I seek a muse, and I suspect you may be exactly what I'm looking for."

The smile returned, as did her attention. I suppressed a smirk—Ellen had no doubt heard tales of women elevated from the lower classes through their association with artists and writers, and sought a similar advancement for herself. Henry's painting again came to mind and my inner smirk faltered. Perhaps I could prevent another tragedy.

"What do you want a muse for?"

I explained my position as a writer, though disappointment rankled me that Ellen had not heard of my work. I told her about Henry's lofty ambitions, and my desire to tell the truth that he could not, and in the course of my narrative, I described his painting.

"It's common enough. Girls get too old or sick and men don't want to know. They can't make any money, so…" Ellen allowed her words to hang in the air but the unhappy conclusion was plain enough to infer.

"It's very sad, but I feel literature could do so much more than art."

Ellen nodded, as if she knew what I meant. I remembered the hooded figure.

"However, there was something a little unsettling about Henry's painting, and I don't just mean what it was about. No, there was a hooded figure in it that Henry didn't remember painting."

The colour drained from Ellen's face and her fingers curled around the edge of the table. Her knuckles turned white and a muscle worked in her jaw.

"The girls fear something worse than the loss of their virtue, sir."

"What do you mean?"

"Oh nothing!" Ellen pasted a false smile on her face. She stood to leave, her hands trembling as she knotted her fingers together.

"Where are you going?"

"I'm sorry, sir."

Ellen disappeared into the gloom of the club. I rose to follow her, but the shadows swallowed her, leaving me with only darkness for company. Two men near the door cast suspicious looks in my direction, and I hurried out of the club and into the cold London night before questions could be asked.

Once outside, I thought again of the peculiar conclusion to our conversation. Ellen spoke of fear, yet refused to divulge the contents of her thoughts. She evidently believed I could offer no aid in the face of some nearby danger, yet I could only speculate as to the nature of this threat. Perhaps one of the local men was to blame, growing fat on the profits of the female bodies he sold, and keen to threaten them if they chose to leave.

I wandered the streets for around half an hour, where I passed furtive men on their way to the Virginia Club, and gentlemen heading home after late-night visits to friends. The hook of a story nagged in my mind, and I found that I turned in the direction of Blackfriars Bridge. As I walked, I turned the topic over in my mind. I wanted to give the fallen women a voice, but I could only do that by speaking to them myself and hearing their stories with my own ears. I needed affirmation of my suspicions about a shadowy underworld figure, intent upon ruling the unfortunate women with a rod of iron.

I approached the bridge in search of another muse, but I spotted blond curls farther up the street. I peered closer and realised they belonged to Ellen. She hurried towards the bridge, her hair loose around her shoulders. She darted glances in all directions as she walked, her arms drawn tightly across her chest. Her boots beat an irregular rhythm in the quiet street as she varied her pace. She was clearly terrified of something. Maybe if I took her somewhere warm and gave her a drink, she might speak. Indeed, I was shocked to see her alone in such a place so late at night, and after her sudden fright at the club, I was concerned as much as I was curious.

"Ellen!"

Ellen stopped and turned. Recognition sparked on her face, but her expression was unreadable. Before I reached her, someone stepped out of the darkness of the alley to Ellen's left. Ellen turned and threw her arms up in a defensive gesture, but a pale hand shot out of a dark cloak and covered Ellen's mouth, cutting off her scream. I broke into a run but Ellen was dragged into the alley.

I reached the narrow lane. I expected to see her skirts bunched around her waist, or the flashing blade of a knife in the gloom. Instead, a hooded figure bent over Ellen's prone body, obscuring her face. Wet, sordid chewing sounds filled the air, and my stomach churned to hear them.

"Hi there, stop!" I found my voice, but it bore a waver that betrayed me. I tried to move into the alley, but my feet refused to obey. They held fast, rooted to the spot, while my knees quivered from the exertion of my run. My heart pounded, and my ribs vibrated within my chest, though from terror or exercise I could not say.

The stranger stood. Blood clotted in the bite marks around Ellen's mouth. The figure leaned down and held its hand—a horrible skeletal hand of bleached bone, over the wound. It tore upwards in one savage motion. For a moment, a white mist, the same shape and form as Ellen, hung from the figure's grasp.

"You there!"

The creature, for it was no human, ignored me, and folded the white mist into a neat square, which it tucked into the folds of its cloak. The figure bent down and caught hold of Ellen by the shoulders. It dragged her out of the alley, and up the quiet street. Shock gripped me, yet somehow it did not surprise me in the least. I did not question this peculiarity, consumed as I was by my desire to help Ellen. I struggled to move in order to follow their progress, but my feet refused to obey my commands. I pummelled my thigh with my fists, helpless and frustrated. My mouth kept moving, my vocal chords straining to cry out, but no noise would come forth. It was as though I were trapped in that terrible sort of dream in which you can see the world moving around you, but you are powerless to intervene.

As the apparition reached the approach to Blackfriars Bridge, my feet broke their bonds. The sudden movement impelled me to stumble forward, hurrying along the pavement towards the unholy pair. Revulsion at the sight raged inside me and I no longer thought of the story that I had originally sought to tell. I sought only to better understand what was happening. I ran towards the bridge, where the monster reached the mid-point. It hoisted Ellen up onto the stone balustrade, and her body tumbled into the freezing waters below. I cried out in despair.

The hooded figure wiped its hand on its cloak, and free of its burden, it drifted towards me. I stared, straining my ears for the sound of footsteps, but there were none. I shouted something nonsensical, I know not what, and while I saw no eyes, I was aware of the weight of its gaze. The malice that this figure bore for me was as apparent as the sensation of winter in December. This was no normal man, ruling and punishing the unfortunates of London. This was something else entirely. The apparition, belonging to some awful class of spectre previously unknown to me, continued down the bridge and turned onto Southwark Street.

I stood in the street, my feet pointed towards the bridge but my body twisted in the direction of the creature's exit. I wanted to recover Ellen's body, but I would surely perish in the cold waters, and that would simply add an extra tally to the creature's card. I had a notion to call for help, but only a priest could help poor Ellen now, and there was naught the constabulary, such as they were, could do. Part of me wanted to turn tail and flee, to run back to my rooms and avoid late night excursions into London's bizarre streets. Yet despite the animosity that the figure clearly displayed towards me, another impulse wanted to follow it, to make sense of what I'd seen, and to quiet the rising voice inside me that sought answers. As I struggled to decide upon a course of action, another voice added its tones to the clamour, raging about what a fine story this would make.

I could not turn myself away once my feet began walking. I kept the infernal creature in sight, and hurried along Southwark Street. My quarry sped on, although I did not think it knew I was following—unless it knew that I was on its trail, and did not care. Indeed, having seen its manner of murder, I scarcely believed that it would consider me to be a threat of any kind. I wondered if I had perhaps seen a wraith of some kind. Indeed, I remembered the novel of Dr Polidori, *The Vampyre*, and speculated that perhaps this was the manner of their feeding.

The creature darted down another street, and I paid no attention to where I was. I kept thinking of Ellen, the beautiful, tragic blonde dumped into the Thames with cruel abandon. Even if she became nothing else, she could have been my muse. Now she would be another sentence or two in the newspaper, a mere footnote to the country's mistreatment of unfortunate women.

I followed the figure along Redcross Street. It reached a pair of iron gates, and drifted between the bars. I approached the gates some moments after, and found them fastened with a large padlock. I grasped the bars, pulling on them with all of my strength to determine the means by which the creature gained access. There must have been some way through to which I was not privy, although I suspect my desire to discover a rational explanation was my mind's defence against the fantastical events to which I had borne witness. I peered between the bars into a simple yard, moonlight falling across its uneven cobbles. The monster made its way toward the centre.

"Hi there, you! Yes, I see you!"

I shouted through the gates. The creature paused at the centre of the yard and turned its head in my direction. An angry hiss filled the yard as it lay down on the bare ground, and melted into the cold night air.

I stared between the gates but there was nothing to be seen. It had simply disappeared. I continued to stare as though it may yet reveal itself, as though the trick might be explained through rational means. I could not allow myself to believe that a being capable of lifting a young woman over a bridge could pass through iron bars and vanish into the cold night air as though it did not exist. An idea flitted through my mind that I had dreamed the entire thing. Perhaps lack of sleep, or a morsel of undigested dinner, had played tricks upon my eyes.

"'Ey up, what are you doin' here?" A gruff voice interrupted my thoughts.

I turned around to see an elderly man grasping a staff in one hand and an ancient lantern in the other. A moth-eaten watch cap perched on his balding head, and a tattered cloak did its best to keep out the chill of the night.

"I was just looking for someone. At least, I thought I was."

"You won't find no one in there, sir," replied the night watchman.

"I thought I saw someone go in."

The watchman frowned. He peered between the bars, and looked down at the padlock. He raised his gaze to meet mine.

"No way to get in, sir."

"I saw someone, I am sure that I did." I peered into the yard, and turned my gaze back to the night watchman. A chill ran down my spine, and I shoved my hands into my pockets.

"Tell me what 'appened, sir?"

I told the watchman about my quest to find a muse, and my need to tell the story of the fallen women. I explained about meeting Ellen, and about what I saw in the alley. I realised the folly of my actions, but the tale poured out in a jumbled rush, and I trailed off into silence when the watchman started nodding.

"I know who you saw."

"Who?"

"I don't know 'er name, but I know 'er lives in there," said the watchman, pointing into the yard. "This weren't always a yard. Many years back, this was a burial ground, yes it were. Only it weren't fer no usual folk. This was fer the geese of Winchester."

"The what?"

"The street women what was put to work by the Bishop of Winchester. They was called his geese. The one what you saw… she's the grand old mother, ain't she? When you saw her bendin' over that girl, she was takin' her soul. She dumps 'em in the Thames so the running water can wash away their sins."

"She does what?" If the watchman had told me such a tale yesterday, I would have called for a policeman and recommended he be taken to Bedlam, but after the events of the evening, I found I was incredulous although not entirely disbelieving.

The night watchman repeated his words. I stared at him, eyes wide and unblinking.

"You expect me to believe that a former prostitute, dead for centuries, is taking the souls of fallen women, and dumping the bodies in the river? I thought they were committing suicide."

"No, sir. It's the Mother Goose. She takes 'em. Frees 'em from a bad life. You know 'er cloak? It's the cloak of all 'er sin when she were alive. She's been quiet for a while, dunno what's prompted her to take it up again."

"I see."

"I reckon yer would be best off goin' home, sir."

I nodded and moved away from the gate, casting a last look into the yard before I walked away down the street. The night watchman waved as I turned the corner. I believed it to be only my imagination when I saw the faint outlines of the street through him.

* * *

The following morning, I browsed the newspaper over breakfast, immersing myself in society gossip and business news until the events of the previous evening seemed naught but a bad dream.

A knock at the door disrupted my reading. I glanced at the clock on the mantelpiece—only eight o'clock, yet I expected no visitors at such an hour.

I opened the door. My landlady stood in the hallway, flanked by a policeman and a well-dressed gentleman. I clung to the door, my knees suddenly weak. I had done no wrong, but the sight of a policeman at one's door is apt to cause discomfort of some kind.

"Yes?"

"Are you Edward Bonneville?" asked the gentleman.

"I already told you he is," said the landlady.

"I just need sir to confirm this, madam." The gentleman's tone was light but firm. He gave her a pointed look, and she pursed her lips.

"If you need me, I'll be downstairs." The landlady hobbled away along the corridor. The third step down creaked, and I assumed she had stopped on the stairs to eavesdrop. Unless I took action, the contents of our transaction would be spread around the parish before lunchtime.

"Perhaps you'd care to come inside?"

I held open the door and gestured for the men to enter and they shuffled inside. I sat in my threadbare armchair, and offered its twin to the gentleman. The policeman took up a position near the door, hands clasped before him.

"Yes, I am Edward Bonneville. What can I do for you, Mr...?"

"Inspector Abbott. I just have a few questions for you, Mr Bonneville, shouldn't take too much time. First, could you confirm your whereabouts yesterday evening?"

"I went to visit my friend, Henry Woollenby. He's an artist, and he wanted me to see his latest painting."

Inspector Abbott nodded to the policeman, who fished a notebook out of his pocket and scribbled down Henry's name.

"What else did you do, sir?"

"I came home, Inspector."

"I see, sir. Did you do anything in between? Did you perhaps visit another establishment on your way home?"

Inspector Abbott stared at me, his gaze pinning me to my seat. A lie withered and died on my lips, and I sank into the chair. It was no use pretending anything other than the truth.

"I did swing by the Virginia Club for a spell."

"Did you talk to anyone while you were there?"

"Yes, a lovely young woman named Ellen. I was doing some research— I'm a writer, you see, and I wanted to get some first-hand impressions to enrich my latest work. I realise it's not the most salubrious club in London, but it was on the way home and it was recommended to me." I ignored the policeman's sneer.

"I see, sir. And did you see this Miss Ellen after you left?"

"Not at all, Inspector."

"It's a pity you say that, sir. Only I have it on good authority that you did see the lady later that evening. Does Blackfriars Bridge ring any bells for you?"

My stomach clenched and an icy weight coiled itself into a knot in my gut. I opened and closed my mouth several times as I fought to find the right words.

"I know what you're getting at, Inspector, but it's not what you think. I did not kill Ellen, and I certainly didn't throw her body in the Thames."

"Ah, so you know what became of her."

I fell silent. Any lies would be useless now as I had given myself away.

"If you didn't kill her, then who did?"

I studied the inspector's face. He had a warm countenance, and a kindly expression that encouraged me to trust him. I sat forward in my chair and spilled the story in an uninterrupted flow. I told him about the hooded figure, the one from Henry's painting, and I described my pursuit of the creature to the old yard. I recounted the night watchman's words, even explaining the figure's strange garb.

"What a to-do! I've never heard anything quite like it."

"Yes, I realise it sounds bizarre, but it's the truth. Go and find the old watchman, he'll back me up."

"We'll do just that, sir. I'm sure he can clear all of this up in a jiffy. One question though, if this creature doesn't like you, why hasn't it done anything to you yet?"

"I do not know. I have asked myself that as well but... I just do not know."

"I see. Well will you excuse me? I just need to speak to my colleague here, double check his notes."

The two policemen ventured into the hall, leaving the door ajar. I leaned forward, straining to hear their conversation. Only snippets floated through the crack.

"I think he did it alright... oh I know he believes all that rubbish... clearly insane... Bedlam."

I leapt out of the chair like a cat on a hotplate at the mention of Bedlam. No, I would not spend my days in a madhouse for anyone. I searched the room for proof of my innocence, but all I found was scribbled notes from the night before. I could not even read some of my writing, so desperate was the scrawl.

"We'll have to get permission..."

Even in my state of panic, I recognised that I had to get away. They would not seek out the night watchman, so I would be forced to do so myself. With his testimony, they would see I spoke the truth, and all would be well.

I hurried to the window, slid the sash up and crawled out of the gap. The yard lay two storeys below me, but the kitchen roof provided a platform of sorts to my right. I inched along the windowsill and jumped across the narrow gap to the sill of the neighbouring room. Flakes of lime wash peeled away from the sill, coating my feet.

"The window!"

The inspector's voice floated out of the open window, and his head poked out into the cold morning air. He looked across at me, his kindly expression grown hard and unyielding.

"Stop!"

I threw myself into open space, and landed on the kitchen roof with a thump. Dazed and winded from the fall, I rolled down the roof and into the yard. I cried out when my knee made impact with a misshapen cobblestone. I looked up and Inspector Abbott disappeared from the window. Shouting came from inside the lodging house.

I forced myself to my feet and made my way across the yard. The back gate stood open, no doubt left unlocked by the coal man, and I limped out into the alley. I hurried towards the street, half-dragging my left leg behind me. My head start gave me just moments to disappear into another alley before the two policemen reached the yard.

I plunged down one street after another, ignoring the stinging cold, and the stares drawn by my flapping dressing gown and mad gait. The morning fog stung my eyes, and I hurried onward, ever mindful for the sounds of commotion behind me.

My stupor cleared when I reached Blackfriars Bridge. The usual throng of people parted as they steered clear of my unusual attire and air of desperation. Two figures remained still, unwilling or unable to move with the crowd. I peered through the fog, and recognised the hooded figure from Henry's painting. My vision cleared and I recognised her companion. The night watchman. He pointed to me while speaking to the creature, and I found I could read his lips.

"He talked." The night watchman knew that I had spilled her secret. Or, rather, their secret. He told me to dissuade me from pursuing the story further, but now I had passed it on. The creature set off toward me.

I turned to flee back in the direction from which I had come, thinking even Bedlam would be preferable to a final encounter with the Mother Goose, but my feet refused to obey. I opened my mouth to shout for help but no sound came forth. Panic fluttered in my mind, turning my thoughts to ice as I struggled to move. I was as frozen as I had been the night before, during the attack upon Ellen in the alley.

The figures advanced. I squeezed my eyes shut but still they came toward me. The night watchman brandished a club, and the hooded figure drew back her sleeves with skeletal hands. I ravaged my throat with silent screams. The hooded figure pushed back her hood. My mind imploded at the sight of the naked skull, and the fires of vengeance burning deep inside the empty eye sockets.

* * *

60

Inspector Abbott scanned the report one last time. The body of Edward Bonneville had been pulled from the river, and the coroner recorded a verdict of suicide—believed to be prompted by guilt. The inspector frowned as he read of the mysterious bruising around Edward's head and shoulders, apparently caused by some form of heavy blunt instrument. The vocal chords were tattered, and bite marks were found around his mouth.

The inspector stood and threw the report in the fire. He placed his mother's rosary in his top pocket, and left a new report on his desk, one which made no mention of bruises and bite marks.

This latest story was the final straw. It was time to pay a visit to Redcross Street.

BURNING
RAYNE HALL

Supper was bangers and mash with mushy peas. Mum had promised me the glossy calendar photo for November—lambs frolicking around Camber Castle—but only if I ate up every meal this month. I disliked greasy bangers, I despised mash, and I hated mushy peas, but I wanted that picture, and it was only the ninth. Half-listening to my parents' grown-up talk about the need for a new church, I stirred the peas into the mash. Instead of becoming more appetizing, the meal now looked like a vomit puddle around dog turds.

Pa's knife sliced a banger; fat spurted. His face shone with enjoyment. My brother Darren stuffed his mouth with mushy peas and smiled as if he liked the taste, which I knew he didn't. I wondered if Mum had promised him the picture, too.

Mum patted her freshly permed hair. "It's almost night." She stood up to pull the kitchen curtains against the approaching darkness, the way she always did during supper. This time she paused. "There's a lot of smoke. It looks like something's burning down by the old harbour. It glows. Holy Mother of Jesus, something's burning proper. It could be the Eversons' shop."

Standing on my toes, I peered out of the window. My breath fogged the cold glass. With the sleeve of my jumper, I wiped a patch clear, saw dark smoke spiralling toward the empty sky. A light glowed a half-mile from our house, like an orange-coloured glimpse of hell.

Pa put his fork down. "I'll go down the road and watch."

"Is it wise to get involved with this?" Uncertainty quavered in Mum's voice.

"I'm not involved." He stood up and took his grey hat and winter coat from the clothes hook on the door.

"Can I come?" Darren asked through a mouth full of blackened sauerkraut. "I've finished my supper."

Pa was already tying a grey shawl around his neck. "Yes, you can come, son." He paused, pointing his chin at me. "I'll take the girl, too."

Frightened by what I'd seen out of the window, I tried to protest. "I don't want to go. Please…"

An angry glance from Pa shut me up. His hard hand pulled me away from the table. "You'll come."

Within moments, Mum had bundled me into my anorak, a thick knitted shawl and a woollen hat. "Stay with Pa, don't catch a cold, and don't talk to anyone."

Darren grabbed his superman jacket and cap and ran down the stairs, and I followed. At least I had escaped from the mushy peas.

Pa forced me into the black metal seat on the bar of his bicycle, so that I was locked between his body, his arms and the handlebar. At seven, I was really too old to travel in the child seat, but he seemed to like holding me captive, and I did not dare suggest I ride behind him on the luggage rack. Darren followed on his own bike.

A few minutes later, we reached the blaze, and faced it from the safety of the pavement opposite. My heartbeat roared in my ears like a locomotive. The fire was real in its frightful intensity. Thick smoke oozed through the roof and curled into grey spark-loaded columns. Hot stink wafted in our faces.

"Smells like we're burning garbage," said a woman with silver spectacles and wrinkly skin. Others laughed; their laughter sounded eerie against the whine from the fire.

Many people had come to watch the house burn. Onlookers stood in small clusters, their hands in their pockets, their faces muffled with shawls.

My mouth was dry and tense; cold prickled on my skin, and I put my hand into my father's coat pocket to hold his hand. "I want to go home, Pa. Please."

"Watch." He grabbed my shoulders and turned me towards the fire. "Watch and learn. Learn about what happens to garbage."

I tried hard not to look, but the glow drew and held me. I knew the house: The shop on the ground floor sold magazines, lottery tickets, ice cream, my favourite Werther's toffee sweets and Mum's cans of mushy peas. Above the shop was a flat, and above that, an attic under a gabled roof.

The façade looked thin and vulnerable. The upper windows contained dark emptiness, and the bow windows of the shop screamed with orange heat. Everything looked black against this orange. The house reminded me of the lanterns we'd been making at school, black cardboard with rectangular cut-outs, with brightly coloured translucent paper behind.

I didn't mind the rows of mushy peas cans burning, but I regretted the Werther's toffee and ice cream chest.

"Are they in there?" a young woman asked in a thin voice. She carried a small white dog in her arms and stroked it incessantly. She tilted her head at my father. "The Eversons and the Arabs aren't still in there, are they?"

"I've only just arrived. I know nothing."

"If they were at home, they'd have come out by now, wouldn't they?"

When he gave no reply, she turned to the tall bespectacled woman. "The fire fighters are taking their time, aren't they?" She stepped from one foot to the other, either nervous or cold. "They've been notified, haven't they?"

"Yes," the other woman said.

"Well, they're volunteers, I suppose they can't be expected…"

"No."

"Still, why…"

The sea breeze whipped the flames into further frenzy. In the distance, seagulls screeched.

"I don't know anything, so don't ask." The older woman turned away. The younger one stopped talking, and pressed her face into her dog's coat.

Not everyone was quiet, though. Darren had met up with other boys from his class. They hurled stones at the windows of the upper stories, smashing the panes the fire hadn't reached yet, chanting something about cleaning up the town. Their teacher stood by, and I expected him to call the boys to order, but held his hands folded behind his back and watched.

Within moments, the sash windows of the upstairs flat lit up at once like a garland of festive lights. Glass crackled and tinkled, a beautiful chiming sound, dotted with poufs and bangs. The smoke grew darker and thicker, turning dirty brown and charcoal black. Plaster blistered and peeled off the wall. Embers flew.

Wind blasted from the site and threw furious heat at us. My face felt like a roasting sausage, but when I averted it, the icy night air made my hair stand up.

Sirens howled, the dog yapped, and people made room on the pavement for a shiny police car. Two uniformed policemen jumped out and shooed people back from the site, including the chanting boys. Then they stood, inactive, hypnotised like the rest of us.

Now smoke seeped from the small attic window, then it lit up as if someone had switched on a hundred lights behind a red curtain. A collective "Aah," rose from the crowd. A couple of people started to clap, but stopped when a policeman threw them a stern look.

I wasn't sure what it all meant. I couldn't believe that people were trapped inside this boiling heat. I scanned the crowd for the woman with the white dog, but she had disappeared, so I asked the woman with the spectacles. "Are there people in the fire? Are they burning?"

"Of course not, dearie," she soothed. "The Eversons are away on holiday. They had a sign in the window, 'Closed until Monday 11th'. And even if there was someone in there, they wouldn't feel a thing. The smoke would get them first. So don't you fret." She fished in her coat pocket. "Here, have a sweet, dearie." I hesitated, because my parents warned me not to take sweets from strangers, but Pa had laughed with this woman, so maybe she wasn't a stranger, and it was a Werther's toffee..

"Come on, take it."

Fearing to offend by refusing, I croaked a thank-you from my dry throat and took the sweet, but put it into my pocket.

Now a red fire engine pulled up with blue flaring lights. Dogs and sirens howled. While the fire fighters opened the hydrant and connected their thick limp hose, the burning house roared like an angry animal. The night sky now appeared deep blue, cool and clean.

I heard one fireman question a group of men. "Anyone still in there?"

"Don't think so. The Eversons own the shop and live in the flat above; they're away on holiday."

"There won't be much left of their shop and their flat when they come back."

"They're insured."

In the meantime, two fire fighters with helmets had rammed the door and gone in, but came out within moments, signalling with large arm gestures.

The fireman standing near us translated. "The staircase has collapsed. Nothing we can do."

Flames leaped high in the air, glowing orange and yellow, red and lilac, and it was the most beautiful and most horrible sight I had ever beheld. In the midst of the tumult, I heard screams from the fire.

Around me, people mumbled and shuffled their feet.

"It's the wood," someone said. "The fire has reached the ceiling beams." Another voice replied, "That's right. Old wood always sounds like that when it burns."

A fat dog howled and strained at its lead. But the people just stood, spellbound by the spectacle. The rumble and roar of the blaze absorbed any further cries. Huge billows of smoke and flame erupted when the roof burnt through and beams and timber collapsed with a crash.

A few moments later, the fire quietened, showing what was left of the building. The floor between the ground floor and the first storey still held. Above it, all was gone, apart from a few sagging fragments of walls, and the timbers on each corner which flamed like giant altar candles.

"That house is lost for good," the fireman said. "All we can do now is stop the fire from spreading."

The acid sting of wet ash got into my nose and into my throat where it scratched and tasted bitter. As best I could, I shielded my face with the knitted shawl. Dancing ashes showered us like confetti from a carnival float.

As the fire withdrew further, the darkness grew silent and cold.

"Time to go home," Pa said to nobody in particular. "The children are getting restless."

* * *

By the time we got home, I was shivering. Although I needed to ask many questions, Mum packed me into bed and told me to be quiet and sleep.

All night images of fire plagued me, and I feared I would burn. The bitter flavours of smoke and fear clogged my throat, and I heard the sounds of crackling fire. My heart hammered and my body was bathed in cold sweat. Many times I touched the floor to check it for heat, afraid that the storey below was burning. Any moment smoke and flames might burst through and engulf me in hell fire.

* * *

In the morning, I was still upset. My hair stank of nasty smoke, and my head burnt from the uneasy night.

Mum put her hand on my forehead while we sat at breakfast. "The girl has a fever. You shouldn't have taken her out in the cold."

"You've been too soft with the children. They have to become tougher." He lit a cigarette and puffed. Normally, he didn't smoke at breakfast. The smoke curled and found its way into my nostrils.

While the others had bread with butter and blackberry jam, Mum served up bangers, mash and mushy peas. In our family, sickness was no excuse for wasting food. I recoiled at the vomit-like stuff, no less repulsive after microwaving than it had been before. Mum sniffed, but not at the food. "Holy Mother, you stink. All three of you. The smoke is in your hair."

I sliced a banger with my knife, and watched the grease run and curl around the peas-mash heap. Darren spread butter and thick blackberry jam on his bread. I glanced at the picture of the jolly lambs and decided it wasn't worth it. If Pa left for work soon, I might get away without forcing the horrid stuff down. Mum sometimes waived punishments.

The letterbox rattled, and a plop told us that the newspaper had arrived. Mum fetched it. She moved the bread-bowl to the side and spread the paper out on the kitchen table, opening it on the first page of local news.

I read the headline, one bold word after the other. "Family Perish in Fire—Hoax Call Leads to Destruction of Shop and Homes."

Perish meant something like 'die'. But surely nobody had died. We'd been there, and everyone had said that the Eversons were away on holiday.

A large photo showed a smouldering ruin, a smaller one depicted fire fighters directing a blast from a hose.

Darren grabbed the paper and read aloud. "Three members of the Maqsoum family died in the fire. They were…" He mumbled the names and ages of the victims.

So people had died. They had burnt like the martyrs in the most frightening stories of *The Children's Book of Saints*. But it couldn't be true. The saints had died in faraway countries a long long time ago, not at the end of our road last night.

The report said that the local fire fighters had been called to a non-existent fire, which made them late to arrive at the site. It described how the charred remains had been found. The mother had cowered under a table while the father and the eight-year-old twin daughters had squeezed into a corner. The man's body was shielding the children with his own, apparently trying to hold off the flames from them until the last possible moment.

Nausea squeezed my throat again. These people had been awake and conscious. They hadn't passed out in the smoke, as the woman with the spectacles had tried to make me believe. With a pang of guilt I remembered the Werther's toffee I had accepted from her, and resolved to smuggle it into the rubbish bin later when nobody was looking.

I realised that the Arabs had seen the flames coming, looked into the deadly orange, smelled that bitter, acid smoke. Perhaps they'd found the exit blocked, but kept hoping that someone would get them out, if only they could retreat from the fire until help arrived. They'd withdrawn, shrunk into the corner, pursued by death. Even as the flames gnawed at them, as smoke clogged their nostrils and bit their throats, even as the flames started to devour their flesh, they continued to hope, even as the father sacrificed himself to gain a few more seconds for his girls... And then they screamed. I had heard those screams of pain and despair and death.

"They suffered," Mum said. "Holy Mother of Jesus, they must have suffered. I thought they'd go without pain, from the smoke. It doesn't seem right. Even for Arabs, this can't be right."

Pa shifted uncomfortably on the corner seat. I thought he would say something to praise the Arab father's courage. Instead, he lit another cigarette and said, "I'll be off in a moment."

Mum recovered and turned her attention to us. "Never play with matches," she lectured. "I've always told you so. Now you know what comes from being careless with fire."

"They were only Arabs," Darren said with the superiority of a twelve-year-old. "Dirty people. It was a dirty flat they lived in, full of clutter. Arabs live like that. I mean, just think of it. Four people in a one-bedroom flat. Decent people wouldn't live like that."

Although I didn't follow his reasoning, I accepted that the deaths had been at least partly the Arabs' fault, because of the way they lived, and because they had probably been careless with matches. I clutched my mug of hot milk.

"Why didn't they get out?" Mum wondered aloud. "They must have heard the fire, smelled something. They can't have been asleep at that time."

"Don't get involved." Pa took his coat and left.

* * *

Because of my fever, Mum made me stay in bed all day and brought me chamomile tea and hot water bottles. I sweated in the heat.

I could almost feel the hot breath of fire on my arms, and closed my eyes against the pain. In my mind, I crowded in the corner with the Arab family. We were trying to shield one another from the inevitable fire, the fear, the stinging leaps, the bites of the flames.

I thought of my own family. Strangely, I couldn't imagine Pa shielding us. I felt a yearning for the kind of love this Arab father had for his daughters.

In the evening, Mum made me sit at the kitchen table, either because she thought my fever had gone, or because she didn't want to annoy Pa. She plunked the plate of old food before me, not even bothering to reheat it in the microwave.

* * *

I was saved when a visitor came: the old woman with the silver spectacles. Mum patted her hair as if to check that the waves were still in place, and swiftly removed the plate with the disgusting food. Instead, she gave me and the woman fresh plates and we ate bread and mustard like the others. Of course talk turned to the fire again.

"Shame about the shop," the woman said. "I know Everson wants to move to more central premises where he can have a tea room, but it's still a huge loss."

Pa smiled. "They have insurance."

I didn't understand this grown-up talk, but had a vague idea that insurance prevented families from getting burnt. "Do we have insurance?" I asked.

"We don't need it. We don't have Arabs living in our house."

The mention of the Arabs made me cry.

"The girl's upset," the woman said. "It's been too much for her. She's so young. How old are you, dearie?"

"Seven," I managed between sobs. Then I asked the question I had wanted to ask all day. "Are they saints now? Have the gone to heaven?"

"No, dearie, they're Arabs. Arabs don't go to heaven."

I cried more. I wanted them to go to heaven.

Mum tried to console me. "Maybe there's something like a lower heaven where Arabs can go. Other heathens as well, if they've been good." She patted my hand. "Remember when your cat died? Maybe there's a heaven for cats and Arabs and other animals."

Darren giggled, and Pa snorted. "There's nothing in the Bible about that."

For a moment, all was quiet. Mum's mouth twitched like she might cry, too.

The visitor spoke into the silence. "If Everson doesn't rebuild, the site would suit our new church."

"We could use a new church." Relief sang in Mum's voice. "Something good is coming out of this after all." She folded her hands in her lap and smiled.

Pa and the neighbour smiled, too, because everything was good and right.

MINISTRY OF OUTRAGE
CHRIS LIMB

The world is a far better and much safer place than it has ever been and continues to improve on a daily basis.

What about the casual horror of urban life in the twenty first century? One only has to watch the news to be sickened almost beyond belief. The constant mindless violence. The murder. The hypocrisy. The disregard for others that has gripped the soul of the human race for the last half century.

I'm flattered that you really believe all of that. No, more than that. I'm actually quite touched. Thank you. That means a lot to me.

* * *

I considered myself an artist. A very highly paid artist, to be sure; an artist working to a very specific brief, but a bona fide creative giant nonetheless. On the other hand, I didn't see why this meant that I had to dress like some kind of bohemian imbecile. Not for me was the scruffy ill-fitting thrift store attire of the bulk of my colleagues. No unkempt hairstyle defiled my skull.

Some of my fellow employees at the Ministry of Outrage had, on occasion, remarked that I looked as if I'd be more at home in a city bank. What they failed to realise was that their faux beatnik look was just as much a uniform as the bowler and pinstripe of the denizens of the Square Mile.

As far as I was concerned what mattered was my work—and I'd never had any complaints about that.

The lift chimed and I stepped out through the opening doors into the Ministry's offices. Here I was again, back at work, enjoying my job, doing what I did best.

For all intents and purposes, the Ministry of Outrage was just another Soho advertising agency. Or so everyone believed. While it was indeed true that we took on any number of bona fide commonplace and lucrative contracts, these were just a front for our true purpose. A very successful front, certainly. Everyone remembers that one with Osama Bin Laden on the tube, not to mention the infamous Baby with AK47 campaign.

I love the way that our name was an elaborate double bluff. *Ministry of Outrage.* Very trendy, very chic. Very Soho. Very genuine ad agency.

Very true.

We never had to kowtow to the Advertising Standards Authority. We weren't answerable to the Independent Television Commission. Our masters were a body far more mysterious and powerful.

Strictly speaking we were civil servants. Personally, I still considered myself an artist.

I sat down at my desk and waggled the mouse. The computer woke from its slumber and, after typing in my password, I fired up NewsMill 2.0.

* * *

I was recruited while still working at Globular Cluster. It was shortly after one of my most daring and successful campaigns had been pulled after numerous complaints from Daily Mail and Guardian readers alike.

I was annoyed, but as far as my boss was concerned, having an advert pulled was a rite of passage. It meant that I was playing with the big boys now.

I had no idea how big until the Cadaver came calling.

It was one of those midwinter days when the watery London daylight barely made it down to street level. I was soaked and in a foul mood when I swept past Julie and started up the wrought iron spiral stairs two at a time.

"Maxwell!" she called after me. "There's a Mr Cavanagh to see you."

When I opened the door to my office he was sitting in one of the easy chairs, bowler hat and neatly furled umbrella hanging from my hat stand. I frowned. He should have been made to wait in the foyer.

He unfolded himself and stood. Topped with steel grey hair, the pale translucent skin of his face was stretched over an angular skull. He looked simultaneously delicate and powerful, older than at first glance. Almost a corpse. An intelligent and dangerous corpse.

"Mr Bruckler. Pleased to meet you. Cavanagh."

Cadaver. His voice was quiet. I shook the papery hand he offered me. It was surprisingly warm and strong. His suit was black and his shirt white. He wore a plain grey tie and regarded me through old-fashioned spectacles.

"What can I do for you?" There was something about him that told me acting on my initial impulse to ask him just what the fuck he thought he was doing would be unwise. I sat down.

"I'll get to the point." The Cadaver pulled a business card from his top pocket. "We wondered when you'd have time for a meeting with us. We have a proposition you might find interesting."

I took the card.

J Cavanagh esq
90 Whitehall
SW1A 2AS

The government.

"Look, if this is about those complaints…"

"Not at all," the Cadaver raised a hand, "Certain opportunities have arisen for someone of your talents. Opportunities that might afford a salary at least twice the one you currently draw. Interested?"

* * *

90 Whitehall was a grey building near the Ministry of Defence. Inside, wood-panelled walls and threadbare red carpet deadened my footsteps. I wasn't quite sure where to go. There was no reception desk.

"Ah, Bruckler," the Cadaver appeared from a door a little way down the corridor, "glad you could make it."

I followed him into a small windowless room dominated by a white projector screen.

"Do take a seat."

The seats were decrepit swivel chairs—state of the art circa 1950—but comfortable.

"I hope you'll find this interesting," the Cadaver slid a piece of paper and a fountain pen across the table, "but you need to sign this first."

Non-disclosure agreements were par for the course in advertising. Never mind government secrets; the shit would really hit the fan if WikiLeaks were ever to get its hands on half of what goes on in the commercial world.

Still, I'd never been asked to sign the Official Secrets Act before.

The Cadaver glanced at the signed document before secreting it within his briefcase.

"You may find this illuminating." He pressed the button on a remote control and a face appeared on the projector screen. A woman's face, contorted in anger, the light of hell burning in her eyes. The eyes. Beneath the fury there was something almost happy about them. A joy at being permitted such anger.

The picture panned sideways and zoomed out, revealing that the woman was merely one of a crowd, all of whom shared the same expression of ecstatic fury.

"This is what we have been tasked to control. Not far beneath the veneer of civilization lurk these barely human monsters." Despite the emotive turn of phrase, the Cadaver's voice sounded measured and calm, a voiceover from a documentary about the twenty-first century from several hundred years hence.

"Where's this from?" It looked familiar but it was the kind of thing you saw in the newspapers on an almost weekly basis these days—I might have just been recognising the look rather than the actual scene.

"A year ago. Outside a courthouse inside which an alleged child-killer was on trial. Look at the crowd's depth of feeling. How angry they are. You would hardly credit that the human brain had the capacity for such sustained negative emotion."

"Alleged?" I was curious about the Cadaver's turn of phrase.

"How many of these people do you think knew the victim or her family?" On the face of it the Cadaver was ignoring my question but I could tell from the intelligent glint in his eye that this was his way of replying.

"Difficult to say, given mob mentality," I thought about it and erred on the side of caution, "Say… less than five per cent of them? Depends upon the size of the community of course."

"An intelligent guess," the Cadaver pulled out a sheaf of papers from beneath the table and leafed through it looking for the answer, "it's Northampton, population approximately two hundred thousand. The size of the crowd outside the courthouse was over five hundred so that's more than a quarter of one per cent of the population. And of this percentage… precisely *none* of them knew the victim."

"Really?" I raised my eyebrows, "How can you be certain? I'm not surprised, given what people are like—but *none*? Really?"

"We can be absolutely certain of these facts," the Cadaver shut the dossier with a snap, "Because there was no victim. The entire case was a fabrication, the officers concerned are in the employ of our department and the perpetrator is an actor, also in our employ. It might surprise you to learn that once these people are supposedly locked up everyone forgets about them, no matter how many of them were vowing bloody murder and threatening dire consequences for them upon release. This is a very… useful amnesia."

"But why? Why bother?"

The Cadaver gestured with the remote again and the picture on the screen changed to a close-up of the woman first displayed.

"Because of this. "He walked over to the screen and tapped at it with a fingernail. "This untapped anger. We have to drain it off somehow."

"But isn't faking these outrages stirring up the anger in the first place?"

"Alas no," the Cadaver shook his head with a kind smile, "Without these distractions the anger and violence inherent in humanity would build up and explode. Probably directed at the government."

"So why…" I must admit I was puzzled. I'd always thought of the human race en mass as toothless cattle, a resource to be exploited by judicious use of pretty colours, pictures and lights. I didn't like the idea of having been wrong about something or having been in the dark. It felt against nature. Against *my* nature.

However, there was something about the Cadaver's demeanour that prevented any resentment building up against him. Despite his benign, almost frail, aspect there was something very dangerous about him. If I crossed him I wouldn't even know about it. I'd just wake one day to discover I'd never existed in the first place.

Besides, who was to say that cattle couldn't be dangerous? Tell that to someone trapped in the path of a stampede.

"It seems to be a property of civilization. Once population and technology reach a certain level, it's only a matter of time before society tears itself apart. A tricky subject to study, given the vast amounts of time and huge volumes of data to process, but our computer models suggest it's something to do with the nature of consciousness en masse. Revolution is nature's way of resetting the civilization clock, cutting the population back, emptying the gene pool and starting again. We can't allow that."

"How long has this been going on?" I had no doubt that what the Cadaver was saying was true. There was an undertone to his voice that forbade disbelief. He'd have made a marvellous politician. I wondered why he'd chosen to bury himself so deeply in the bowels of the civil service instead.

"Our control of this phenomenon started shortly after World War Two. Students of history could see that the revolutions and the rise of extremism of one stripe or another was the beginning of the end. If we weren't careful our two thousand-year-old civilisation was going to start tearing itself apart in a pointless war. People needed something else to get angry about. Something other than their own governments.

"For a while they used other governments or ideologies as an external threat, but that never really worked. For every five people who swallowed the line about the Soviets there were five more who'd decide to join them. Even when they dismantled that particular structure and chose groups such as Al-Qaida instead there was always the danger that people would see them as an attractive alternative. After a while these organisations became far more popular than they otherwise would have."

"But surely that's quite recent?" I was confused, "Have you only just changed your mind?"

"Ah no, forgive me" the Cadaver raised a skeletal hand in apology. "That was the external wing of the ministry, in liaison with similar ministries all over the world. But the internal office has been active just as long and with a greater degree of success I would say. You see, whilst there is always a possibility that external threats could divide the people we want to unite, what *we've* been doing is finding enemies within; enemies that no one in their right mind would want to support.

"We made some mistakes at first, of course. In the fifties and sixties we thought that drugs and the counterculture would be suitable candidates for demonization but they proved more attractive than repulsive. We hadn't taken the Beatles into account. They were a real wildcard.

"So we turned our hand to declawing popular music—although one operative thought we just needed to get the right angle on it. He tried again in 1976 and nearly succeeded but even a phenomenon as nihilistic as punk was attractive to some. So we had to find something else. We stripped drugs of their glamour and introduced cheap heroin into the country. This seemed to work for a while. You may remember?"

"*Heroin screws you up*," I smiled, "Those scary public information films were one of the reasons I wanted to go into advertising in the first place."

"I can see we've picked the right man." The Cadaver smiled and I felt good. Why did I find his approval so pleasing? Perhaps he was adept at speaking a very reassuring dialect of body language.

"After a while it became clear that even though it was an effective enemy to have chosen and one that did frighten people, it didn't make them angry. And bleeding off the anger was central to maintaining the control we required. Fear wasn't enough.

"Then we discovered the ideal demon. The paedophile, the kiddy-fiddler, the molester. Even vague rumours of such monsters were enough to whip the voters into a massive frenzy of anger. Have a look at this expression." With a gesture the Cadaver brought the close-up of the angry woman's face back into focus on the screen. "Can you see any empathy or sadness here? Is she thinking of the child she believes has been abused and killed? Absolutely not. She is revelling in the knowledge that she has been *allowed to hate*. Allowed to express violent, sadistic urges in an arena where none would dare censure her.

"For our purposes it's the perfect stimulus. If paedophiles didn't exist it would be necessary to invent them. The appetite for such bile is staggering.

"And it's not just paedophiles that are useful. Anything that drives self-styled right-thinking individuals to subhuman mob frenzy can be used. Pensioners mugged for twenty pee. Happy slappers.

"If you come across a news story that makes you wonder how human beings are able to sink lower that you ever thought possible—you're probably right. They didn't. We crafted the story to syphon off negative energy. If you've ever wondered why some crimes remain unsolved it's because they never happened in the first place. Handcrafting a solution as well as the crime would take far too much effort when all we need is the outrage."

"I see," I replied. I was excited, as if a curtain had been lifted and I was seeing the ropes and pulleys back stage. This was how the world worked. It made sense. People were incapable of committing heinous enough crimes and yet not intelligent enough to realise that if they couldn't then only the most deranged could.

"It takes artistry and a certain kind of imagination. We have software to predict where and when the pressure needs to be relieved, but how to release that pressure… Well, that's where individuals such as yourself come in. Artists. Creatives. Art is a lie—and the best lies are ones that people believe. People are becoming cynical about advertising, but most of them still believe what they hear on the news. The ultimate commission for a true artist. Are you in?" The Cadaver stood up and reached out a hand. As if he needed to ask. Of course I was in.

"Absolutely." I shook his hand.

"Welcome to the team." From the expression on his face the Cadaver had never been in any doubt as to the result of my recruitment.

* * *

I had developed an almost symbiotic relationship with the NewsMill software. Like the brush in a painter's hand, it was the tool of my trade, an extension of my brain. It was connected to a government database somewhere, but I had no idea from where this database obtained its information.

Every morning I studied a colour coded map of the United Kingdom. Red indicated the hotspots: the regions to which I should pay the most attention, the regions where intervention was needed, the regions where anger engineering was required.

Drilling down into the details for a particular area, I had access to an array of supporting variables with intriguing names like Strategic Social Spectrum, End-means Coefficient and Political Mobility Rate. It had taken a while, but I now had an instinctive feel for what kind of intervention was needed when I looked at the pattern of the numbers. On this particular morning I noted that a red spot down in Brighton and Hove required a medium sized media intervention. A newspaper report or a few lines on a website would not be enough; we'd need to fake some footage.

The eggheads over at the ministry were working on NewsMill 3.0 which would automatically generate the footage using CGI. This would save time. I had worried that my own skills might one day be superseded, but the Cadaver had reassured me that this wasn't the case. They'd tried automatically generating the stories in response to the figures but had ended up with nonsense—one scenario suggested by the computer was that a gang of toddlers had terrorised a war veteran with a syringe full of HIV positive blood.

No, for the stories to retain the ring of truth and to be palatable enough for the masses to swallow them, human creativity was required. Artistry. I was, above everything else, an artist. I took pride in my work. I was, in many ways, an auteur—a director whose artistic vision and deft hand imprinted his work with his own personal stamp—and was free to dream up and implement scenarios that fitted perfectly to the societies for which they had been designed.

I hoped one day to be put in charge of a major project with national scope. These events happened every year or so; the population as a whole required checks and balances to be applied. I'd advised and worked on smaller areas of bigger national campaigns, but had yet to be given one of my own. I lived in hope. It was only a matter of time; I already knew that individuals higher up the chain of command than the Cadaver had begun to notice me.

There was a risk with the bigger jobs of course. The terse manuals I'd read containing the history of such ministries worldwide mentioned their widespread failure in Eastern Europe at the close of the nineteen eighties. The last thing we needed was for that to happen here—and it was a risky business. One push in the wrong direction, a misjudgement of the mood of the people and we could have a revolution on our hands, no matter how many jubilees, Olympics, or royal weddings we threw at them.

I looked into the Brighton and Hove case. A three-minute news slot on BBC South Today (with associated web coverage) would suffice. Sneaking something onto the BBC was often the best thing to do as many other news agencies stole from them. We had contacts in all the regions, people working for the police and media who would do whatever was required of them without question.

With the control we had over the way the people saw the news we could have brought down governments if we'd wished. But there was no need. The government and the ministry were synonymous, even though they were officially unaware of us. It was all about plausible deniability.

We had our own artisans and actors. Our professional liars. They'd all signed the Official Secrets Act and were paid very well. Furthermore they'd been informed, without having to spell it out to them, that to blow the whistle on the ministry would have ended their lives—literally. But why would they? Our employees had to work at most a couple of months a year and were able to live like celebrities on the results. Any kudos that running to WikiLeaks would have given them was far outweighed by the loss of everything up to and including their brain function.

Besides, we had WikiLeaks in our pocket. An illusion of press freedom was very important. As long as the public believed there was someone digging out the secrets that governments preferred to keep hidden then they wouldn't go looking for anything themselves.

It wasn't perfect. Some of the higher profile public performances had serious continuity problems if you looked closely enough, and I was aware that on occasion heads had rolled in the higher echelons of the ministry and its foreign equivalents.

I wouldn't have to arrange anything on a national scale this time. For what I had in mind I'd need one actor—preferably an elderly lady—and a makeup artist. Our agents in the BBC and local police would do all the rest.

I typed the requirements into NewsMill using the usual terse abbreviations and went for a coffee. It wasn't required for me to be on the spot, but I preferred to oversee things, albeit from the shadows. Besides, I needed to indulge myself occasionally in order to flex my creative and intellectual muscles, to make sure my manipulative skills were finely honed and that I remained at the top of my game.

It wouldn't do for my work to fall below par. I didn't know what happened to people when they no longer were of any use to the ministry but imagined that there wasn't much room for promotion; I'd filled a very large pair of shoes, but what had happened to their original owner I had no idea. People went so far out of their way to avoid mentioning him—I was absolutely sure it had been a man—that there was a person shaped hole in my knowledge. It was a hole of such precise location and dimensions. If I looked hard enough I'd be able to find out not only his name and address but what his favourite film was, and where he went for breakfast the day before he died.

He was dead. Of that I had no doubt.

I had no intention of ending up dead. I had confidence in my artistic ability to produce reams of convincing reality substitute for decades to come. By the time I was ready to move on, no doubt death would have claimed some of the head honchos and I'd be able to step into the smart suit and shoes vacated by, say, the Cadaver himself. It would be a fitting way to spend my twilight years, inducting and teaching those like me so that my philosophy and mindset would live on.

Our methods were a small price to pay for security.

* * *

The makeup artist had done a sterling job. Half of the frail old woman's face was discoloured with a frightening bruise, brown and purple. They'd even managed to redden the whites of her eyes. A memo had gone around about the use of CGI instead of makeup, but I was sceptical. The verisimilitude of these reports could only be damaged by post-production; many of the people involved—including the camera operator—were unaware of the fact that they were taking part in an elaborate fabrication and it was best to keep things that way.

The woman stood at the bottom of Adelaide Crescent, the wide sweep of Georgian Terraces forming an impressive background, and told in a shaking voice how an assailant wearing a hood had mugged her on the doorstep of her flat. Thankfully he hadn't got hold of her door keys—which she wore on a lanyard around her neck—but had snatched her handbag and given her a kicking before running off. The ironic thing, she said, was that she had less than two pounds in cash on her and nothing else of any real value in there.

What was the world coming to?

Once the filming had wrapped up, the star of our piece was whisked away in a private cab, not to the imaginary flat in Adelaide Crescent but to a large property at an undisclosed location somewhere in the mid-Sussex countryside. The BBC packed up their equipment and drove off leaving me standing on the seafront.

I began walking towards the city centre and my hotel, setting sun at my back. I wasn't staying anywhere ostentatious, just a small family run hotel down in Regency Square, somewhere the ministry always took its business when in the area. A hotel with an exclusive private bar.

After three or more hours alone in the bar I was bored. Despite how much I'd downed I didn't feel in the slightest bit drunk. Alcohol never affected me that much, especially when I had other urges to satisfy.

I marched downstairs and out into the night.

It had been a warm enough day but the air was now beginning to cool. I checked my watch. It was one AM, the ideal time for this kind of thing. I turned one way then another, trying to lose myself in the narrow maze of residential streets along the sea front. My hand clutched at the object in my coat pocket, the object I always carried with me when out and about, just in case the opportunity presented itself.

And then I saw him. An old man, shuffling uphill along a narrow street. I sped up and within seconds was only a few yards behind him. I glanced about. There were no CCTV cameras in range.

I reached forward and grabbed him by the shoulder, spinning him round, making sure he was fully aware of the tyre iron I clutched in my other hand before I brought it crashing down on his skull.

The expression on his face was worth it. That delicate balance between confusion and terror. It was perfect—as was the way his skull split and he collapsed to the floor, a stream of thick arterial blood trickling across the pavement and into the gutter.

I was an artist and while I employed my skills in the service of my job, there was nothing quite like the thrill of working with genuine materials. Faking it was only so satisfying; eventually you had to express yourself for real.

The thrill faded and I dropped the tyre iron back into my coat pocket. The lining was waterproof; I'd be able to remove all trace of the event later. I turned away and began walking back down the street when a figure stepped out from behind a parked van. My heart stopped. At first I could only see the silhouette, but then its identity became clear.

It was the Cadaver.

My life was over. I had become a liability and was sure that he was going to remove all trace of me either now or at some point over the next twenty-four hours. There was no escape.

And then he smiled, removed one of his gloves and held out his hand for me to shake.

"Welcome to the next level," he said.

MAID OF BONE
TOBY BENNETT

The teeth in Allie's pocket were chattering with the cold. She slipped cautiously between the crooked rows of stone lining the mist choked graves. With only stars to light her way, progress was difficult but she was careful never to put a foot out of line; it was unthinkable that she might step over a verge and disturb what slept so lightly in the looser earth.

Keep to the path. Keep to the path.

The words clacked like ticker tape in her head. Not just anyone could approach the ossuary; there was a prescribed way to do things, if you wanted to be received—if you wanted to be able to leave once you got there.

Each footfall mattered; you had to be soft and quiet and come when the night was darkest. No one had ever directly told her these rules, she relied on dreams and omens. The sudden flight of birds, the turn of wrinkled cards, the way sediment lay in old cups; like all love affairs it came down to murmurs and instinct.

She would not deviate from her path, could not put a step wrong for fear of the consequences. Consequences she could only vaguely imagine. Horrors that were whispered to her from the moonless sky; warnings that slipped between her legs, on the stray vapours of the mist, caressing her with a chill that tightened her belly into a hard knot.

Allie could smell the dank moss, the not quite dead vegetation that rotted close to the small spring trickling from the hillside with winter's wash. She was getting closer, almost there now. The teeth rattled in anticipation. The screech of insects answered the sound from the darkness.

She had had her first kiss in the shadow of the ossuary, her back pushed hard against the torn breast of a saint, watched by the stone devils that plagued him. She never knew who had kissed her, she'd kept her eyes firmly shut just as she'd been told—it was the only time her love had ever talked to her directly.

The memory of that encounter called her back, especially on the cold nights, laden with offerings and ready to make wild promises, anything to be free of the fear she felt beyond the cemetery walls. Allie knew she would be allowed to stay, one day, when she had laid enough before the iron bound doors. Yellow ivory, white bone, things both new and long dead; things made clean by worms, kept hidden from the sun until ripe.

Her betrothed craved sacrifice, but what lover didn't?

Her worn boots began to squelch in the deepening mud and a few drops of icy water flew up to soak through threadbare skirts.

A shiver ran through her so reminiscent of the touch she yearned for. A moment dimly remembered, pain and fear, a weight against her. Was it wrong to promise yourself to a stranger in the dark? Allie didn't have an answer, all she knew was that she would keep making offerings until her love returned. Right and wrong, smart or stupid didn't matter, it wasn't like she'd been given a choice. The wind was rising, chasing away the low mist and whipping her dark hair into streaming chaos. She ground her teeth and mashed her hands deep into her pockets.

Allie had spent so long getting herself to look just so, it wasn't fair. Her beloved never saw her as she wanted to be seen. The wind seemed to push against her, as if to drive her back from the brooding mausoleums ahead of her.

I will not be denied.

She reached out and took support from the crooked angel that stood over the sunken and forgotten grave of Thomas Rilley, nineteen thirteen to nineteen sixty-three.

"Thank you," she whispered to the angel. The cracked stone stayed expressionless but she knew that she had done the right thing to speak. Angels could be vengeful—standing alone for so long bred spite.

"Sorry to disturb you, Tom," she added as an afterthought.

An owl hooted its approval of her manners, winking at her from the velvet night with lambent eyes that missed nothing. Before too long the wind blew itself out, the owl returned to the hunt and she could move forward once more. She felt a growing warmth, an eagerness to her stride as she stepped into the shadows of the taller monuments that snaked over the older, moister parts of the graveyard.

Here a century had spilt its favoured children, holding them close in clinging clay. The shadows were long and stubborn here. Great horses rose above old generals and cherubs squatted like vultures over the tombs of babes. Each chisel stroke upon the weathered stone spoke of agony, ground into marble and granite with grim resolve; so that those who stole new years from their betters might remember. Lost brothers, wives and mothers, scattered in the darkness, hidden from the sun.

None knew all the secret names now. Allie only knew a few.

No one risked the cold or dared to walk between the frozen watchers for long. The statues set to guard old secrets, all better left buried.

The ground rose, becoming drier and now her damp feet sounded on bared paving stones, scoured by the sulking wind that made the grave dust dance in tiny, ever decreasing circles. She smoothed her hair, her fingers catching in the knots that unseen fingers had tied as she walked the path. The dead would have their little jokes.

The ossuary stood on the top of the hill. Her heart was pounding—a rhythm to prick up the ears of all but the most sated of night time wanderers.

A row of trees had once adorned the last sweep up towards the low building that squatted at the top of the hill but, like teeth in an old man's mouth. Many had fallen leaving the avenue ragged.

The bleached bodies of the trees had never been removed, just shifted to the side of the path where their splintered bodies lay half buried, holding back the coiled brambles and darting thistles that had long harboured designs on the pale stones that lead to the house of bones.

Before she knew it, Allie stood before the great doors. The saint and his demons stared at her with hollow, deep carved eyes. They watched as she reached into her pocket and began to lay out her gifts before the door.

A bird's skull, small and light. The feet of the cat that had killed it.

Last of all, she laid out the teeth, still alive with the aching cold. Gold glinted from one of the molars as she set it in a fan-like pattern over the pale bones that she had spent so long picking clean; that was a special prize, gold for her love as precious as the moments they would share soon when she was heard, when the door groaned open and she was taken below.

Allie was so lost in making everything just so that she almost didn't hear the approach of the night watchman. At the last moment she noticed the scrape of boots and the muted glow of his approaching light.

She panicked and scurried on all fours into the shelter of a carved tome that had cracked and toppled from the stone pedestal that marked a long dead scholar's grave. She squeezed herself into the narrow space between the plinth and the stone pages, all the while whispering apologies to the one who slept beneath.

The watchman came closer and she had to stifle her prayers.

Her entreaties were silent now.

Please make him go away.

Let him not see.

Make him blind. Make him scared. Make him pass quickly.

The unwelcome torch came on regardless, robbing the shadows of their mystery and freezing the unquiet statues into position.

The watchman, himself little more than a tramp, was drunk, walking unevenly. Allie knew that the old man only took the job in exchange for a meal and somewhere warm to sleep. He was as lost in the world of the living as she was. He was probably the only one closer to the dead than Allie, though she hated to admit it. The watchman, like all of the living, was too hot, dirty and loud. The one time they had encountered each other before had not been pleasant. He'd made all sorts of threats and terrible, burning promises about what would happen if he found her again.

Allie forced herself further back into the shadows, wincing at the touch of the stone through her thin jacket.

If I push too hard and the old book shifts…

She closed her eyes for a second and forced herself to breath regularly.

When she opened her eyes Allie was greeted by a terrible sight.

Her prayers had been answered, at least in part, the drunkard had not seen her gifts. At least that is what she assumed because he was pissing right on them. A night's worth of drink dribbled out in steaming drops. The old despoiler even had the gall to up end his bottle into his maw, while he was shaking himself dry over her hard won gifts.

It was too much. She rushed him, a wordless howl spilling from her lips.

It didn't take much to tip him over, the watchman had never been steady on his feet.

Allie hadn't really had much of a plan, she just wanted to make him pay, she'd imagined him falling into the door, flopping in his own piss., She'd hoped to give him a good scare and a kick before he could pull himself together, but she never got the chance.

The door. *Her* door.

The one that had always been locked, swung wide as the watchman fell against it. He teetered for the merest instant then tumbled down into the darkness. He landed with a wet *thunk.*

Alley cast about for the fallen man's torch, her hand recoiling from the fresh, warm, mud. At last she grasped the rubber handle and sent a thin beam into the cavernous blackness in front of her. That moist darkness— something that she longed for and at the same time something she had hoped never to see. The torch beam stabbed down, as noticeable as a pure soul in hell, and illuminated the pool spreading out from the watchman's bald head.

She was trapped. Part of her filled with longing to slink into the hollow stillness of that tomb and another part of her queasy with the realisation of what she had done. This was no cat, no bird—that was a man cooling on the stones below her.

As much as she wanted to respond to the clear invitation of the open door, there was the terrible miasma of the fresh kill stopping her from crossing the threshold into the sanctuary she had dreamed of for so long.

Piles of pale bones lined the walls, their yellowed exteriors made purest white by the torch's stabbing beam.

"Go," A thin voice echoed from the neatly arrayed piles of decay. The densely packed skulls and long femurs caught the splash of the torch's light, but there was no one living to be seen.

Allie stood her ground for a second, fighting the fearful urgings of her pounding heart. Her skin prickled. They were so close, so full of expectation. Her legs felt like they might not hold her as she turned and ran back into the night. Ghosts followed her all the way home.

* * *

She had to wait for the moon to dim again before she felt their call. The weeks had not been easy. The world of the living was sharp and jarring enough; her stepmother's shrill calls, her father's rough touch. Allie had been a ghost among them for so long, now she felt displaced from the only world that made any sense to her.

The birds and the cups, the cards and bones, all agreed that it should have been her lying at the bottom of those stairs. The watchman had stolen her place. Left her to deal with the mess he left behind.

The dead had only anger for her now. She felt their contempt even beyond the cemetery. In the guttering of candles and the crackling hiss of flickering bulbs. There was rage at the edge of light; resentment in the darkness from those she had betrayed, polluted.

At first she feared that the watchman would be missed. She watched the bone house for days hidden in the long grass at the top of the hill. None of the other visitors to the cemetery noticed her. She felt like everyone must know what had happened. How could they not hear the dead railing against her?

She need not have worried. The ossuary held its secrets well. No one went close to the ossuary and no one looked up at the dark girl standing on the hill. Mourners had eyes only for their own dead anyway.

The loss of the watchman had no outward effect on the cemetery, except that they padlocked the gate at night. The living, ever deaf, didn't mourn with the dead.

Allie had long ago found ways to breach the crumbling walls.

What with guilt and worry, there had been less time to find proper gifts than she would have liked. She felt empty handed when she returned. A child's doll with a missing leg, some blood-stained glass from outside a pub and feathers, bound with spider's web, were all she had to offer. She had considered some part of her own body, but she knew that there was already enough blood. The graveyard was alive with it.

There were scratching sounds emanating from every grave she passed. The dead had known the watchman well and they could smell him on her, scent her guilt.

Allie didn't know if she feared or hoped for the chill touch of some ghoul on the lonely trek up to the ossuary. Would it be *him* or some other, angrier phantom? Did it really matter? Would *he* even want her anymore? She had never been at peace with the living, the way they hurt you, judged you. It had always been the dead that she had turned to for comfort.

They'd buried her real mom far away, but one headstone was much the same as another. Allie had recognised the fellowship of death from the start. When she was a girl she'd pictured bony fingers stretching from one coffin to the next like roots; everyone holding hands in the dark. No matter where her father moved them or how hard things got she could always find a trace of the life she had lost in death.

A child's dream, she saw deeper now, but there was still cool solace in the cemetery's shadows and the hissing of its leaves, elusive whispers in the night.

The voices had never been hostile before. Some were angry or confused but she had never heard them direct that rage at her. Now it was like crossing a room after her father had been drinking, the slightest noise might set them off and there was no knowing what they might do to her. Her haven had turned sour.

It was a slow walk; Allie had to make so many apologies. She knew they were only just accepted. Rilley's angel bared long fangs at her when she passed and the cherubs puffed out fat cheeks in disapproval. With the watchman lost the path was becoming overrun with new growth. Allie had never realised how much a part of the place the old ogre was.

I've hurt them all, stolen the one who looked after them.

It was hard to know what to feel. She would not have harmed her sleeping family for anything, but he'd been so loud and disrespectful.

He'd forced her to do something.

She'd only wanted to teach him a lesson after all.

If... It was no good making excuses. She knew what it was like to have someone who hurt you tell you that they never meant to do it. How many times had she wanted to scream back, 'You're not sorry, you're never sorry'? What people did mattered and there was no point trying to tell yourself that there were excuses.

Allie balled her fists and swallowed back tears. Her failure was hers to accept; if the dead made anything clear it was that at some point you have to stop running.

Another tree had fallen and she was forced to step over it. Jagged branches snatched at her skirts and despite her best efforts, wooden claws scored her calves. More blood in the graveyard—she could feel the air thicken with the scent. Allie made the best she could of it, mopping at the thin trails on her legs with the bundled feathers. Feathers, spider webs and blood; blood on glass and childhood lost.

Will it be enough?

The door had not been relocked. She had no torch this time but her eyes drunk in the starlight, picking out details that should have been hidden to mortal eyes. Each step of the shadowed stair was clearly defined, even down to the spider-web cracks that permeated the worn stone. Further down, a monochrome world spread before her, its boundaries defined by the neatly stacked bones that lined the chamber's rough stone walls. The white bones radiated pale light, an eldritch gleam that only her eyes could see.

The first step down was slippery and the railing next to it was jagged, corroded. The next step had crumbled slightly when the watchman hit— she could feel the indent with her foot. The third was smooth with use.

Four

Allie didn't know why she was counting; it wasn't much farther to the bottom.

Five

The numbers kept the other voices out, she realised. It had been subtle at first but as she neared the bottom of the stairs the sounds bloomed in her head like she was in a crowed auditorium. Snatches of old conversations and flashes of regret, forgotten grudges and secret joys threatened to overwhelm her.

Six

It was too much; she was being torn in too many directions.

Eight? Or was it nine? There couldn't be many more than that could there?

Allie had once imagined that only one person spoke to her from the dark but now she knew that there were many. A voice for every skull; every skull speaking as one; each whispering a greeting or demand.

The watchman was not where he had fallen. Dried blood told her that his body had been dragged across to the wall. That's where she found him, thinner than he had been; the skin already drawn tight, his teeth bared in greeting… just like all the rest.

"He must be cleaned." The voices whispered.

"Prepared."

"Made one of us."

"Flesh does not belong here."

"I can't," Allie protested. Her voice echoed through the hollow chamber and something shifted deep in the brittle piles.

I'm going to be sick. Please don't make me.

"You brought him here, it is your job." There was no room for argument.

"You put him among us."

"You must clean him, hold things together."

The breath hissed between Allie's teeth.

You can't ask me to do this… I won't!

She flinched, expecting more anger—ready for the inevitable pain, but there was only silence.

"You did this." The skulls said, "You placed him amongst us. Do you deny it?"

If they had shouted, threatened, she would have known how to handle that. It was a lesson long learned. It was the simple expectation that disarmed her.

Allie's stomach heaved and she turned as if to go... but at last she nodded. She lay the blood soaked feathers and the doll in the centre of the room, but she kept the heavy piece of glass.

Pretend you are not here—it's someone else doing this. If they want it done so badly let them...

But they need you, you did this. You killed a man, you have to make it right.

First, she peeled off the man's uniform. It was hard to work the buttons because her fingers had gone icy and numb. The greasy cloth crackled as dried blood flaked away. Next, she reluctantly disrobed herself. The work would be messy.

But you don't have to notice.

The image of one of the few holidays they had taken when her brother was still alive flitted through her mind. Her brother grinned at her, and laughed at her embarrassment about being seen in a swimming costume. She wished she was free like he was now.

"Don't look," she said, blushing at the thought of them seeing her. It was as much apprehension as cold that studded her pale skin with goosebumps. She laid the watchman flat and straddled him, raising her improvised blade. Her first cut was tentative and the jagged glass barely broke the skin.

God help me I can't do it again.

"Harder." The dry voice from beyond the bones ordered.

Allie gulped and thrust the glass hard into the watchman's distended belly.

A cloying stench rose up, curling over her naked flesh like the long fingers of some lascivious wraith.

"Again!"

Her hand obeyed without thought. Allie winced as the blackened glass nicked her finger, but that didn't stop her from stabbing again and again.

At last the yellow fat was rolled back and the stubborn tendons had been individually severed.

She was only vaguely aware of it; she was lost in memory, watching her brother play with his red beach ball, he was still so small.

Allie retched as she became aware of her surroundings again for a moment. She didn't look down, her hands worked automatically, so clever in the dark, even without eyes to guide them.

"It has to go."

"Dirty." Another voice added.

"We are all clean here."

"You must do as he would have."

Allie reached out and plucked at the slimy mess with thin, cold fingers. She felt something slide from out of her grip like a thick worm. She chased it, squeezing to get a better hold and pulled. The stench intensified. Allie's eyes watered but she kept tugging and she was rewarded with a sudden release in tension that sent her spilling backwards with an armful of gore. Heavy wetness sloshed against her chin, covered her upper body and dribbled down her naked thighs.

She sobbed and held onto a scream.

"Take it away!" A distant voice whined.

"Bury it away from us."

"Give it to the gnawing worms."

I'm not here.

Allie plunged back into the security of her memories, but the miasma found her even there. The stench rose.

Mum had told them to not to swim close to the outflow pipes on the other side of the beach.

Allie regained her feet, her arms still cradling what she had drawn forth.

Wet sand for the castle.

She deposited the heavy mass in the watchman's long coat.

She took it all for burial, leaving the watchman hollow, his ribs protruding. She washed herself in water from the spring on the hillside by the first rays of the sun. When she came back for her clothes no one spoke. Sunlight made them nervous, but she knew she would have to come again.

* * *

A month has gone; another moon has died.

* * *

Allie came back with a knife. Her offerings were also better prepared this time. Twisted wire bound a mannequin made from old chicken bones, a token of her intent. Coloured ribbon from three lost kites, a wedding ring thrown from a window, and a bottle containing a note that would now never be read.

She reached the door without feeling any menace this time. The memories of the dead are too focused on things that happened long ago for any short term grudges. Besides they knew how much she had already done for them.

Allie reached into her pocket and drew forth the small blade, the one that she used to skin cats and cut the heads from birds. She would finish things tonight, she swore to herself as she stepped into the gloom. The bones provided their own light again.

Time had done a lot to make her work easier. The flesh was soft and slipped easily from bone. Allie couldn't help but notice there were also large bites take from the corpse. She glanced at the skulls but they were quiet tonight, silenced by guilt. She could read their expressions though.

You brought him here you left us alone with him… what did you expect? It's been so long since we chewed.

Allie shook her head and got to work.

She tugged and cut at the corruption that covered the watchman, making him clean and pure with practiced strokes. Maggots spilled and squirmed from the putrid stuff. Allie ignored them and continued to scrape with her knife. Before she knew it the last of the meat was cut away.

She tore away the scraps of flesh with her fingers; rasping away the last stubborn strands with her nails. Polishing until the bones were as fit as any offering she had ever made. The bones now gleamed with their own light.

"Good."

"Rest now."

"Lie with us."

"Accept your place."

Allie piled the bones just as the others were piled, they were still a little raw but only the keenest eye would notice that they were fresher than the others or pick out the nicks left by the pocket knife.

Allie lay down beside the new pile, her hand caressing the smooth ball of a knee joint. Finally she would be welcome in her true love's house. He would come to her, given time, she knew it. Maybe he already watched her through hollow eyes, one more faceless suitor in the smiling rows around her. It was hard to know where he might be, yet she felt him all around and hungered for his touch. She would not mistake his touch for any other. She rubbed the silken tip of the bone.

Time meant little here. It was enough to know her groom was waiting.

She slept deeply and woke at dawn's first light. It felt so good to have been accepted, to have a proper home again at last. It was a feeling that stayed with her through the next day. The living world seemed like a translucent dream. The awkwardness and the fear that she had while dealing with the world beyond the cemetery evaporated. There was no more need for concern, no more waiting.

The watchman had been an accident, a bad one. It still made her shiver to think what she had done, how close she had come to losing everything. The memories were almost enough to dim her euphoria—almost. However upsetting the means had been, Allie had no doubt that she had pleased everyone waiting for her in the ossuary. She belonged with them now.

Allie was so confident that she had done all that was needed that she went back to the cemetery the next night, she didn't wait on the moon or try to find offerings. That was all in the past. They would accept her now—they had to after all she had done. The watchman owed her most of all.

Whatever she had taken from him when she pushed him, she had also given him a home. He would have to return the favour. She came back to the graveyard with all the eagerness of a bride, slipping through the graves, past the wretched angels and over the carcass of the fallen tree. Careless of wraith and thorn, she skipped up to the door.

She could feel them summoning her and she was overjoyed that her work had been well received and that she would once more know the cool calm of the ossuary, an end to the loneliness she felt among the living. She flashed a smile at the saint and the demons he played with.

She pushed. The heavy wood didn't budge.

She pushed again, as hard as she could.

"More to do." She heard them whisper from the dark.

"There is a tree on our path."

"And dead flowers on the graves."

"You must attend these things."

"That's not fair." She shouted but they gave no response and the door remained locked.

She hammered and pleaded. How could they be so cruel? How could they deny her when she'd made such an offering—done so much?

They want more.

Allie's foot hit something in the dark. She bent down to retrieve it and found herself holding the watchman's torch. It didn't have to mean any-thing, but then birds could fly at random, tea could settle and mean noth-ing, cards and coins might flip to chance. Allie clicked the torch on and off. Was this all they'd offered her?

She pounded as hard as she could, left fresh blood on the rusted iron of the door.

"Let me in, you can't make me do this."

Nothing.

Were they even there?

Had they ever been?

Surely they could see what they were doing to her. The terrible cycle they were asking her to be a part of.

"Open up or I'll never come back," she threatened, but of course it was a lie. Where would she go if not here?

She would do anything, anything they asked and they knew it. Allie had never been able to deny her love, no matter what it cost her. Other people might not understand, but *they* did. Allie knew they could be ruthless and she knew that when they were, she would accept it.

How could anyone in love do any different?

Allie didn't like to think about the other reason she would come back despite their cruelty—she had nowhere else to go.

She would clear the tree and clean the graves; she already knew how to pacify the angels. With the watchman gone, she was the only one who could, and she'd keep doing it until they unlocked the door for the last time. Her sacrifice was still not enough—she would give more, they knew that, trusted her. She could not fail them without failing herself. She had made herself the final offering—as much part of them now as the watchman's polished bones.

No going back.

Anyone with a soul would have understood how desperate she was, how much she needed an end to her pain. Anyone who could feel would never have asked her to walk the lanes of graves at night alone. Anyone with a heart would have relented, swung the door wide and held her close—but there was only silence. The silence of the long sleep until the moon was dark again and a new supplicant made fresh offerings. She was a fool to think he would give himself so easily, that enough had been given and their courtship was done. His love was yawning, infinite and insatiable.

Allie understood now, the one she loved and the ones she cared for did not have heart or soul or feel another's pain—they were, after all, made of bone.

SHADES OF MEMORY
S.G. LARNER

Patrick reined Constance to a halt to study the bent metal sign. It should have said 'Miriam Vale', but some unknown vandal had gouged at the paint, so that it now proclaimed: M an Vale. Beside the sign, an upside-down, blackened ute rusted by the crumbling highway. Black sand drifted against the useless vehicle, carried on scorching winds from the endlessly burning coal seam gas fields to the west.

The tightness in his chest might have been from anxiety or exhaustion. This was the first town he'd seen in the past three days of horseback travel under a blazing Queensland sun. Razed homesteads littered the verges of the highway, remnants of the Upheaval. Patrick licked cracked lips, his throat dry, and longed for decent food and a bed.

Patrick gave Constance a gentle kick and her hooves thud-clopped on the disintegrating road.

They passed a rotting old Queenslander, its roof missing, lantana strangling the walls. Parched dust and spiky weeds filled the space once occupied by lawn.

Down the road a mangy yellow dog barked and then disappeared behind a large black object. Patrick squinted through the orange haze of sunset, but couldn't make it out. As he approached it resolved into a giant fibreglass crab, charred and twisted and riddled with bullet holes. It blocked the doors of what had once been a petrol station, but was now a burnt husk. The bowsers had melted into blackened lumps from the heat of the conflagration.

A tiny smear of yellow caught his eye. He nudged Constance closer, although she snorted and trembled. A scraggly dandelion flower lay between the crab's claws. His belly curdled. "Strange place," Patrick said, ignoring his gut. He patted Constance on her sweaty neck. "I suppose it's to be expected, out here near the gas fields."

Empty buildings stretched the length of the highway that cut through the town. A skinny boy of about eight burst out from behind the crab, chasing the yellow dog. The dirty child ran in front of Constance's legs, glanced at Patrick with wide eyes and dashed away. Constance reared, her ears flattened. Patrick soothed the skittish horse and turned her head in the direction the boy had gone. The street sign said 'DOUGALL ST', and as he rounded the corner a stranger crossed the road and entered a large building ahead.

MIRIAM VALE HOTEL. The paint was faded but the building was sound. He was surprised by a large solar panel perched on the roof above a tattered awning, but smiled in anticipation of a hot shower. The smell of roasting meat drifted from the open windows and his stomach rumbled. He dismounted and wrapped Constance's reins around a pillar. She flicked her ears and whinnied as he opened the ochre door.

An old-style jukebox stood against a wall, lights flashing. Nearby a grandfather clock ticked. Three scraggly men sat at the bar. Two were Aboriginal, with black curly hair and dark skin, and one was bald with blond whiskers. All three had hunched shoulders and worn spirits. They turned as one and glared at him. The publican, a stout man with an angry burn scar across one side of his face, raised an eyebrow.

"Don't see many of your kind 'round here," he said.

Patrick touched his dog collar. "Am I able to get a drink? Lemonade, I mean." He flushed, emasculated under their combined stares. Lemonade. Not a real man. "I've travelled far."

The publican shrugged and poured the cloudy beverage then slammed it onto the bar. "It's your business what you drink, God-man."

Patrick perched on a stool and sipped the lukewarm lemonade. It wasn't sweet enough. "Has there been illness?"

Mutters. The blond-whiskered fellow frowned. "No illness."

Patrick blinked. "Oh. I just thought, with how empty it seems…"

Blond-whiskers shifted on his stool. "It'll fill up soon enough." Laughter from the others that quickly died as they lapsed back into brooding and gulped their beers. The publican glanced at them then back at the priest

"Are you wanting a room?"

Patrick nodded. "I'm heading to Calliope tomorrow, but I'd appreciate a bed for the night. Is there anywhere to stable my horse?"

The publican poked his head in the kitchen and yelled something. After a moment the child from earlier scurried out, glanced sidelong at Patrick and disappeared out the front door.

"Charlie will deal with your horse. What's your name, lad? Is this your first posting?"

"Patrick. Yes. O'Malley." His cheeks warmed again. "I've travelled from Bundaberg. From the seminary. The priest in Calliope died. They sent word asking for a new one. The Bishop thought it would build my character." Patrick remembered the Bishop's face as he'd said that. The others had sniggered; Davvy had said it was a good way to get rid of dead wood.

"It's rough out there," the publican said and reached across the bar. "The name's Bailey."

Patrick shook his hand. "Thanks for your kindness, Bailey. God smiles on you."

Blond whiskers grunted at that. Patrick ordered food and slunk off to a table in a shadowy corner.

* * *

The grandfather clock struck midnight. Patrick woke with a start, a puddle of cold drool under his cheek. The pub was full of tense men. Each careworn face stared toward the entrance, and as the last *dong* faded an expectant hush descended.

The door opened and a middle-aged woman with a round figure in a blue dress strode in. She was followed by a teenaged girl with blonde hair and a beaming smile, and then a little girl who was a younger version of Charlie. Still more women entered.

Patrick waited for the scolding to begin. Instead, smiles and hugs were exchanged, and Patrick's breath misted in the suddenly frosty air.

Music blared from the jukebox. Townsfolk danced to songs Patrick hadn't heard since he was a child. He sidled along the wall to the bar.

"Shouldn't those children be in bed?" he asked Bailey as he scratched his head, unable to figure out what made him so uneasy about the scene. The publican stood with his hand resting on the bar, a slack expression on his face. He shook himself at Patrick's words.

"You should take *yourself* to bed," he said with a frown.

"But..." Patrick leaned forward and studied the women. "Where were all these people before?"

Bailey tensed. "The God-man needs his rest," he said, raising his voice above the din. The revellers paused in their merrymaking and regarded him with suspicion. His skin prickling, he took his room key and retreated upstairs.

* * *

Sleep eluded him. The sounds filtered up through the carpeted floor until the first pale light of pre-dawn smudged the room with charcoal shadows. When quiet finally reigned he drifted into a fitful slumber.

He woke, his heart pounding. Hot air blanketed him, his skin coated with sweat.

Patrick sat up and kicked the damp sheets off his legs as the significance of the dandelion lying on the dirt in front of the burnt, pocked crab hit him. A child's offering in remembrance. Could the women be ghosts? "Stupid fanciful dreams," he muttered, but the disquiet lingered. The Good Book mentioned spirits, of course, but he'd never thought they could be real.

A snippet of history from the seminary seeped into his consciousness, something he'd tried to forget.

He'd joined the Church to make a difference in the post-Peak Oil world. As society collapsed during the Upheaval people had turned to organised religions to piece together some semblance of community. In Queensland the Church of Reclamation became the biggest institution, coordinating food deliveries and redistribution of resources. Big business had funded the formation of a rogue Church whose primary function was to hamper the unifying efforts of the Reclamation, all in the name of bottom line. The rogue group had called itself the Brothers of Mercy and targeted small communities.

While the communities had suffered at the hands of the Brothers, the Church of Reclamation, lacking the ability to apprehend them, did nothing. Eventually the Brothers disappeared as their benefactors fell victim to the realities of post-Oil life, though not until after they'd destroyed many smaller towns in rural Queensland. Women were often prime targets, persecuted as the source of society's ills, tortured and killed while the Brothers cited Eve as their justification.

The Bishop said spending too much time near the gas fields, breathing the tainted air, had driven the Brothers crazy. If the townswomen had been murdered by the Brothers, their souls may have been too shocked to cross over. And if their men refused to let them go...

Patrick pushed himself up and dressed before he slunk downstairs. Bailey called out to him. "It's best you leave today."

"That was the plan," Patrick replied, not meeting Bailey's eyes. "I thought I would leave closer to dusk and travel at night—the heat is unbearable so close to the gas fields."

"Our version of Hell on earth." Bailey pursed his lips and studied Patrick. "Best you keep to your plan."

Patrick's gaze flickered to the jukebox. He cleared his throat. "I need to check on my horse. Where is she stabled?"

Bailey hollered for Charlie. The boy scurried from the kitchen and grunted at Patrick. Outside he could smell the bitumen baking in the sun. A dog barked but nothing else moved on the street. Everyone must be holed up in their houses, as was sensible in such heat. Charlie led the priest to a house with broken windows and peeling paint.

The boy unbarred the door and pointed inside. Patrick shuddered as goosebumps rose on his skin. He peered in.

The room must have been a lounge room once, but the carpet had been pulled up, exposing the concrete floor, and all furnishings had been removed. Constance, still saddled, was hitched to a long metal railing that had been installed at some point since the house had been abandoned. A single shattered window let sunlight into the room, and the other window was boarded up. A basin half-filled with water had been set on the floor beside the railing, and some attempt had been made to strew dried grass on the hard concrete.

Patrick's cheeks grew hot and his chest tightened. He'd neglected his duty to his horse. She'd carried him through a desert wasteland with stoic endurance, and would carry him to his destination without complaint. She deserved better.

He crossed the floor and unsaddled her, then stroked her side, checking for signs of stress. She whickered softly and turned to nuzzle at his ear. Patrick rubbed her down and cursed himself for his stupidity. Charlie was too small to tend to a horse, and these people would know little about tending them. He hadn't seen any since leaving Bundaberg.

One of the panniers carried grain mash, and Constance snorted eagerly and buried her muzzle in the bag when Patrick offered it. He tied it around her neck and let her munch for a while, internally berating himself.

If she became unwell he would be forced to stay in Miriam Vale. Or he'd have to leave her behind and continue on foot. The former made him uneasy, the latter was suicide. Patrick tried to convince himself that his duty was paramount, that God would protect him, but he was a long way from the seminary and the people here were hostile, the town decaying.

He put his arms around the horse's neck and breathed in her earthy scent before he untied the pannier and gave her a last pat. Constance whinnied as he headed back to the pub for food. The sun glared down, bleaching the colour from all he could see. The streets gasped for moisture, cobbled with rock and broken bitumen and sand.

Bailey grunted when he saw the priest.

"Could I get a bite to eat?"

The publican pointed to a blackboard. "I do a noon special. Hope you're not fussy."

Patrick prayed it wasn't rats. "Not at all."

Time dragged on, each minute reluctant to give way to the next. A slender fellow with mutton-chop sideburns pushed the door open but let it shut again when he saw Patrick at the bar. The next man to enter was short and dark with curly hair, and he too left at the sight of the priest sitting alone.

"You're bad for business." Bailey glowered as he set a bowl on the bar and pushed it across. Patrick inspected the contents. The brown sludge steamed, and smelled of unidentified meat and pepper. The priest sampled it. It was decent enough, better even than some of the food he remembered from his novice days.

The door whooshed inward. Light and dry air invaded the pub. The man, silhouetted in the entrance, stood at the threshold and called out.

"Had enough of this, Bailey. Want him gone."

"Yeh, Morgan, I know," the impassive barkeep replied. "He'll be leaving this evening. Now off with you."

The door swung shut. Patrick stared into his stew. "I'd like to help you," he said.

"Ain't nothing the likes of you can do for us." Bailey slammed a glass onto the bar, the burn on his face flaming. Liquid sloshed over the edge and splattered on Patrick's hand. "Lemonade?"

"Thanks." Patrick took a cautious sip. Still warm and sour. "When were the Brothers of Mercy here?"

Bailey shook his head. "Best you stop, now." He leaned over the bar and looked into Patrick's eyes. "You're not like them others, I know that but I ain't the majority here, you understand. Folks here are angry, and seeing you has flared it up again. You just eat your food and be on your way and don't be talking to nobody."

Patrick swallowed. The mouthful of stew he'd forgotten to chew slid painfully down his throat. "For what it's worth, I'm sorry."

"It ain't worth much, God-man."

Patrick hunched over his bowl and shovelled the hot stew in as fast as he could. The sounds of Bailey tidying, sweeping, the clinking of glasses, the squeak of chairs, all melded into a meditative hum as Patrick contemplated his options. The sharp scent of vinegar roused him from his reverie as Bailey ran a rag along the bar.

"Finished?"

The priest handed his bowl over. Bailey disappeared out the back with it. Patrick tapped his fingers on the bar and recalled his lessons. Souls that didn't cross over were trapped in purgatory, repeating the same movements over and over. It was difficult to free them, doubly so if their loved ones clung too tight. He scrunched his face, the quandary almost defeating him. These men were living for their dead womenfolk, not for God.

The men of Miriam Vale must be brought back to God's will. His face smoothed, and he straightened. As Bailey returned Patrick pushed the chair back. It screeched on the wooden floor. He hurried to the stairs.

The man called Morgan blocked his way. He grinned, showing broken teeth. A crimson smear marred his cheek.

"What do you want?" Patrick asked, his heart hammering.

Morgan held up his hand, a twisted red claw. "Have you ever seen a human candle?"

Patrick backed up, shaking his head. "It wasn't—"

"Your kind did nothing to stop 'em. They herded our girls into the claws of the crab, claimed they were sinners, tied 'em up and burned 'em alive, even the young ones. We got the bastards, killed 'em all. Was too late, though, wasn't it? Had to put a bullet in my wife's brain, put her outta her misery. You ever had to do somethin' like that, God-man?"

His bowels loosened. "I'm sorry."

Morgan leaned in, his foul breath made Patrick's eyes water. "Yes. You're all good at saying sorry." Then he pushed past Patrick and went into the bar area.

Patrick's body was hit by tremors as he trudged upstairs. It was one thing to speculate, another thing to have his suspicions confirmed. Nothing in his training had prepared him for this. In his room he knelt and prayed, asking God for guidance and forgiveness. As afternoon fell toward sunset the words came to him, planted in his mind by divine will. He knew what he must do, knew the time and place.

Patrick wiped the sweat from his brow and sat on the bed. "Thank you, Lord." He stretched his shoulders. "I won't fail you."

* * *

The timing had to be just right. Dusk was the liminal time between day and night, one of the transition points that caused the veils between the worlds to thin. The spirits would be able to escape purgatory to enter Heaven—or Hell, if that was their fate—but they needed a priest to entreat on their behalf.

Patrick could see the train station from his room. The site of many departures and arrivals would be the best place to send the spirits on their final journey. Patrick tiptoed down the stairs, his breath shallow. He slipped past the entrance to the bar where the room swarmed with patrons, and then he was out into the street and running across toward the train station.

The sun had not yet sunk below the horizon. Patrick exhaled, his throat tightened with nerves as he climbed the stairs to the platform. He took a deep breath and focused on the rusting train tracks.

"Holy Father, bring these women forth from Purgatory so you may judge their sins." The air froze. His skin pebbled with goosebumps and he opened his eyes. Ghostly apparitions stepped forth onto the platform, as though alighting from an invisible train. The women of Miriam Vale, old and young; beautiful and not, their ethereal forms clad in the garb they'd been wearing in the pub the night before.

They were not happy to see him. The face of the one nearest was set in a soundless scream.

"Forgive me," Patrick said, his chest hollow, "you must understand. It's necessary. This is *His* will."

She shook her head, radiating a sadness that shredded his heart, then pointed behind him. The spectres watched as he swung around.

The boy, Charlie, stood in the parking lot across the road, peering at him. He disappeared into the Hotel.

Patrick took a deep breath and the words spilled out. "Forgive these women their sins and receive them into Your Heavenly Kingdom. Allow the survivors a chance at living."

As he stumbled over the last words Patrick threw himself down the stairs. He tripped over the uneven ground, aiming for the derelict house Constance was stabled in. His blood thundered in his ears and his lungs burned as he neared the gutted shack. The forlorn apparitions trailed after him, fading as the daylight dimmed.

Patrick flung open the door to carnage. Blood streaked the walls, and Constance—a whimper strangled his throat. He bent and stroked her soft muzzle. "I'm sorry," he said as the tears flowed. He heaved the panniers over his shoulders and walked to the doorway, weighed down by sorrow and fear.

"You won't take them from us again."

Bailey hefted an axe, flanked by the rest of the townsmen. The transparent women stood in a line in front of them. One by one they raised their hands, and each blew a kiss to the men. Then the sun slipped below the horizon, dragging the unwilling ghosts down with the last rays of light.

"It's too late," Patrick said, sobbing. "They're gone."

"What have you done?" Bailey's face paled as he turned. Cries of despair rang out from the throng of men behind him.

"They're gone!"

"Veronica! Ronnie!"

"Bring them back!"

Ice snaked down Patrick's spine. He sniffed but snot leaked from his nose.

"I sent them to our Heavenly Father, to receive his judgement. You all need to move on with your lives."

"You should have left well enough alone."

"I was only trying to help!"

Bailey's eyes narrowed. "I told you there was nothing you could do for us, God-man." The husbands and fathers and sons and brothers who'd watched their womenfolk die fanned out on either side of Bailey as he lifted the weapon.

"Why did you have to kill the horse?" Patrick could barely see through the watery haze.

Bailey swung around, glared at Morgan. "We could have used a horse," he said, teeth gritted. Morgan scowled.

Charlie ran to Bailey's elbow. "Make the bad man go away, Papa," the boy said.

"With pleasure," Bailey replied. The men of Miriam Vale surrounded Patrick. His voice quivered as he prayed loudly, breath coming in gasps. He'd done as the Lord instructed, hadn't he? The Lord would save him. He would. *I don't want to die.*

The decrepit buildings of the town were tombs in the purple light of dusk, and Patrick realised that the shades of their memories were all these men had of the women they'd loved, twice taken.

Patrick heard the wailing lament of the women of Miriam Vale in the whistling passage of the axe.

REASONS TO KILL
J.C. MICHAEL

No one paid much attention to the stranger when he moved to town. What a costly mistake that was.

We couldn't even say for sure when he moved in. Of course, a group of us went to welcome him once we noticed someone started to clear and tend the garden, but when he saw us coming he shot inside and declined to answer the door. We only bothered once more, at Christmas, but again he decided he didn't want to respond to our knocking. We left him a gift all the same. Some of the townsfolk felt uneasy, but the majority of our small community said live and let live. The town was ample, big enough for all of us, and there was no reason to impose ourselves upon the man. But that was before spring came. Before the Watson kids went missing. With those three unaccounted for, the youngest of them only seven, our feelings toward the stranger in our midst developed from a mild curiosity, to a worrying concern.

* * *

"We've searched everywhere," said Peter Harrison, for what seemed like the hundredth time.

"You can't have, otherwise you'd have found them."

It was a fair point—and you could expect nothing less from the children's mother—but all the same, Harrison had done all he could to try and find her two sons and daughter. We all had.

"We all know we haven't searched everywhere so let's quit gabbing and go knock the bastard up out of bed. And if he doesn't answer I'm busting the fucking door down."

I took another drink. God how I missed proper beer. It was Paul Robertshaw who'd spoken, and his sentiments were no doubt shared by the majority of those present. It was virtually a full gathering of the town, thirty out of the thirty-six of us. Other than the three missing children, and the stranger, only old Clifford and his daughter were missing; him housebound, her laid up with flu.

"We know nothing about the man," said Harrison. "What if he's armed and doesn't take too kindly to us breaking into his home in the dead of night?"

Paul stood, and I knew what was coming. Harrison may have organised us into the self-sufficient community, and by doing so become our un-official leader, but Paul had known his own mind ever since primary school. If he'd decided to do something, no one was going to stop him.

"Then I'll take my own gun and give him fair warning. He answers the door and lets us check it out, or he'll let me in—at gunpoint."

"And if he answers the door with a gun of his own? What then?"

Paul looked at the young woman who'd spoken and shrugged. He and Sarah had never seen eye-to-eye over much.

"Fuck knows, I'll cross that bridge when I come to it."

* * *

Ten minutes later we were walking across town, both of us armed, both of us nervous, neither of us willing to show it.

"You know as well as I do we've been lucky this past year," said Paul as we walked through the deserted streets. The quiet was sinister, like those first few weeks. It was a feeling whose return was unwelcome.

"I know."

There was no option but to agree. The world had come to a standstill, yet we'd buried our dead, and carried on. The movies would have you be-lieve that there'd be post-apocalypse anarchy, the countryside awash with murderous gangs pillaging what was left. It wasn't like that at all, as far as we knew. In some ways, now was better than before. Less people. Less stress. Less noise.

I guess I was lucky, having no family to lose when the outbreak hit. Still, it wasn't a bad life for the survivors, even those who'd lost their nearest and dearest. Growing your own food was hard work, yet rewarding, and the sense of community was something which had been absent in the modern world. Harrison, who'd studied history before going into 'retail manage-ment' and running the local newsagent's, reckoned it had been exactly the same after the Black Death. The same natural resources, but far less people. I'd no idea if he was right, but either way, life wasn't that bad. To be frank, I preferred growing my own food and trading with my neighbours, rarely leaving town for anything more than a walk through the countryside, com-pared to the forty mile daily commute I'd once endured just to sit in an of-fice staring at a computer screen.

* * *

When we reached the house we could see the light from a candle flicker-ing in one of the downstairs rooms. We stopped at the garden gate.

"How you want to do this?" asked Paul.

"Buggered if I know. It was your idea."

"Well, I've been thinking," he said.

"First time for everything," I couldn't help but reply.

"There's no point stirring things up too much. Why don't we just shout from here? Tell him there's some missing kids and the town needs to know he isn't involved. We want a quick look round, and then we'll be on our way."

"And if he doesn't respond?"

Paul looked at me, fear and resolve in his grey eyes. "Then I'm going to shoot out one of his upstairs windows so he knows we mean business."

As it was, it didn't come to that. Paul shouted out that we were looking for some lost children and, after a twitch of the curtains, the front door opened. We looked around the house, upstairs and down, attic and basement, garage and garden shed, and saw nothing out of the ordinary beyond the stranger himself. He was far from ordinary. The desiccated and cracked skin covered in yellow scabs gave us a whole new topic to worry about—the stranger was infected.

* * *

Everyone was still at The Boar's Head when we got back. None of them took the news well.

"How the hell can he be infected?"

"I don't believe it."

"Can we catch it?"

"Oh God!"

"Is it a new strain?"

"We need to get rid of him!"

"Why is he still alive?"

There was a whole raft of questions and statements, but no answers or suggestions. The outbreak, to our knowledge, had lasted seven weeks. People fell ill by the thousands, their skin drying out and cracking before oozing with a mixture of blood and pus which scabbed over like miniature mountain ranges across the skin. From the formation of the first yellow scab death came within seventy-two hours. The whole process didn't appear to be that painful, physically, although the mental anguish was undoubtedly torturous. The infected just got drowsier until they fell asleep and their heartbeat slowed to a stop. Nobody got better. Isolation made no difference, nor did excessive contact. The theory was that the infection had spread weeks, months—maybe years—previously, and simply taken a long time to incubate before showing any of the symptoms which heralded Death's imminent arrival. That was why neither quarantining the victims, nor locking yourself away, did any good. If you had it, you had it, and you'd had it—simple as that. Infected before you even knew it existed.

Why did some of us survive? Was it genetics? Luck? Or even divine intervention? No one knew. Maybe we'd just missed the infection when it had first spread. We all had ideas, but with the vast majority of the world's scientists and doctors suffering the same fate as everyone else, there were no definitive answers.

I drank another beer, and excused myself to resume my personal search for the Wilsons in the nearby woods. It would be another twenty hours before I finally succumbed to exhaustion, the kids still missing.

* * *

It may have been a glorious spring that year but, figuratively speaking, a cloud hung over the town. It had been two weeks since Adrian, Jason, and Cassidy vanished. We'd carried on searching but our sustainable style of existence prevented us from putting the day-to-day tasks entirely to one side. Some felt that, in the absence of any bodies, the only explanation was that the three of them had run away. I admit, I was starting to think that way myself. As for the stranger, he was still alive and still tending his garden. We'd kept a close eye on him and, besides the fact he should have been dead, nothing appeared to be out of the ordinary. It was a situation which was about to change dramatically.

* * *

Paul and I were in The Boars Head playing darts when Harrison came in and called us over.

"I need to speak to you two. Now."

His tone indicated something serious, as did the fact he immediately headed upstairs.

We exchanged a quick glance, put down our darts, and followed him. He'd headed into one of the smaller guest rooms at the back. The pub had been run as a hotel when people tended to travel a bit more. We'd had people visit town over the past months, we were by no means completely cut off from the rest of the world, but the couple of rooms at the front had been sufficient for that trade, plus the odd occasion someone drank too much of the homebrew and didn't feel like the walk home.

The room smelled musty from lack of use, and I'd have preferred it if Harrison hadn't shut the door behind us as soon as we walked in, but it was comfortable enough. I took the armchair, Paul the stool by the dresser, and Harrison perched on the end of the bed.

"I'm concerned by our infected friend," Harrison said.

Neither of us said anything, giving him the floor for whatever he had to say.

"I've been going through the town archives, partly as a hobby, more recently in case we'd missed anything that could help find the Watsons." From out of his pocket he took a sheet of paper and began unfolding it. "And before either of you even think it, I know damn well most folks have given up, but that doesn't mean I have too. People have become desensitised after all we've been through, but those kids could still be out there, suffering. Their mother needs to know one way or the other."

His speech over, he paused, as if daring us to contradict him or tell him he was wasting his time. When he was satisfied we were waiting for him to proceed, he continued.

"This is the town map from nineteen forty-six. You can see the church, market place, town centre, largely unchanged. We're here. The modern estates obviously aren't shown."

"Right," said Paul. "So what are you actually showing us?"

"This," said Harrison. "An air-raid shelter next to what was a convalescent home that was demolished in the early 'fifties."

"Shit," I said, causing Paul to look at me. Harrison was unfolding another map but I didn't need to see a more modern town plan to know where the shelter was. It was in The Groves estate. Right where the stranger had claimed his plot.

"Bang on where he's living. You think it's still there?" I asked.

Harrison sighed. "I don't know. You'd have thought we'd have heard about it, if it was. We've lived here all our lives."

"Why?" said Paul. "Do you know where any other shelters were? If I could ask my granddad I'm sure he'd say he knew about it, but if it was in the grounds of a hospital, and then had an estate built over it, it's hardly interesting enough to go telling people about. And," he was on a roll, "think about who owned that house. Isn't it the one deaf and dumb Edwin used to live in? You don't think the bloke could be that nephew of his that used to turn up now and again do you?"

Of course it was that house. Double-D Ed had been one of those characters every small town has. A bit of an oddball, but harmless, as far as anyone knew. He'd lived there for as long as I'd known, and could have quite easily bought it as new. As it happened he'd died about six months before the outbreak, and the house had sat empty since. If he'd an air-raid shelter in his back garden he wouldn't have told anyone—couldn't have, to be blunt—so there was every chance it was still there, which begged the question.

"So what now? You think those kids could be down there?"

Harrison and I looked at Paul. He'd just said exactly what we were thinking.

* * *

I needed a moment to think, so I offered to grab another round of drinks. My friends were nothing if not predictable. Paul would propose something forceful; Harrison would advocate caution. For me, the whole situation was increasingly uncomfortable. It wasn't just the missing kids, although that was the prime concern. The fact that the stranger was clearly infected, yet somehow had kept death at bay, was another mystery that demanded consideration. Not only that, but the stranger wasn't showing any signs of the usual lethargy the illness brought on. He was still tending his garden, and working on the exterior of the house. We'd even seen him putting up a shed a day or so back. Other than his appearance, which was still only a few steps up from a walking corpse, he seemed right as rain.

"So what's the plan?" I asked when I got back to the room despite knowing that there was no way the two of them would have reached a consensus.

"Paul thinks we should seize him, stick a twelve bore in his face, and force 'the truth' from him," said Harrison.

"And this pussy thinks we should politely enquire if he's kidnapped any kids lately and if he'd mind us taking a peak in his dungeon," said Paul who was, unsurprisingly, the more agitated of the two.

I took a breath, and took a drink, "This isn't the Wild West, but it isn't the civilised society we grew up in either. None of us know a damn thing about this sort of thing, and Paul, TV doesn't count so don't even go there." Both of them were listening, which was a start. "If we try to snatch him we could make a real mess of things, and someone could get hurt. By someone I mean one of us or the kids; as well as him—he could still be innocent, by the way. It isn't like we can pop to the hospital if any of us get injured. It's what, thirty miles to the nearest doctor? And that's if what we heard still holds true. Besides, do we really want to start torturing people? This isn't bloody Guantanawhatsit Bay. Let's try something a bit more creative."

Paul sat forward, he would be the most receptive to what I was about to propose. Harrison leant back. He'd be harder to convince, but I wanted both of them onboard.

"I'm happy to sneak round the back of the house to see if I can find anything out but we need to distract this guy's attention if I'm going to be able to have a decent scout around."

"A diversion?" said Paul, "like what? Setting fire to the twat's house?"

"That's a bit drastic," I said, "but we could set fire to his shed."

* * *

The sun had set and the twilight world of dusk was holding off the night in the daily battle it was forever doomed to lose. It was the perfect time to execute our plan—dark enough to afford us some cover, light enough for us to be able to see what we were doing.

The plan was for Paul and I to hedgehop our way along the row of properties leading to the stranger's house before splitting off—me, into the back garden, and Paul into the front. Once there, he'd light a small fire beneath the shed. Harrison, along with his German shepherd, would just happen to be walking by and, seeing the blaze, would alert the stranger. With no running water—we all got our own from the local river—tackling the blaze would be impossible, but efforts would need to be made to prevent the fire from spreading. Fortunately the shed stood apart from anything other than a stone boundary wall, yet Harrison would argue that both he, and the stranger, would need to keep a close eye on things in case any stray sparks looked likely to start secondary fires elsewhere.

I checked my watch, the firestarter would be striking the match any time soon, before high-tailing it back next door to where he'd stashed his shotgun. Harrison may have had Holyfield with him, but if things went tits up Paul was there as backup.

"Fire! Fire!"

Harrison's shouts ruptured the air before I saw any smoke. I hesitated, how would I know if the stranger responded? It was too late to worry about that.

* * *

The back garden was covered in a mixture of paving and gravel. Planters were dotted here and there, and a raised bed ran alongside the fence, but overall there was more stone and concrete present than organic matter. It explained why such a private individual had established his veg patch out front. I cast my eyes over the layout for a second time, not knowing what I was looking for. What the hell had I expected? A corrugated iron hut half sunk into the ground? A pair of cellar doors, swinging in the wind? The light was fading, as was my confidence, but there was no way I could turn back when the lives of those kids could well depend upon how our half-baked plan panned out. My intent was to take a quick look around, so I'd left my cumbersome gun on the other side of the wall, sacrificing security for speed. Now I was vulnerable. The night was mild, but I started to shiver. I admit it, I was scared. To make matters worse an acrid smoke was blowing around the side of the house and into the back garden, stinging my eyes and catching in my throat. The endeavour was proving to be futile, and I determined that getting out of there, and having a rethink, was the best option.

Why I didn't go back the way I came I can't tell you. Panic probably. I'd been on the verge of a heart attack ever since we'd left the pub and started walking towards this part of town.

As it was I headed across the garden, up onto one of the planters, and pulled myself up onto the top of the wall. As I swung my legs over to the other side my line of sight shifted back into the garden I was leaving. That's when I spotted it. There, on a paving stone underneath a wooden bench, was a brass ring large enough to fit your arm through, or pull on with both hands. I dropped back down and scurried over. I nudged the bench out of the way and grasped the cold metal. The slab slowly groaned upwards on a metal hinge as I pulled. Below, a ladder headed down into the darkness. Part of me wanted to close the damn thing and get the hell out of there. We could come back tomorrow and force the stranger to let us take a look, but we could have done that this evening. The whole aim of the plan—torching his shed aside—was to find out what was going on without antagonising things. I had to see it through, and lowered myself into the hole. My feet found the rungs and I reached up to shuffle the bench back over the opening. My tracks covered I ducked down and closed the lid. I was in complete darkness, and wondering just what the fuck I was playing at.

It took a few deep breaths to regain control of myself, and get the panic back in check. There was a torch in my pocket, the end of the world still a recent enough event for us to have a stash of working batteries, but using it while climbing down the ladder would've been awkward. Instead, I descended in pitch blackness. When I reached the bottom I quickly turned on the torch and was struck by a vision I would try to forget for the rest of my days, but which would haunt me for eternity.

The room was large, with a row of bunk beds down either side, most of which were clearly occupied. Tentacles of panic wrapped themselves around me once more, constricting my chest and making breathing difficult. Despite those slumbering either side of me, my attention was locked to the far wall. Three naked blood stained bodies were hanging there from chains which glinted in the torchlight. I've no idea how long I stood there, rooted to the spot and taking short, sharp, breaths, but although the forms moved in their sleep none of them awoke. Eventually, I edged forward past a total of eighteen sleeping figures, male and female—all infected. The oppressive atmosphere of the pit began to conspire against me, leaving me nauseous and disorientated. My panic only held at bay by some inner strength I'd never known I'd had. I made it to the far end; my boots felt like lead weights and my body heavy, as if I'd just reached the summit of Everest rather than crossed the floor of a room that would've normally been traversed in seconds. I'd needed no confirmation the three bodies were those of the Wilsons. They were alive, their chests slowly rising and falling, and I whispered my thanks to God. They were also riddled with puncture wounds: small holes, in pairs, dotted all over their torsos and limbs, each set ringed with an angry bruise. Only their faces, porcelain pale in the darkness, appeared unblemished. My murmuring prayer of thanks darkened to a curse upon those who had inflicted such injury upon these innocents.

Rage was building inside me and I almost threw myself at the man who slept peacefully only a few feet away. How could these bastards sleep contentedly while the abused bodies of children adorned the wall of their quarters? It was inhumane—the actions of monsters, not men. The urge to pull the nearest of them from his bed and dash his brains out on the cold stone floor was almost irresistible. Yet sanity retained the upper hand in this most insane scenario, and I maintained what composure I still had. To attack would be suicide. I was outnumbered, and I had no wish to tangle with the type of lunatics who, sick or not, could visit such pain and suffering upon innocents.

The extent of these people's guilt compared to that of the stranger may have been unknown, but I was certain that some amount of guilt belonged to each and every one of them, and for that they would need to be held accountable. Such concerns, however, were for another time. I had to save the children, and that priority needed to be my prime concern. I returned my attention to them and pulled at their chains, but they refused to budge. Even when I pulled at their slender ankles and wrists, viewing further injury as the lesser of two evils, I still couldn't slip them free of their bonds.

I was ashamed by the futility of my efforts, both now, and even more so by the fact that Paul and I had missed this hellish pit a fortnight ago. What suffering must have been endured since then? And what degree of fault for that could be apportioned to me? I was crying, and my sense of judgement and reasoning was collapsing under the weight of the situation. How I found the inner strength to provide me with the resolve to deal with the hand fate had dealt me I cannot say, but I thank God I did. I wiped away my tears on the sleeve of my jacket, and turned to leave.

As I made my way back through the room one of the figures turned over in their sleep and yawned. It was a woman, middle aged, and with a face criss-crossed with the lines of scab so indicative of the infection. As she yawned I saw her skin stretch tight, and in some places split, a thick yellow pus oozing out of the wounds like tree sap. I forced my gaze away and in doing so it fell upon the small table to the side of her cot. There was a book on it, and at first I didn't believe it when I saw that this was a Bible, but the absurdity of that paled in comparison to the equipment next to it— a set of steel fangs. I couldn't resist, and gingerly made my way over to pick them up. If I had to hazard a guess I would have said the cold, shining, metal, was surgical steel. As I studied them in one hand I crossed myself with the other, even though I'm neither religious nor superstitious. An unusual act, but these were unusual times. The fangs looked like they would slip in front of the teeth, like a gum-shield, the razor sharp prongs clearly the instrument which had been used to puncture the skin of the children and let forth their blood into the wearers waiting throat. I was sickened, and hastily put them back down. A quick look around the room confirmed that there was a set by each bed. Some of those sleeping still had blood around their lips.

I fully expected a blow to the head as I crawled out, a single strike that would knock me out cold only to wake up hanging by the children, my blood being drained so that they could stay alive. I'd joined the dots, and it was the only thing that made sense, that the blood somehow held the infection in check. Fortunately, no such blow came. There was no noise from the front of the house, but the air was still laden with smoke and an orange glow permeated the falling darkness of dusk. I had to do something. *We* had to do something. The stranger would no doubt be suspicious. He could kill the kids and escape, with or without the others. It was time for me to regroup with Harrison and Paul, but as I began to head for the wall my gaze turned for one last time to the house, and there he was.

The stranger was sprawled out on a recliner, just the other side of the patio doors, basking in the light of the rising moon. A glass of what looked like wine, but which could have been something else, sat next to him. It looked syrupy on the side of the glass.

If I'd had a gun with me, I'd have shot him there and then.

* * *

Five minutes later, I was sitting with Harrison and Paul on a set of swings a street away.

"What do we do? We need to get those kids out," I asked as soon as I'd recounted my adventure to them.

"And the rest?" said Paul, "That cunt must be some kind of guardian for them, unless they take turns? Move around from place to place?"

Harrison shook his head. "I don't think he's as sick as they are from what you've said. He took quite a risk letting you look around before, and it makes me think he's tougher than he seems. And they must've known about the shelter when they pitched up here. Maybe one of them actually is Edwin's nephew?"

"I don't think it matters who they are," I said. "What's important is what they are, and that we get those kids out safely."

"Listen," said Harrison. "What if they feed the same time each day? They never woke when you were down there. He never came out when I was shouting "fire". What if they feed and then go into a trance, or just pass out. That gives us a window of opportunity. We can come back at dusk tomorrow and…"

"Wait another day? Those kids are barely alive!" Paul was incredulous. "You don't have a clue what you're talking about. I say kill the lot of them, they're like fish in a fucking barrel down there."

"We're not assassins, Paul," said Harrison, his own voice rising a notch. "And as much as I don't know what we're dealing with—neither do you. What if shooting them doesn't work?"

"I don't think…" I began to say, but Paul got there first.

"They aren't fucking vampires, for God's sake! We don't need a silver bullet or a stake or whatever. They'll go down just like anything else."

"I can't allow it," Harrison's voice was lower now and I could see that an internal conflict was battling within him. "Just because what they have done is abominable it doesn't give you the right to execute them."

"That's bullshit."

"If you kill them I can't allow you to stay in town. You'll be cast out as a murderer."

"That's not your decision. Why not see what everyone else thinks?"

"And march a mob up here with flaming torches? This isn't the dark ages. These people are sick."

"Yeah, in the fucking head."

"Head, body, both. It's an illness, Paul. They are just trying to survive, however wrong their way of going about that may be. They need to be punished, but maybe they could also be helped."

"You think illness is an excuse? A reason to defend these bastards? For fuck's sake, Harrison. Why don't they just ask for a transfusion? They're a bunch of psychos, simple as that."

"Listen to yourself. A transfusion? Who knows how to do one of those these days? Think about it, man. If they'd asked you to bleed in a jar for them would you have done it? Or driven the poor unclean bastards out of town?"

I'd heard enough, and could see both sides of the coin. It was an argument far older than this evening. The degree to which people should be punished for their sins. The circumstances which could be called upon to in some way explain, even if not to justify, such sin. Can sickness ever be an excuse for inhumanity towards your fellow man? For cruelty to others? Cruelty to children? It was an argument for which I had neither the time, the inclination, nor the right answer.

Paul was of the old 'hang 'em and flog 'em' persuasion, Harrison of a more liberal bent. Me? Nothing could justify what they had done; I had to agree with Paul on that score. The fact it was children made it worse. Hell, if it had been adults it would still have been wrong, but I just wanted the kids safe. Retribution was a more troublesome topic. We couldn't arrest them. We couldn't lock them up. But if we sent them on their way how many others would suffer? My thoughts were tying themselves into knots of Gordian proportions. I slipped the swing out from under my backside. "I'm going back. Who's coming?"

* * *

I'd started walking as soon as the words were out of my mouth and Paul followed immediately, Harrison only seconds after that. They were like chalk and cheese but I was glad to have them both with me. Them and Holyfield who'd sat licking his paw throughout our recent debate.

"So what's the plan?" said Paul. It was four words which suddenly made me the leader of our little trio. The problem was, I didn't have a plan. I didn't have a fucking clue.

"I don't know, but we can't go home to our beds and sleep on it. We don't go in and start killing people, but we don't leave those kids a moment longer than we have to. First things first; the stranger."

After a quick detour to a few sheds, we eventually found some bolt cutters, and headed back to the house. The stranger was still sprawled out on his recliner, and the patio door was unlocked. We slipped inside and looked at him, his eyes open yet unseeing, the glass of what was now congealed blood sitting half drank by his side.

"What do we do now?" hissed Harrison.

I was making it up as I went along, and was about to suggest that we bound and gagged the man to take him out of the equation. I don't think Paul had thought ahead either, but while I took a second to think, he acted. He dropped his gun to the floor, grabbed the heavy bolt croppers out of Harrison's hands and cracked them against the side of the strangers head.

To this day, I believe that the intent had been to do no more than incapacitate him. The blow was not delivered with as much force as Paul was capable of, but the impact shattered the stranger's skull like the shell of a boiled egg. I can only think that the infection had caused his bones to weaken, as the way his cranium collapsed was more akin to some third rate special effects in an eighties horror movie than anything you'd expect in real life. The whole side of the stranger's face caved in as though it was nothing more than a poorly inflated football.

One eye hung loosely from its socket; blood and yellow pus streamed from the fissures which had been rent open and poured from his nose and mouth. A guttural gurgle emerged from the stranger's blood-filled throat. Unbelievably, he tried to stand. I stumbled backwards into Harrison who was busy vomiting on the tiled floor. Paul looked at me, his eyes betraying the fear of what he had done irrespective of his earlier 'kill 'em all' stance. The stranger's head hung to one side, and he spat blood and what could have been curses while his left hand groped around for something, anything, to defend himself. When his hand happened upon the blood-filled glass by his side I realised two things with instant clarity: he was going to thrust it into Pauls face, and he was a blood-drinking monster that needed to be destroyed.

"Fucking hit him again!" I screamed.

The order snapped Paul back to the matter at hand. He lashed out at the stranger—no, the creature—once more, and with an awful ripping sound its head was almost torn from its shoulders. The thing staggered, and reached for Paul who had backed away and was lining up another swing. It was Harrison who shouted this time demanding that Paul kill it, his earlier sensibilities torn away by the horror now being played out before his eyes. Paul swung again, a blow which tore the monster's head from its shoulders, leaving the body to crumple to the floor. It didn't get up. Nor did the head continue to chatter its teeth, or snarl at us. We weren't in a zombie movie. We'd just killed someone.

When someone is beheaded right in front of your eyes it isn't an easy thing to deal with. The three of us were so fixated on what we had done that none of us noticed that the occupants of the shelter had silently scurried out like rats from a nest. Realisation only came when the first of them launched themselves against the patio doors with a thud and a crack. By the time we had turned, the next pair had thrown themselves against the glass. This time it failed to hold.

I can recall how the moonlight glinted off their steel fangs. The chaos as they charged us on all fours, like animals. And the blood, I can remember the blood. The coppery tang of it on the air. The way it sprayed from wounds and decorated the room in a crimson overcoat.

Paul managed to grab his gun and let off both barrels, the pellets shredding the bodies of the two he hit, but he had no time to reload. I can recall how he used the gun as a club, how each blow crumpled flesh and crunched bone. The creatures were both strong, unfeeling of pain, and weak, their bodies clearly rotting from within as the infection caused decay in place of death. But there were too many of them, and one eventually clamped its jaws upon his face, tearing off his nose and shredding his cheeks. Holyfield took out a few more, but as he concentrated on one fallen victim two more pounced onto his back, tearing through his hair and into the back of his neck with fangs and clawed nails. I shot one, blowing an arm clean out of its socket and across the floor. The anaesthetic effect of the infection numbed the pain but provided no respite when I fired my remaining shot directly into the bastard's face. Reloading was out of the question so I grabbed the hot barrel in my hands and swung the stock in a whirlwind of blue steel and walnut.

For all the details I do remember, right down to the Ralph Lauren logo on one of those monster's shirts, there are large gaps in my memory. From the point at which I resorted to using my weapon to bludgeon those around me to the point at which I finally realised that I was merely beating unmoving corpses into an ever bloodier pulp, I remember little. Everyone bar me was dead. Only I survived.

I didn't see, or don't recall, exactly what happened to Harrison. Sometimes I wake at night after reliving those moments in my dreams, hearing him screaming my name, "Mitch! Mitch!", as he battled against them. The memory of those screams are enough without any visual accompaniment. I know they killed him; I found his body behind the sofa as I wearily stumbled out of my own, murderous, frenzy. I know he fought; as there was blood on his fists and boots, on his knees and his forehead. He must have scrapped like a kid in a playground brawl, but it hadn't stopped the creatures tearing a hole in his chest and spilling his intestines across the floor. I remember seeing that. I wish I didn't.

Even though I lived, a part of me had died, for I had become a killer. Harrison was right, we weren't murderers, but that was what I became that night. Dehumanised as they had been, in deed and in my own perceptions, they were still people. Sons and daughters, mothers and fathers, human beings just like me, but sick. Sick with an illness that was of no fault of their own, and which may have also been responsible for the depths of madness to which they had plunged. I legitimately call it self-defence, and attempt to reconcile it as retribution for what these—these *vampires*—had done, but at the end of the day I put them down like rabid dogs, and in doing so, I was changed. To the town I was a hero; the children had been saved. Their physical scars had healed, and their mental scars seemed only superficial as the blessed fog of amnesia clouded all but the vaguest notions of what had happened to them. To me, my heroism was tainted by a homicidal villainy, a destructive darkness that would stain my character, and plague my thoughts for the rest of my life.

It's been hard to adapt, and impossible to forget. I'd always been a quiet one, but following that I withdrew even further. My accountant's fingers were now killer's hands, appendages which no longer belonged in the town I had always called home. I was as altered by my actions as the outbreak had altered the world, and the infection had altered those whom I had brutally dispatched. It wasn't long before we heard stories of a vampire clan which had been roaming the countryside, taking children, and draining their blood. To start with, we thought it may have been those that had come here, and that we—that I—had rid the world of this new evil... but the stories continued.

One day a man came. He said he was passing through, but he had come with a purpose. He sought me out, introduced himself as Harry Atherton, and told me he was hunting them. He explained how he'd found a number of nests, and taken them out by placing explosive charges on their chests as they slept. The timed detonations killed them all at once, and he told me that this was the best way to do it, as waking one wakes them all. It was this which had been our big mistake.

We talked long into the night. About how these groups could have come into being; if they had evolved independently, or if they were part of a whole.

We talked. We drank. In the morning Harry offered that I could travel with him, work with him. And I have accepted.

DIGGING DEEP
RAMSEY CAMPBELL

It must have been quite a nightmare. It was apparently enough to make Coe drag the quilt around him, since he feels more than a sheeted mattress beneath him, and to leave a sense of suffocating helplessness, of being worse than alone in the dark. He isn't helpless. Even if his fit of rage blotted out his senses, it must have persuaded the family. They've brought him home. There wasn't a quilt on his hospital bed.

Who's in the house with him? Perhaps they all are, to impress on him how much they care about him, but he knows how recently they started. There was barely space for all of them around his bed in the private room. Whenever they thought he was asleep some of them would begin whispering. He's sure he overheard plans for his funeral. Now they appear to have left him by himself, and yet he feels hemmed in. Is the dark oppressing him? He has never seen it so dark.

It doesn't feel like his bedroom. He has always been able to distinguish the familiar surroundings when any of his fears jerked him awake. He could think that someone—his daughter Simone or son Daniel, most likely—has denied him light to pay him back for having spent too much of their legacy on the private room. However much he widens his eyes, they remain coated with blackness. He parts his dry lips to call someone to open the curtains, and then his tongue retreats behind his teeth. He should deal with the bedclothes first. Nobody ought to see him laid out as if he's awaiting examination. In the throes of the nightmare he has pulled the entire quilt under him.

He grasps a handful and plants his other hand against the padded headboard to lift his body while he snatches the quilt from beneath him. That's the plan, but he's unable to take hold of the material. It's more slippery than it ought to be, and doesn't budge. Did his last bout of rage leave him so enfeebled, or is his weight pinning down the quilt? He stretches out his arms to find the edges, and his knuckles bump into cushions on both sides of him. But they aren't cushions, they're walls.

He's in some kind of outsize cot. The walls must be cutting off the light. Presumably the idea is to prevent him from rolling out of bed. He's furious at being treated like this, especially when he wasn't consulted. He flings up his hands to grab the tops of the walls and heave himself up to shout for whoever's in the house, and his fingertips collide with a padded surface.

The sides of the cot must bend inwards at the top, that's all. His trembling hands have flinched and bruised his sunken cheeks, but he lifts them. His elbows are still pressed against the bottom of the container when his hands blunder against an obstruction above his face. It's plump and slippery, and scrabbling at it only loosens his nails from the quick. His knees rear up, knocking together before they bump into the obstacle, and then his feet deal it a few shaky kicks. Far too soon his fury is exhausted, and he lies inert as though the blackness is earth that's weighing on him. It isn't far removed. His family cared about him even less than he suspected. They've consigned him to his last and worst fear.

Can't this be another nightmare? How can it make sense? However prematurely eager Simone's husband may have been to sign the death certificate, Daniel would have had to be less than professional too. Could he have saved on the embalming and had the funeral at once? At least he has dressed his father in a suit, but the pockets feel empty as death.

Coe can't be sure until he tries them all. His quivering fists are clenched next to his face, but he forces them open and gropes over his ribs. His inside breast pocket is flat as a card, and so are the others in the jacket. When he fumbles at his trousers pockets he's dismayed to find how thin he is—so scrawny that he's afraid the protrusion on his right hip is a broken bone. But it's in the pocket, and in his haste to carry it to his face he almost shies it out of reach. Somebody cared after all. He pokes at the keypad, and before his heart has time to beat, the mobile phone lights up.

He could almost wish the glow it sheds were dimmer. It shows him how closely he's boxed in by the quilted surface. It's less than a hand's breadth from his shoulders, and when he tilts his face up to judge the extent of his prison the pudgy lid bumps his forehead. Around the phone the silky padding glimmers green, while farther down the box it's whitish like another species of mould, and beyond his feet it's black as soil. He lets his head sink onto the pillow that's the entire floor and does his desperate best to be aware of nothing but the mobile. It's his lifeline, and he needn't panic because he can't remember a single number. The phone will remember for him.

His knuckles dig into the underside of the lid as he holds the mobile away from his face. It's still too close; the digits merge into a watery blur. He only has to locate the key for the stored numbers, and he jabs it hard enough to bruise his fingertip. The symbol that appears in the illuminated window looks shapeless as a blob of mud, but he knows it represents an address book. He pokes the topmost left-hand key of the numeric pad, although he has begun to regret making Daniel number one, and holds the mobile against his ear.

There's silence except for a hiss of static that sounds too much like a trickle of earth. Though his prison seems oppressively hot, he shivers at the possibility that he may be too far underground for the phone to work. He

115

wriggles onto his side to bring the mobile a few inches closer to the surface, but before his shoulder is anything like vertical it thumps the lid. As he strives to maintain his position, the distant phone starts to ring.

It continues when he risks sinking back, but that's all. He's close to pleading, although he doesn't know with whom, by the time the shrill insistent pulse is interrupted. The voice isn't Daniel's. It's entirely anonymous, and informs Coe that the person he's calling isn't available. It confirms Daniel's number in a different voice that sounds less than human, an assemblage of digits pronounced by a computer, and invites him to leave a message.

"It's your father. That's right, I'm alive. You've buried me alive. Are you there? Can you hear me? Answer the phone, you... Just answer. Tell me that you're coming. Ring when you get this. Come and let me out. Come now."

Was it his breath that made the glow flicker? He's desperately tempted to keep talking until this chivvies out a response, but he mustn't waste the battery. He ends the call and thumbs the key next to Daniel's. It's supposed to contact Simone, but it triggers the same recorded voice.

He could almost imagine that it's a cruel joke, even when the voice composed of fragments reads out her number. At first he doesn't speak when the message concludes with a beep, and then he's afraid of losing the connection. "It's me," he babbles. "Yes, your father. Someone was a bit too happy to see me off. Aren't you there either, or are you scared to speak up? Are you all out celebrating? Don't let me spoil the party. Just send someone who can dig me up."

He's growing hysterical. These aren't the sorts of comments he should leave; he can't afford to antagonise his family just now. His unwieldy fingers have already terminated the call—surely the mobile hasn't lost contact by itself. Should he ring his son and daughter back? Alternatively there are friends he could phone, if he can remember their numbers—and then he realises there's only one call he should make. Why did he spend so long in trying to reach his family? He uses a finger to count down the blurred keypad and jabs the ninth key thrice.

He has scarcely lowered the phone to his ear when an operator cuts off the bell. "Emergency," she declares.

Coe can be as fast as that. "Police," he says while she's enquiring which service he requires, but she carries on with her script. "Police," he says louder and harsher.

This earns him a silence that feels stuffed with padding. She can't expect callers who are in danger to be polite, but he's anxious to apologise in case she can hear. Before he can take a breath a male voice says "Gloucestershire Constabulary."

"Can you help me? You may have trouble believing this, but I'm buried alive."

He sounds altogether too contrite. He nearly emits a wild laugh at the idea of seeking the appropriate tone for the situation, but the policeman is asking "What is your name, sir?"

"Alan Coe," says Coe and is pinioned by realising that it must be carved on a stone at least six feet above him.

"And where are you calling from?"

The question seems to emphasise the sickly greenish glimmer of the fattened walls and lid. Does the policeman want the mobile number? That's the answer Coe gives him. "And what is your location, sir?" the voice crackles in his ear.

Coe has the sudden ghastly notion that his children haven't simply rushed the funeral—that for reasons he's afraid to contemplate, they've laid him to rest somewhere other than with his wife. Surely some of the family would have opposed them. "Mercy Hill," he has to believe.

"I didn't catch that, sir."

Is the mobile running out of power? "Mercy Hill," he shouts so loud that the dim glow appears to quiver.

"Whereabouts on Mercy Hill?"

Every question renders his surroundings more substantial, and the replies he has to give are worse. "Down in front of the church," he's barely able to acknowledge. "Eighth row, no, ninth, I think. Left of the avenue."

There's no audible response. The policeman must be typing the details, unless he's writing them down. "How long will you be?" Coe is more than concerned to learn. "I don't know how much air I've got. Not much."

"You're telling us you're buried alive in a graveyard."

Has the policeman raised his voice because the connection is weak? "That's what I said," Coe says as loud.

"I suggest you get off the phone now, sir."

"You haven't told me how soon you can be here."

"You'd better hope we haven't time to be. We've had enough Halloween pranks for one year."

Coe feels faint and breathless, which is dismayingly like suffocation, but he manages to articulate "You think I'm playing a joke."

"I'd use another word for it. I advise you to give it up immediately, and that voice you're putting on as well."

"I'm putting nothing on. Can't you hear I'm deadly serious? You're using up my air, you—Just do your job or let me speak to your superior."

"I warn you, sir, we can trace this call."

"Do so. Come and get me," Coe almost screams, but his voice grows flat. He's haranguing nobody except himself.

Has the connection failed, or did the policeman cut him off? Did he say enough to make them trace him? Perhaps he should switch off the mobile to conserve the battery, but he has no idea whether this would leave the phone impossible to trace. The thought of waiting in the dark without knowing whether help is on the way brings the walls and lid closer to rob him of breath. As he holds the phone at a cramped arm's length to poke the redial button, he sees the greenish light appear to tug the swollen ceiling down. When he snatches the mobile back to his ear the action seems to draw the lid closer still.

An operator responds at once. "Police," he begs as she finishes her first word. "Police."

Has she recognised him? The silence isn't telling. It emits a burst of static so fragmented that he's afraid the connection is breaking up, and then a voice says "Gloucestershire Constabulary."

For a distracted moment he thinks she's the operator. Surely a policewoman will be more sympathetic than her colleague. "It's Alan Coe again," Coe says with all the authority he can summon up. "I promise you this is no joke. They've buried me because they must have thought I'd passed on. I've already called you once but I wasn't informed what's happening. May I assume somebody is on their way?"

How much air has all that taken? He's holding his breath as if this may compensate, although it makes the walls and lid appear to bulge towards him, when the policewoman says in the distance "He's back. I see what you meant about the voice."

"What's wrong with it?" Coe says through his bared teeth, then tries a shout, which sounds flattened by padding. "What's the matter with my voice?"

"He wants to know what's wrong with his voice."

"So you heard me the first time." Perhaps he shouldn't address her as if she's a child, but he's unable to moderate his tone. "What are you saying about my voice?"

"I don't know how old you're trying to sound, but nobody's that old and still alive."

"I'm old enough to be your father, so do as you're told." She either doesn't hear this or ignores it, but he ensures she hears "I'm old enough for them to pass me off as dead."

"And bury you."

"That's what I've already told you and your colleague."

"In a grave."

"On Mercy Hill below the church. Halfway along the ninth row down, to the left of the avenue."

He can almost see the trench and his own hand dropping a fistful of earth into the depths that harboured his wife's coffin. All at once he's intensely aware that it must be under him. He might have wanted to be reunited with her at the end—at least, with her as she was before she stopped recognising him and grew unrecognisable, little more than a skeleton with an infant's mind—but not like this. He remembers the spadefuls of earth piling up on her coffin and realises that now they're on top of him. "And you're expecting us to have it dug up," the policewoman says.

"Can't you do it yourselves?" Since this is hardly the best time to criticise their methods, he adds "Have you got someone?"

"How long do you plan to carry on with this? Do you honestly think you're taking us in?"

"I'm not trying to. For the love of God, it's the truth." Coe's free hand claws at the wall as if this may communicate his plight somehow, and his fingers wince as though they've scratched a blackboard. "Why won't you believe me?" he pleads.

"You really expect us to believe a phone would work down there."

"Yes, because it is."

"I an't hea ou."

The connection is faltering. He nearly accuses her of having wished this on him. "I said it is," he cries.

"Very unny." Yet more distantly she says "Now he's aking it ound a if it's aking up."

Is the light growing unreliable too? For a blink the darkness seems to surge at him—just darkness, not soil spilling into his prison. Or has his consciousness begun to gutter for lack of air? "It is," he gasps. "Tell me they're coming to find me."

"You won't like it if they do."

At least her voice is whole again, and surely his must be. "You still think I'm joking. Why would I joke about something like this at my age, for God's sake? I didn't even know it was Halloween."

"You're saying you don't know what you just said you know."

"Because your colleague told me. I don't know how long I've been here," he realises aloud, and the light dims as if to suggest how much air he may have unconsciously used up.

"Long enough. We'd have to give you full marks for persistence. Are you in a cupboard, by the way? It sounds like one. Your trick nearly worked."

"It's a coffin, God help me. Can't you hear that?" Coe cries and scrapes his nails across the underside of the lid.

Perhaps the squealing is more tangible than audible. He's holding the mobile towards it, but when he returns the phone to his ear the policewoman says "I've heard all I want to, I think."

"Are you still calling me a liar?" He should have demanded to speak to whoever's in charge. He's about to do so when a thought ambushes him. "If you really think I am," he blurts, "why are you talking to me?"

At once he knows. However demeaning it is to be taken for a criminal, that's unimportant if they're locating him. He'll talk for as long as she needs to keep him talking. He's opening his mouth to rant when he hears a man say "No joy, I'm afraid. Can't trace it."

If Coe is too far underground, how is he able to phone? The police-woman brings him to the edge of panic. "Count yourself lucky," she tells him, "and don't dare play a trick like this again. Don't you realise you may be tying up a line while someone genuinely needs our help?"

He mustn't let her go. He's terrified that if she rings off they won't accept his calls. It doesn't matter what he says so long as it makes the police come for him. Before she has finished lecturing him he shouts "Don't you speak to me like that, you stupid cow."

"I'm war ing ou, ir—"

"Do the work we're paying you to do, and that means the whole shift-less lot of you. You're too fond of finding excuses not to help the public, you damned lazy swine." He's no longer shouting just to be heard. "You weren't much help with my wife, were you? You were worse than useless when she was wandering the streets not knowing where she was. And you were a joke when she started chasing me round the house because she'd forgotten who I was and thought I'd broken in. That's right, you're the bloody joke, not me. She nearly killed me with a kitchen knife. Now get on with your job for a change, you pathetic wretched—"

Without bothering to flicker the light goes out, and he hears nothing but death in his ear. He clutches the mobile and shakes it and pokes blindly at the keys, none of which brings him a sound except for the lifeless clacking of plastic or provides the least relief from the unutterable blackness. At last he's overcome by exhaustion or despair or both. His arms drop to his sides, and the phone slips out of his hand.

Perhaps it's the lack of air, but he feels as if he may soon be resigned to lying where he is. Shutting his eyes takes him closer to sleep. The surface beneath him is comfortable enough, after all. He could fancy he's in bed, or is that mere fancy? Can't he have dreamed he wakened in his coffin and everything that followed? Why, he has managed to drag the quilt under himself, which is how the nightmare began. He's vowing that it won't recur when a huge buzzing insect crawls against his hand.

He jerks away from it, and his scalp collides with the headboard, which is too plump. The insect isn't only buzzing, it's glowing feebly. It's the mobile, which has regained sufficient energy to vibrate. As he grabs it, the decaying light seems to fatten the interior of the coffin. He jabs the key to take the call and fumbles the mobile against his ear. "Hello?" he pleads.

"Coming."

It's barely a voice. It sounds as unnatural as the numbers in the answering messages did, and at least as close to falling to bits. Surely that's the fault of the connection. Before he can speak again the darkness caves in on him, and he's holding an inert lump of plastic against his ear.

There's a sound, however. It's muffled but growing more audible. He prays that he's recognising it, and then he's sure he does. Someone is digging towards him.

"I'm here," he cries and claps a bony hand against his withered lips. He shouldn't waste whatever air is left, especially when he's beginning to feel it's as scarce as light down here. It seems unlikely that he would even have been heard. Why is he wishing he'd kept silent? He listens breathlessly to the scraping in the earth. How did the rescuers manage to dig down so far without his noticing? The activity inches closer—the sound of the shifting of earth—and all at once he's frantically jabbing at the keypad in the blackness. Any response from the world overhead might be welcome, any voice other than the one that called him. The digging is beneath him.

Outside In
Brett Rex Bruton

6

I swing my feet from beneath the warmth of the covers and down onto the cold, hard copy of the opening paragraph. I slip a cigarette from the crumpled packet lying on the bedside table and light it with a shielded flame from a beaten, copper lighter. A thick cloud of smoke and vapour drifts from my open mouth and disappears into the darkness of the bedroom. The shape beneath the covers behind me stirs. I reach back with one hand, trace the depression where the waist meets the curve of a buttock, then stand. A robe hangs from the back of the bedroom door. I lift it from its hook and slip it over my shoulders as I leave the room.

Is this all going as planned? Hell, who knows? I'm not even sure I *have* a plan anymore. Private investigators—private dicks—we're a resourceful lot. Always got a card up our sleeve. Trust a woman to muddle the narrative.

I move towards my desk, past the open window that looks down upon the glowing lights of the Old City District. Far below, long strings of winding halogen mark the steady progress of city traffic as it winds between the towering arches of the magno-rail. The hum of Higgs-Boson engines drifts up from the streets far below, and a glowing snake of light slips by almost silently as a rail carriage winds its way between the rooftops on its cushion of air.

The landscape of lights and curious architecture momentarily distracts the narrator. By the time his attention returns to me, I'm stubbing out my cigarette in an old, brass ashtray and opening the top-right drawer of my desk. I ignore the folded bundle of oilcloth and the .38 snub-nose it contains and instead remove a small, carved box. The light of the desk lamp catches the intricate engravings, and as it flows across their edges, their shapes ripple and change. They swirl across its surface. Their clusters grow tighter. As I lift the small clasp and open the lid, I feel reality re-align. A compression of gravity warps the text around me. I hold the maguffin up to the light. Something in the narrative goes '*click*'. As does the hammer of Starla's revolver.

The glowing tip of her cigarette reflects in the polished gold of her .22 Purse Protector. Accessory *haute couture*. Never leave home without it. Silhouetted in the bedroom doorframe; the lights of the city turn her hair into a faint halo. She's left the sheet on the bed.

"I'm sorry, baby," she says, her voice the whisper of a Hollywood starlet, her lips the colour of cherries, "I told you that thing was no good."

Damn. This is too early for a twist.

1

A field mouse walked through my door a week ago. A tiny thing with large eyes made larger by the glasses they hid behind. The old dirt on her shoes said one of the rural districts. Her modest blouse said maybe one of the outer burbs instead. Either way, she hadn't been in the city long.

My receptionist, Connie, brought her tea, no sugar, while she sat across from me and begun her story. She introduced herself as Tabitha Berg. I said: "Hi, my name is Hank Jewel", daring the narrator to contradict me. Tabby passed me a picture of an angel—hair like spun gold and lips the colour of cherries—and told me: "She's my sister, Starla Berg, though she's called herself Starla Bright for about as long as I can recall. Always had a head on her. Thought the world was just waiting to be her oyster. Couldn't wait to crack it. We lived out on a turbine farm by the Plateau. That was before Starla disappeared."

I backtracked a paragraph or two, mentally underlined my first guess, then politely asked her to continue.

"Almost five years ago, Starla vanished. We searched everywhere—even dragged the river—but she was gone. Then I see this in the newspaper." She handed me a clipping of the angel on the arm of Four Fingers Kennedy and a dart of jealousy stuck me in the gut. "I asked around," she said, "That's the Kennedy Club. And that's Keith Kennedy."

Four Fingers Keith Kennedy. One time goodfella, now a top-ranking untouchable. I whistled in through my teeth and slid the photograph and snippet of newspaper back towards her. I told her in my best condolence voice that if her sister wanted to stay lost, that was her concern. Tabby knew where she was. If she wanted Starla back so bad, she could fetch her herself.

Tabby's wide, mousy eyes closed to thin, hard chips and I began to re-think my previous assumptions. "She can stay dead," she hissed, each word hitting the page with the clink of broken glass, "but when she left, she took something from me. I want it back."

I leant back in my chair as the story suckered me in, then told her what it would cost.

She paid.

2

The Kennedy Club was a hornet's nest painted a pretty shade of maroon. Goodfellas, oldboys and made men crawled in every corner, while top dollar alley cats strutted their heels between the tables. The bartender served me a whiskey in a crystal tumbler worth a little more than my suit, but a fifty slid back beneath the glass got me directions and a password through a green door at the back. Powerful men in an assortment of fedoras locked eyes with poker-cube retina lenses, matching their willpower with equally despicable personas across the globe. No smoked spectacles here.

"What can I get you?" asked bartender number two, and I gazed up at the pantheon of bottles ranked behind him. No green glass here either. Prism bottles climbed the wall, the colours of their contents shimmering, their ostentatious names too numerous for the narrator to list. I pointed and mumbled. I could hear my credit chip sobbing. The tender poured me a glass of ember spirits and sparkles, but before the credit link registered, a voice beside me said; "Put it on my tab, Deek."

The picture hadn't done her justice. Her hair was a sunrise. Her eyes were twin storms of grey. The narrator's description made it as far as the delicate crease where her slender neck met her clavicle before he had to stand up from his desk and pour himself a glass of water. When he returned, he found us at a booth away from the noise. She'd heard I was looking for her. She lit my cigarette and I lit hers, and we laughed as the liquor did its work.

Maybe her hand was a little too close to mine when Four Fingers' goons rocked up. They had me sliding along on the toes of my boots before my glass had the time to hit the ground. We were almost to the back door when Starla put a candle to the corner of an antique Irma Stern and people started shouting. One meathead turned to investigate. The other I doubled up with an Italian heel to the goonies. As he crumpled, I saw the fine impressions of an adrenal augment spider-webbing beneath the skin of his neck. I took a moment to register how lucky I was before scrambling down to the end of the paragraph and slipping around the edge of the page.

3

"She's really been looking for me all this time?" Starla asked as we sat in the bucket seats of my vintage Vitron. We'd been stealing time since that night in the bar. At first, I couldn't find the heart to tell her our meeting hadn't been coincidence. But that night, I'd convinced her to slip her handlers and meet me in the alley behind Four Fingers' home, and I came clean.

"Yeah," I said. I thought of the look in Tabby's eyes and lied through my teeth. "She misses you. Seems they thought you were dead." I waited the appropriate amount of time, then continued; "She also says you took something. Something she'd like back."

She leant her head down. The light of the old car's panel display cast her face in a pale blue light. I kept my eyes forward. She may have been smiling. She may have been crying. Then she took my hand in hers and everything was ok.

"I was never much of a farm girl," she said, "Mucking around with generator couplings and CO2 sieves... I knew there was more for me. More to me. Then one day, Tabby and I are walking through the north field and the world begins to feel... thin. False.

"Tabby almost trips over this small box. It's just lying there, like it was waiting. We open it up and I'd swear that every blade of grass in that field bent towards us. People talk about being the centre of the universe, but to actually *feel* it? To know it? By the time we began walking home, I already knew I was leaving.

"I met Keith my first day in the city. Took him a single evening to wine and dine me. He was small time back then—part time bookie, occasional wise guy. With me by his side, he was made in three years. Four years in, I told him about the maguffin."

And then she did begin to cry, small tears that slid silently down to her chin then vanished. "It was exciting, at first. Everything began happening so quickly. Keith went from small fry to big fish. We went from down-town to up-town. The cars got bigger and the guns got flashier. But after a time, something didn't feel right. The world was happening around us, not *to* us. A bomb in Keith's car went off a few seconds too soon. Keith walked away with a graze and a smoking suit. His wingman, Vince, spent five minutes trying to screw his own legs back on before collapsing onto a pavement littered with shrapnel. I went to visit a friend in Kingsville. A botched robbery of the first class carriages sent them tumbling off the rails. Thirteen died. I was treated for a graze on my forehead that was gone three days after. Wherever I looked, I found us in the midst of adventure, but never a part of it." She paused to wipe her eyes. "When I told Keith this, he smiled. Told me I was being silly. Then he took the maguffin from me and locked it in his office safe. That was a year ago. I haven't seen it since."

She looked at me then, and I remember being amazed at how fast a person can fall in love.

"I'm tired, Hank. I'm grateful, but I'm tired. I want to be a part of the world again." She smiled then, and I honestly believed everything was going to turn out ok. "I know the combination to Keith's safe. His new boy Jesse keeps it on a paper slip in his wallet, in case anything ever goes wrong. Phone Tabby. Tell her we'll bring her the maguffin."

4

The ocean air cut to the bone. A chill breeze rolled off the waves and over the docks, ruffling the pages, and I pulled my jacket tighter around me. I checked my watch, stumped out my cigarette and lit another. The clouds hung low in the night sky. The tip of my smoke burnt like a small meteor.

The tock-tock of heels turned me around. A silhouette emerged from the gloom, a slender apparition. I opened my mouth to call, but a suspicion made me swallow my words. Where was the mousy, young woman who had stepped into my office six days ago? The shadow approaching moved like a knife through the fog, its footsteps measured, the vapour trail of its breath a series of controlled crotchets floating in its path. Then the breeze caught the fog and tugged it from a pair of dark-rimmed spectacles and Tabitha emerged from the text.

"Do you have it?" she asked, "Is it here?"

"I do. It's back in the car. Just wanted to make sure that you were you." I shrugged. "Habit."

I held up my hand and flicked the flint of my lighter twice. Back in the gloom, an engine started up. Twin headlights crept around from between the corrugated, dock warehouses. They swivelled towards us, pinning us in a circle of light.

Then everything went wrong.

The car leapt forward in a squeal of clichés. I grabbed Tabby and swung her aside, tumbling us out of its path just as the hurtling vehicle punched a Vitron shaped hole through the fog where we had just stood. I scrambled to my feet as the car swung back around, yelling at Starla to stop, screaming; "What the hell are you doing?" But when my trusty old wagon leapt forward a second time, it wasn't me Starla aimed it at. Three pops rang out. Two spiderwebs blossomed in the windshield of my baby, and one of her headlights exploded. I turned towards the gunfire and found the field mouse striding towards the charging car, both hands extended forward, the luger in their grasp throwing fire and lead before her. Four shots. Sparks flew from the Vitron's bonnet. Five shots. The driver's side mirror disintegrated. Six shots. The bullet went wide as, at the last second, the car veered to the right and into a spin. Its rear caught a stack of wooden crates and the last I saw of Tabby were two shining points of rage set behind a librarian's lenses before she vanished beneath an avalanche of boxes and timber.

The passenger side door flew open.

"Get in the car!" yelled Starla, miraculously unscathed.

I looked to the splintered crates. I looked to the car. My feet refused to move. Then:

"Get in the fucking car, Hank! That's not Tabby. That's not my sister!"

5

"Maybe we should keep it," she said as our car sped through the dark towards the final act. I nodded. *Yeah, hang onto it for now. Get back to the apartment. Grab some cash and the .38 in my desk. Make like a tree and get the hell out of this shit-eating town. Set up somewhere else. Stick the maguffin in our pocket and wait for life to happen. Let it throw us a couple of bones. Maybe a town house. Ditch it in a lake when we're done.*

Yeah, we could do that, I thought as we tumbled into my apartment and the adrenaline of the last hour got the better of us.

We could do that easy, I thought as Starla pulled me down onto the bed.

7

My head snaps back as the goon—Jesse, it seems—drives Four Fingers Kennedy's point home. His adrenal augment is buzzing away happily in the side of his neck, its tiny tubes twitching and pumping, his teeth grinding and his veins popping, the micro Higgs-Boson drive happy to churn out energy from now until the universe goes pop.

"He'd have found us", Starla had said as Jesse the Goon yanked me from Four Fingers' sedan and stuck a semi-automatic in my ribs. *"Keith's a part of this story, Hank, and stories like this don't end with a pleasant drive into the sunrise."* She opened The Kennedy Club's service door with a four digit code and a vocal scan. We stepped into the covered alleyway. As the thick door clicked closed behind us, she turned, signalling Jesse to wait. *"A tale like ours; it needs a villain, and villains don't let bygones be bygones. The story won't let them."* She put a hand on my face, then drew from her jacket the small, carved box. She held it between us. *"I'm sorry, Hank. This is the way it's got play out."* Then she turned and was gone. And I was dragged back into the hornet's nest.

Jesse's second punch takes me in the kidneys, and I almost piss myself there and then. Four Fingers is waking me around in circles, cracking his knuckles. He's a big guy, still carrying a lot of his wise-guy meat—hasn't had the time to get soft. But a guy in his position has to have a Jesse. A made man keeps his knuckles clean. Then a right hook from five carefully manicured digits topples me and the chair I'm taped to, and the last few sentences go blurry.

"You got nerve," says Kenedy, slipping off a heavy ring and massaging the finger underneath. "Takes a lot of balls to come in here and try to take what's mine." He takes a seat in front of me as Jesse rights me up. We're back in the green room, and I'd kill for a drink. But the doors are locked. The poker-cubes are dark. Even the bar staff are ghosts tonight.

"You think you're the first?" he continues, "You're not the first. There's a joker like you around every corner. The pretty box draws 'em like flies.

Each with a dream. Each with a scheme. Each of them buried six deep in foundations across this sinkhole of a town." He steeples his fingers and dips his head, as though praying. Then he's standing and his heel's in my chest, making that sound you get when you punch a pillow real hard. The back of my head cracks against the floor and I think a rib just popped my left lung.

I can hear Kennedy yelling, but the sounds are muddy, the sentences strange, the words are wrong, letters come apart, unwrap, a rap-tap the tapping upon my key strokes as they hammer toward an ending when the cold hits me in the face, ice-cubes and bourbon, and I have no fucking idea where I am until Four Fingers Keith Kennedys fill my vision, so I pick one and I focus and he's shouting; "It's mine! Mine! You fucking street jockey! You plodding dick!" His hair's gone wild and his face is red. He's standing above me with an empty glass and a firmly placed boot is all it would take to retire me permanently. "My box, in my safe! It's mine! I'm the hero of this fucking story! Me!" He's sweating like he's run a marathon. He's grinding his teeth. His eyes are wide and shiny and there's too much white and I realise that, back behind the scenes, away from the newspaper cameras and celebrity clientele and mobster high-life, Keith Kennedy has gone insane. Fruit Loops. Loonie Tunes. *Th-the... th-the... That's all, folks.*

This is my story, I think he whispers, then the door opens.

I look up from my comfortable spot on the floor. A field mouse just walked into the room. She's wearing new glasses and a fresh change of clothes. And a nasty bruise down the right side of her face. The docks are no place for a lady.

"You've met Irene," Kennedy says, suddenly composed (but yes, if you squint, you can still see the crazy). "She's smarter than you. Know's which side to pick." He beckons. She moves to his side, all pretence at timidity vanished. Here again is the shadow I'd seen cutting the fog along the water's edge. But when he takes her chin in his hand and turns her head so he can see her bruises, does she flinch?

"Maybe she had ideas of her own. But maybe she changed them. Maybe, after her own plans went bad, she took a long, hard think about who she was fucking with, then decided to call me and spill the beans about your little... arrangement."

Jesse lifts me back up. I loll forward against my restraints. There's a warmth spreading across the back of my head and trickling down the sides of my neck. I open my mouth to say 'Hi' to Irene but spit blood onto the floor instead.

"So I check my safe, of course, and when I see the space where my pretty box should be, I almost forget the deal I've made with little Irene here. But then who should call but my runaway kitten, come to her senses. Saved us a lot of looking. Probably saved Irene a lot of hurt too."

I check my bonds, but they're as tight as ever. I square my shoulders as best I can, sneer up at the two through a swollen eye and a cracked tooth and quietly gurgle, "Let me guess; she figured that, if she couldn't have it for herself, maybe she could manage some trickle-down fortune. Hell, it's not just the main characters who get to live happily ever after, right?" I turn my attention to Irene. "Hey, has he told you about Vince? Bet he thought he was getting lucky too. They buried him in three boxes."

Kennedy steps in with his fist raised and I figure this is the one that finally does it for me, but then the door opens again and my angel walks in. She's got the box in her hands. Her jacket and blouse are gone. She's in a dress the colour of a winter sunset and the silk shimmers like oil on water as she moves. How can you stay mad at a woman like that?

She glides up to Four Fingers and plants one on his mug. His hand finds that curve oh-so-recently described. She giggles. If she's faking, she's doing a damn good job. Kennedy takes the box with one hand, gives one last squeeze with the other, then turns to me. Big smile.

"My girl," he says as he lifts the small, carved lid, "My box".

Then the box goes bang. Four Fingers becomes Three Fingers. The narrator laments the loss of alliteration.

The ruined case falls to the floor with the remains of Kennedy's left thumb. Starla's .22 Purse Protector bounces out as the box lands. It takes Kennedy a second to start screaming, but once he does, he's in it to win it.

Jesse the Goon's on the move. He's got Starla by the neck. But Starla, ever prepared for the dangers the late night city streets might hold, plants a thin tazer into the side of his neck. There's a flashing blue light and a string of bright pops, like miniature machinegun fire, then a crack and the strong smell of burning insulation as something tiny in Jesse's adrenal augment explodes. He leaps back, flailing at his neck where already the veins are beginning to swell and distend. He's trying to scream but his jaw has clenched tight. *Hneh! Hneh!* he goes, until two of his front teeth shatter outwards and suddenly we can hear him more clearly.

Starla's behind me, cutting at my binds. Irene is gone, the door to the main club swinging shut after her. My hands come loose, then my feet. I strip away the last of the tape from around my waist just in time to hear Kennedy scream; "You bitch!"

He's coming at us like a bull. The made man is gone. The goodfella is sitting this one out. Even the wise guy is looking the other way. The ninety-five kilos of rage and old muscle barrelling down on us was used to garrotting pensioners for rent money long before any of this maguffin business began. Starla and I aren't both getting out of the way in time, so I knock her aside and brace for impact. Then Kennedy slips on his thumb. He topples forward and I take his weight. I twist to the side and he's rolling past us, stumbling as he tries to regain his balance, then colliding with the thing that, only moments ago, was Jesse.

The goon's neck has swollen up to engulf his chin. Across his shoulders, where his jacket has begun to split, his muscles are growing muscles. Just below where his right ear used to be, the flesh is leaping and bubbling. Buried deep inside the rapidly expanding muscle tissue, where the augment hides, the micro Higgs-Boson drive must have slipped its bearings. Millions of perpetually spinning particles just got re-introduced to gravity. All that energy's got to go somewhere.

The thing that was Jesse roars as the synthesised adrenal cocktail courses through it. A hand, now the size of a dinner plate, takes Kennedy by the top of his head as he tries to pull himself upwards. A short squeeze turns it to pink jelly and red mist. The stitching along the soles of its shoes splits as not-Jesse steps forward. Realising its legs still work, it roars again, then begins lumbering towards us, intent on tearing us apart before its rapidly swelling muscles do the same to its body.

I turn to Starla, stare into those great big eyes, and scream, "Where the fuck is it? Give it to me, quick!"

She doesn't hesitate. She reaches in between her breasts, and gravity does that weird, reverse concussion. She draws out the maguffin. Reality realigns. I snatch it from her and the universe wraps around me. I cock back my arm and time bends. I throw.

The maguffin sails towards the warping monster of messy death charging towards us, carrying the weight of reality with it. As it flies, the adrenal augment, borne by the tiny Higgs-Bosson drive, erupts from the beast's chest in a spray of viscera.

I grab Starla. Together we leap for the safety of the bar.

They meet.

The world goes thick. Reality slows. Across the room, items rise from their surfaces. An ashtray hovers. A chair lifts from the ground. Behind the bar, the bottled liquids become floating bubbles of myriad hues.

They touch. Gravity meets *gravitas*.

The universe goes pop.

8

We scramble through the hole in the Kennedy Club's wall and into the night. My left lung is on fire and I'm breathing hard in the smoke and dust. Miraculously, Kennedy's sedan has remained intact, minus a couple windows. Starla helps me over the last of the rubble and up to the driver's side door. But as we're climbing in either side, she puts her hand on my leg and motions for silence.

A field mouse creeps from the ruins of Four Fingers Kennedy's club. Her head shoots left and right as she scans the smoke and shadows. The glasses are gone. Her eyes are wild but sharp. She clutches something tight to her breast with both hands as she climbs through the cavity in the blasted, brick wall and flees down the alley. Words tumble after her into the night.

"Do we follow her?" asks Starla beside me, "Do we go after it?"

I knock some loose nuggets of glass from the side window, clear a porthole through the soot on the windscreen, then pump the break a few times to check for irony. Satisfied, I light a cigarette.

"Let her keep it," I say. I reach beneath the dashboard and set the engine humming as the story races away from us. "We don't need it anymo

Hope Is Here
Karen Runge

THE SUNSHINE GROUP:
WE ARE HERE TO MAKE THE WORLD
A CLEAN AND HAPPY PLACE!

The proclamation screams in bright blue, the background cream-yellow. The bottom of the sign is printed with a child's drawing, or maybe a drawing done by an adult pretending to be a child, depicting round green hills and nose-less, orb-faced boys and girls, all standing in a line and holding hands.

Beneath the edict, above the drawing, it reads:

HOT FOOD
HOT SHOWERS
HOPE IS HERE!

The script is fresh, natural. It's hard to tell if it was stencilled on or drawn by hand. I stare at the words, and then look again at the drawing of the children. In their stiff, finger-linked line, they look as though they are marching forward. Maybe this was the idea. When children sing or play games, they're always standing or sitting in a circle. I remember that from the days when I used to go to the playground in the park, and watch them in their brightly-coloured groups, pushing each other down slides, sometimes screaming and laughing; sometimes crying, or being made to cry. I'd spend whole afternoons there, often mornings, too. Seated on that bench by the gate, comfortable beneath the shade of the tree, my sturdy old backpack leaned against my legs.

This was before one of those parents noticed me, and looked at me as though I were a shark in a swimming pool. I remember her. The dyed hair and the too-tight jeans, her face full of makeup papered over the creases that spread across her face. I remember the loose folds of her neck flushing red, the lipstick caught on her teeth, that forefinger raised with its painted fingernail, stabbing at the air, at me, until I mumbled my apologies and left, never to return. She looked at me as though I were a wolf. That witch. I was just a man with an empty day and nothing else to make me smile.

I wanted to scrape the makeup off her face with the rough edges of my bitten fingernails. Take some of the skin off, too.

But that would make the kids scream and cry.

There are no adults in this picture, either. This picture on the sign, with its children wearing scribble-smiles, caught in the colours of eternal sunshine. There are no adults, though the place this sign was made for is an adult place. A place for adults like me, who have lost children, forgotten children. Who are not allowed near children anymore.

Are they trying to tell us children are our salvation? That children are the ones reaching out to us, and not people with bank accounts and fundraising plans, and lists of volunteers?

If I were to go in, would it be little boys and girls laced up with aprons, standing in a row behind the service table, dishing out watery potatoes and plates of over-cooked pasta?

'Budget food', I think, is the term. Staples bought from wholesalers in bulk.

If I were to say this out loud to anyone who listened, they might look at me as though I shouldn't know the difference. As though it's ungrateful of me to even bring it up. This is how, even when people think they're being kind, they're being cruel. They forget that those like me have had our time among people with grocery lists and well-stocked kitchens all of their own. I used to be one of them, didn't I? The only difference is that I've had to accustom my tastes to the contents of trashcans and discarded sandwich crusts. The only difference is that I know what *real* hunger is now, and how joyful the idea of having my own plate is. My own plate, filled, the contents of which would slide into my belly and ease the slow burn that nests there like a hungry demon, scrabbling at my insides with needle claws and teeth.

Staring at that sign from across the street, with its cheerful promise and its shiny glass doors, I avoid my reflection and try to move my feet. Beyond those doors stands a row of clean-cut faces, smiles spread to wide, white-toothed grins. Voices come in smooth, welcoming tones of condescension. Their eyes melt with pity, a thin film layered over the look of disgust they're so desperate to hide. They sniff a lot, as though they have colds. They'll try anything to cover their noses, for whatever brief moment, and make it look innocent.

This is the razorblade hidden in the apple. This is the paradox of help and harm.

* * *

It's going to rain later. I smell it in the air, a faint electric damp. I see it too, the way the sky is slightly darkened at the edge of the horizon. A storm blue, bleeding into pale pastel shades. On the high street, women in sleeve-less summer dresses click down the pavement in strappy high heels, swing-ing their arms as they step. Businessmen carry their jackets slung over their arms, their long sleeves rolled up, top buttons undone.

They are absolutely oblivious to the changes in the sky, the threat rolling in on them.

I sit on the bench outside the coffee shop, waiting for Mandy. When it's busy in there she sometimes takes a little longer, but for now the weather is still warm and people don't want to drink hot coffee. They want to go down to the beach and eat ice-cream; maybe candy apples, sweet and red. They want to knock off work early and head to one of the bars on the quay. Later, when it starts to rain, they'll come crowding back along here.

Mandy comes out after she spots me through the window, her dark hair tied up off her neck, her apron smeared with chocolate sauce.

"Having a messy day, today!" she smiles, and hands me the small latte and jam pastry she probably pays for herself. I don't know, I never asked. "This is the second apron I'm gonna have to change."

"You're still beautiful," I tell her, cramming the pastry into my mouth and softening it with a swig of hot coffee. I do this to keep my eyes water-ing. I do this to keep from staring at her breasts, those soft mounds sheathed in fabric, her waist laced in tight.

She giggles, moves to hit my shoulder, then stops her hand mid-motion. She blushes, smirks, folds her arms. "I can't stay," she says.

"You'll be busy later," I tell her. "When the storm comes in."

"Storm?" She squints her eyes and cranes her neck, looking up into the sky. "You sure?"

I nod, slurping coffee, already turning away. "See you around," I say.

I do not thank her. I have never thanked her. I don't go there for the coffee, you see.

* * *

Down under the bridge, Manxy is up on one of the rocks, mid-speech, mid crazy-eyed roll. "You gotta check it out, man!" he says. "They got piles of pasta—you know, *spaghetti*. Not dry noodles with a spoon of boiled to-matoes, I mean *spaghetti*. With pork and mushrooms. I asked them, 'Where's the garlic bread?' and the guy there laughed, and he told me, he said, 'Next time, friend!' He said *next time*. He said 'Tell your friends!'"

The dog that's always at his feet sits gazing up at him in adoration. It's a small thing, small enough to send flying if you were to give it a kick. It's got patchy fur and a busted ear, but its eyes are always wet and soft, especially when it's watching Manxy talk. It sees me coming, turns its head a little, and starts yapping.

I glare at it and saunter over to the water's edge.

"Gee," he calls me. Forgetting that my name used to be Gary. Forgetting that I hate any other name. "Hey, Gee! They got pretty girls there, too!"

What has Manxy been smoking? I wish he wouldn't talk to me.

"Gee, you like the pretty girls! The girls there are all in short skirts and tit-busting shirts. And they lean over when they dish the food out. You wouldn't believe it! You'd go wild!"

When I was new out here, I once made the mistake of telling Manxy how I got to be this way. There's nothing wrong with swapping stories, we all need to do it sometimes, but I was dumb and didn't know how to choose which people are the right ones to tell. Manxy isn't the right person to tell anything to. He's like the town crier of the underbelly. Every time I see him, he'll say something like this, something to remind me. Something to make me want to gut him and his dog both.

"Fuck off, Manxy."

"No serious, Gee. You gotta go. It's called Hope is Here, and it's run by this new group, a charity or something. They call themselves The Sunshine Group. Their place is all brand new, up on Wyle Street. Big shiny windows. The showers are all new, too. Fresh built. The place smells like paint and plaster. And they're not like those big communal ones either. Each one has its own stall. A *stall!*"

"I'll shower in the rain," I tell him. Then, remembering my manners, I add, "Thank you."

"That's why you smell so goddamn bad," he says. "Like shit smeared on rotten eggs. You wanna be like this the rest of your life? You've gotta take what's offered. Everyone else does!"

Shit smeared on rotten eggs. Fantastic. I remember Mandy and her hand getting stuck mid-air. The chocolate sauce drying over her left breast. The way she smiles at me and then steps back. No razorblades in that apple.

Still, it hurts. The rain's coming.

"What's the catch, Manxy?" I ask him. "Do they stick you with needles, give you lectures about drugs?"

"No," Manxy shakes his head. "Just get you to answer a few questions. They're doing data collecting, something like that. Standard practice, man. Standard. They're devoted to getting us all off the streets."

I wouldn't know what's standard or not. The closest I've ever been to a soup kitchen or shelter was the Christmas drive, when the Church van came to us, came right down here to the bridge with boxes of food and piles of clothes. Teenage girls with pimpled chins and elf hats tried not to sneer when they handed the stuff over. They just wanted to go home and watch their parents get trashed, then sneak out to smoke joints in the back garden. Their mothers were right behind them, though. Fat ladies flashing gold jewellery, dishing stuff out with plastic smiles, sniffing like they all had colds.

The sneers are more honest. I gave those girls the widest grins.

Everybody said "Merry Christmas!" at least a hundred times, until it was ringing in my head like a goddamn chant. Then they packed themselves up and hurtled back to their homes to carve turkeys and drink wine.

It wasn't so bad. After all, it's my door they were knocking on, and not the other way around.

* * *

I head back along the high street, and stand across the road from Mandy's coffee shop. It's hard to see her through the distance, through the crowd. The rain picks up and chills the warmth out of the air, and the people passing by start ducking into the coffee shop. Through the mess of moving heads, I sometimes glimpse her face. She's moving fast behind the counter, working the till, grabbing pastries. Her eyebrows tight with concentration, her lips curled into a smile. Mandy, she's always smiling. It doesn't matter what it is she's looking at.

* * *

I should've stayed at the bridge. Manxy and his fucking dog. The rain hits my shoulders like small icy bullets, bleeding in through broken seams. These shoes I'm wearing, they used to be classic black. I used to wear them to the office, Monday to Friday. Now I wear them pretty much twenty-four-seven, and they're stuck to my feet like a sheath of living leather, lined with layers of peeling skin. When I do take them off, they slide away with a shower of black dirt and the smell of vermin rotting under wet leaves. Underneath, my toes are blue and black and the nails are curling in. I peel the ends off while they're still soft with grime and sweat.

I used to have nail clippers, but they got stolen out of my bag.

I used to have a pair of rubber slippers, too.

I used to have a lot of things.

I forget where I'm going and take the slip road that cuts behind that restaurant, *Salvatore*, just as the chef comes out for a cigarette break. I round the corner on him, and the moment he spots me his eyes bulge red and his arms fly out. He sends his lighter soaring, skittering out through the rain and toward the piles of rubbish.

"Get the fuck out of here!" he yells. "You fucking disgusting scum! You fucking low-life! Get the fuck away!"

I bend to pick up the lighter, close it in my hand.

He moves like he wants to fight me, but steps back at the last minute. His arms flail.

"I know what you are!" he screams. "I know what you fucking are!"

I keep walking until his tirade is lost beneath the sounds of the rain.

* * *

WE ARE HERE TO MAKE THE WORLD
A CLEAN AND HAPPY PLACE!

Big words, those. Big Promises.

I push open the doors, and step into a reception area with a welcome desk and rows of plastic chairs bolted into the floor. The walls are papered with pictures of smiling children and matching slogans.

A BRIGHT FUTURE!
A FRESH TOMORROW!

Rain leaks off of me in a steady, sliding trickle. The girl behind the desk stands up, grabs a towel out from somewhere I can't see, and walks over to me, all smiles. She's wearing a miniskirt and I imagine the place behind the hem, beneath the fabric, that slide of warmth and wetness nestled between her legs.

"Welcome to Hope is Here!" she says. "Isn't it a beautiful day?"

"Not really," I say, taking the towel.

"Why don't you dry off?"

She's already fetched a mop, a washcloth. She steps outside to clean off the smudge I left on the door when I pushed it open. She mops off all evidence of my footsteps, hands me a pair of rubber slippers. My classic blacks disappear into a plastic bag.

"We'll get you some clean clothes after you've had your shower," she says, then briefly wrinkles her nose. "You smell really bad, you know? Worse than any of the others."

"That's not very polite," I tell her.

"We believe in honesty, not condescension."

"I can get behind that," I nod.

At least, I think I can. No hidden razorblades here, so far. Still, it hurts.

She takes me into a small corner office, picks up a clipboard and a pen, and smiles at me. "Comfy?"

"I'm out of the rain."

"We need to do a quick assessment for our records," she says. "Top scorers get a chance at rehabilitation, so let's hope you'll join our club."

I'm still wearing wet pants and my ass is starting to itch in this chair. "Will this take long?"

"That depends."

She clicks her pen, and smiles at me with slightly yellowed teeth. Too much caffeine? Nicotine? I wish she'd offer me some. I'd kill for another of Mandy's little lattes.

"How long have you been on the street?" she asks.

"Two years, somewhere around there."

"Where were you before?"

"A city far, far away."

"You don't want to tell me?"

"No. You don't want to know my name?"

She shakes her head. "Not yet. We need to get past the important stuff first."

The important stuff.

"How would you rate your level of happiness on a scale of one to ten?"

"Ten below fucking zero," I say. "It's fucking cold in here."

She smiles, flips her hair over her shoulder, letting her fingers snag carefully through the strands. "You swear a lot, too," she says. "Is that something you always did?"

"I don't remember. Not to pretty girls like you. Not before. Not usually, anyway."

"You like pretty girls?"

I stare at her. "Who doesn't?"

"Lots of people!" she says. "So you used to swear at pretty girls, sometimes?"

"If they were being bitches, yes."

"Do you think I'm a bitch?"

"I don't know yet."

She makes marks with her pen. Not writing. Ticks and crosses. She wasn't kidding. I'm being scored.

"How did you get to be on the street?"

"A pretty girl took everything away from me."

"How?"

"It's ancient history and I'd rather not say."

"Two years ago isn't ancient history. Are the police looking for you?"

"Why would they be looking for me?"

I rub my ass around in the seat.

After a while, she looks back down at the clipboard. "Okay," she sighs. "How about animals? Do you like animals?"

"I hate yappy little dogs with busted ears."

She sighs. "So that's a no?"

"I don't know."

I take the lighter out of my pocket and start to flick it. It flashes tiny sparks that glow against the dark creases of my hand. When she sees it, her eyes widen.

"You smoke?" she asks.

"Can't afford it."

"Would you, if you could?"

"Yes, I think so."

"Do you ever light fires?"

"Every night."

She laughs. "No, I mean to burn things. Like buildings or… something."

"Do you mean am I a pyromaniac?"

"Oh!" she beams. "You've got a good vocabulary!"

"What? I'm not a fucking idiot."

She shakes her head to herself. "Pity about that attitude."

"Listen," I say sharply, staring at the plump arcs of her breasts. "If you'd lived like…"

"And about that temper." She stands up suddenly. "Follow me," she says.

* * *

I'm back out in the rain with a slip of paper in my hand. I'm wearing plastic slippers and I don't have socks. I still smell like shit and rotten eggs, and the rain is still hitting me like a million tiny bullets of ice.

The piece of paper says, "Congratulations! You've reached Phase Two of our Rehabilitation Programme!"

Beneath this is a drawing of happy little children, joined at the hands and looking like they're all about to start marching forward with their scribble smiles and eternal sunshine colours.

They want me back here at ten tonight.

* * *

I catch Mandy as she's closing up. She looks different out of her apron. Tight jeans, snug black top, her hair loose and shining down her shoulders. She turns and sees me, and she smiles.

"You came to say goodnight?" she asks.

"Mandy," I say. "I got into this rehabilitation programme. I want you to know that I'm gonna be okay. I want you to know that I'm grateful for everything you did for me. For smiling at me every time we met."

"A programme? That's great, Gary!" she smiles, opening her umbrella and pulling me beneath it. She smells like roasted coffee beans and cinnamon rolls.

"And when I've got myself straight, I'm taking you to dinner. Okay? I'm taking you to *Salvatore's*, and you can order anything you want."

"*Salvatore's*?" she laughs. "You're kidding!"

"No, I'm not. I mean it. I really mean it. You don't have to believe me just yet, but I'll prove it to you. Just remember, okay? Just remember."

She slides her arm through mine, like we're lovers, like we're friends.

Her steps slow a little. "You smell really bad," she says. "You know that?"

* * *

Ten at night, and the doors are closed, covered from the inside by a thick heavy curtain. The door isn't locked, though, and when I step inside I see the room is lit with dim, flickering lights. Around the room, there are hundreds of candles. They line the reception desk, they stand in corners, collected on small tables. As I move inside, I see shapes shuffling in the dark. The room smells like dead things, rotten things; things smeared and stained, and then forgotten. The shapes, of course, are all the other guys who made it into the programme. They're hunched over under blankets, scattered through the seats. The girl I spoke to earlier comes over, the one who didn't tell me her name and didn't ask me mine. She takes my backpack and hands me a blanket.

"Take a seat," she says. "The Head Coordinator will be along shortly to give you all a little speech, and then we can begin."

She's in a dress, a long white dress with long, loose sleeves. There are about seven or eight other girls like her, too, with shining hair and soft smiles. Angels in the light.

"What's with the candles?" I ask her.

"They're beautiful!" she says, "And they're cheaper than electricity."

I take a seat in the middle, not wanting to be too close or too far. Not wanting to seem overeager, or too absent.

Nobody talks. It must be the light, reminding some of us of Church. There's always something about candles casting shadows in the dark that brings a kind of hush, makes things feel more sacred. I used to make use of that, before, with all those other girls.

A few more street guys come in, and I count about thirty of us. Manxy isn't here, or any of the other guys from under the bridge.

Damn right. I wouldn't want them here, messing the place up with their shitty jokes and that yapping dog.

After a while, a man in black jeans and a long black coat comes in through another door. His hair is dark, greased back in stiff spikes. He has a strong jaw, a perfectly symmetrical face. He's clean-shaven, almost baby-faced. But his eyes are alert, sure. He walks with purpose and power. This man is the boss. The girls all smile at him, and move to stand in neat rows on either side; like they're all ready to hold hands, march forward, maybe sing.

"Welcome to Hope Is Here!" he says. "I'm Aleister, head of our little group."

A few of the guys clap. One of them whistles, and Aleister puts his finger against his lips. "Let's have some respect, some silence," he says. "This world we live in is a crazy, chaotic place without adding to the noise. Which is why our dream is to create a centre of tranquillity, happiness, cleanliness, and hope. Our goal is to expand beyond these walls, until every one of you is off the streets, and the world can be a perfect, sunshiny place." He beams.

One girl steps forward, and in her hands is a long scroll. It's a poster, and she unrolls it. Another bends down in front of her, holding the bottom down so that we can all see.

"This is our happiness metre," she says. "Our city is an affluent one, with beautiful weather and bright clean beaches. We feel that no matter what your situation is, everyone should be able to score at least a Dawn on the scale."

And this is how it's scaled. Kids' drawings of the sun, set to the time of day. Dawn, a slightly glum silver, sleepy-eyed. It shades up to Noon, which is a wide, smiling sun with lots of red and orange flames framing its face. Then the smiling suns begin to fade, smaller and weaker, until at the very top is Dusk, a miserable, fading sun smothered with blue and the smoke-black of falling night.

"*We're* all Noons," she says. "But in your assessments, you're the ones who all scored a Dusk. Now we don't know why that is, but we do know that even if we feed you and clean you up, we still can't make you happy." And she smiles at us sadly, a soft curve of the lips. This is Mandy's smile, when she's too busy to look up and see me watching her through the window.

Aleister takes the poster from her and rolls it up smartly in his hands. "We're always looking for new recruits to join our little club," he says, "but none of you fit the criteria, with the attitudes you displayed."

One of the guys towards the front stands up. "What the fuck are you saying?" he says.

Aleister smiles again, a wide grin of perfect white teeth. "This is why we can't have you," he says. Patient, but commanding. "Anger, bad language, bad attitude. People offer to help you, and *this* is your response. We think that the less of you there are, the more room there'll be for people to be happy. The more room for us to help the people who would actually *use* it."

Behind me, someone stands up, heads for the door.

"Can't go out that way!" Aleister says. His voice is loud and bright; a wave rolling through boiling syrup.

This is when uncertainty and confusion move in to panic. One of the guys stands up, grabbing at his chair, maybe to throw it, but it's bolted to the floor.

"You litter our streets with your filth and your stink, but worst of all, you spread disgust!" Aleister says. He's shouting now, over the sounds of the other voices, people moving. "You turn our beautiful streets into trash heaps. *You* are trash heaps, and we're the only ones with a plan and the will to do something about it."

From his coat, he pulls out a long silver blade. It glows in the light of the candles, takes on the brightness of flames, as though it itself is a flame, a sword of fire instead of metal. The girls reach into their robes. In their hands, they now hold straight razors.

I don't look at their faces, but the force of their smiles beats down on us, brighter than sunshine. Sunshine and happiness. Sunshine eternal. For them, but not for us.

And they all march forward.

They find me at the bottom of the heap, lying with my face pressed to the floor, pretending to be dead, taking shallow breaths. The weight of the bodies piled across my back is smothering. My nose is thick with the sick, copper-sweet smell of blood, the hot acidic tang of fresh urine. The stench of scorched skin and burning fabric from when the candles fell, and spread small fires. Underneath me a pile of intestines lies uncoiled, turgid, wet, and slowly cooling.

My mouth burns with the bitter aftertaste of bile.

"One more," Aleister says. Finding me, who had not moved. Who had lain so still, and heard and felt the bodies falling around and over me. Who had played possum, biting my tongue to keep from screaming.

"I love children," I hear myself sob as he bends close. "I love children, and I love a girl called Mandy... and I can tell the weather. I can tell the weather better than a weatherman."

A light flashes into my eyes. Staring up into the beam, I make out white robes stained red. My heart hammers in my chest as I try to focus, to process what I see. The curves of cheeks. Soft-smiling faces. Steady hands moving, reaching down for me.

"Oh that one," a girl says, her voice familiar. "He's the worst pervert of them all."

"Lift him up," Aleister says, his voice soft and smooth and very gentle. Arms reach around me. Two girls. Just two of them, their robes washed red. The wet fabric clings to their bodies, their bodies pressed against mine. All my strength, it's drained out of me. I stand off-balance, trembling, staggering on a pile of torn limbs and opened guts. Something rolls beneath my heel, and I glance down to see a head. It's torn back from its shoulders, the throat a gape of bloody disarray, the last unsnapped tendons and the tight clasp of vertebrae yearning to pull it back into place. My stomach spasms, my balance swerves away from me, but the hands that grip me tighten, and I don't fall.

I want to fall.

Aleister's eyes gaze into mine. Patient. Commanding.

"Dusk is just a dying day," he says. "So go into the night."

His blade, once bright and white, is thick with blood and matted hair. He raises it to my throat.

Behind him, rows of girls hold hands, swaying on their feet.

They're angels in the glow of dying fire. They smell like cinnamon, like candy apples. Like life.

Would To God
That We Were There
Tom Dullemond

When I was young I was struck by the lines of a Lord Tennyson poem:

> *Would we not, when glancing heavenwards*
> *On a star so silver-fair*
> *Yearn, and clasp the hands, and murmur:*
> *"Would to God that we were there"?*

"Yes!" I would think. "*Yes?*"
Now I'm here and everything is falling and I think, *No.*
No no no—Fuck no.

* * *

The final stage of the Mars500 project started in June of 2010, and in November of 2011 the six crewmen emerged little worse for wear. Being locked up in a set of rooms for all that time is supposed to prepare you for this trip, and they always come out fine. On-call comms to help with psychological problems and real kiss-the-earth gravity will do that to you; it'll fill you with a cockiness that only hard vacuum will suck out. And yet Diego Urbana came out of Mars500 and said, "Hearing people talk live means a lot. It is the best gift you can get."

He was so right. I came out of a similar project just fine; I can keep myself entertained. I'm a nice guy. The isolation wears you out but you know all will be well in the end.

Oh, it's Cynthia! Sometimes I catch a glimpse of her when I sneak a glimpse through the observation port and the sun spins past. It's always *down*; the old walls are now *down*. Cynthia and Blake are tethered so I usually can't see them, but I guess the orbit has curved around enough now so the sun reflects off their suits. Donovan is always out of view. I think Cynthia wanted it that way.

Their suit jets can be remotely activated. It's how I induced a three-rpm spin on the module. It was a small improvement; instead of falling forever I weigh about a kilo now, and now I get sunrises and sunsets every twenty seconds through the little observation port. I've boosted the filters so I can't see the stars wheeling eternally. It just feels like a little lamp is orbiting me in a black room. It's amazing how that keeps the terror away for minutes at a time. I have to stop when it gets the better of me, hold onto something and just breathe. That's the funny thing about fear. Your heart pounds in your chest, your palms break out with sweat—but eventually it subsides; eventually you become numb to it. Eventually you can breathe.

It's important to drown out the stars. I remember there was a cosmonaut on one of the space stations who came to think the stars were watching him. There's nothing to see out there except the swirling streaks of stars, and I don't want them watching me either.

Three rotations per minute would normally mess with your inner ear; we're too bound to gravity not to detect the artifice of centripetal force. But I stay down low, mostly; I try to keep my head away from the rotational axis. When I lie pressed to the thin wood veneer of the capsule wall and close my eyes, it almost feels like I'm lying face down on the solid ground in my kitchen at home instead of falling to Mars through this black infinity.

* * *

When the communications shorted out three months into the journey, it was Donovan who cracked first. He'd slipped into a twenty-five hour day. I'd read about that in Mars500 too. About twenty percent of the time he was the only crewmember awake. That's no way to live.

It was silly of him, really. And unprofessional. We'd all done this before; we'd each spent six months inside OPSEK, completed EVA training and yawned through half-trip versions of the Mars500 project in the early twenties. We knew there was a fully automated base on Mars waiting for us; I'd watched the videos of the robots assembling the damn thing. There were supplies and radios and orbiters to relay our signals via the Interplanetary Internet. There was plenty of research to do, and the promise of other settlers on their way, eventually; a Hohmann transfer orbit like ours needs Earth and Mars to be aligned just *so*, and that only happens every two years, so it would be a while before they came. We literally fall around the sun to reach Mars, a straight line through curved gravity wells. Ain't physics grand?

We passed all the psych tests. We did our solitary confinement. We drilled our exercise routines to make sure we kept our bodies toned as well as we could.

But there's something about where we are, where no human being has ever been, that seared away our preparation.

OPSEK drifts a hundred miles or so above the earth. The proud astronauts who walk on the Moon are three days away, no more than a light second.

145

But we're *far* away; we're far away and a tiny, insignificant bubble of heat and life and thoughts. Mission control would take minutes to reach us. All that's left to remind us of home is the little network handshake light that blinks on the navigation computer, but we can't communicate. We're now further from Earth than the Earth is from the Sun. There's not another soul for over a hundred thousand thousand kilometres around me.

No one can catch us; no one can stop the ship. It has to fall all the way to Mars. A rescue mission can't be launched for another twenty months or so. We were pioneers with no recourse, only the promise of an automated welcome when we reached Mars.

* * *

There's…

There's something about the void.

Donovan took an overdose a month after our comms went down. I heard him choking in the medical capsule and floated across to see what was happening but it was too late. I vacuumed up the spinning globules of vomit while Cynthia tried her best not to be sick herself, but it got me thinking. About all that extra air he left behind. About how much we might need in terms of supplies if, say, we decided to spin in Mars orbit for nine months until the planets aligned again and we just kept falling back to Earth.

Blake was outside trying to fix the comms array at the time. He did it every day, went out to hang in the void to spend time alone and fix the comms. I didn't think that was healthy but we really needed those communications; during Mars500, the crew bickered over who received more messages from their loved ones. In later fake missions, it was the communications experts like Donovan who were responsible for making sure every team member received the same number of emails and video messages. I wondered how many he had been trashing for the benefit of the rest of us. I hadn't received too many.

As the medical doctor, I didn't really know what he expected to achieve after a month of fruitless repair attempts; I didn't understand electronics nearly as well as Blake, but maybe it kept him sane. He was the one relaying all the news from earth before the malfunction. It's very important to have someone trusted filtering the news. After an extended period of isolation we humans become psychologically delicate, you see. In the absence of psych professionals on the mission team we need that team of psychologists back on Earth monitoring our behaviour. Otherwise it's too easy to miss the signs. That would've helped Donovan, I'm sure, and I would not have needed to change the mission parameters so much. Things would've turned out better for Cynthia and Blake, too, obviously.

Cynthia went for EVA to gather her thoughts after we said goodbye to Donovan. I helped her put him in his spacesuit with the seals open and she tethered him to the outside of the capsule. The plan was to pull him back in when we reached Mars orbit. He'd be perfectly freeze-dried eventually, and none of us felt like keeping company with a rotting corpse for the next five months.

It's easy to abstract the reality of this trip. The Mars500 project was the perfect example of this folly. Five hundred days in a sealed environment with a handful of fellow astronauts, but always there's hard gravity to remind you that you're home. And you know there are fellow humans mere metres from your fake capsules. And you know that if anything were to go wrong that only minutes would pass before human voices and human arms wrapped you tight.

I held Cynthia close as she died, because I knew it would be the last human contact I'd have for more than a year and because she struggled a little, even in sleep. Afterwards, I worried that there wasn't enough morphine left for Blake. But there was. Now they're tethered to the hull alongside Donovan. It was better this way. They were getting flaky. They never would've made it.

Cynthia had a terabyte of music on an expensive little player and she used to plug it into our speaker system. She had a taste for thirty year old German doom rock, and so on occasion our little tin can would float through the soundless void with a soundtrack of angry thrash guitar and screaming vocals. I had joked we should watch *2001: A Space Odyssey* on the projector and replace *Also Sprach Zarathustra* with metal where appropriate.

In the first month of being alone I would play those songs on repeat; the wall of sound and thin fake gravity masked the careless void for a time. Eventually something blew in the speakers and the rage turned tinny.

Blake used to laugh at me plugging away at orbital and spin gravity calculations on my Mac after Donovan died. "The ship's too small to give it meaningful spin gravity, doc," he'd laugh. "And this baby's Mars orbit is all pre-programmed, you're not going to find any mistakes there."

I was just the doctor, after all. I didn't know anything about spin and orbits, right? Well, I picked three rpm, Blake. Just enough to pretend that there's a *down* without succumbing to the nausea and dizziness of the Coriolis Effect, as long as I stay flat to the floor and crawl everywhere. Bet you didn't know *that*, with your fancy electronics training that didn't help you fix the comms board. And I've got the return trip all worked out now, too, because they never thought we'd need one, but I *changed the mission parameters*, Blake. And you should thank me that I didn't need any practise on how to administer intravenous sedatives, being a doctor and all. How's the view out there, by the by?

I told him it was something to keep me occupied, something to fill my head and crowd out the dark thoughts. He just laughed and somersaulted down to medical. The living quarters are a three metre wide cylinder that goes for twenty metres before it opens onto the medical capsule, so his was a beautiful demonstration of aerial skill. Cynthia watched him sail past, smiling. It was the first smile I'd seen from her in weeks.

I finished the last of the calculations eventually, alone, pressed flat to the fake wood in the pretence of gravity. Once I reach Mars next month I only have to hang in orbit there for another four months before I can fire off most of the attitude adjustment booster and kick on, in the reverse dance that brought us here. It will take the four of us on a gentle spiral back down to the inner Solar System and eventually… eventually… back to Earth. And now there's enough air and food to last me all the way back home, if I'm careful.

Careful? I'm a doctor. I got this.

* * *

I read a lot of Lovecraft when I was a kid. He liked to populate the universe with horrible inhuman alien entities; things that sat just outside our awareness, on the thin edge of Euclidian space. I suppose he considered it a horrific thing, these creatures.

But I don't even have *them*.

I'm the loneliest human who ever existed, two hundred million kilometres from earth, and all around me is infinitely *down* and the closest humans are my three dead friends, puppets on strings around the capsule.

Nietzsche said *'if you stare into the Abyss long enough the Abyss stares back at you'* but every day I crawl-skim over to the observation port and I stare down into the void in hope and *nothing looks* back.

Nothing.

So I close my eyes and clutch at the ever-so-slightly curved floor, and I pretend it's Earth, and I wish to God that I were there.

And I dream…

* * *

…In my dream the capsule passes close to home on its slingshot trajectory to Mars, and I've stopped it spinning now, so Earth looms comforting and steady below, large as the view from the ISS. I slide into the airlock and take a deep breath, then dive, wings wide, into the cool breeze of space.

Behind me the capsule spits free of air and spurts and spirals onwards and out, a shuddering balloon, trailing Cynthia, Donovan and Blake on their tethers. They wave at me with big smiles, their helmets tipped impossibly open so they can yell their best wishes and condolences that I couldn't come with them. They fly back and finish their mission on that tiny red dot in the distance.

I smile; I exhale gently as I dive closer to the Earth, cool wind hissing in my ears and making them pop. There's no other sound but the excited beating of my heart. Mountains spin into view below me and I curve my approach to glory in the white peaks and fractal slopes, white-capped tops, the scent of vegetation and mountain spring water filling my nose. Cities drift by, streets filled with banners and flags and crowds waving and cheering and ready to embrace me.

And then, as I drift gracefully as a dove over the peaks of the Himalayas, I turn my face to the black-blue sky. Returning to the mote that is my home, I scream a mad defiance at the void.

* * *

I'm woken by a series of dull thuds. Probably Blake bumping against the hull. He's tethered a little closer than the others and it happens from time to time. He always was a pain in the ass. I don't want to go crawl down and out but I need that gravity. He'll just need a little push.

Always there is that light on the navigation console flashing. The network handshake.

Someone, somewhere, is thinking of me.

NEGATIVES
WENDY HAMMER

"Remind me again why I'm out in the middle of nowhere at this ridiculous hour," Maddy said, wriggling in the passenger seat. She reached over and cranked up the music. The sudden thunder of bass shattered the relative peace of the countryside. A flock of birds took flight, bursting out of the tall grasses in blurry black clots. Their indignant cries were lost in the noise and wind.

Viv turned the volume down and said, "First—most people get out of bed before noon, so let's be real about the time complaint. Second—you insisted, remember? It's a twin's sacred duty, or something, wasn't that what you said?" She forced herself not to smile, kept her lips firm and set.

"Right," Maddy grinned. "I couldn't let you go off and have all the fun alone. I'd lose my claim as the evil one." She stretched and sighed like a cat nestling into a sunbeam's warm embrace.

I don't think that's quite how it works," Viv said. She would have continued, but Maddy turned the music up again. It was an old tussle, one not worth fussing about. Viv concentrated on her driving instead. If she missed the turn, they'd never find their destination in time to catch the perfect light.

Vivian Madeline Gates and Madeline Vivian Gates were identical twins, and nearly perfect doubles. They had the same hazel eyes—brown shot through with eddies of olive green and flecks of amber. They traded clothes without a second thought because everything fit perfectly, every curve and hollow aligned. Even their unruly curls fell into the same patterns.

But scratch the surface and all that changed. 'Different as night and day, those two,' people said, usually with a baffled shake of their heads. Like there were rules governing their twinship. Like it was somehow unnatural.

The outsiders were wrong. The twins' differences were their strength: one dark, one light. They had one to jump into the rapids, and one to watch and record from the safety of the banks. With one to balance the other, the two could weather anything.

Maddy stuck her head outside to catch the wind. Sometimes the open convertible wasn't enough to contain her. She whooped with joy.

"You're going to swallow a bug," Viv said. She kept her eyes on the road. The turn was going to reveal itself any minute.

* * *

They pulled into the remains of the old parking lot. The car bumped and heaved as it crawled over patches of weeds and buckled blacktop. Viv pulled up close to the entrance. She turned off the engine and stared at the scene before her.

"You have got to be kidding," Maddy said. "What a dump."

Viv turned to her twin. "What did you expect? I did say it was an *abandoned* amusement park." She snorted and climbed out of the car.

Maddy met her at the back of the vehicle. "Sorry. Didn't mean to put a damper on your fun. I guess I didn't expect it to be so… empty looking." She tilted her head and added, "I know. Duh. Now what can I carry?"

Viv pointed to the mini-cooler, stocked with snacks and water bottles. She pulled out her small backpack and shrugged into it. She unzipped her camera from its case and slipped its strap over her head. She was ready.

They faced the park together. Neither could deny that Professor Future's Fun-Land had seen better days. Thirty years ago it had drawn thrill seekers from all over the country. Coaster fans in particular had made the trip to the remote site's featured ride, a mammoth structure called The Orbit. Old pictures showed it towering over the park, twinkling with artificial starlight. It still loomed, but had gone dark and cold.

Viv had done some research before she chose this site as her subject. It helped that it was isolated and mostly forgotten. It was funny, how the quirks in geography had figured into the park's fate. At first, it was a bonus. They'd been able to put on a nightly fireworks display—had lit up the dark skies with dazzling sparks of color. They'd built an impressive go-cart track that wound its way out through the surrounding grasses and hills. There'd even been plans to build a sister establishment: a water park.

Professor Future's fun seemed like it would never end. Then the hard times hit. Highways were re-routed. Weather turned. Financial hardships led to safety slips. Tragedy stacked on calamity, and the park died.

New attractions sprang up elsewhere with bigger and better amusements. The Fun-Land was left behind, and soon slid out of mind. It didn't take long for its memory to fade. The park had been all but erased, and that was just as Viv wanted it. The odds of them getting caught or having to compete for the best spots, were slim.

Viv and Maddy picked their way through the debris. They climbed over turnstiles frozen solid with rust and their feet crunched over old glass. They soon found a section where the fencing had collapsed and they slipped through into the park itself.

Here and there a few echoes of the old theme could still be seen: a dully gleaming comet or two, the tail section of a rocket ship, a ray-gun gripped in the tentacle of a cartoonish alien. Maddy couldn't resist saying in her best imitation of a B-movie space invader, "Take me to your leader, puny human." There was laughter in her voice, but she stayed close to her twin—so close she stepped on her heels at least once.

Viv kept working. The site was everything she'd hoped for. She was already composing potential photographs and her fingers twitched. "It's wonderful," she said. Viv was drawn to lost places. She craved the stillness and melancholy beauty of decay. The poignancy of abandoned dreams moved her like nothing else.

"It's creepy," Maddy said. She turned to look at Viv and her grimace turned into a smile. "Guess I'll have to wait for you to show me the good in it. Like you always do."

The camera's clicks and whirrs served as Viv's response.

* * *

The girls found a spot of shade to shelter in while they took a water break. Maddy gulped down the cold liquid, and let the overflow spill down her chin and neck to soak her shirt. Viv sipped for a while, then shrugged, and did the same. The air against the wet fabric cooled them down, refreshed them. They sat in comfortable silence.

Viv was glad they'd made it in time to take advantage of the bright light. Sometimes she liked harsher contrast. The brutal shadows and distorting orange glare suited the ruins. It brought out a fierceness, a kind of stubborn refusal, even as it highlighted the inevitable victory of time.

She'd photographed an old spin ride—a Scrambler—half collapsed and rusted out, covered in choking vines. She'd found the torso of a robot on the ground. His face was cute and resembled an old boom box. He had speakers for eyes and a bow tie made from floppy disks. His arm was extended in a stiff salute to the sky. Viv had discovered his other half a short distance away, standing sentinel by a sign that read, "You Must Be This Tall to Ride." Birds had built nests in the cradle of its waist.

Viv had taken many other shots, seen many other things, but kept returning to the roller-coaster. There was something about how the black metal dominated the space above them that fired her imagination. Maybe it was its size and engineering, or the contrast of the gaping holes within the tracks. Maybe it was how the fallen pieces twisted and snaked along the ground like vicious offspring. It was menacing, but lovely all the same.

"So, how much longer?" Maddy asked. She pulled her heavy curls away from the back of her neck and rubbed her water bottle on the exposed skin.

"I need just a bit more time. I want to capture this place in softer light. We need to wait until dusk."

"It makes that much difference?"

Viv nodded. "Definitely. Photos taken at the right time will glow—the edges will soften. The sadness of this place will be like something you can almost touch. You can't miss that kind of beauty."

Maddy shrugged, trusting her sister.

Viv dug in the cooler and found a chocolate bar, Maddy's favorite. She tossed it over to her. Maddy had been a great sport. She'd amused herself with songs and games, and had even found a few choice spots for Viv to photograph. She'd not praised the park directly, but Maddy got close when she'd remarked, "This place was probably pretty awesome back in the day. I wish I'd seen it then." But even that happy daydream couldn't hold up for long.

Viv could tell Maddy was starting to fade, but figured she had another hour or two left to work with. Maybe three—if she'd packed enough chocolate.

* * *

"You were right about the light," Maddy said. "Even I can see how it changes everything."

Viv nodded and snapped another photo. She had only another few minutes before the last of the golden light was gone. The cooler blues and violets of twilight were gorgeous in their own way, but she preferred to view that with her own eyes instead of through the lens.

"Hey, how about one of us? Can you do that?" Maddy posed, super-model style, all awkward angles and curves. She pooched out her lips and sucked in her cheeks. Maddy gave great duck-face.

Viv didn't do a lot of portrait work. She preferred to stick with landscape and still-life photography, but she owed her sister. A memento of their day would be a perfect thank-you gift.

Viv set up the camera. They would be framed by the coaster overhead. Their curls would mirror its loop de loop turns. The light would make the highlights in their hair burn like they were on fire. They'd look like they were part of the park—like it had folded them in. It would be a fine picture. She set up the camera's timer and ran over to Maddy.

The twins linked arms and grinned.

The camera clicked.

And then the music started.

It was faint at first, almost a whisper, but it grew steadily louder—a whine of synth and a driving beat. The sisters took a few steps toward the sound.

Maddy recognized the music first. She turned to Viv and said, "I love that song!"

Viv gave her sister a blank look.

Maddy snorted and said, "It's Split Enz, dummy. From the eighties?" She scrunched up her nose and added, "Doesn't matter—let's check it out." Maddy turned and walked in the direction of the noise. She belted out the chorus to "I Got You" as she picked up the pace.

153

Viv had to jog to catch up.

They followed the music to the base of the Robot Ride Guardian and stopped.

The area beside the robot's leg shimmered and shimmied with waves of distortion. It looked like pebbles thrown into a reflecting pond. As the seconds ticked by, the waves grew more violent and then the image tore in two. A sliver of blackness grew in between.

The rift opened wider, as if to welcome them.

Viv gripped Maddy's shoulder and leaned on her. Her legs had gone weak and wobbly.

Suddenly, cold neon blinked and glared out of the hole—first pink, then orange, then green. A whiff of popcorn and sweet toffee wafted through.

Maddy shook off Viv's restraining hand and moved toward the light. "Holy shit! Do you know what I think this is?"

Viv shook her head.

"I think it's like a door in time. Viv, I think this goes back to the park's past."

Michael Jackson's "Thriller" blared from somewhere inside the rift.

Maddy squealed and clapped. "Can't you hear it? Won't you come see?"

A chill crept down Viv's spine. Her limbs went heavy and numb. But, yes, she could hear the music—and underneath that—the sound of metal rumbling on metal. It was the unmistakable plunge and rattle of a rollercoaster. The delighted screams of riders provided harmony.

She loved that sound. She feared it too.

Maddy picked up a chunk of rock and tossed it through the rift. The air shimmered and then the rock landed with a dull thud. Nothing else happened.

"We have to go through," Maddy said.

Viv shook her head. "No way. Why the hell would we do that?"

Maddy gaped at her. "To avoid a lifetime of regret? To say "yes" to adventure? To experience magic—like all those kids we envied from stories? Or how about a chance to have some fun?" She pointed to the rock. "See? It's safe. And we don't have to go far, right? I just want to see what happens. Please?" She took a step forward.

Viv hesitated.

Maddy shrugged. "Suit yourself. I'm going." And she stepped through.

The hazy glow obscured her form for a second, but she made it. Maddy stood on the other side, spread her arms wide, and laughed. "It's amazing!"

Viv took a step and stopped. She looked at Maddy, then closed her eyes and ran forward. She felt a harsh bite of cold, a kind of curious folding sensation, and then the warm body of her twin.

Maddy hugged her. "I knew you wouldn't let me down," she said.

* * *

The robot stood tall and proud—whole again. Maddy and Viv both measured up, well above the minimum height requirement for riding.

The rift had stabilized. It stood wide open. Viv could see the decaying future through the door.

Around them, the park's past buzzed with activity.

Nobody noticed them. The crowd broke just before it reached the rift. They flowed around it like a stream washing around rocks. The twins and the entryway were as good as invisible.

Maddy waved, pulled faces, and gestured at patrons as they passed by. Nobody even blinked.

The twins linked hands, nodded at one another, and merged into the park's traffic.

At first they took cautious steps, kept glancing back at the rift every few seconds. It held steady, and remained unnoticed by all but the two of them.

Maddy whirled around in a tight circle. "I want fairy floss!" She stopped. "Wait, no, let's go on some rides. Or…"

Viv held up her arms in surrender. "Okay, okay. But damn, girl, take a breath. You're going to bust a blood vessel. Let's just take it as it comes."

Maddy grinned and said, "Lead on."

All around them colored lights winked and spun. The air was filled with music, happy voices, and the constant whirr and groan of the rides. Fried dough, cinnamon, roasting nuts, and other tantalizing scents tempted them. It was the best mix of all the fun of an amusement park.

The crowd was a kaleidoscope of neon bright patterns, popped collars, and big teased hair. It was too authentic, too varied, to be a costume parade. Maddy elbowed Viv. "Told you! Time travel." She made a little fist then popped it open, spreading her five fingers wide. "Mind. Blown."

Viv nodded and reached for her camera, but came up empty. She groaned. It was back on the other side. She'd left both it and her smartphone on top of the cooler. Maddy wouldn't have one either. She never carried it when she was with her sister.

There goes proof.

"Come on, Grumpy. Let's try a ride. Please?" Maddy's tone held the same musical note she always used to wheedle and cajole.

Viv wanted to cave in, but had to be practical. "With what?" she said. "It's not like we can use our money or credit cards."

Maddy pouted.

"Hey, pretty ladies! You can ride this one for free!" A man working the Scrambler waved and smiled. He was wearing a purple flight suit—it seemed to be the basic uniform of the park.

The twins jumped back in shock. He was the first to have noticed them.

"No strings attached."

Maddy peered at him. "Who says? I mean, won't you get in trouble?"

The Scrambler-Man laughed. "Pretty and nice. You're quite a prize." He bowed. "I'm the Night Manager, at your service. I say who rides and who doesn't. I run the park."

Viv opened her mouth to ask a question.

He pointed to his uniform. The words NIGHT MANAGER were embroidered on his right breast in gold thread.

Viv swore they hadn't been there a second ago.

"C'mon. What are you waiting for?"

Maddy bit her lip, but succumbed. "Thanks, man!" She pulled Viv toward the ride.

Maddy had been dragging them into adventures from the time they could walk.

Why fight it now?

Viv laughed and said, "Race you!"

They were swept up and away in a whirl of motion. After that it was all height, spin, speed, and sugar.

They saved the rollercoaster for last.

It pulsed with simulated starlight. It hummed with promise. The twins made their way into their seats and held hands. For luck.

* * *

Viv started to regret their choice to ride the coaster the moment their car made it to the apex of the first rise. The view was beautiful, but Viv shivered. Her mouth went dry and her breath caught in her throat. She looked down. They'd been suspended above the park for far too long. Something had shifted.

Maddy squealed and raised their arms in victory.

The car plunged forward and down.

The speed was exhilarating and wind whipped through their hair. They were mashed into the seats and then they floated, at the mercy of physical force. They twisted, turned, and went upside down.

They screamed, half in terror and half in delight. The sound was matched by other cries. When the ride stopped the girls fell silent.

But the screams went on.

The park filled with them.

Viv and Maddy struggled in their seats and fought against the safety harness. They didn't know what was happening around them, but they didn't care—not in that moment. Nothing mattered except getting free. Viv pounded against the restraint. Finally, the automatic unlocking mechanism fired and the bars popped up in every car.

The twins leapt out.

Metal screeched and there was a tremendous crash somewhere in the distance. A huge fountain of flame shot up into the air. The stink of burning plastic and fuel filled the park.

The screaming continued.

The platform stood firm and still, but the noise punched forward. Any peace they had sheltered in would shatter on contact.

Viv and Maddy looked at one another, pointed toward the exit, and nodded.

The teenage couple from the car directly behind them came up to stand by the twins. The boy said, "That was totally rad. We're going again!"

Viv whirled. She was about to ask him how he could say that when something awful was obviously going on in the park but her words died on her tongue. The skin of the boy's face sagged, melting down his face to pool and jiggle at his jawline. His lips had sloughed off to reveal a wad of purple chewing gum lodged in his braces. He grinned and a fat yellow worm wriggled out from a hole in his cheek.

Viv gasped and Maddy made a whistling, moaning sound.

The teenage girl winked. "Too much for you, huh? Chicken!" She snorted with derisive laughter. Her breath was hot, thick with peat and the cloying sweetness of rot.

Her eyelid had slipped off and sat on her cheek, mired in a thick layer of base and rouge. The girl's clumped lashes, heavy with navy blue mascara, stood stiffly at attention. Her naked and staring eye rolled around with lazy oblivion.

The twins didn't answer. They just ran.

* * *

Some kind of switch had been thrown. The pleasant hum of one impossible and magical summer's night had become a whirlwind of violence and fear. It was as if every terror, every disappointment, and every calamity that had darkened the history of Professor Future's Fun-Land had come home to roost all at once.

The girls ran, their fingers white with the strain of holding on to one another's hands so tightly.

Viv prayed that they could find the robot. She prayed the rift was still open. She prayed they could make it there in time to get through the door.

The black night burned orange in the distance. Pockets of darkness held sway when bulbs burst. Gunshots popped and echoed over by the Ferris wheel. A gunman stood poised before it. He picked off passengers at his leisure. A body dropped from the height of the ride. Viv couldn't tell if the person had been trying to escape or if they'd fallen victim to a bullet. It didn't matter—the gunman hit the body twice as it fell.

All around them, the crowd turned to corpses. The stench of decay and the copper tang of blood hung heavy in the air. Some of the people had wounds—stabs, slashes, and punctures. Some were burned. Others were covered with dust and debris—probably victims of the tornado that had howled through one spring afternoon.

Viv was sure that so many couldn't have died in the park while it was up and running.

Her heart stuttered in her chest. *What if they had died after? What if they too had walked through the door and had been trapped?*

"Faster, Maddy!"

Maddy was wheezing, but she found more speed. "Viv! What the hell is happening?" she gasped.

"Worry about that later. Now? Run."

Behind them, the roller-coaster screeched and moaned. A section collapsed and plummeted to the ground with a deafening crash.

Viv regretted glancing back and took the next turn as fast as she could. She remembered the snow cone stand and its floating astronaut mascot. She recalled the pleasure of the sugary sour lime cone she'd feasted on a half hour before and had to swallow a sudden surge of nausea.

"Almost there, Maddy!"

Her sister squeezed her hand.

They turned another corner. Viv could see the robot. It was still on guard duty. The rift shimmered, marking the doorway home. It was smaller now, dimmer, but it was there.

A hitch had developed in her side, a stabbing pinch of pain, but she powered through it. She ignored the heat in her left calf, was determined to deny the possibility of cramp.

Her sister wasn't so lucky. She lurched and nearly fell. Maddy let go of Viv's hand so she could clutch her leg. Her face twisted in pain.

"We're so close, Maddy. Don't stop now."

"I know Viv, but it's seized up." Her voice rose in panic.

Viv hauled her sister to her feet, and half-carried her as they inched forward.

They'd almost made it to the rift when a voice cut through the chaos. "Hey, pretty ladies. Where do you think you're going?" It was the Scrambler man—the Night Manager. He eyed the pair of them and spat onto the ground. It was a casual, almost contemplative gesture.

Viv was surprised there was no visible damage on him. Not a single a spot marred that purple flight suit.

Lightning struck the carousel fifty meters away. The terrified cries of children mingled with the calliope music. The air smelled scorched. Meaty.

The Night Manager continued as if nothing had happened. "The fun is just beginning. Why, the fireworks haven't even started yet."

It was Maddy who spoke first. "We've had enough for tonight, that's all. We just want to go home." Her voice only trembled a little, right at the end. She mustered up a smile. It wasn't as bright as usual, but she'd put all the charm she could into it. "We thank you for your generosity."

The Night Manager inclined his head.

The girls started to move again.

"The cramp has loosened, Viv," Maddy said. "I can walk by myself."

They separated.

Viv jerked her head toward the way home. It was only a few meters farther. Maddy nodded and they scurried forward.

The first firework exploded overhead. Viv ignored it and stepped into the zone by the rift. It felt quieter, protected. The exit was smaller now, but they could still make it if they were fast enough.

She turned to motion Maddy through.

Maddy stood half in the protected circle and half out. She was looking up at the fireworks.

It was a dazzling display. It lit up the dark skies overhead in showers of red, blue, green, and gold. Beautiful as it was, they had no time for it. Viv spoke with urgency. "Come on, Maddy. We have to go. Now." She reached, grabbed Maddy's hand, and tugged.

Maddy didn't cooperate. She stood firm.

Viv pulled again, but was surprised when Maddy jerked in the opposite direction.

"I can't see you, pretty girl, but I've got your sister, sure enough." The Night Manager's voice was soft, self-satisfied. "Now what would happen if I pulled harder? What would happen if I took my other hand away from this pretty mouth? Would I lose my prize?"

Maddy's muffled cries erupted into a shriek. The noise was tamped down.

"That is no way to show gratitude to your host. Not when we won you, fair and square," the man said.

Maddy squeezed Viv's hand twice in rapid succession.

For once, Viv couldn't understand what her sister was trying to tell her. She squeezed back and tried to pull Maddy toward her. It was no use.

The Night Manager chuckled.

Viv dropped her twin's hand and stepped back into the park. Fireworks still crashed and boomed overhead. Purple streamers rained down from a cluster of red orbs. They were bright red, like those syrupy cherries that perch atop ice cream sundaes.

The lights turned from vibrant to garish and obscene the instant Viv fixed her attention on Maddy.

The Night Manager was leeching away all her color—all her light and life. It was as if Maddy was turning into a negative image before her eyes.

"She's with us now," the man said. "You will be too."

Maddy and Viv looked at each other. They'd almost always known what the other was thinking. This was no different.

Viv shook her head. Pleaded and denied. But the color kept fading. Darks turned bright. Bright faded to black.

The Night Manager took his hand away from Maddy's mouth.

His cruel laugh rang in Viv's ears, but it wasn't enough to down out Maddy's whisper. "Go, Viv. Go," she said. The last of the color drained from her. The light in Maddy's eyes dimmed and went out.

The Night Manager let go and lunged for Viv.

She was too quick. Desperation gave her speed.

The Night Manager only managed to brush her arm with his fingertips. His touch was so cold it burned.

She dove for the rift, almost missed, almost got tangled up in the robot's salute, but got her balance back in time. She had to twist sideways to fit through the collapsing exit. She felt the pinch, the fold, and then warmth again.

A voice followed her out of the rift.

The Night Manager shouted, "That's okay. We're not greedy. When you play the crooked game, one pretty lady is better than none. And we're going to have such good times. Every night is fun night at Professor Future's Fun-Land."

Viv shut her eyes. She'd expected a taunt.

They flew open when she heard Maddy cry, "Go! Viv! I lo—"

The rift slammed shut.

Viv finished the sentence for her. "—ve you." She fell to her knees and cried. "Love you too, Maddy." She clutched her arm. The frostbite didn't hurt nearly as much as the rest of her.

Viv stayed by the ruins of the robot's legs until the first fingers of dawn crept up and warmed up the light. It was only then that she could force herself to hobble back to the cooler. She was ashamed that her first impulse was to gulp down water and to choke down a chocolate bar. But she did it anyway.

Then she made the call.

* * *

Maddy Gates' body was never found. The official story was that the twins had been attacked during their exploration of the ruins. The tragedy became another sad point in the park's history.

When she found the courage, Viv developed the photographs from that day. They were beautiful and terrible. Her exhibition was a smash success and she sold hundreds of prints.

There was one photo she kept only for herself—one she hid away from everyone. She'd cried over it—the last one she'd taken that day. Viv made two prints. One positive. One negative. She needed two images: one dark, one light. One for before, one after.

Viv had to try to be whole, but she felt so empty—felt less than half.

She suspected she always would.

Viv found some comfort in the portraits. She liked seeing the life in Maddy's eyes and the brightness of their smiles. She stared at the pictures for hours, soaking up every detail.

Sometimes, she swore she could see, off in the distance, high atop a curve of the roller-coaster, the shadow of something that looked like one of the coaster's cars. Sometimes she could see two arms, clasped together, raised in victory.

Maybe Maddy was there, still riding.

Or maybe it was just a trick of the light.

FIT CAMP
SHANE MCKENZIE

Baxter sat on the couch, staring at his stubby fingers. His parents stood over him, arms akimbo, the harsh words aspirating from their frowning lips. He couldn't look them in the eye, not while they announced his punishment. Of course, they said it wasn't punishment, but Baxter knew better.

"What do you think, honey?" Mom forced a smile.

"I don't know."

"It'll be good for you, son. I promise." Dad placed a strong hand on his shoulder and squeezed.

Fat camp.

They were sending him to fat camp, just like they always said they would. It wasn't his fault he liked candy so much; or cheeseburgers or chilidogs; or cake or soda. It was in his genes, it was who he was. His grandfather had been morbidly obese, so much that he died of a heart attack at the age of sixty. Baxter looked down at his midsection, making note of how tightly his shirt fit. Like saran wrap over a rump roast.

"When do I have to go?"

"Tomorrow," they both said, more to each other than to Baxter.

* * *

They pulled their SUV into the gravel parking lot, the tiny pebbles crunching under the rubber of the tires. Baxter pressed his face against the window and watched the other chubby kids waddle around. Their parents held their soft, plump hands, all doing their best to look excited. There weren't as many as he had expected. Baxter wanted to scream.

"Are you really gonna make me stay here?"

Dad sighed, hesitated, then said, "It's only for a couple of weeks, son. Just think of how much weight you could lose, how much lighter you'll feel."

"Yeah, honey, it'll be great. Plus, you could meet new friends. Doesn't that sound like fun?"

"I see some girls walking around. In a couple of weeks, maybe they'll be less fat and more pretty." Dad grunted as Mom jabbed an elbow into his side. "I mean, they're pretty now, but…"

"It's gonna be great, honey. You'll see." Mom returned her disapproving gaze to her husband.

Baxter opened his door and slid from his seat, but his foot hit the ground awkwardly. His ankle twisted and sent a jolt up his leg. He yelped, collapsed to the ground and grabbed his ankle, rocked back and forth.

"Whoopsie-daisy!"

A pair of hairy legs stalked toward Baxter, beige socks pulled up tight, red stripes at the tops. An equally hairy hand shot toward him.

"Easy does it."

Baxter squinted toward the baritone voice and accepted the hand though he wasn't sure if his ankle would hold him up. He was pulled to his feet with authority, his shoulder popping, and he hopped for a second before settling his weight on the ankle. It hurt but not as bad as he'd expected.

The sasquatch hand moved to his head, messed his hair, pushed down on his scalp with uncomfortable force.

"Hello," Dad said.

"Hello, folks. I'm Randy, the head counselor here at Fit Camp." The hairy man shook hands with Dad, then Mom. He smiled down at Baxter, but Baxter looked away.

"We're the Stephens' and this is our son, Baxter. He's here to shape up." Dad squeezed Baxter's shoulder again.

"Is that right?" Randy said as if talking excitedly to a toddler. "Well, I guarantee we'll take *real* good care of him."

Mom and Dad smiled and looked down at Baxter. Other parents were saying their goodbyes to their little chubby bundles of joy all around him. Other counselors were trying to sound as enthusiastic as possible.

Baxter couldn't say a word to his parents. Their faces were lit with anticipation, as if the camp would make him a better person, make them love him more.

He craved a candy bar.

* * *

They sat in the cafeteria. Their chunky arms and legs rubbed against each other as they huddled together at the cramped table. The counselors smiled at the fresh meat, whispering to each other. Baxter still couldn't believe he was there. It all felt like a bad Disney movie.

"Hi." A voice came from his left. "I'm Chris."

Baxter turned toward the voice and was met by a smiling oval face. Though Baxter knew he was overweight himself, this kid actually made him feel good about his own appearance. The boy's face looked tiny surrounded by so much cheek and chin, his breasts pouring over his stomach, stomach pouring over his groin. His arms rested on the sides of his belly which pushed them outward as if he wore a heavy coat. Labored breaths rattled from his throat, causing Baxter to feel out of breath himself.

"Baxter," he said, trying his best not to stare.

As he looked around the room, his spirits continued to rise. He had always seen himself as the chubbiest kid around, but now he seemed to be the smallest. At least at Fit Camp he was.

"Your parents make you come, too?" Chris said.

"Yeah. I can't believe I'm here right now," Baxter said.

"Me either. I don't think I'm *that* big."

Baxter cleared his throat to hide his chuckle.

The counselors stood shoulder to shoulder at the head of the room, facing the kids. Randy walked into the cafeteria and slammed the door behind him. He faced everyone, his teeth glistening under the fluorescents.

"Welcome to Fit Camp, everyone! I can't tell you how excited I am to see all these new chubby faces here today."

Baxter wondered why he would use a word like *chubby*. He didn't like Randy, or the camp, at all.

"We have a special treat for all you newcomers. A specially prepared feast."

Murmurs erupted from between the kids' saliva-slickened lips. Randy had their full attention now.

"Now, I want you all to really enjoy this. Consider this your last meal, you know, like people about to be executed."

Baxter didn't like the tone of Randy's voice or the smirk on his face at the mention of execution. Chris bounced up and down, waves of fat rolling under his shirt. He smacked his lips and breathed heavily.

Two swinging doors burst open and another group of counselors pushed stainless steel carts out: four carts in all, each one piled high with food. Food that normally would make Baxter go crazy. One cart was full of doughnuts, all shapes and colors piled on top of one another, the glaze glistening. Pies and cakes of all varieties littered the next cart. Another cart contained what looked like fried food, though Baxter had no idea what some of it was. All brown and crispy, sweating grease. A mountain of pizza, cheeseburgers, hot dogs, and other delicious-looking delights rode the last cart.

The symphony of aromas in the cafeteria was almost too much for Baxter to take. As hungry as he was and as good as the food looked, there was no way he was touching it. Seeing the bouncing anticipation of the other kids, along with Randy's gleaming rictus, had evaporated his appetite.

The rest of the kids giggled and licked their lips as they ogled the food, unable to contain themselves with the promise of stuffing their chunky faces.

"All right, everyone. Dig in!" Randy yelled.

The counselors stood back and watched as the jiggling stampede roared forward. Spongy fingers grabbed and shoved. They stuffed deserts into their mouths as they piled more onto their plates, licking custard and glaze flakes from their moist lips.

Baxter just sat there, unable to move, stomach roiling as the kids gorged themselves. Chris rocked and whimpered in his seat beside him. Baxter hesitated to look toward the boy next to him as more moaning oozed from Chris's lips. The bench's metal legs scraped across the floor and the boy wiggled his body. An image of the fat kid with his hands deep in his pants as he stared at the mounds of food flashed through Baxter's mind, and he shook his head to rid himself of the thought.

But when Baxter finally turned to face his neighbor, he realized the boy was just stuck in his seat. Chris rocked his body back and forth, his labored breathing rattling in his throat, but couldn't get himself free. His eyes looked like black gumdrops shoved into the dough of his head, and they darted from the food, to his seat, to Baxter.

"You need some help?" Baxter said.

Chris answered with his eyes and a jiggling nod of his head. Baxter shoved his arms under Chris's armpits and lifted as the boy rocked his body free of the table and bench imprisonment. Without issuing a thanks, he waddled toward the carts, wiping sweat from his face as he swiped a plate.

Baxter sat back down and rested his chin in his palms. If his parents were hoping to scare him straight, it was actually working. *Is this what I look like to Mom and Dad when I eat at home?* Sure, compared to the blimps in front of him, he seemed pretty normal, but what about when he left this place? To the rest of the world, he was still a fat ass.

Hairy fingers wrapped around his shoulder and squeezed. "Aren't you hungry, Baxter?"

Baxter flinched, glanced up at Randy. He tried to shrug the hand away, but it held strong. "No."

"It's your last chance. Are you sure?" The hand squeezed harder.

"I'm sure, okay?"

Randy didn't say anything more. His hand never left Baxter's shoulder as they watched the kids gorge themselves. Wet smacking and slurping sounds swam through the air.

* * *

Baxter lay on top of his stiff mattress and dreaded the horrible activities he was sure the counselors had planned for the kids. He ended up getting a bunk with Chris, and gladly gave the boy the bottom bed. Baxter wondered how much sense it made to have overweight kids sleeping on bunk beds. The thought of one crushing another almost made him laugh.

The door crashed in and a blond counselor rushed inside, a green hose clutched in his fists. He held his thumb over the end and sprayed the kids.

"Wakey wakey, hands off your snakey!"

The boys covered their faces with blankets, arms, anything they could to avoid the freezing water. Most were unable to move, their thick bodies rocking in their beds, as the water splashed over them.

"Time to get moving, you fat tubs of shit!"

"Hey, man. You can't talk to us like that," one boy said. Water dripped from his multiple chins.

"I can't?" The blond man stomped his way toward the boy, yanked him to a sitting position by his hair, then slapped him across the face. The boy's cheeks jiggled with the force of the blow. A red handprint glowed like a neon sign.

The room went silent. The only sound coming from the boy was his heavy, snotty breathing.

"Here at Fit Camp, we do what it takes to get you fat fucks in shape." The counselor grabbed the boy's flabby breast and squeezed it. The boy thrashed and whimpered. "And if any of you have a problem with that, speak up now."

Nobody said a word. The boy screamed as he tried to escape the man's pinching, but he couldn't get away. Tears ran down his plump cheeks.

The counselor finally let go and stood in the middle of the room. "I'm Kyle. Nice to meet you all. Now get the fuck outta bed and get outside."

The sound of movement filled the room as the boys rolled themselves out of bed. The crying boy rubbed his chest as he gathered himself.

Kyle watched and shook his head as the boys struggled to get their clothes on, especially when it came to their shoes. Most had to help each other, unable to reach their feet.

Already knowing he'd need it, Baxter jumped down and helped Chris. The boy kept glancing toward Kyle, then back at Baxter, his breaths rattling, chest heaving.

They followed the counselor out of the cabin toward the clearing outside where the trees swayed in the crisp, cold wind. The girls were outside too, the female counselors ushering them along to join the boys. They lined up, Baxter unable to see what lay ahead through the bulky bodies of his peers.

"What's going on?" he asked Chris.

"I can't see anything."

The counselors walked up and down the line, smiling at the kids.

The line moved, little by little, and Baxter eventually saw what they were doing. Weighing them. A stainless steel scale stood at the front of the line, and the counselors forced each kid to strip down to their undies. One boy, his stomach draping over his crotch, stepped onto the scale. His back folded at the sides and freckles stippled his skin.

"Jesus Christ, boy." Kyle moved the metal pegs and wrote down the boy's weight on a clipboard. "I can't even see your balls."

The boy's head drooped as he shuffled away.

The girls stood just behind Baxter, their half-naked bodies making him blush; he'd never seen a naked girl before, not in person anyway. He tried to avert his eyes to the ground, but they kept springing back toward the feminine flesh. A large black girl shifted her weight from side to side as she wiped tears from her eyes. Her bra looked ready to snap at any moment, hanging on to her frame by a thread.

"Your turn, fat ass." Kyle pulled Chris forward. "Strip down."

"I-I can't."

"You can't? What's the matter, you got a pussy down there?"

Chris just stared at his feet, or maybe his stomach, and said nothing. Kyle sprang forward, grabbed Chris's shirt and ripped it off. Chris's entire body jiggled, his breasts bigger than most of the girls'.

"Want me to do the rest, piggy?" Kyle tossed the tattered shirt to the ground.

Chris shook his head and pulled his pants off. A very visible brown streak ran down the back of his sagging briefs.

After Chris was finished, Baxter stripped without having to be told and stepped onto the scale. Kyle nodded his head and wrote down the information, then slapped Baxter on the ass when he passed.

"Next!"

* * *

They stood in an open field, lined up shoulder to shoulder, the girls mixed in with the boys. Randy walked back and forth in front of them.

"Today is the day you make a change. A big change." He stood in front of Baxter and smiled. "I'll give you all a choice. You can come with me or you can go with your assigned counselor." He pointed to the men and women standing at attention, lined up opposite from the kids. "I'll be doing exercises and showing you how to eat healthy. It's something you can take with you and use in everyday life. Those of you who don't wanta put in the effort, that want the easy way out, your counselor will take care of you. You come with me, it'll take hard work and dedication. It can be done." His eyes landed on each kid's face, one and a time, then stuck on Baxter's. "Or, you can go with your counselor, and they will show you the Fit Camp secret. Something that'll change you forever."

The kids looked around at each other. Baxter had already made his choice. Whatever Fit Camp's secret was, he wanted nothing to do with it. He could lose his weight. He could do the hard work.

"For those of you ready to exercise, ready to put in the effort, follow me." Randy walked past the kids and nodded to the counselors. Baxter stepped out of line and followed, mortified when he realized he was alone. Not a single other person moved.

Randy locked eyes with Baxter and smiled. "I thought you might come, Baxter."

"All right, you fat, lazy sacks of shit!" The counselors stomped toward the queue of kids. "You come with us, one at a time! Step forward when you hear your name!"

Baxter knew that whatever this place had in store for the others was not the easy way out. Nothing about the camp was easy. He stared at the back of Randy's head as they walked past the trees and toward the cabins.

"You made the right choice, Baxter. Good exercise and a healthy diet is all you need. You know I used to be fat, too?"

"Really? How long ago?"

Randy laughed. "Oh, not too long ago. I made a decision and it changed my life. I think you can do great things, Baxter."

They stepped through the doorway of a cabin that was far bigger than all the others. Workout equipment lay everywhere: free weights, treadmills, bicycles. Baxter had never used anything like that before.

Randy showed him a routine, using the treadmill to work up a sweat, then moving to the bicycle, and eventually some weight training. Sweat poured down Baxter's face, his shirt stuck to his body. As hard as the work was, he felt good. He had never felt so good in his life, so alive.

"That was a great first day, Baxter. You keep this up and the results will be very rewarding. You hungry?"

"Yeah."

"Go take a shower, then meet me in the cafeteria, all right?"

Baxter nodded, noting to himself how friendly Randy was all of a sudden. He couldn't help but wonder what the other kids were going through.

He jumped in the shower and sighed as the scalding water rinsed away the sweat glaze coating his fat rolls. Squeezing handfuls of belly, he vowed to himself to lose the weight. The sight of Chris and all the others was enough to make him sick, and he could suddenly feel the lard hanging off of him. The methods of the counselors were intense, but effective.

He dried himself off and wrapped the towel around his waist. The air bit at his damp skin as he trudged across the gravel trail toward his cabin. A boy sat on the bottom bunk just inside, staring into his lap.

"Hey," Baxter said as he passed, then stopped and stared.

The boy smiled up at him. It was the same boy from that morning, the one Kyle had given the titty twister to. His face was leaner, his torso shrunken in under his now loose-fitting shirt. The smile never left his face as he glared at Baxter.

Baxter threw some clothes on, then hurried out of the cabin, leaving the creepy boy behind. He walked toward the cafeteria where Randy was waiting for him.

"Feel better?"

"What are the counselors doing to the others?"

Randy's smile faded. "You don't need to worry about that. You made the right choice, Baxter. Let's get you something to eat."

They walked into the cafeteria where a steaming plate of grilled chicken breast and vegetables awaited, which to his surprise, wasn't too bad. He ate it all, but made sure to pace himself.

"How was it?" Randy asked.

"Good."

Randy patted him on the back and said, "I think you'll go a long way, Baxter. You've got the right attitude."

"Thanks. I feel a lot better."

"And that feeling will only keep growing if you keep this up. I'm proud of you."

The doors burst open and a line of kids walked in. Baxter gasped at the sight of them. The thinner kids marched in, a robot-like emptiness in their eyes. Bandages were wrapped around their arms and legs.

Randy patted Baxter on the back again. "You made the right choice, kid."

* * *

"What'd they do to you guys?"

"They fixed us, or at least started to," Chris said from his bottom bunk.

Baxter couldn't help but stare at him. The fat surrounding Chris's face was gone, as if it had been carved away. His clothes hung loose from his thinned-out torso. He must have lost 100 pounds, but Baxter knew that was impossible. What could the counselors possibly have done? Baxter thought. Why the hell am I exercising and eating bland food if I can lose the weight in a day?

"Did it hurt?"

"It was wonderful."

Chris's voice was soft, like he was talking to himself. The look in his eyes made Baxter avert his own. He looked around the room and saw that all the kids looked this way, as if lost in a dream. They mumbled to themselves, smiling stupidly.

"You really should come, Baxter. It's magnificent."

They all turned their heads to stare at him. Smiling.

One boy stepped out of bed and walked toward Baxter's bunk. He scratched at his bandages, his smile turned upside down. "Leave. Run away."

The others swiveled their attention to the boy, their smiles stretched wider.

The bandages grew darker as the boy scratched them, blood seeping through the fabric and dripping to the floor.

"What's the matter?" Baxter asked.

"Run...!"

He fell to the floor as he twitched and convulsed. Blood gushed from beneath the bandages and pooled around him.

Baxter jumped out of bed and ran to the boy's side. He couldn't get a hold of him as the boy's body shook and writhed. Blood coated the boy's arms, made it impossible to get a grip.

"Someone help me! Get some help!"

The kids stayed on their beds, grins tight over their faces as they watched the boy buck in his own blood on the floor.

"What's wrong with you people?" Baxter jumped to his feet and ran out the door. The night air chilled him, turned the blood on his hands cold. "Help! We need help!"

An owl hooted above him, but no other sound came besides bugs and wind.

"Randy! *Help us!*"

He ran around the camp, passing cabins and banging on doors. Nobody answered.

"Hello? *There's a goddamn hurt kid over here!*"

He rounded a corner, and finally found a cabin with lights on inside. Shadows moved in the windows, and as Baxter ran toward it, the sound of voices and laughter became audible.

He burst through the door without knocking. "Someone's in trouble! We need—"

The counselors. All of them. Naked.

They danced, laughed, sipped from plastic cups, smoked from glass pipes. They stopped their dance and watched Baxter enter the room.

"What the fuck you want, fat ass?" Kyle said from the corner. He stood and unveiled the female counselor that had been under him, her legs spread wide. Kyle's glistening penis pointed at Baxter, bounced as Kyle walked toward him.

"One of the k-kids. He... he needs help. He's bleeding badly."

"Another bleeder. There's always at least a couple of 'em," one of the other counselors said, then sucked on a pipe and blew the cloud of smoke toward Baxter.

Kyle stood in front of Baxter, grabbed the pipe from the other counselor, and put it to his lips. He blew the smoke directly into Baxter's face, stinging his eyes and inducing a round of coughs. Kyle held the pipe out and offered it to Baxter. "Go ahead, lard ass. We won't tell."

They all laughed, continued their party as if all was well.

"Did you hear me? *We need help!*"

Kyle's fist smashed into the middle of Baxter's face.

Baxter felt his nose crack under the force of the knuckles, and his body hit the ground as his legs gave out from under him. Stars sparkled at the edge of his vision as blood rushed from his nostrils and into his mouth.

Bursts of laughter were barely audible behind the ringing in his ears. Kyle stood over him, his erection still at full salute. He raised his fist again, and Baxter covered his head with shaking arms.

"Leave him alone!"

Baxter recognized Randy's voice. His spirits rose, hoping Randy would end this craziness and help him. Baxter sat up, wiped the blood from his face, and searched the room for the head counselor.

Randy stood at the opposite end of the room, also fully nude, his body covered in coarse black hair. He stared at Kyle with disgust on his face.

"He made his choice. You don't touch him, you know the fucking rules."

Kyle backed away to his corner where he hopped back on top of the girl. Within seconds, his hips were thrusting and the girl was moaning. Through all the pain in his face, Baxter's pants began to tighten.

Randy stepped past the counselors and held his hairy hand out. "Come on, let's get you cleaned up."

Baxter took his hand and stood. His nose throbbed and his mouth was coated with blood. Randy pulled Baxter toward the rear of the cabin, away from the front door.

"A boy needs help. We have to get him some help."

Randy turned his head. "We can't help him."

"But he's bleeding—"

"You need to see something, Baxter. You weren't supposed to see it yet, but you have to see it now."

His grip tightened around Baxter's hand as they entered a room. As soon as they walked in, Baxter felt a sense of well-being, like nothing bad could ever happen to him. The room was dark except for multiple black lights hanging from the ceiling. A slurping sound came from somewhere.

"What is this?" Baxter said, unable to stop smiling.

"It's our mother. She's feeding."

They walked toward the center of the room where a soft whimpering could be heard between the slurps.

A creature sat cross legged on the ground, tentacles writhing from its torso, its pebbled skin glowing blue under the black lights. A long straw protruded from its featureless head, the other end stuck into the stomach of a girl. The black girl who had stood behind him in line earlier that day.

"What's happening to her?"

"Mother is relieving her. Taking away her burden. She is merely cattle, Baxter. You shouldn't worry about her."

The creature slurped mouthfuls of fat as its tentacles waved in the air with delight. As Baxter stared, he realized that Randy was right. A creature

171

this beautiful, this magnificent, deserved it. The girl was nothing. The boy bleeding back at the cabin was nothing.

"She's wonderful," Baxter said.

"We want you to join us, Baxter."

"Join you?"

"With a kiss and an embrace from Mother, you'll live forever. We want you to join our family, Baxter."

The creature slurped once more, then a tentacle reached up and pulled the straw from the girl's body. Baxter saw that the straw was attached to Mother's face, and she retracted it into her mouth where it disappeared behind thick, bulbous lips. The girl lay unconscious before Mother, a small giggle escaping her lips. The gaping wound in her belly dripped yellow and pink globs onto the floor.

"She's ready for you, Baxter."

The creature's tentacles opened, as if welcoming Baxter for a hug, a soft cooing sound tickling his eardrums. He stripped off his clothes and climbed into Her warm embrace.

"I love you, Mother."

* * *

"But we drove all this way, honey," Mom said.

"I know, and I'm sorry, but I love it here. Can't you see it's working?" Baxter spun, showing his slimmer body to his parents.

"You look great, son," Dad said. "I say we let him stay. It couldn't hurt."

Mom hesitated, then smiled, reached out to Baxter and ran her fingers through his messy hair. "Fine. I guess this is why we brought you here in the first place."

"Exactly," Baxter said.

"You like it that much?"

"It's wonderful." A toothy grin spread across his face. "I could stay here forever."

QUARTER TURN TO DAWN
SARAH READ

Andrea drank, and savored the sweet toxins. *The ocean is a toilet,* she thought. *A vast fucking toilet where a trillion creatures shit every day and Mother Nature flushes away her unwanted pets. Still. Can't beat the view.*

She pulled the crepe umbrella from her rum and stuck it in her hair, too drunk to remember she'd done that with the last few—a bright, boozy tiara pinned down her salt-stiffened brown curls.

The waiter, Santino, continued to bring drinks, on the house, crowding them onto the small table by her deck chair. *He's probably hoping I'll black out before the police are done and the reporters move in. Maybe I won't remember a thing in the morning.* But his eyes were warm as he winked at her and grinned.

Rob's voice carried from the lobby, a tight throaty tone to it that the police wouldn't know meant *back the fuck off.* Another few minutes of questions and they'd learn the hard way, like she had. She rubbed at the sore lump under her hair.

The trip was supposed to fix everything—get away for a while, get to know each other again. It had been a bad idea. *Better off not knowing. Still. Can't beat the view.*

She had let her glass sit too long. Fine black silt settled in it, clung to the tops of ice cube rafts, and stuck to her teeth so that they crunched when she clenched her jaw. Best to keep the glass tipped, let the ash fall on the bottom. The empties, their bases full of ice in various stages of melt, were fogged with ash.

The sunset over the sea, through the haze, cast a brilliant red glow over the beach. Coastal officers swarmed over the sand, hauled wreckage, and lined narrow black bags along the shore. The palm leaf-coated nylon awning, collapsed on one side, formed a lean-to over the deck that blocked her view of the street where flashing lights and sirens whizzed past. Footfalls crunched on broken glass behind her. Rob stepped through the frame where the glass door used to be.

She squeezed her eyes shut and felt the sting of the sharp grit collected in the corners, felt the horrible pull of his stare on the back of her head.

Rob pulled a toppled deck chair back onto its legs, dragged it through the glass to her side, and dropped into it. A wooden slat from the back clattered to the deck.

"They're leaving. I told them what you saw. I guess they'll match it up with whatever they find down there," he said, shaking his hand at the beach.

"You told them what I saw?"

"Well, yeah. I told them what you thought you saw. What you thought it looked like."

"They were swimming."

"Those wrecks are old. You're not even supposed to swim close enough to see the bodies. Have some respect. And you've been drunk, like, all day." He bounced his left leg on the ball of his foot, rapidly, shaking the dilapidated frame of the deck.

"I have *not* been drunk all day. And my O2 tank was full. When that boat moved—"

"The *Fenix.*"

"When it turned over and started coming up, there were people swimming out of it."

"They were probably just sharks."

"They had faces. Some had *hair.* Are you telling me sharks have hair, Rob?"

The bouncing leg sped up. "No, what I'm telling you is—" The chair joints creaked and unfolded, and dumped him onto the scattered shards of glass.

Andrea's body shook with restrained laughter; a cloud of fine ash rose from her shoulders.

Rob pulled himself off the deck. His ash-smeared white linen Bermuda shorts were now speckled with blood. He plucked at shards, swearing, face as red as the smoke-cloaked sun.

Andrea snorted and choked on the grit in her throat.

"Fuck you," he said, and flipped the small side table. Her collection of glasses flew into the awning. "And quit drinking. I'm not carrying your drunk ass to safety if there's an aftershock, or if that mountain blows again."

"What about the dead people?"

"Jesus Christ, what about them?" He pushed his hands through his hair, flashing the white line of scalp where the fake orange of the tanning lotion hadn't reached.

"Will you carry my ass to safety from them?" She raised her eyebrows.

"Why did I even bring you here?" His flip-flops slapped at his heels as he stomped back into the hotel lobby.

"To fuck me," she said, and took another drink.

Probably going to try and get his money back, she thought, *as if it's the hotel's fault the country is trying to shake itself off the map.*

She pushed herself out of the chair and stumbled down the sloping deck to the railing.

Fire trucks lined the beach and aimed their floodlights at the work crews. A hulk of rusty metal and twisted wood had been hauled up onto the sand, dragged from the shallows where it had resurfaced in the quake. Figures in reflective jackets swarmed the wreck, pulling apart old seams and draining pockets of brackish water.

The line of narrow, slick, black bags stretched beyond the reach of light.

Andrea shivered. The sun was gone—just a red glow left on the water. She turned, steadied herself on the railing, and climbed back into the hotel.

The whir of generators around the lobby drowned out the rising tide of commotion that washed up on the shore.

* * *

Rob slept facedown on the bed, above the covers, his blood-speckled butt bare to the room. If he'd shown any sign of humor, she'd have spanked him. Instead, she pulled a crepe umbrella from her hair and slipped it between his cheeks. He snorted.

The ice bucket full of water sloshed when Andrea set it on the floor. She pulled the sink plunger up and filled the basin from the bucket. The washcloth turned grey from the ash she scrubbed from her face. Salt crumbled from her swimsuit as she peeled it off and stepped into soft cotton shorts. She pulled on a tank top Rob had given her that said 'BITCH' across her tits. A 'token of affection'. She wore it because he thought she wouldn't.

Her fingers caught in the tangles of her hair as she tried to tame the curls. She pulled it back into a knot and a small red barb of coral tumbled from a curl. The coral's sharp tine sunk into her thumb as she retrieved it from the floor.

The pain was slow to travel to her foggy brain. She pressed the cut to her lips, soothed it with her tongue, and tossed the barb in the toilet.

The room was already soaking up the equatorial warmth. She opened the balcony doors, and swung them to move some air.

The beach had gone dark. Only a few dim lights shone at the resorts lavish enough to have generators, the rest of the town pitched into darkness. The mountaintop glowed, reflecting its fire off the underside of ash clouds.

The clock flashed twelve; her fancy dive watch had failed in the deep water; her phone sat on her pillow back in New York—a condition of their retreat. *He's got a condition, all right. Or a disorder.* She yawned.

Rob's form sprawled across the whole bed. There was no space left for her—not unless she wanted to spoon up next to him. She didn't. She slipped out onto the balcony, shut the door, and settled into the plush deck chair, her head spinning into sleep as she listened to the splash of the ocean two floors below.

* * *

A shrill screech shattered her dream and she flung her eyes open. *Santino...?*

A sepia morning glow had settled over the ocean. Sunlight filtered weakly through smoke, its peace cut through by the sound of something scraping at the glass behind her. She spun around in her chair.

Rob crouched on the floor inside the glass door. He clawed at the glass, his nails folded back to the raw quick. His jaw hung slack, saliva stringing from his lips.

She leaped from her chair and reached for the door handle. *Is he hurt?* She flinched back. He banged on the glass, but the shrieks continued behind her. His breath did not fog the glass.

What's wrong with him, Jesus, what's going on?

She backed away from the door, reached behind, and grasped the balcony railing. Her eyes slid to the side, over the low wall.

Below, the ground seethed with bodies. Men in reflective jackets fled coral-crusted skeletons that dragged their slick black bags behind them. Tourists ran as shuffling, grey-skinned creatures leapt at them. Blood sprayed from tan flesh that squirmed as the grey figures fell on them and ripped them with rows of serrated fangs.

Andrea puked sweet and sour rum over the rail. She fought for breath against the tide of nausea and the tightness in her throat.

There was a bang against the balcony door and Andrea spun to face Rob again.

A web of cracks spread across the glass door. Rob's mouth pressed against the center of the spiral fissure, gnawing. A tooth dropped to the carpet trailing pink froth behind it, and a bloody fang burst through the gum in its place, spraying the door in a fine mist of blood.

Andrea screamed and pressed her back to the low cement barrier at the balcony's edge. There was a privacy wall separating their balcony from the one adjacent and she sidled along and leaned around it. She planted one foot firmly in the corner of the balcony and hugged the dividing wall. She reached her other leg over the edge—over the bloody chaos below—then swung it around into the neighboring balcony.

Rob's hand burst through the door in a coruscating shower of glass and her stomach churned at the thought of the drop to the pavement below.

Oh god. Now, Andrea. Now!

Jump.

Andrea threw herself over the wall and slammed into a deck chair with a crash that sent her sprawling. As she scrambled to her feet, Rob's bloody arm reached around the dividing wall, tattered, bloody fingers grasping at the air.

"Not today, asshole! Or ever again."

She picked up a wooden deck chair, and threw it through the glass door. Fragments of glass fell around her as she leapt through the jagged hole.

She crouched—waiting, listening. The room was silent. Bathroom empty. Fresh sheets folded on top of a bare mattress. She should be safe for a minute.

Andrea sat on the bed. Rob flailed and grunted wetly but made no progress. *What the hell had happened to him?*

There was a loud thud in the hallway and Andrea ran to the door and pressed her ear against the crack.

A door slammed in the distance. A scream.

The hinge on the bar bolt screeched as she rammed it in place. *I've got to find help; I've got to get out.*

She grabbed the phone receiver from the nightstand and pressed it to her ear. The line was silent, but for a slow buzz of static. She pressed the button for the desk, and held her breath. It rang.

A voice burst through the line, a staccato of rapid Spanish.

"Hello? Santino, is that you?" Andrea said.

"Mrs. Renato! You're alive!" Santino's grin slid through the phone, the way it had slid up her legs the first night she stretched out on the beach. The way his fingers slid over hers when he handed her a drink.

"I am *not* Mrs. Renato. Santino, what's happened? What's going on out there?"

"You were right, Miss Andrea. They just walked right up out of the sea." He laughed.

"Santino, are you drunk?"

"Yes, I am, señorita. Locked myself in the store room behind the bar."

"How do we get out of here? Rob is… I climbed over the balcony to the next room…"

"Stay where you are. Get drunk if you can! One got me last night, but I'm still myself. Not like the others. I think it's the tequila!" He cackled and hung up the phone.

The line clicked back to static. Andrea slammed the receiver down. *So much for her knight in shining armor.* The cut on her thumb itched.

Rob's arms still waved around the partition, his throaty moans floating in through the broken door.

She sat on the bed. Her stomach growled. The screams outside grew distant.

She raided the mini-fridge, and washed down a tube of peanuts with a fist-sized bottle of scotch. A tiny wheel of shortbread was her dessert.

She stepped out onto the balcony, and hugged the wall away from Rob's bloody reach. His movements grew more erratic in her presence, his moans frantic. She stepped within a few inches of his fingertips, watched him grow rabid as he clawed the air for her.

"Some things never change."

The strip of boardwalk below the balcony lay in ruin. Scattered garbage, crushed bicycles, and bloody piles of bones littered the paths. Sharks threw themselves at the shore after the gory piles. Desiccated segments of ships that had risen with the Fenix bobbed in the waves, covered in rough corals. Calcified bodies streamed from their fissures, marched up onto the beach, and poured around the resorts into the city. Where they stepped, bright corals bloomed. Distant sounds of chaos ebbed and flowed with the wind. The world smelled like the dead insides of a shell.

A deep roar filled her ears. Waves began to flow backward, curling back toward the sea. The balcony swayed, the bright concrete cracked, and crumbled away from its rebar ribcage.

Andrea stumbled back through the doorway. She fell on the bed. Pictures tumbled off the walls.

A deep explosion rattled her teeth. All the glass in the room shattered. The sky grew dark, the air ripe with sulfur.

Andrea buried her face in the pillow, coughing, until the shaking stopped. Her own trembling shook the bed long after the earth had stilled. The roar of the volcano continued; the sky grew darker.

A low moan sounded from the balcony. The shelf of concrete hung by warped strands of metal. The partition had crumbled. Rob was scraping his way up the slope of debris toward the empty doorframe.

Andrea jumped to her feet. Sharp glass fragments pierced the soles of her feet. *No time for pain.*

She reached up and grasped the ornate brass wall sconce by the bed and hung from it, tugged on it till it ripped free from the wall.

Rob's twisted fingers wrapped around the metal frame of the door. He dragged himself forward over the crumbled concrete and shattered glass. His skin had faded to a sickly grey, painted over with his expensive rusty bronzer.

Andrea cleared a path of carpet and found her footing. She stretched her shoulders.

"Fucker," she whispered. "You want to finish our fight here in paradise? *Here I am.*" Rob pulled himself up, shuffled into the room, and stumbled toward her.

She lashed the sconce at him and raked it across his face. Teeth and blood flew, scattering across the far wall. He turned back to her, eyes rolling. Sharp yellow triangles sprung from the empty gums, spraying her face with blood.

She swung again. The impact shocked her arm, and she felt his bones give.

When his face whipped back to hers, his jaw hung below his nose, swinging from pale tendons. Serrated teeth ran in rows along the meaty crescent. His left eye bulged over a concave cheekbone.

Andrea struck him again. He staggered back. His reaching fingers brushed the fabric of her shirt. Thick, dark blood ran down his twisted neck. He spun, looking for her. His head was wrenched, stuck around backward. Bloody arms grasped again, reached the wrong way. A frothy growl bubbled from his throat. Dark, necrotic flesh spread from the wounds the broken glass had left on his rear.

Andrea lunged, and brought the sconce down hard on top of his head. It punched through the bone and sunk deep. The air filled with the scent of spoiled oysters and he dropped to the ground in a crumpled heap.

She lay back on the bed, panting, and listened to the rumble of the mountain and the silence of the boardwalk. Her feet throbbed. Her heart skipped.

This time I finished it—for both of us.

Blood seeped from shallow cuts across the calloused soles of her feet.

No no no. She sat up and looked at the small cuts. *Running is going to hurt but I can't stay here. I need to get to Santino.* She stood and yelped at the pain in her feet. *I need my shoes. I need supplies.*

She ripped a pillowcase from the pile of sheets on the bed and stumbled to the mini-fridge. She snapped the lid off a tiny bottle of vodka, clamped it between her teeth, and tipped her head back to slosh the liquor over her tongue as she scooped the contents of the fridge into the pillowcase.

The balcony platform sloped away from the shattered glass door. The deck chair dangled, caught in the rebar of the crumbled barrier. She spat the empty vodka bottle out. It tumbled, and splintered on the ground two floors below. Her head spun.

Her sticky fingers curled around a steel spoke that stuck from the wall and she stepped out onto another metal spine. She whimpered as her cuts wrapped around the gritty metal. Powdered concrete fell away from the walls around her. She scrambled over the rubble and into the room she'd shared with Rob, stepping over the pool of blood where he'd burst through the glass. She ran straight to the hall door and slammed the bolt in place.

Their mini-fridge was still full. Rob hadn't let her touch it—told her it was all fattening garbage. *It's the last thing you need,* he'd said. She grabbed a bottle of liquor and downed it.

The water in the sink turned red as she scrubbed at her feet. The skin around the cuts had darkened. She poured weak yellow beer over the wounds. They stung and foamed, hissing.

"Damn it," she said, scraping slivers of glass from the cuts. She limped to the phone and dialed the desk.

"Miss Andrea! You still kicking, *macha?* Staying *jumo?*"

"Santino, I cut my feet. Will that do it? Am I fucked?" She wrapped her feet in strips of bed sheets.

"How should I know? Either way, stay drunk."

"I've just got the mini-fridge."

179

"You're fucked."

"You have more there?" She pulled her sneakers on over the bandages and cinched them tight.

"Yeah, I've got the whole store room. If you can get here. I'm not coming up there."

"Right. Asshole. See you soon."

"Sure, *macha*. My love to you. Bye." He sounded sober.

* * *

Rob's backpack bulged with mini-fridge snacks, travel-sized toiletries, and a blanket from the bed. She'd drunk two more mini bottles of booze and refilled her empties with water from the bucket. The pockets of her jeans stretched around the sconces pulled from the wall. She leapt around corners, swinging half a curtain rod in each hand. She gritted her teeth with each footfall as the insoles grew spongy with blood.

The halls were dark tunnels, lit only by dusty corner windows. The loud hum of the generators rattled the walls but lit only the exit signs above the stairwell doors.

Andrea crept along the wall. She peered through a rectangle of glass in the stairway door. The space beyond was empty, but the single naked bulb that hung over each landing didn't do much to illuminate the long slopes of stairs between.

She pressed the bar and slipped through the opening. A siren shrieked through the stairwell. Her feet echoed off the concrete stairs.

At the ground floor, on the last landing before the dark pit of basement, lay a pile of slick skeletons. At least three skulls poked from the nest of bones in the putrid puddle. Andrea dropped the curtain rods. She cupped her hands over her nose and mouth. Jagged fragments of a gnawed pelvis crunched under her sneakers as she edged toward the door.

A scrape and moan sounded behind her from the dark stairs cutting into the hotel's underground space.

She kicked the bones out of the way, felt blood slosh in her shoe. The door didn't budge. Locked. She bit her tongue against the scream rising from her gut and pulled a sconce from her pocket. The impact of the brass against the reinforced glass knocked her teeth together, rattled her joints. The glass held, fogged over with her rapid breath.

The smell of rotting fish filled the stairwell. Something rough scraped against the steps and splashed in the puddle behind her.

She turned for the stairs. A pale, lumpy figure reached the edge of the ring of light cast by the dim bulb above. It hissed, and she saw the flash of fangs before she threw herself onto the door lever. She felt the lock strip— heard the mechanism crack. She tugged at it till it swung open, scattering fragments of the lock around her feet.

More wet bones filled the dim hall. They smelled salty, like the fried pork skins she'd eaten, unknowingly, before her dive. *The* dive. She'd enjoyed them until Rob told her what she was eating. *Flesh.* He'd laughed.

She ran through the hall to the lobby, and the shrieking siren followed her.

The white tiles were smeared with red. No movement or signs of life. She slipped around the corner, into the open foyer.

The smell of stagnant tide pools made her eyes water. Sulfurous ash clouds drifted in through the open entryway. The roar of the ocean mingled with the growling of the mountain, the crash of falling debris. Cracks threaded through the walls and ceiling. In the floor, fissures ran with blood.

Andrea inched around the perimeter of the lobby. She kept her back to the wall, holding the sconce in front of her.

At the back of the lobby lay the wide hall leading to the restaurant and bar. To Santino, with his warm eyes and lingering fingers.

She turned and ran.

Bloated figures lay across the floor, their skin grayed, their limbs convulsing. Their eyes reflected dull silver like tarnished nickel. Bloody wounds, necrotized and oozing, covered their prone forms. They moaned as she passed them, reaching out for her ankles, but a spreading slime stuck them fast to the floor.

The thick, grey metal door behind the bar opened a crack.

Andrea jumped, nearly stumbling into a pool of rot.

"*Macha,*" Santino called.

She ran to him and slid into the room. He slammed the door and locked it behind her.

"I heard you coming," he said.

She turned to him.

"*Ai, Jesus,*" he shouted. He grabbed her hair at the back of her head, pulled her face skyward.

When she opened her mouth to scream, he jammed the neck of a bottle between her teeth and tipped it. A corrosive tide of tequila stripped her throat.

She dropped to the floor, her hair wrenched from his grip.

"Andrea, can you hear me?"

She moaned.

"Shit," he said.

"Goddammit, Santino." She slapped him. She forgot she was still holding the sconce.

He ripped into a stream of foul Spanish.

She pulled herself up, gripping a wall that felt like it rolled in the surf.

He rubbed his face. "Your eyes, *macha*... you're turning."

She squeezed her eyes shut, shaking her head. The room spun.

"Where are you hurt?"

She reached down and pulled off her shoes. Black blood poured from the soaked leather.

He poured liquor over her feet, and sponged away the blood with a bar rag. She didn't feel a thing. He handed her another bottle. "Keep drinking. Nothing can grow in you with that in your veins."

"Is tequila all you have?"

"Only the best. Top shelf." He pulled down another cardboard box from a chrome rack.

She sniffed the rim of the bottle, flinched, squeezed her eyes shut and drank deep.

"This doesn't look good, *macha*," he pulled the blanket from her pack and set it behind her head. "Drink till you pass out. I promise, if you turn, I'll kill you in your sleep."

* * *

Crabs pinched her toes. Slick sea-worms slid under her clothes, like Rob's roaming hands, and pushed themselves into her wounds, chewing at her insides. She opened her mouth to scream, and warm, salty water rushed in.

* * *

Her head weighed heavy as an anchor. She moaned, but stopped short, her raw throat burning.

Water touched her lips. Not the hot, salty seawater of her dream, but cool water. Fresh. It burned her throat.

"You still in there, *macha?*"

She opened her eyes. The dim light had grown cloudy. Santino's face shifted in and out of focus. She rubbed her eyelids.

"There you are," he said. He smiled. One of his teeth was missing, and a sharp point poked through the gum.

"Santino…" She reached for his face.

He pulled back from her touch. "It's not a good look for me, I know." His grin wavered.

"How long was I out?" She asked.

"Don't know. I fell asleep, myself."

"You were supposed to be watching me."

"Oops?" he shrugged, and held up an empty bottle. "Besides—when I look at you, how can I tell if I'm dreaming?"

Andrea shook her head, waved away his flirtation. "Your skin…"

"And you're as silver as a fish belly. We're turning, *macha*, both of us. It's a race."

She stared at her arm. Her skin had lost its glow.

182

"If I was a gentleman, I'd let you win." He brushed her hair back from her forehead.

"You're not?"

"I guess we'll find out."

She looked down. Her feet were black to the ankles, the skin of her legs grey and scaly. She'd had her first wax for this trip. *Another condition. Waste of money, either way.* She sniffed.

"I don't smell like one, yet. Neither do you."

He tipped another bottle to his lips, then passed it to her. "At the finish line, one of us will smell like fish, the other fish food." He grinned. The serrated tooth slid further through the puckered skin of his gum.

"Well, no point in running our race sitting down." She reached up to the chrome bars of the shelves and pulled herself up. Her numb ankles shook.

"What? Where are you going?" he stood, swayed on his feet, reached out and steadied her.

She grasped his wrist. "I don't want to be eaten alive in a closet. And I don't want to eat you. I guess I'll go for a walk on the beach. Feel the sand between my toes."

"*Macha loco*, you'll never make it to the beach."

"Better than sitting here. And I only saw one *thing* walking around on my way here. I think they're all in town, now."

He stared at her, his eyes dull. "You're right, let's go." He picked up the pack and dropped two more bottles into it. He dug around on the floor for the sconce she'd hit him with and stuck it in the waistband of his khaki slacks. "With all the tourists shuffling off to town, maybe I can finally see my beach."

"You don't have to come," she said.

"If I'm to be a staggering fish corpse, better to do it where the action is, not locked away in here to starve."

She nodded. He took her hand and squeezed it.

Sooty air rushed in through the open door, burning their eyes. They squinted through the smoke and stepped out into the bar.

The bodies on the floor had sprouted. Fine filaments of purple, yellow, orange sprung up from their mouths and eyes. Calcified protrusions burst from the skin at their joints. Cloudy pools of water spread from where they lay.

Andrea and Santino wove a path around the reef bodies, down the wide hall to the lobby. The piles of bones had grown over with green fuzz. The earthy smell of chlorophyll combated the sulfurous smoke.

They stepped out of the open entryway. The sky was the color of charcoal, glowing red from the hidden sun and burning mountain. Smoke poured off the bright forest on the slopes to the north, and ran down to town. To their left, surf roared.

They turned toward the beach.

A dozen wrecks bobbed in the shallows, tossed in the waves of an encroaching tide. The waves lapped at the edge of the parking lot and nudged cars into scattered piles. Bodies stuck to the boardwalk, sprouting bright corals. Small fish flapped in the new pools, and nibbled at the clouds pouring off the corpse reefs.

Shuffling fish-figures, their bleached coral bones branching out from fissures in scaly skin, splashed along the flooded path, a new ecology blooming in their footsteps.

Andrea waded into the water. Santino hesitated, then grabbed her hand and followed.

"They're ignoring us," he said.

"I don't think we smell like food anymore."

"But we don't smell like they do."

She lifted his hand to her nose, breathed him in. "You smell like tequila."

He grinned. A wide, serrated triangle grazed his lower lip, drawing a line of dark blood.

She pulled his face down to hers and licked it clean, sucked gently, drawing more, tasting the warm salt of him. He pushed his hands through her hair. Her curls came away in his fingers. He shook them free into the waves.

Water lapped at their chests as they walked deeper into the sea. The scales on her legs rippled with pleasure in the tug of the current.

She pulled Santino under.

Bubbles trailed from slits in their necks as they kicked through the dark water, silver eyes darting through the cloudy debris of an era at its end.

Pink crepe umbrellas floated on the waves like paper lanterns.

A Keeper of Secrets
Benjamin Knox

By the third day, Anna had long since given into the restless boredom of children her age, and decided to explore the house. It had been, until recently, her grandmother's house. Her parents had come to organize the old woman's effects and prepare the wake. Anna thought that it was a silly name for it. Grandma wasn't about to wake up, even she knew that. Adults were so weird.

She had been left mostly to herself, however, and since it had been raining relentlessly since they had arrived, her exploration would have to be limited to the house. The long sloping back garden was 'off limits' her father had told her. It was a pity—she was sure she could see, through the rain streaked window panes, an old weather-worn tire-swing hanging from the large oak at the far end of the garden where the sloping grass and shrubs met the stream that marked the edge of the property. There were probably crabs and even fish in that stream, but the sky had wept continuously and kept her from finding out.

Besides, her mother would go on and on at her if she got even the smallest smudge on her new dress. At first she'd been excited at the prospect of a new dress. Then she saw what her mother had in mind. "It's respectful," her mother had told her, but Anna thought that it looked like a big black hanky, with frills. She wasn't a baby anymore, but her mother was impervious to her protestations. In the end she found herself draped in the silly thing which puffed out at the sides and was itchy all over. She even had to wear the silly little white socks and shiny black shoes. The black bow in her hair was the cherry atop the cake of her humiliation.

Her parents said that she looked lovely and that Granny would have been proud of her. Evidently they didn't remember Grandma Harris very well.

Hence Anna—trapped in the silly itchy dress and feeling more like a doll than she ever had in her whole life—took it upon herself to count the rooms on all three floors of her Grandmother's house.

* * *

It was by accident that she discovered the attic; and the door on a string, with its folding stairs. It wasn't difficult to open at all. The mechanisms were all well-oiled. At first the darkness of the attic had made her feel nervous. It looked to her, at least for a moment, like the yawning maw of some strange beast. It reminded her of a nature programme she had seen on television where crocodiles would lie in the sun with their mouths open and birds would wander between their jaws oblivious of the danger. She felt a little like that bird now, as she mounted the attic stairs. A naked bulb hung from the darkness, and the image of the attic doorway being a mouth came back to her, the bulb the beast's uvula, and the steps the creature's tongue.

The air of the large and dark space was cloudy with dust and smelled musty. Mould, dust and old wooden scents writhed in the newly disturbed air. Anna reached up and tugged the cord. The light cast by the bare bulb was sickly and weak but enough to navigate the attic space by.

Square ghosts of draped luggage loomed out at her in the electric glare. These ghosts were accompanied by racks of old plastic-sheathed clothes and even older furniture.

Anna made her way through the gloomy maze of the attic. The wooden beams of the roof acted as a reference so she didn't get turned about amidst the looming shadows. It was kind of like navigating by the stars she thought.

She worked her way through the narrow spaces slowly, careful not to touch anything. For some reason she could not fathom, she felt that if she touched anything her courage would abandon her to the nightmares of her imagination. This became more difficult; her resolve was tested the farther she wound away from that lonely bulb by the attic stairs. She studied the shapes, trying to guess what lay beneath the shadowy sheets. Not everything was covered. There were ornaments piled high upon boxes and old trunks with big brass clasps. Tiny black spiders weaved gossamer webs that undulated as she moved by, her body disturbing the air. A mapped globe of the world stood at the end of the narrow passage she was traversing. A dead end. Anna didn't want to think about anything dead at all. Not in this place. Even if it was only an expression. She'd had enough thoughts about death, and enough talks about it from the adults in her family. Their voices always quiet and solemn.

Turning, she made her way back the way she had come and took a different path where several met. She turned a few more corners, avoiding precariously placed heirlooms. *This must be the right one*, she thought, as the path took her farther towards where the end of the attic should be. This she knew, was where all of the oldest stuff would be. Her Grandmother's keepsakes from many years ago, when she was still young. These were the types of things Anna was particularly interested in. Quickening her pace, eager for what she might find, she was not expecting the figure standing tall in her path before her.

So sudden was she upon the figure that she let out a startled cry. Shrouded in long cloth, the figure stood still and ominous in her way. Anna

186

moved back the way she came, eyes fixed on the silhouette, watching for it to move or give chase. But it didn't. Anna squinted her eyes in the gloom of the far attic, trying to get a clearer view. Working it out, she moved forward to touch it. She held her breath, ready to bolt if needs be, and reached her hand out.

It was cool and rough.

No warmth.

It wasn't alive.

Anna tugged at the sheet partly covering the figure in front of her. As she had guessed; it was a mannequin. Well, not quite. It wasn't like the ones she saw when her mother took her shopping, all plastic with hair on and painted faces to make them look real. This one was missing its head and limbs. It was merely a torso on a sturdy pole. A bonnet had been placed atop it giving the impression, from a distance, of having a head.

Relieved, Anna breathed out, unaware that she was still holding her breath. Removing the old dust cover had stirred up a lot of dust. She could feel it now tickling the back of her throat and her nostrils. She slinked by the old dressmaker's mannequin and further on towards the farthest end of the attic. This was where the real treasures hid. A tall grandfather clock stood like an absurd mechanical headstone surrounded by old wooden chests. The type Anna had seen on television and in movies, with metal bindings and padlocks holding them shut; the type that always held treasure.

She tried the padlocks, checking to see if carelessness or age had opened one. Unfortunately they all held fast. With a disappointed sigh Anna left the padlocks, but stood stock-still when a scratching noise came from behind one of the trunks. She focused her mind, straining to hear the slight sound again. A moment later she heard it. A light scratching coming from a large trunk pushed against the far attic wall. All of a sudden she wondered what she might have wandered into. This place had remained untouched for decades. Even in her earliest memories of her grandmother, she was too old and frail to make it up the folding attic stairs, never mind navigate the labyrinth attic itself. She became startlingly aware of how far from the light and the exit she had come.

What was that scratching? Was it rats? Oh, she hoped it wasn't rats. Had she stumbled into the secret realm of the attic-rats? Her mind populated the attic then with phantom scuttling things hiding just beyond her view, sneaking around her, watching her with their tiny black beady rat eyes.

It came again, that light scratching sound.

She steeled herself, ready to run at even a hint of fur, and moved towards the old chest. The closer she got the more she saw that the huge old thing hadn't been push up against the wall as it appeared. There was a small gap between them. Nervous, her fingers scrunched the lacy hem of her dress as she peered behind the trunk.

There was no rat there—only a small pile of lacy black rags.

She squinted against the deep gloom and peered closer, trying to visually decipher the shape she had found. All of a sudden, like those silly 3D images her father loved to show her, it snapped into view. It was a doll, long discarded. It lay with its dresses coiled around it. It must have been sat on the old trunk, then at some point collapsed behind the trunk and never been recovered.

She reached down to pick it up, when it moved further into the dark corner. Anna shouted with fright. All of a sudden she was half way back to the dressmaker's mannequin when her reason returned. *I must have seen things, or knocked it somehow. It couldn't move by itself. Could it?*

Unless it wasn't a doll.

Slowing her panicked breathing, she forced herself to turn back and venture another look.

What she saw she couldn't quite believe, but it left any fright she'd had behind. It was *not* a doll she had seen. There, pressed against the back corner, tiny and clutching at the wall with fright, lay a tiny girl. She was impossibly pale and thin, and her chest heaved with quick terrified breaths. Her wide eyes were black like spilled ink. Anna's heart went out to this fragile creature.

"It's alright," she said, "I won't hurt you."

The little girl in the black lace dresses kept her distance. She looked so small and thin, like she was starving.

"Are you hungry?" she asked.

No response.

"Please don't worry, I won't tell anybody you're here. You won't get in trouble, honest."

Strangely enough, this worked. The expression of abject terror softened to one of mere exhaustion. Anna backed up, hoping to encourage the tiny girl to come forward a little at her own pace.

"Really it's alright, I promise I won't tell." She smiled crouched down sitting on her knees. She was careful not to get her dress under her; the attic was dusty and her mother would not be impressed. The tiny girl with the black eyes seemed to calm down a little but made no move from the safety of her corner. The girl had calmed down when Anna told her she wouldn't tell anybody that she was there. Maybe she was scared they'd send her away. Though what on earth she was doing here in the first place Anna couldn't even guess, but it gave her an idea.

"I'm not even supposed to be up here anyway. Nobody knows I'm up here, but it'll be our secret okay?" she said, hoping the girl would trust her sincerity.

Slowly, and very carefully, the tiny girl in her ratty black lace dress sat up and moved a little closer along the tunnel between the trunk and the wall. *She looks like a frightened animal from one of my nature programmes the way she darts her head around like that, looking for danger,* she thought. As the girl got a little

188

closer and her confidence grew that there was no immediate danger, she leaned forward and in a dry whispery voice said, "Nobody?"

It took Anna a moment or two to work out what the little girl meant and marvelled at the fact that this tiny thing had spoken. It made the girl seem more real to her somehow.

"No, nobody knows I'm here. They're all downstairs, talking quietly and being sad. So, it's just the two of us."

"Promise?" came the little voice again. To Anna it sounded like several voices whispering to be heard as one.

"Promise," Anna beamed.

With this the tiny girl stood up to her full height, a little over a foot. She was whip thin and chalk white and her dresses were dirty and torn. She looked like a fairy tale peasant girl, except for all the black. The girl climbed up the back of the trunk and sat on its edge. With Anna on her knees they were almost eye-to-eye now.

The tiny girl seemed much more at ease than she had been only moments before. This encouraged Anna and she smiled when she spoke, "My name's Anna," she asked, "what's yours?"

For a moment the girl looked confused. As if she had no idea of what Anna was talking about. She kinked her head to the side, like a bird.

"*Slou'ha,*" said the tiny girl in her strange little whisper. It was Anna's turn to be confused. She tried to repeat the sound, working her mouth around the sounds slowly.

"Slooo-a," she attempted.

"Slou'ha," the little whispers came again. This time delighted.

Anna tried again: "Sloo-Ah'" she said phonetically; then again, "Slou'ha."

The tiny girl smiled and spoke again, "Ah-na."

There was a slight sing-song lilt of an accent in the way the girl spoke.

"That's right," she said, "I'm Anna, you're Slou'ha. It's nice to meet you." With this, Anna slowly extended her hand out towards the girl, Slou'ha.

The girl retreated a little at first, unsure of her intentions. Perhaps she thought it was some form of trick? Then she leaned forward and extended her own fragile limb alongside Anna's. Anna took the girl's hand between her fingers, careful to be gentle, and shook her hand. She didn't want to hurt her. After all, she was so very small and frightfully thin. She seemed so delicate that any wrong move might break her. But she didn't break.

"Nice to meet you," Anna said again.

The girls smiled at each other. They had both made a new friend today.

* * *

They spent a few minutes together, before Anna heard movement from downstairs and her mother's faint call. She didn't want to have to go and leave her new friend. But she knew that if she didn't go now her mother would come up to the attic, and Anna had promised Slou'ha that she'd keep her presence a secret; a promise she'd break if her mother came and found her here. Besides, her mother wouldn't approve of Anna being up here by herself, particularly in her special dress. Not with all that dust.

Anna promised Slou'ha that she would visit her tomorrow, assuring her that this would remain their little secret. She said goodbye, and wormed her way through the maze-like attic back to the lonely bulb and the bright opening leading down into the house proper.

She had just gotten the attic stairs folded up and slid them back into the ceiling, when her mother came down the corridor.

"Anna, there you are," her mother scolded, "where have you been? Didn't you hear me calling you?"

Anna didn't know which question to answer first.

"You weren't trying to get into the attic were you?"

"No," she said quickly, "I was just bored, so I decided to explore Grandma's house."

"Oh," said her Mother, "Good, I wouldn't want you going up there anyway. It's so old; I don't know when someone last went up there. It's probably not safe, and all that dust besides." Her mother took her by the hand, taking her back downstairs. "Try not to wander off in future, I want to introduce you to your Great-Aunt Talitha."

As they went back down to the sombre proceedings, Anna cast a long yearning look behind her, wanting to return to her new friend already.

* * *

The next day all Anna wanted to do was to go up to the attic and visit her friend again. To visit Slou'ha again, and bring her some food. She was so small after all, and thin too. She *must* be hungry. Anna's heart went out to the tiny pale girl she had found up there alone in the dark and dusty attic. Her parents, however, had different ideas and she wasn't able to steal even a minute to herself. Today was her Grandmother's Wake. Anna still thought it sounded silly. Tomorrow they would bury her in Ashwood Cemetery, next to Grandpa. For that they'd all have to go to the church. Which was another silly thing too. In all the time Anna had known her Grandma, she had never once gone to church.

But her parents insisted, and she was forced into the scratchy and uncomfortable dress yet again. Once more her mother brushed her hair straight back and placed a band on her head to keep it that way. Then came the silly white frilly socks and the shiny beetle-like shoes.

This wasn't fair—it wasn't even raining today! But heaven forbid that she went outside, or had any fun. She was sad that Grandma Harris had died, she really was, but she didn't think that Grandma would want any of this fuss. And she didn't see why *she* had to suffer. All the adults got depressed, and stood around being respectful. Funny how respectful and quiet seemed to be the same thing.

How many of them actually wanted to be here? Anna wondered.

Not many most likely.

She looked at them all now, assembled in the large downstairs sitting room of her Grandmother's house, dressed in black, the ladies with their big silly hats. They all stood still; a few talked in dangerously low whispers, but most just stood around being quiet.

Anna wanted her jeans and sneakers. She wanted to go outside. She wanted to see her new friend again. But none of these things were to be. Her mother had a list of tasks she wanted Anna to be on hand for. She helped lay out the heavy silver trays of snacks. Not real snacks Anna noticed, but crackers and grey gooey stuff. Adult snacks; serious snacks with no flavour that were low in *clories*—whatever those were.

Anna huffed and puffed, but if her mother heard her she paid no heed. On the third heavy tray run, Anna made a break for it. Instead of going back to the kitchen, she snuck out the hall exit. She stood there in the main hallway a moment, listening. No tell-tale footsteps, and no one in sight. She was clear to make a run for the stairs, when she felt a hand on her shoulder and the high-pitched warbles of her aunt Helen.

"Oh Anna, dear Anna, is that you?"

Of course it's me, do you see any other people still in grade school? She thought, grumpy at being caught. She turned to face the massive form of her aunt Helen. The black-clad planetoid loomed about her, a giant veiled radar dish of a hat pinned to her head. Her painted face a mixture of gossip and grief.

"Oh Anna, how you've grown," said Aunt Helen as she touched Anna's hair, resting her small clammy hand on Anna's cheek. It made her skin want to crawl off her body.

"Yes," was all Anna could think to say with her aunt's hand cradling her cheek like that. She didn't want to move. It was like finding a horrible stinging insect already on you—you had to stay absolutely still and hope it would leave of its own accord.

"Oh, how long has it been? You must be what… thirteen by now."

"Ten," Anna said, unmoving.

"Oh I know your Grandmother would have been so proud to see you all grown, almost a woman." Her aunt began to cry a little and moved her hand from Anna's shoulder to wipe her eyes on a small lace handkerchief.

I'm free! The wretched hand had gone, the insect buzzing away to sting someone else. She had to get away quickly. If she encouraged her aunt, she'd be trapped all day with her. A fate worse than kitchen duty.

"I know, I miss her," Anna said casting her head down and making whimpering noises. She wasn't going to tell Aunt Helen that she'd seen Grandma Harris only a month ago.

"Oh dear, it's alright to cry young Anna, you let it out. Come to your Aunt Helen."

Oh no! Backfire! Quick—think, Anna. Think!

She turned to look at her aunt and said, "It's alright I can be brave. Grandma would have wanted me to be brave. I just need a moment in the bathroom. I'll be fine." Anna walked a few steps down the hall then added, 'Thanks, Aunt Helen.'

The monolithic woman smiled, and her eyes welled up with tears again. *Perfect.* As Anna went into the small bathroom beneath the stairs and closed the door, she heard her Aunt say, 'Aw, bless that child. So brave, and not half as bad as her mother.' Then she heard the tap of Aunt Helen's shoes (she had such tiny feet for such a big woman) cross the hall then fade away into the carpeted silence of the lounge.

Yes, I did it! I knew that'd get her. Ha, the perfect getaway. She still had to make it out the bathroom and up the stairs before anybody saw her though. Her mother was, no doubt, already wondering where she was. Anna waited a second or two longer, just to make sure Aunt Helen had gone, and readied herself to make a dash for it.

A last minute idea struck her. She quickly unbuckled her shiny beetle-like shoes, tucked them under her arm, then opened the door and *ran.* Up the hallway she bolted, catching the wooden banister. Anna swung herself around it, her socked feet sliding as she turned. By the time she registered the impressive move she had just pulled off, she had already quietly yet speedily, padded halfway up the stairs.

She had been right to remove her shoes. She had moved faster, and more importantly, much quieter. Now that she was on the first floor landing, Anna slipped her shoes back on but didn't buckle them. It'd take too long and she had another flight to go.

She crept up the second flight. She heard voices, male voices, muffled and deep coming from the second floor. *Damn it!* she thought, recognising her father by his tone rather than his words. As she reached the top she peered around down the hallway in both directions. No one. But the muffled male voices were coming from the same direction as the entrance to the attic. *Double Damn!*

In the wallpapered and carpeted hallway, Anna felt like a spy from an old movie, sneaking about trying to hear the secret meeting that would reveal the villain's plot. But she wasn't a spy. She couldn't just blast away anyone who discovered her, with the small silenced pistol she kept—strapped to her thigh, of course. No, she was just a girl, and if her father saw her, he'd probably send her back downstairs to help her mother. *Back to the gulag with you!*

The voices were coming from an old office to her right. The attic entrance was just beyond it at the end of the hall, with its little pull string dangling, tempting her. The door to the office wasn't wide open, *thank goodness*, but it was ajar, which meant they might see movement outside if they were looking in that direction. Anna crept up and peered through the crack between the doorframe and the hinges. Through the sliver she saw her father and two other men, all in their dress suits, huddled around something, their backs to the door. She still couldn't make out what they were saying, or doing for that matter. What on earth were they huddled around? A moment later she found out.

A muffled voice again, and all the men cried out, "Aww, no!" she heard her father say, "Damn it."

The men moved a little and spoke to each other their faces a mixture of enjoyment and concern. Her father patted who she reckoned was her uncle Marty on the shoulder. As they moved, Anna saw it. An old transistor radio. They had tuned it in to a station and were listening intently. There was no music, only another man's voice. *Was it a secret communiqué from their organisation's evil commander?* Nope, it was sports. They were listening to the game on the old radio.

With their attention fixed, Anna had no trouble sneaking by. She pulled the cord which brought down the attic stairs slowly. Then, very carefully, she unfolded the lower steps and began to climb. As she got half-way up she reached down and pulled the lower steps up. She didn't want to get caught. When she got to the top, the lower steps already lay folded up against the upper set. Now all Anna had to do was tug the trap shut, which she did. She hoped her father and the others didn't hear the click as the steps popped back into place.

Anna found herself in near complete darkness. She searched with her hands above her, found the cord and pulled it. The lonely bulb came on, its weak light stark to Anna's eyes, which had just begun to acclimate to the darkness.

Without waiting, she moved through the towering labyrinth of ancient objects and dust-cover ghosts, almost making a wrong turn, but catching herself at the last moment. Anna was so excited to see her friend again that she paid no attention to the fact that she was running through the near darkness. Spotting the old tailor's dummy with her bonnet head, Anna smiled. Yesterday it had frightened her thinking it an intruder, but today it was like an old friend. Squeezing by it Anna went up on her toes to pat the top of the bonnet hello. A few steps later Anna found herself at the far end of the attic, facing the mammoth trunk again. She crept over to the small space behind the trunk and called softly.

"It's me Anna, I came back like I said."

But there was no response and nothing behind the trunk. Just a gloomy narrow space littered with a few hiding dust-bunnies. Anna's heart sank. Where was her new friend?

"Slou'ha?" she called, a little louder than before. The dust-filled darkness of the attic yawned wide, swallowing her words. Yesterday the girl had been right here, hadn't she? At that moment Anna started to doubt herself. Her mother was always going on about how her imagination was getting the better of her. But she hadn't imagined it, and it certainly wasn't a dream. Anna slumped down to sit on the old heavy trunk, uncaring of the thin layer of dust that would surely mark her dress.

"I didn't imagine it, I'm sure," she said to herself. Hearing her words made it more real. As crazy as it was, she *had* met a tiny girl yesterday, whip thin and chalk white.

At that very moment she heard a collection of tiny whispers come together to form a tiny voice.

"Anna."

She looked up, and from behind the tailor's mannequin stepped the girl. She was not quite so tiny as Anna had remembered her. Yesterday, with Anna sitting and her new friend on the trunk, they had been eye-to-eye. Today, with Anna slumped on the trunk and Slou'ha standing they were again at eye level.

"Anna," she said again, coming further out from the shadows, "you came back." The not so tiny, yet still small girl had a smile on her face. It made Anna happy to see her smile. Yesterday she'd been so terrified.

"Slou'ha," Anna began, "here, I brought you a sandwich. I thought you might be hungry." Anna fished out the small triangular tuna sandwich she'd stolen from the silver trays. As she offered it to her, Slou'ha stepped closer still. *She is taller?* Anna wondered. Her hair was messy, but less tangled too. Her dress had somehow grown with her, but she was still gaunt and frighteningly pale, with eyes shiny and black like Anna's shoes.

She reached out and took the small white triangle from Anna. She seemed curious of it, but unsure as to what it was, or what to do with it. First she sniffed it, then tasted it on her little grey tongue, then just like that the sandwich was gone. Slou'ha smiled at Anna, her cheeks puffed up and moving. Anna noticed a smudge of tuna on the girl's curved lips. Her grey tongue darted out to retrieve the little morsel.

"You were hungry," Anna said.

Slou'ha moved closer to sit alongside Anna on the huge old trunk, then said, "You came back."

"I told you I would," she beamed. "It wasn't easy either. My aunt Helen almost got me, and then I had to sneak by my Dad and some of my uncles." Anna said, proud of herself.

"So no one saw you come here?"

"Nope." Anna said, "I told you it was our secret."

Slou'ha was pleased and she relaxed with a smile. The smile looked strange on the pale girl's face, yet quite beautiful at the same time.

"Can you stay long?" asked Slou'ha in her whispery voice.

"Not too long, but for a little while," Anna said and realised she'd been vague.

"Good," said Slou'ha.

"You haven't had any company for a long time have you?" Anna asked.

"Not really. I used to talk with Ida, but after a while she stopped coming." Slou'ha seemed touched briefly by a wave of sudden melancholy, but quickly brightened, "But then you came."

"Ida?" Anna wondered, "You mean Ida Harris?"

The other girl nodded.

"You mean Grandma Harris, you knew my Gran?" Anna had been thinking more out loud than meaning to state the obvious, but Slou'ha smiled and nodded again.

"And her mother before her." The simple statement made Anna's mind whirl. *She knew my Great-Grandmother!*

"You must be old to have been around so long," said Anna then clapped her hand over her mouth. "Sorry, I didn't mean to say that you're old."

"It's alright," said the girl, "I'm not really. I just stay the same. I don't feel old, especially not now." Again that cute, slightly crooked little smile graced her tiny, pale, perfectly curved lips.

Anna's mind was so full of questions she didn't know which one to ask first. They'd all gotten into a traffic jam before they reached her mouth. She just sat there gawping at her new friend.

Sensing her distress, Slou'ha decided to answer a few of Anna's unspoken questions. "I came over on the boat with Elena, we were best friends back then. We spent most of the voyage sneaking about the boat, spying and hiding and then telling each other what we had seen. Mostly we went together though."

"How long was the trip?"

"On the ship?"

Anna nodded her head.

"It took a little over a week, but it felt like forever."

"Wow," said Anna. She'd never been on a boat in her life. She'd been on a plane once or twice for family holidays, but she thought that they were probably very different. Anna found herself desperately wanting to go on a long sea voyage. An adventure on the High Seas.

"Wait," said Anna, 'if you knew my great grandma when she was a girl, then you must have known Grandma Harris all her life?" Anna found this amount of time difficult to imagine. She understood the quantity but just couldn't wrap her mind around experiencing it.

"Not really," came Slou'ha's reply, "when I sleep, I sleep for a long time."

"Like a bear when they hibernate for the winter?"

"I suppose it is a little like that, yes."

They sat there again in silence before Anna eventually spoke again.

"What was she like? Grandm—Ida?"

"She was much like you are now," said the pale girl, her smile still on her lips. It wasn't what Anna had been hoping for. She wanted long rambling tales about her Grandmother's exploits as a child. But her new, extraordinary friend seemed unwilling to go into too much detail about the past. Anna floundered as to what to say. Perhaps the obvious was best;

"You're taller than yesterday, I'm sure."

"Yes," said Slou'ha, the whispery voice warmer now, "I feel a little better, thank you."

"Thank me? What did I do?"

"You could have told everybody about me, but you didn't. I surely would have vanished had you done that."

"What?" Anna was shocked at the revelation. "Really?"

Slou'ha nodded her head.

Anna couldn't believe that, with a simple secret, she had unknowingly held this girl's life in her hands.

"That's why you were so frightened—you thought I might tell?"

Again Slou'ha nodded.

"But you didn't, and that secret you kept for me helped me to feel better."

Anna marvelled at what she was being told.

"You're not entirely better yet are you?" but Anna already knew the answer to her question. Yesterday Slou'ha had been truly tiny and starved, ready to disappear. Today she seemed taller and healthier, but this was only by comparison. Slou'ha was still deathly thin and pale. She knew then what she must do.

"My father and my two uncles are listening to the old radio in my Grandfather's old study, but they're supposed to be downstairs with the other guests."

Slou'ha looked up, slightly confused by the sudden shift in topic.

Anna continued, "My aunt Helen keeps a flask of brandy in her handbag. She's probably three-sheets-to-the-wind already." She wasn't sure what the last saying actually meant, but it felt right in the context and she had heard her mother use it for drunkards before. She liked the way it sounded as she said it.

She thought quickly then started again, "My mum doesn't like my dad to smoke, but I know he does. I saw him one morning with his pipe sneaking into the pantry. I went in afterwards. It didn't smell like cigarettes, it was sweeter. I don't think he knows I saw him. I never told mum.'

Slou'ha was beaming a big gleeful grin. A the self-assured type that just lit up her entire face. Spurred on by this, Anna thought of another.

196

"I did my friend Amy Reynolds's essay at school last year, and she got top marks for it. We didn't get caught."

And another—

"When I was six I lost the class pet, he was a hamster—we called him Mr. Wiggles—and I blamed Ricky Timms for leaving the latch undone. He got sent to the corner, and no one ever suspected me. Always felt a little bad for Ricky though. No one believed him."

And another—

"Tally Rimbald and I went skinny-dipping in her parent's hot-tub one afternoon when her parents were out. She wasn't allowed to go in. But we didn't care. The bubbles felt nice, but the water was all chemically."

The two had begun to giggle at the stories Anna was telling. They giggled a little more with each one she told, until holding their bellies and with tears in their eyes, they collapsed together in a fit.

* * *

They spent the next hour and a half talking and telling secrets the way girls do. But this was better. It was gossiping and her mother told her that it was rude to gossip. But this was for a good cause. By the time Anna snuck back out of the attic, Slou'ha already had a touch of rose to her chalky cheeks. Anna couldn't wait to see her again tomorrow. It was supposed to be their last day in the old house, but she didn't want to think about that right now. She hadn't meant to spend so long up in the attic, her mother would be looking for her for sure. She'd have to think of a good excuse.

* * *

Her final day at her Grandmother's house arrived and Anna was up early. She was sad that they had to go so soon, and sadder still that she couldn't explain why she wanted to stay longer to her parents. Today was also the day of the funeral. They would all have to go to Ashwood Cemetery for the service and burial. It would take up so much of the day as well. She wanted to go and pay her last respects, but she didn't think that Grandma Harris could hear her. If she could then she'd hear her anywhere, but it was more for her parents. They wanted her there, she knew that. After all Grandma Harris was her Mother's mum. She thought about that.

Will I do the same if—*when*—*mum passes on?*

So Anna went with her parents and family, to Ashwood Cemetery. The service in the chapel was monotonous and long. Everyone who came up to speak said pretty much the same thing, and ended up crying. Up by the coffin were wreaths of flowers surrounding two large photographs. One of Grandma Harris as Anna had known her, perhaps a little younger. The other, for the benefit of her older friends gathered here and to illustrate the long full life she had lived; an old black and white of Ida (Jones at the time, not yet Harris) at roughly twenty. They barely looked similar. White curls in one, long black waves in the other. Anna's mother remarked on the resemblance between Anna and the old black and white image, and told her that she would look very similar when she was twenty to the large image at the front. Anna didn't know what to say or think about that.

Eventually, after the long boring speech by the priest and some truly awful organ music, the congregation moved outside behind the coffin. Her father was one of the pallbearers. All the adults, except her aunt Helen, had their heads down sombrely. Aunt Helen was whispering away in a gossipy fever to a reluctant family member.

They laid Grandma Harris to rest beside her husband's grave, which Anna thought was creepy as hell. The Priest said more things Anna didn't quite understand, and people cried and threw flowers as they lowered the coffin. Anna imagined what the Grandma Harris she had known would say about all this. No doubt she would stand for none of it. She'd think all this weeping and wailing was a waste of time and breath. Anna had liked her Grandma, and would miss her. She would always recall the mischievous wink she'd sling Anna, when the others weren't looking. That wink reminded her a little of Slou'ha. It was the same cheeky nature.

Once the ceremony was complete, the adults spoke briefly and then filed away in their black clothes to waiting black cars. She was relieved to hear that they were heading back to Grandma's house, something to do with lawyers and the reading of the Will.

For this her mother and father wanted her to stay in the house and to keep herself patiently amused. She couldn't believe it—they'd given her free reign! The few adults that would also be around would all be huddled in the same room. Effectively, Anna would have the run of the house to herself. She thought of the attic and the perfect opportunity to say goodbye to her friend. Perhaps she could even persuade Slou'ha to come with them. The girl could live in their attic if she wanted. Anna would hide her in the car boot, she was so small after all. She'd fit with plenty of space left over.

* * *

The attic door pulled shut behind her. She had once again made a perfect getaway. No one had noticed her once she'd left the adults in the study. Anna the Spy was as invisible as ever. Her game made her think of the old films on television where the female spy in the wonderful dress always had a tiny silver pistol against her thigh, for emergencies. Small but deadly.

Anna tugged the cord several times, but the bulb didn't light. It must've blown. She made her way to the rear end of the attic, and said hello to the kindly tailor's mannequin with her bonnet head as she passed. This time

Slou'ha was waiting for her in the small space at the very end of the attic, sitting atop the old trunk.

As Anna rushed to her friend, Slou'ha stood up. Anna stopped. Slou'ha had once again grown since last she had seen her. Now she was identical in height to Anna. That wasn't the only thing that had changed about her either. The lacy black rags she had worn had transformed into a flowing black dress. Her hair, once all messy and dirty, was freshly combed and a shiny, glossy black wave. She smiled at Anna and took her hand. They both marvelled at her transformation.

"Wow," Anna said, unable to contain her shock and joy. Slou'ha smiled back at her. "Is this all because of yesterday? Because of the secrets?"

Slou'ha smiled excited and giddy. She looked more like a little girl than ever before. It pleased Anna to see her friend so happy and healthy. She was also more than a little proud of herself for having something to do with it.

Then she remembered that she was going home today. It must have shown on her face, as Slou'ha with a clear soft voice—the whispers now gone—asked her, "What's the matter?"

Anna sat on the trunk. "Today is my last day here. In a few hours my parents are taking me back home."

"Is it far?"

Anna nodded solemnly.

"So you won't be coming back to visit me?"

Anna shook her head.

"I was hoping that you might come with us. We could hide you. It'll be more difficult now that you're bigger, but I can sneak you into our attic at home. You could live with me." Anna already knew the answer, but she had to ask. She'd never forgive herself if she didn't.

"I can't," said Slou'ha, 'If anyone were to even catch a glimpse of me… I'm still too weak. I'm sorry."

"Yeah, I thought so," Anna moaned. A thought occurred to her then. "Who are you going to talk to once I'm gone, who will tell you secrets?" Anna couldn't stand the idea that her friend would wither away again to that small frightened creature she had first found. She was so beautiful now, and she wanted her to stay that way. She wanted to stay here with her too, but both things seemed impossible.

"New people will move in, I'm sure. Hopefully they'll have someone as nice as you with them."

"But what if they don't, won't you starve." Anna was being a pessimist, but she couldn't help it. She was angry at herself for spoiling their last day together.

"I was thinking about that, and I have an idea," said Slou'ha with a touch of mischief. Anna couldn't help but smile.

"Yeah?"

"I'll need your help."

"Anything!" Anna said, excited now.

"You'll have to give me a secret, a big one. A really big one in fact. Something so big that it'll last me a long time, just in case no one moves in. Can you think of anything like that?"

Anna thought about it. She thought about it hard. She could think of lots more little things, but nothing huge. Not the kind of thing that she knew Slou'ha meant.

"I've got one."

Anna looked up at her friend a little confused.

"You do?"

"No one knows that you've been coming up to the attic right?"

"No, I was careful."

"Good, then this one will be the biggest secret of all."

Anna didn't know what Slou'ha was getting at, but any idea was better than nothing.

"What will?"

"Where Anna is."

"What?"

"It's a very big secret indeed—*where, oh where, has Anna gone?*"

Anna figured it out. "I could stay here!"

Slou'ha was in her own little world now, "Oh they'll look and look, but no one will find her. They'll think all kinds of crazy things, but none of them will ever know, none of them will ever suspect."

Anna didn't like the way she said '*her*'. It was as if she had forgotten Anna was even there. She wasn't talking to Anna, she was talking to herself. It frightened her a little bit.

"What ever happened to Anna? It'll be such a big secret!'"

Slou'ha turned to Anna now a wicked grin replacing the cute one. Her slim white hands snapped to Anna's shoulders, holding Anna tight. Her hands were still cold to the touch.

"Wait, Slou'ha, what are you doing? Let me go!" Anna wrestled, but failed to break free from the pale girl's iron grip. Slou'ha's big black eyes got bigger and her smile impossibly wide. "Let go of me! You're hurting me!"

But Slou'ha paid no attention. Her beautiful black dress had grown and quivered in the dark like a living shadow. When she opened her mouth it opened too far, and stretched right down to her chest, like a gaping black hole. Anna screamed and kicked, but the dark tendrils of the girl's shadow dress wrapped around her. They were the coldest things Anna had ever felt. They dragged her towards that huge mouth and wicked gleeful eyes.

Then just like that, Anna was gone. Swallowed up by the darkness in the heart of the pale little girl who lived in the attic. Slou'ha was right too; people would search and search. They would come to think the worst. But no one would ever know, none would even suspect. For years they would wonder, 'Whatever happened to dear young Anna?' But they would never know because it was her secret. Just hers.

Forever.

SPIRITS HAVING FLOWN
JOHN EVERSON

It was never so sterile. So polished.

So bereft of life.

The old frame house once sighed with his tortured breath, spoke with his aching lips, stumbled from thunderstorm to snowfall with his unsteady feet.

No more.

I move from one room to the next, noting the forest green granny-square afghan folded neatly on the back of the second-hand couch, its cushions, (for the first time?) perfectly fitted together. The thick, dripping grease spots have been wiped away from the small orange and brown tiles above the Donna Reed-era Amana gas oven range, the sloppy spaghetti stains painting the wall by the garbage can scrubbed down to faded shadows. I can see the patterns in the yellowed linoleum. Bundles of daisies. Given Mac's and my inattention to housekeeping, I'd never seen the flowers before.

The family has come, has cried, has cleaned, has gone.

Leaving me. The caretaker. The tenant.

For now.

And there is only one more thing to do.

* * *

Mac said he was only lying down for a nap on the perpetually rumpled couch. Those were his last few words to me. His breathing had been labored all week, and I worried. "Go down to The Last Chance later?" he whispered the question, and I nodded. He grinned a small grin and slipped off his heavy glasses as he curled into the cushions and afghan on the couch.

Nodded at me.

Caught his breath.

Wheezed.

And was sleeping.

I left the room, figuring to wash the car. While it was a gloomy shade of overcast in Mac's living room with all the heavy hand-me-down curtains drawn, it was 85 and sunny outside. Out there, life was dancing. In Mac's house, life moved slower, if at all. Maybe it was the smoke, or the low light. Or Mac. But sitting in his living room was like being trapped in a bubble of amber. Everything was still, and stained in sepia.

When I came back into the house an hour later, wet with sweat and stray hose water, Mac didn't stir. I went to the bathroom, rinsed my face and arms, combed back my hair, and then pulled on a fresh shirt. The house was quiet. Nothing too strange there. Mac didn't go for loud music, and only clicked on the TV at night. But this felt different, even so. At first I put the sense of stillness down to the absence of the screams and laughter of the kids outside, running through sprinklers and shooting at each other with water guns that looked like they'd come from a SWAT armory.

But no, that wasn't it.

The absence, the stillness in the house was a missing constant—that sighing whisper of air trickling in and out of Mac's lungs. The ever-present wheeze that meant Mac was at home. It had been the background sound-track to my life here these past six years, for if Mac wasn't with me, drink-ing away the pain at The Last Chance, he was here, wondering how it had all come down to this. From a gentle mother's arms to the edge of the hard Chicago streets to the arms of another woman and her kids and then, not. Loneliness. Only this small house at the edge of a roughed up and left be-hind farm town with a migrant worker as a roommate and a minute-to-minute struggle just to breathe.

"Life is a bitch," he'd often said to me in a low voice at the edge of a slanted smile.

"Then you die," I'd answer.

He'd squint back at me, take another sip and nod.

"Then you die."

* * *

The first time I met Mac was on a barstool at The Last Chance. He was emptying a tall can of Old Milwaukee, and flirting with the bartender with the shadowed eyes. Those shadows came from lack of sleep; she put in time as a receptionist at the Feed Store to make ends meet for her three kids. Still, she humored him, laughing and patting his hand as she emptied the ashtray that had filled up near his right hand.

"In your dreams," she answered some off-color comment of his, rolling her eyes.

"And what exciting dreams those must be," I said, edging my way into the conversation with a compliment to her. Never hurts to flirt with the barkeep—she'll pour better for you.

"What do you know of my dreams?" Mac growled and turned away.

Strike one.

"You're a man. You have the same dreams we all have."

A glare from the evil eye. He started talking to the woman on the other side of him, a haggard thing with long painted nails and a mouth that stretched from ear to ear. She looked 70 but was probably really only 45. He showed me his back and said nothing more.

Strike two.

I finished my whiskey in two slugs and left the bar—and Mac—behind.

* * *

I was new to town then, having slowly worked my way down from well-paid insurance suit in Chicago to minimum wage bag boy at the last two-horse town 20 miles north. Seemed I couldn't cure the itch in my soul, and neither could the bottle. I began seeing Mac almost every night at The Last Chance. Where else was I gonna go after a day working the fields? Sweat and forget, that was my new motto.

One night not long after my first brush with Mac, I pulled up a stool next to him and ordered a Seven and Seven. Mac turned his head to gaze up at me sideways, one eye open, the other squinted near-shut.

"What you wanna do with a highbrow drink like that," he said. "You gonna drink at this bar, you order some Jack Daniels straight up, or have Ginny pull you a beer."

Ginny had stopped to see my reaction, and I shrugged. "Is a Jack and Coke acceptable?"

"Suit yourself."

From that day on, I was Mac's barstool buddy. And eventually, house-mate.

* * *

There was no funeral.

Mac wouldn't have it. He wanted cremation with no ceremony whatso-ever. The family compromised and laid him out in a box to wake for one night. Some people probably wanted the chance to say goodbye, they felt; and they were right. The family was amazed at the turnout, but not sur-prised when the bulk of the bodies walked straight down the street to The Last Chance afterwards.

I found one of my old Chicago business suits that almost still fit for the occasion, and stood sentinel by the casket as nurses and waitresses and rummies and friends from his growing-up days in Chicago streamed by the body. An old flame with a fake eye that was downright creepy if you looked too long probably cried the most. Word is a knife fight with the man who'd been with her before she'd came and went on Mac had taken half her sight. I wondered if she still had phantom sight on her right side, like when you lose a finger but still feel its presence on the end of your hand. A high school buddy holding forty extra pounds in his belly who probably wished he could slide his beard up *above* his forehead helped her away from her increasingly loud casket-side conversation with the dead body.

But mostly, none stayed too many minutes, or cried too hard. Many were amazed he'd lasted so long.

His face looked like softly brushed wax, his fingers molded in plastic. That thin brown mustache made him look a downright dapper mannequin lying there in his brother's suit. He'd never owned one of his own. You don't need a suit to drink at The Last Chance.

"It's so sad," his family members murmured, talking in whispers in the back of the room. "But it's for the best," they reasoned. "What kind of life did he have? When you're that far into the bottle, what kind of dreams can you have left? He'd drowned them all out."

I stifled a sad smile and turned away. If they'd only known; it was the dreams that sent him to the bottle, not the bottle that stifled them. And no matter how hard he tried, he'd never managed to drown them out.

Nobody sent flowers to Mac's wake. One plant sent over by the local Christian church marked the head of the casket, and I watched it walk down the street with the family, when they left Mac's body to be burned. Their cars were packed with salvaged items from his dresser and cupboards. Memory holders, keepsakes, pictures. The solid imprint of his life on the world, dispersed with more transience than his dreams.

As the funeral parlor locked its doors, I realized that all that I had now of him was a piece of glass and the empty shell of a house. And even that would soon be denied, once the family sold it. Even his ashes wouldn't remain; those would be shipped north for burial once the cremation was complete.

*　*　*

I have to laugh as I think of the reactions in those first hours after his death. The phone calls. The tears. The shock. The first hurried clearing of the house. When his sister arrived late in the afternoon from up north, she barely said a word to me, but instead performed a silent reconnaissance of the house. She peeked into all the cupboards, knelt to peer under the couch and felt between his mattress and box spring. Finally, she got up the nerve to just ask.

"The guns, the knives...?"

"He left me instructions," I said. "I disposed of them all."

A troubled smile, and a nod. One less detail for her to worry about. The last thing the family needed at this stage was police interest in Mac's unlicensed hobbies.

If she'd only known of the one important thing I had yet to dispose of. But, I suppose, she wouldn't have understood. Hell, five years ago I wouldn't have understood. Just a few months ago, I wouldn't have been ready.

It's time now though. For me. I have to be ready.

In his bedroom, I shove aside the ancient metal frame of his single bed, and with a screwdriver pry up the loose board beneath. There's an echo of a child's scream as I lift out the small wooden box buried there, under the dead man's bed. Is the echo from the children outside, down the block? Or is it from the delicately filigreed box, from the faces peeking out there from amid the slim vines and trees embossed in its lid? It too, had lacked for a funeral.

I replace the board and the bed, and returned to the kitchen. On the strangely clean table, I lay them out. One violent glass frame after another. They are small things that the box divulges. Country housewives hang similar glass shards from strings above their windows to catch and bend the sun.

Mac used them to catch and bend dreams.

Bad ones.

Nightmares.

I spread the myriad shards of mottled glass until the entire table was covered. The fake woodgrain surface came alive with twisting, writhing shades of flame, of blackness, of blood. Reaching to the middle, I lifted one that I recognize as mine. An ancient face stared back at me through the slender trap of glass. An old man, by the look, and gentle. But I knew better. This father figure was a haunt who'd chased me through back alleys in the night, all teeth and black nails and rusted razorblades thirsting for my neck. It had been years since he'd plagued my sleep. Mac had trapped him here, along with so many others.

There was the malformed, hideous child that his sister had never borne. There was the grisly red-smeared traffic accident that once woke his niece up nearly every night, shaking and sweating with fear and grabbing at her belly to see if it was still whole. There was the nephew's family dog, dragging its twisted body away from the road, trailing its lifeblood and back legs behind it. And there was his other sister's late husband, a cold thin greying man with a tight fist that beat and beat and then stopped, as his leg sprang to motion, dealing out his love in sharp hard blows to the ribs. Monsters and madmen and murder.

Hard dreams to handle.

These visions and so many more Mac had captured and held from his family and friends over the years, until his box was full and his power stretched thin as an old man's skin.

Only his will held these dreams here, and that will was gone now. Already some of the dreams had discovered that the cage that had bound them for so many years was gone, and I could see the shape and color of the woodgrain pattern through the clear glass they'd left behind. As I surveyed Mac's collection, his life's work, I began to cry. It wasn't the emphy-sema, or the Old Milwaukee, or the cigarettes that had killed him.

It was the dreams.

Wiping the water from my face, I hefted the screwdriver and considered. The dreams would escape, no matter what I did. Dreams can't be killed; can only be stopped for a while. Mac had taught me this: dreams are forever.

But if they can be trapped, can they be maimed? I wondered. Hobbled?

I looked down at the table and saw a miniature Ginny, being raped after hours at The Last Chance by a thug with long black hair.

"No," I cried, and brought the heavy end of the tool down to crush that vision. It shattered and sent other dreams flying off the table to crack and litter the floor. In the air, a scream, and a sparkle, and then… nothing. I repeated my attack on glass holding a monster intent on rending the limbs from a blond boy I recognized from last night's wake; he'd grown at least a foot since this dream was captured. A slight flash, like the faintest slide of a prism, and he was gone. Again and again I brought the screwdriver down, shattering nightmares and adding crumpled dents to the fake grain of the plywood table. The air filled with the angry twinkle of freed visions, and I felt my heart stumble as they surrounded my head, a chattering, screeching host of untouchable teeth and talons. When all the glass was shattered, I spun about the room and swung the point of the tool like a dagger at the air, alive with nightmares and dream deaths. Tears ran down my cheeks as I begged the dreams to follow their catcher.

"Die," I begged.

"Die."

At last, the room was quiet, and I rose from where I'd fallen on the floor, surrounded by empty, clear shards of glass.

I left it all, and went back to my own room, far down in the shadows of the long hallway.

From beneath my own bed, I pulled out a single triangle of glass. I'd fashioned it from a broken attic window, smoothing its dangerous edges carefully with sandpaper and spit. It was the first talisman of my graduation from apprentice to dream catcher. I lay back on the bed, wondering how I could ever be as strong as Mac, to steal and seal so many dark visions. It was up to me now to carry on his work, to lighten lives of three a.m. heart-ache and sleep-stealing succubi.

I held up my one shard of glass to the light, and felt the weight of its pull on my heart.

Mac's gasping face met my own.

"Let me die," his dream whispered. "Please just let me go."

Just days ago, I had captured this shade as he gasped and trembled in a troubled sleep.

Now I hold his dream to rue and remember forever.

It is the first weight in what will become my own collection of imprisoned dreams.

And I think that it will always be the heaviest.

For Jerry

THE WAY OF ALL FLESH
ANGELA SLATTER

Since everything went to hell, Sweet Bobby Tate had found some—indeed, all—of his preferred activities curtailed. This vexed him no end. He was fond of travel—although he could take or leave the big cities; not that there were too many of them anymore—but what he really liked, where his heart truly resided was small towns. The smaller the better as far as Bobby was concerned; easier to meet people, get to know folk. Faster to get around and finish the conduct of business.

In small towns, Bobby would tell anyone who stuck around long enough to listen, people did you the courtesy of conversing. Taking the time to listen. People there were trusting, and Bobby liked that too. He liked how small towns had a layout that was easy to figure, and how they almost always had pleasant and interesting graveyards. Small towns had little old churches of wood, with peeling paint, flower beds awash with colour, prayer books lined up neat and tidy, all manner of altar cloths handmade by the local ladies. There were stone walls around such bone yards, not so high that climbing over them caused a pulled muscle or torn seams in tight jeans, but high enough to give a little privacy.

Cities had less space and so leaned towards crematoria, with niches and so forth, less cadavers, more urns of ashes. While Bobby was not averse to a barbeque on occasion, he preferred things *fresh*.

Bobby's Momma had often told him, *Fresh is best* and her words were a sermon he took to heart. She didn't get out much in her later years and she hated travelling as much as her boy loved it. She looked forward to his visits, though, hearing him tell of his adventures as he crisscrossed the great nation like some latter day Johnny Appleseed, sowing darkness wherever he went. The last time he dropped in on her—before the world had started to fall apart—he'd found her still and cold in her easy chair. No more cosy chats and homey wisdoms, no more games of cheating chess, and that loss hit Bobby hard. He was grateful it was winter and she'd not paid her heating bill.

He made himself a feast she'd have been proud of, ate every last morsel. She would have wanted it that way, he thought; hadn't she fed his infant mouth with slivers of her own flesh and quenched his thirst with her own redness? Every time he'd seen those scars on her arms, in the places where the flesh was softest, he choked up, knowing he was so loved. Whenever he came into a new town and saw a woman who reminded him of his mother, he made sure she was his very first acquaintance.

So when Sweet Bobby Tate stepped across the boundary into Wolf's Briar, West Virginia (Population: 332), footsore and hungry, the primary thing he cast around for was a bakery. On any day not Sunday, that was where you found ample women with grey hair, heavy breasts and loose cotton shifts, smelling of lilac toilet water or lily of the valley. Later on he'd try the church.

* * *

Annabel Adams—sixteen and pretty with only a slight overbite that barely anyone ever commented on anymore—sat on the porch swing and gently kept it rocking with the occasional tensing of her leg muscles. The breeze was agreeable and cool as it rustled through the branches of the old lemon tree. It hadn't brought any awful sort of smell for weeks now, so Annabel figured that whatever had been rotting in large quantities some distance from Wolf's Briar had finished its decaying. The weather was nice, almost on the turn from summer to autumn, and she thought it was her favourite time of year. Behind her the big white house was quiet; no voices, no music radio, no hum of a refrigerator or air conditioner coz no one had heard that for almost a year. Just as quiet as the church and god-acre next door; just as quiet as dust falling.

Annabel did a quick calculation and figured it was more than a year—closer on eighteen months. The power gave out the day before her brother Tim went the way of all flesh. Annabel didn't like to say 'died'. She hadn't thought about it too much before what her Grandma Eileen called 'the Great Retribution' came, but when it got to the point that so many folks she'd known all her life just weren't there anymore, she decided a new term was needed. Slowly but surely, just about everyone went the way of all flesh. She was happy her family had stayed with her though, after everything that had happened, even if they didn't say much anymore.

Sighing, she stood and the swing banged back against the wall, taking out another chip of paint. Annabel stretched, long black hair trickling down her back. Her gaze flitted over the dusty length of the street, the lonely-looking houses, and overgrown lawns, and saw what she saw every day: precisely nothing new.

"Back to the books," she said, so her mother might hear and know she wasn't slacking. It was important, Melba Adams said, to stay up-to-date with all the subjects she'd need for her SATs, because surely one day things would get better and she'd want to go to a good school.

That was Melba's mantra: *things would get better.* Her mother had been certain, so absolutely convinced that one day all the bad stuff would be done with. That one day the power would magically come back on, that they'd

get something more from the landline than petulant silence, that their mo-
biles would once again start pinging signals from towers, and hallelujah, the
tiny gas station at the end of Abel's Road would be pumping petrol into all
the SUVs currently standing idle in people's drives. None of that happened,
though Melba said they should just be grateful none of those walkers mentioned on the radio—back when the batteries still had juice and some places
had generators that let them broadcast—ever came near Wolf's Briar.
Annabel didn't share her mother's faith in the Restoration of Everything,
but she kept up her studies for Melba's sake.

"Back to the books," she said again, and stepped into the cool interior
of the house.

* * *

Much to his chagrin, Sweet Bobby found no trace of either portly ma-
trons or working bakery. Indeed, there was no trace of anyone anywhere.
The shelves in the supermarket had been picked clean for the most part
except for a few unloved tins of peas, ravioli, beets, and thirty-two packs of
Junior Mints.

He wondered if the dead walkers had been through, but there were none
of the usual signs left when those locusts on two legs paid a visit: no empty
bullet casings scattered like metallic fruit, no bodies in various stages of decay littering the streets, no houses hastily fortified and then broken open
like Easter eggs. Everything was just quiet and empty and filled with different degrees of dust.

Perhaps the inhabitants of Wolf's Briar had decided to head to one of
the safe zones early on—but surely they'd have taken their vehicles, as long
as the gas held out? Without much hope, he decided to give the rest of the
town a once-over. Who knew? He might get lucky at the cemetery, find
someone buried not *too* long ago and not too deep.

He wandered up the deserted main street, past empty-eyed shops until
the shops became cottages, then cottages grew into larger houses as they
got closer to land that might be farmed. Soon enough he spotted it: a stone
wall, not too high, not too low, the tips of grave-markers peaking over the
top, and the pale yellow-painted planks of a tiny church. Bobby put some
pace into his step, a smile pulled up one corner of his mouth like a fish-
hook.

He vaulted the wall, his boots kicking up an awful lot of dust and dead
grass. With a keen eye he looked over the simple headstones and the
mounds in front of them, saw that most of them were sunk with age instead
of reaching upwards. Some had metal grilles over them, slowly rusting. In
disgust, he kicked a largish rock and heard it strike against the timber of the
church. Sweet Bobby stalked along one side of the graveyard, then turned a

right angle and paced the distance to the opposite wall. As he got to the next corner, he stopped.

A large white house, three stories high, with a broad veranda. Colourful curtains fluttered in and out of windows. A place that did not look empty or deserted; and then, flitting from one set of open French doors to the next, was a girl. Thin, knobbly knees, a white and black polka dot skirt, and tiny breasts under a washed-out t-shirt. She was singing to herself, off-key, some song he didn't recognise. Her voice cracked partway through the last word and it made him laugh.

He hitched the satchel firmly on his shoulder, and made a beeline for the tall house.

* * *

"Now, Daddy, don't look at me like that. I'll make him welcome."

Her father's expression was the one she thought of as his 'sermon face', just like he used when in the pulpit, talking about the lack of a moral compass in their community. He'd given her the heads-up, turning his mostly-bald head towards the front door just moments before the stranger's lean shape darkened the rectangle of light. Annabel stretched away from the kitchen bench so she could see all the way down the hall and take in the visitor. She kept her breathing calm, although her heart skipped, just a little.

"Hi there," he called. "Mind if I come in out of this heat?"

"Of course," she said like a polite young lady, not contradicting him about the weather coz it really was quite pleasant outside. "Would you like some lemonade? It's from our very own lemons."

"I did notice that tree hanging over the cemetery wall," he called while he paused and removed his boots before crossing the threshold. Annabel took the opportunity to gather all the condiments she needed for his beverage. By the time Bobby had sock-footed it into the bright kitchen, Annabel was pouring a tall glass of lemonade from an old crystal pitcher.

"I'm Bobby Tate," he told her—he didn't tell anyone that he was *Sweet Bobby* until the very last minute.

The girl held out the glass; rough-torn leaves of mint contrasted with the pale yellow liquid. Her hand didn't shake as their fingers brushed, and he was kind of disconcerted by that. Then again, he thought, folks had become strange since the changes; some got friendlier, some got braver, some more easily spooked.

"I'm Annabel Adams and I'm sorry the lemonade's not so cold," she said, sweeping her hair back from her face, carefully knotting the strands into a fat bun at the back of her head, then took up one of the pencils that lay on an open exercise book and jammed it through the thickly wound ball.

The girl smiled. "How do you come this way, Mr Tate? Wolf's Briar's so far from anywhere."

"Oh, I'm just a roaming soul. Besides, there's not much left out there," he said and gestured in the general direction of 'out there'. Bobby took a swig of the lemonade, then another—it was good, sweet. The girl busied herself tidying, lining the exercise book up with the edge of the counter, then closing the text book next to it.

He took Annabel Adams in like a butcher assessing a calf. She hadn't been eating particularly well, but she *had* been eating. He thought about the long-bladed knife in his satchel, but decided that could wait; he liked to get up close and personal with his food first of all. This girl was slender; she wouldn't prove too much of a challenge. Bobby knew from past experience that he would prevail—it was one of the things he liked best about himself.

He put his now-empty glass gently down on the slick surface of the bench. Or he thought he did; there was a moment when it seemed settled, then it was falling, falling, and next it was in pieces on the cool floor of grey tiles. Sweet Bobby stared at the remains as they caught the last of the light from the wide window above the sink. He could have sworn he'd placed that damned cup firmly, solidly, down on the flat expanse.

The girl was unperturbed by the loss of her glassware. She smiled at him and behind her, figures started to appear. Bobby blinked hard, once, twice, trying to focus, to make those pale pasty white things *sharpen*. But they remained quite stubbornly insubstantial—almost swirly. A big-boned man, a thin woman, two young boys—maybe twins—a girl not much older than Miss Annabel here, and finally an old woman with what looked like a shawl of cobwebs thrown jauntily around her shoulders. They looked light as gossamer, pale as angels.

"Don't worry about that, and don't worry about them—although don't you think Daddy would look best with wings? Did you like the lemonade?" asked Annabel. "Not too much sugar?"

Bobby shook his head like a dullard, tried to say 'Just right', but his tongue felt thick and slow, didn't want to form words. He grunted, which the girl was too polite to comment upon.

"Coz," she continued, "you need the sugar to cover the taste of the powder." She saw his expression and laughed. "Oh, hell, it's not poison, if that's what you're thinking, Mr Tate—that would ruin the meat." She addressed the hefty vaporous man, "Sorry, Daddy, I didn't mean to curse, I just got carried away."

The spectre nodded patiently. The woman beside him looked like an aging cheerleader and pointed at Sweet Bobby.

"Yes, Mama," she said with barely veiled impatience. "Miz Melba May Adams, pointing, pointing, pointing, just like she did in life." But Annabel stubbornly refused to pay attention, which is why Sweet Bobby fell so hard, hitting his head on the corner of the bench. Melba's movements headed into semaphore.

Annabel sighed and nodded. "Yes, Mama, I should have listened to you."

She bent over and the shades leaned forward too, so all Bobby saw was a circle of faces, staring down with various degrees of curiosity.

"It was nice to talk to you, Mr Tate, if only for a little while. My family don't say much—well, nothing really. But I do appreciate them sticking with me even after all that happened. I left them til last, you realise, because I love them; did not touch them until no one else was left in Wolf's Briar for me to take in the night. They were kind in life, and very forgiving in death. They gave up the ghost for me, so I could keep my strength up until things get better."

Bobby's eyes drooped and drooped.

"That's the temazepam, it's a hypnotic to send you off to dreamland. Tastes awful bitter though—that's why the lemonade needs so much sweetening."

Bobby tried to talk, although what he might have said he wasn't certain. He might have cursed, or maybe offered his admiration for a game well-played. He thought he might have said *You're the girl I always dreamed of.* The light from the window was dimming, the dusk creeping in like a heavy secret.

"Don't you worry, Mr Tate, you won't even know what happens to you, and I won't be so cruel as to tell you. You'll sleep forever—" She broke off, distracted by the waving of her father's head, then nodded, "You'll sleep like an innocent baby taken up to paradise. Now, isn't that the best gift anyone's ever given you?"

She smiled and as he drifted off, Bobby heard Annabel Adams's final words on the matter: "He shouldn't have thrown that rock and made all that noise."

Her family nodded in agreement.

"Nice round buttocks, juicy and firm. He'll keep in the cellar with some salting and drying. I'll get a year off him if I'm not greedy—yes, Daddy, I learned that lesson. Going to be heavy, though; pity none of you have the wherewithal to help me."

And because the words had lost all meaning for him, they sounded, to Bobby's drowsing ear, like the sweetest lullaby in the world.

ABOUT THE EDITOR

Simon Dewar ~ was born and bred in Canberra, Australia. He lives there with his wife and 3 daughters. He has fiction published in the *Bloody Parchment: The Root Cellar and Other Stories*, as well as the forthcoming anthologies *The Sea* and *Death's Realm*, from Dark Continents Publishing and Grey Matter Press, respectively. By day, he is an ICT systems engineer; by night he writes, and edits, the literature of anxiety.

You may find him on twitter: @herodfel
http://simondewar.wordpress.com

About the
Authors

Alan Baxter ~ *Author of dark fantasy, horror & sci-fi. Kung Fu instructor. Personal Trainer. Motorcyclist. Dog lover. Gamer. Heavy metal fan. Britstralian. Misanthrope.*

Alan is a Ditmar Award-nominated British-Australian author. He writes dark fantasy, horror and sci-fi, rides a motorcycle and loves his dog. He also teaches Kung Fu. He is the author of the dark urban fantasy trilogy, *Bound, Obsidian* and *Abduction* (*The Alex Caine Series*). *Bound* was released by HarperVoyager Australia in July 2014. *Obsidian* and *Abduction* are forthcoming from the same publisher.

His short fiction has appeared in *Fantasy & Science Fiction (forthcoming), Beneath Ceaseless Skies, Daily Science Fiction, Postscripts, Wily Writers* and *Midnight Echo*, among many others, and more than twenty anthologies, including the *Year's Best Australian Fantasy & Horror* (2010 and 2012).

You may find him on twitter @AlanBaxter

Or on his website: www.alanbaxteronline.com

Anna Reith ~ lives behind a keyboard in the far southwest of England, drinks far too much coffee, and writes across a range of genres, with particular emphasis on fantasy and speculative fiction. On the rare occasions she isn't writing, Anna enjoys taking long, muddy walks with her dogs, playing guitar really badly, and falling off horses. Not all at the same time, obviously.

Her website is: www.annareith.co.uk

Armand Rosamilia ~ is a New Jersey boy currently living in sunny Florida, where he writes about everyone around him getting eaten by zombies. He has over 100 releases currently available, including a few different series, like his *Dying Days* extreme zombie books. He also loves to talk in third person... because he's really that cool. He's a proud Active member of HWA.

You can find him at http://armandrosamilia.com for not only his latest releases but interviews and guest posts with other authors he likes! And e-mail him to talk about zombies, baseball and Metal: armandrosamilia@gmail.com

Icy Sedgwick ~ was born in the North East of England, and lives and works in Newcastle, where she teaches design and social media. She has been writing for over ten years, and has had several stories included in anthologies, including *Short Stack* and *Bloody Parchment: The Root Cellar & Other Stories*. She favours Gothic horror, but is not averse to writing fantasy, steampunk or historical fiction!

Icy had her first book, a pulp Western named *The Guns of Retribution*, published through Pulp Press in September 2011, and re-published through Beat to a Pulp in May 2013. Her latest novella, a horror fantasy called *The Necromancer's Apprentice*, was published by Dark Continents Publishing in March 2014. Sequels to both titles are in the pipeline, and she is also in the process of editing her YA ghost adventure about a Cavalier named Fowlis Westerby.

She spends her non-writing time working on a PhD in Film Studies, considering the use of set design in contemporary horror, with a focus on haunted house films. Icy also knits, crochets, and makes jewellery, including a new merchandise range to support her published titles. She spent some time working on paranormal investigations and is keen to infuse her fiction with the supernatural wherever possible.

She spends a lot of time using social media, so you can email her at icy@icysedgwick.com, or follow her on Twitter @IcySedgwick. Her blog is at www.icysedgwick.com, where she posts weekly free fiction, and you can find her on Facebook at www.facebook.com/miss.icy.sedgwick.

Rayne Hall ~ has published more than fifty books in several languages under several pen names with several publishers in several genres, mostly fantasy, horror and non-fiction. She is the author of the bestselling *Writer's Craft* series and editor of the *Ten Tales* anthologies.

Having lived in Germany, China, Mongolia and Nepal, she has now settled in a small dilapidated town of former Victorian grandeur on the south coast of England where she enjoys reading, gardening and long walks along the seashore. She shares her home with a black cat adopted from the cat sanctuary. His name is Sulu and he's the perfect cat for a writer—except when he claims ownership of her keyboard.

Facebook: www.facebook.com/RayneHallAuthor

Twitter: @RayneHall

She posts advice for writers, funny cartoons and cute pictures of her cat.

Chris Limb ~ is a writer and designer based in Brighton, UK. After many years hovering on the periphery of the music industry -originally just going to gigs but eventually graduating to selling t-shirts and badges plus operating the lighting rig for bands—in 2011 he published a pop memoir *I Was A Teenage Toyah Fan* which went down well with its core-audience, received good reviews and continues to sell at a steady rate.

Chris's full length novel *Comeback*—in which the UK music industry and the mythological underworld collide—is currently being submitted to agents and publishers and he recently completed work on the first draft of the follow up *Ghostdance*.

Chris reviews books and audiobooks for the British Fantasy Society and has blogged on a regular basis since mid-2009. In addition he writes short stories a number of which have been published over the past 18 months with more to come over the next six months.

When time allows Chris also plays bass guitar in a couple of bands as well as performing random acts of web and graphic design for a diverse selection of clients in the comedy and theatre scenes.

You can find him at www.chrislimb.com or on Twitter @catmachine

Toby Bennett ~ was born in 1976 in Cape Town, South Africa. He holds a degree in philosophy from the University of Cape Town. Like many writers he has had a varied career that has included graphic and web design, database administration and technical writing. His true passion lies in creative writing and to date he has written eight novels and appeared in a few collections of short stories, including the *Bloody Parchment* and *Dark Harvest* anthologies. He has a story in the upcoming anthology *The Sea* and is looking forward to the release of his serialized novel—Viral, co-written with Benjamin Knox. (Release date to be announced).

His website is www.thedragontower.co.za.

S.G. Larner ~ is a denizen of sunny Brisbane, Australia, where she wrangles three children and complains about the heat. As an antidote to her relatively mundane life she revels in exploring the dark underbelly of the world through her short fiction and poetry.

Her work has appeared in Aurealis, SQ Mag, Tincture Journal, Vine Leaves Literary Journal, and the Grey Matter Press anthology *Equilibrium Overturned*, among others. Upcoming publications include *Fictionvale Episode 4* and *Phantazein*, a new anthology by Fablecroft Publishing.

In her non-existent spare time she knits, sews, runs, bakes, grows things and co-ordinates a school library.

You can find her at http://foregoreality.wordpress.com and on twitter: @StaceySarasvati.

J.C. Michael ~ lives in rural North Yorkshire with his wife, who encourages him to write, and his young son, who distracts him from getting on with it.

His debut novel, *Discoredia*, was published by Books of the Dead Press in 2013, and his flash fiction piece, *Insufficient*, won the 2014 St. Valentine's Day Massacre Competition run by Grey Matter Press.

Ramsey Campbell ~ The *Oxford Companion to English Literature* describes Ramsey Campbell as "Britain's most respected living horror writer". He has been given more awards than any other writer in the field, including the Grand Master Award of the World Horror Convention, the Lifetime Achievement Award of the Horror Writers Association and the Living Legend Award of the International Horror Guild.

Among his novels are *The Face That Must Die*, *Incarnate*, *Midnight Sun*, *The Count of Eleven*, *Silent Children*, *The Darkest Part of the Woods*, *The Overnight*, *Secret Story*, *The Grin of the Dark*, *Thieving Fear*, *Creatures of the Pool*, *The Seven Days of Cain*, *Ghosts Know* and *The Kind Folk*. Forthcoming are *Think Yourself Lucky* and *Thirteen Days at Sunset Beach*, and he is working on a trilogy, *The Three Births of Daoloth*. *Needing Ghosts*, *The Last Revelation of Gla'aki* and *The Pretence* are novellas. His collections include *Waking Nightmares*, *Alone with the Horrors*, *Ghosts and Grisly Things*, *Told by the Dead*, *Just Behind You* and *Holes for Faces*, and his non-fiction is collected as *Ramsey Campbell, Probably*. His novels *The Nameless* and *Pact of the Fathers* have been filmed in Spain. His regular columns appear in *Dead Reckonings* and *Video Watchdog*. He is the President of the Society of Fantastic Films.

Ramsey Campbell lives on Merseyside with his wife Jenny. His pleasures include classical music, good food and wine, and whatever's in that pipe. His web site is at www.ramseycampbell.com.

Brett Bruton ~ writes exclusively during the hours that are most inconvenient for him. As such, the majority of his editing process involves removing curse words. Brett writes horror because comedy is too difficult and 'blood' is easy to spell.

Find him on twitter: @BrettRexB

Karen Runge ~ was born in Paris, France. The daughter of a diplomat, her family lived in France and then Gabon before returning to their native South Africa when she was a young child.

She is a horror writer, sometimes an artist, and works teaching adults English as a second language. Her works have appeared in Shock Totem, Pseudopod, Something Wicked, Pantheon magazine, Structo, and Sirens Call, among others. She lives in Beijing, China, with a wonderful Italian. You can find her at karenrunge.wordpress.com.

Tom Dullemond ~ stumbled out of university with a double degree in Medieval/Renaissance studies and Software Engineering. One of these degrees got him a job and he has been writing and working in IT ever since. Tom writes primarily short fiction across all genres, including literary fiction and the occasional poem. He co-authored *The Machine Who Was Also a Boy*, the first in a series of philosophical fantasy adventures for middle-grade students, and writes a regular flash fiction column for The Helix science magazine.

He is currently involved with the www.streetreads.com project, delivering a Choose-Your-Own-Adventure style location-based story for the Brisbane City Council, as well as featuring in the forthcoming *'Unfettered'* anthology by Tiny Owl Workshop.

His website is www.tomdullemond.com and he can be found on Twitter @cacotopos.

Wendy Hammer ~ teaches literature and composition at a community college. Her stories can be found in the anthology *Gaia: Shadows and Breath* (Pantheon Magazine) and on *Crooked/Shift*, *Liquid Imagination*, and *Every Day Fiction*. Her trilogy of dark urban fantasy novellas, *Cross Cutting*, has been acquired by Apocalypse Ink Productions.

She can be found online at her website www.wendyhammer.com and on twitter @Wendyhammer13.

Wendy lives in Indiana with her husband.

Shane McKenzie ~ is the author of *Infinity House*, *All You Can Eat*, *Bleed on Me*, *Jacked*, *Addicted to the Dead*, *Muerte Con Carne*, *Escape from Shit Town* (co-authored with Sam W. Anderson and Erik Williams), *Fat Off Sex and Violence*, *Pus Junkies*, *Stork*, *Fairy*, *The Bingo Hall*, *Parasite Deep*, and many more to come. He also writes comics for Zenescope Entertainment.

He wrote the script for a short film entitled M is for Matador, filmed by LuchaGore Productions, which was selected by DraftHouse Films to be included in the DVD *The ABCs of Death 1.5*. LuchaGore Productions will be filming a short film based on the first chapter of his novel *Muerte Con Carne*, entitled *El Gigante*.

He lives in Austin, TX with his wife and daughter. He will find you and he will cut you.

His website is: www.shanemckenzie.org

Sarah Read ~ writes, reads, and knits near Rocky Mountain National Park. She is fiction editor for Pantheon Magazine. Her work can be found in Black Static, Revolt Daily, Vine Leaves Literary Journal, and forthcoming in anthologies from Dark House Press and Thunderdome Press.

You can follow her on twitter @inkwellmonster.

Benjamin Knox ~ rogue author, wanders the post-apocalyptic landscape that is modern publishing, never staying long in one place lest the degenerate mutants get his scent and devour him to the bone. Relying only on his wits and armed with his trusty keyboard he flits from the outposts of genre press, braving the radioactive, cannibal infested, wastes of indie publishing that lay between. During his adventures he delivers up tales of the strange, eerie and unsettling. Dare you open those pages and glean what is within?

For further strangeness find him at: benjaminknox.net
Pulpocalypse.tumblr.com

John Everson ~ is the Bram Stoker Award-winning author of the novels *Covenant* (2004), *Sacrifice* (2007), *The 13th* (2009), *Siren* (2010), and *The Pumpkin Man* (2011). All of these novels were released in paperback by Dorchester/Leisure Books. Limited hardcover editions were also issued from Delirium Books, Necro Publications and Bad Moon Books. Covenant, Sacrifice and Siren have been translated or are in the process of being translated and released in Poland, Turkey, France and Germany.

John's sixth novel, *NightWhere,* was released by Samhain Publishing in 2012.

Over the past 20 years, John's short fiction has appeared in more than 50 magazines, including Space & Time, Dark Discoveries and Grue, as well as in a couple dozen anthologies, most recently in *Necro Files: Two Decades of Extreme Horror, The Green Hornet Casebook, Kolchak: The Night Stalker Casebook, Best New Werewolf Tales (Vol. 1), Best New Vampire Tales (Vol. 1), Best New Zombie Tales (Vol. 2)* and *Fell Beasts.* His short stories have also been translated and published into Italian, Polish and French. A wide selection of his short fiction has been collected in five short story collections: *Deadly Nightlusts* (Blasphemous Books, 2010), *Creeptych* (Delirium Books 2010), *Needles & Sins* (Necro Books, 2007), *Vigilantes of Love* (Twilight Tales, 2003) and *Cage of Bones & Other Deadly Obsessions* (Delirium Books, 2000).

"Letting Go," one of the short stories from *Needles & Sins* was nominated for a 2007 Bram Stoker Award and three other short stories from the collection have been included in the Honorable Mention List of the annual *Year's Best Fantasy & Horror* anthology co-edited by Ellen Datlow.

Angela Slatter ~ specializes in Dark Fantasy and Horror fiction. She is the author of the Aurealis Award-winning *The Girl with No Hands and Other Tales*, the World Fantasy Award finalist *Sourdough and Other Stories*, and the Aurealis finalist *Midnight and Moonshine* (with Lisa L. Hannett). Angela's short stories have appeared in such writerly venues as *The Mammoth Book of New Horror #22, Fantasy*, Nightmare and Lightspeed *Magazines*, Lady Churchill's Rosebud *Wristlet, Fearie Tales, A Book of Horrors, Steampunk II: Steampunk Reloaded*, and Australian and US Best Of anthologies.

She is the first Australian to win a British Fantasy Award (for "The Coffin-Maker's Daughter" in *A Book of Horrors*, Stephen Jones, ed.).

In 2013 she was awarded one of the inaugural Queensland Writers Fellowships. She has an MA and a PhD in Creative Writing, and is a graduate of Clarion South 2009 and the Tin House Summer Writers Workshop 2006.

Forthcoming in 2014 are the collections *The Bitterwood Bible and Other Recountings* (a prequel to Sourdough and Other Stories) from Tartarus Press, and The Female Factory (with Lisa L. Hannett), the last in the Twelfth Planet Press "Twelve Planets" series.

Angela has recently finished an urban fantasy novel Vigil, (based on the short story Brisneyland by Night) and has started the sequel, Corpselight. She is also completing work on her Queensland Writers Fellowship mosaic novel, The Tallow-Wife and Other Tales.

AVAILABLE FROM
BOOKS OF THE DEAD PRESS

Tonia Brown - Lucky Stiff: Zombie Gigolo
Peter Lyles was unremarkable in life but unforgettable in death. After over-dosing, Peter's friends turn him into a zombie with the help of "sex-magic" Voodoo. His unforgettable adventure takes him from bedroom to bed-room, giving him a career as the hottest gigolo not quite alive, while he de-nies his hunger for human flesh.

Justin Robinson - Undead On Arrival
Glen Novak is a dead man. Unfortunately for the scumbag who killed him, Novak will keep on cracking skulls until he finds the piece of trash that set him up, or is turned into a walking sack of rotten meat.

Steve Kuhn - We Are The Plague:
Dext of the Dead, Book 1
Dext is a regular man in an irregular situation. The undead plague has deci-mated the population, but pockets of survivors still remain. A battered mili-tary search for survivors while scientists work frantically to control the spread. The clock is ticking… if he can keep running.

Steve Kuhn - We Are The Infected:
Dext of the Dead, Book 2
Dext and his crew are reeling from the losses incurred during their stay at The Haven and are on the run. A military unit known as Kilo Company appears to be the group's best bet for survival, but they are miles ahead and the gap is widening. Everything is not what it seems.

Steve Kuhn - We Are The Entombed:
Dext of the Dead, Book 3
The dead have permeated every square inch of the country, leaving the sur-vivors desperate for commodities. Roving bands of raiders and small, inde-pendent communities pose serious threats to one another, much like the increasing numbers of ravenous, shambling corpses.

Steve Kuhn - We Are The Extinction:
Dext of the Dead, Book 4

Tensions mount for Dext and his crew as they travel west in search of the elusive military unit known as Kilo Company. Characters, both good and evil, affect the course of events. Threats wait around every corner. A truth has been revealed: mankind is more monstrous than the living dead.

Steve Kuhn - We Are The End:
Dext of the Dead, Book 5

The battle for Vegas is done, but not without heavy casualties and broken loyalties. Dishonesty within the group and mental instability weakens the bonds of family, making them vulnerable. One member will break an unspoken rule and thrust the entire group to the brink of self-destruction.

Duncan McGeary - Death of an Immortal:
Vampire Evolution Trilogy 1

The most powerful and feared vampire disappeared at the height of his powers and passed into legend. Most vampires think he's dead. He is not dead.

Duncan McGeary - Rule of Vampire:
Vampire Evolution Trilogy 2

Jamie is on the run. Nobody taught her how to be a vampire; no one told her the Rules of Vampire. How was she supposed to know her limits? Now the vampire hunters want her dead.

Duncan McGeary - Blood of Gold:
Vampire Evolution Trilogy 3

Terrill was the most ruthless vampire, but he evolved into a Golden Vampire, renouncing violence. He didn't know that the evolution was directed by forces bigger than himself.

Duncan McGeary - Led to the Slaughter

Trapped in the Sierra Nevada without food, The Donner Party are led to the slaughter. After being manipulated into a string of bad decisions, the travelers, frozen and abandoned, are preyed upon by werewolves in their midst—the very people they thought were friends.

TS Alan - The Romero Strain

A group of New Yorkers is chased into the city's underground by a zombie horde. Along their subterranean journey, they gather survivors while traveling to Grand Central Terminal, where they believe help will be found.

John F.D. Taff – Kill/Off

When David Benning is blackmailed by a shadowy organization known only as The Group, he's thrust into a world of guns, payoffs, and killing unknown, seemingly ordinary people. As he becomes more enmeshed, he begins to grasp The Group's true motives.

J.C. Michael - Discoredia

As the year draws to a close, a mysterious stranger makes a proposition to club owner. It's a deal involving a drug called Pandemonium. The good news: the drug is free. The bad news: it comes with a heavy price. Euphoria and ecstasy. Death and depravity. All come together at Discoredia.

James Roy Daley – Authors & Publishers Must Die!

No punches are pulled in this nonfiction title, which is filled to the rim with straightforward, practical advice for writers while exploring what it's like to be on the other side of the desk. A must read for every author.

Weston Kincade – A Life of Death, Book One

Homicide detective Alex Drummond is confronted with the past through his son's innocent question. Alex's tale of his troubled senior year unfolds revealing loss, drunken abuse, and mysterious visions of murder and demonic children.

Weston Kincade – A Life of Death, Book Two: The Golden Bulls

Detective Drummond traces his steps in the years since his childhood, but a mysterious serial killer is on the loose, annually performing ritual sacrifices. Alex's skills at reliving the brutal murders are put to the test when so little is left of the victims.

Julie Hutchings - Running Home

Death hovers around Ellie Morgan like the friend nobody wants. She doesn't belong in snow-swept Ossipee, at a black tie party—but that is where she is, and where he is: Nicholas French, the man who mystifies her with the impossible knowledge of her troubled soul.

John F.D. Taff – The Bell Witch

A historical horror novel/ghost story based on what is perhaps the most well-documented poltergeist case to occur in the United States. The Bell Witch is, at once, a historical novel, a ghost story, a horror story, and a love story all rolled into one.

Justin Robinson - Everyman

Ian Covey is a doppelganger. A mimic. A shapeshifter. He can replace anyone he wants by becoming a perfect copy; taking the victim's face, his home, his family. His life. No longer a man but a hungry void, Ian Covey is a monster. Virtue has a veil, a mask, and evil has a thousand faces.

Mark Matthews - On the Lips of Children

A family man named Macon plans to run a marathon, but falls prey to people who dwell in an underground drug-smuggling tunnel. They raise their twin children in a way he couldn't imagine: skinning victims for food and money. And Macon and his family are next.

Bracken MacLeod - Mountain Home

Lyn works at an isolated roadside diner, where a retired combat veteran stages an assault. Surviving the sniper's bullets is only the beginning. She establishes herself as the disputed leader of a diverse group that is at odds with the situation. Will she—or anyone else—survive the attack?

Gary Brandner - The Howling

Karyn and her husband Roy had come to the peaceful California village of Drago to escape the savagery of the city. But the village had a most unsavory history. Unexplained disappearances, sudden deaths. People just vanished, never to be found.

Gary Brandner - The Howling II

For Karyn, it was the howling that heralded the nightmare in Drago… the nightmare that had joined her husband Roy to the she-wolf Marcia, and should have ended forever with the fire. But it hadn't. Roy and Marcia were still alive, and deadly… and thirsty for vengeance.

Gary Brandner - The Howling III

They are man. And they are beast. They stalk the night, eyes aflame, teeth flashing in vengeance. Malcolm, the young one, must choose between the way of the human and the howling of the wolf. Those who share his blood want to make him one of them. Those who fear him want him dead.

James Roy Daley - Into Hell

Stephenie Page and her daughter Carrie pull off an empty highway at a gas station. Carrie enters the building first. When Stephenie steps inside she discovers that the restaurant is a slaughterhouse. There are dead bodies everywhere. The worst part is… Carrie is suddenly missing.

James Roy Daley - Terror Town

Hardcore horror at its best: Killer on the warpath. Monsters on the street. Vampires in the night. Zombies on the hunt. Welcome to Terror Town. The place where no one is safe. Nothing is sacred. All will die. All will suffer.

James Roy Daley - The Dead Parade

Within the hour, James will witness the suicide of his closest friend, be responsible for countless murders, and become a fugitive from the police. In the shadow of his mind, a demon lurks. Bloodlust is a virus and it's infecting his logic. Survival is not an option.

Tonia Brown - Badass Zombie Road Trip

Jonah has seven days to find his best friend's soul, or lose his own, dragging a zombie across the country with a stripper who has an agenda of her own, while being pursued for a crime he didn't commit... and dealing with Satan. Two thousand miles. Seven days. Two souls. One zombie. Satan.

Matt Hults - Husk

When Mallory moves to a small town, her new home won't be as boring as she'd feared. Who is the dark figure watching her? What is the shape hanging in the shadows of the barn? And why has someone begun digging up graves? In the end, one night will decide if the dead will rise.

Tim Lebbon - Berserk

On a dark night Tom begins to unearth the mass grave where he hopes— and fears—that he will find his son's remains. Instead, he finds madness: corpses in chains and dead bodies that move. And one little girl, dead and rotting, who promises to help Tom find what he's looking for...

Best New Zombie Tales - Volume One

Award winning authors and New York Times Bestsellers come together in this fantastic zombie anthology. Includes great tales by Ray Garton, Jonathan Maberry, Kealan Patrick Burke, Jeff Strand, Robert Swartwood, Gary McMahon, Kim Paffenroth... and so much more.

Best New Zombie Tales - Volume Two

Award winning authors and New York Times Bestsellers come together in this fantastic zombie anthology. Includes great tales by David Niall Wilson, Rio Youers, Nate Kenyon, Tim Waggoner, Narrelle M. Harris, John Everson, Mort Castle... and so much more.

Best New Zombie Tales - Volume Three
Award winning authors and New York Times Bestsellers come together in this fantastic zombie anthology. Includes great tales by Simon Wood, Joe McKinney, Tim Lebbon, Nancy Kilpatrick, Paul Kane, Jeremy C. Shipp, Nate Southard... and so much more.

Best New Werewolf Tales - Volume One
Award winning authors and New York Times Bestsellers come together in this fantastic werewolf anthology. Includes great tales by Jonathan Maberry, John Everson, Michael Laimo, James Roy Daley, Douglas Smith, David Niall Wilson, Nina Kiriki Hoffman... and so much more.

Best New Vampire Tales - Volume One
Award winning authors and New York Times Bestsellers come together in this fantastic vampire anthology. Includes great tales by Michael Laimo, David Niall Wilson, Tim Waggoner, John Everson, Don Webb, Jay Caselberg, Nancy Kilpatrick... and so much more.

James Roy Daley - Zombie Kong
Big. Bad. Heavy. Hungry. While a 50-foot tall zombie gorilla smashes the hell out of a small town, Candice Wanglund drags her son Jake through the hazardous streets in an attempt to get away from the man who is determined to kill them.

John F.D. Taff - Little Deaths
Named the #1 Horror Collection of 2012 by Horror Talk
Named Top 5 books of 2012 by AndyErupts
You think you've got bad dreams? Consider author John F.D. Taff's nightmares. Taff has the kind of nightmares no one really wants. But it's nightmares like these that give him plenty of ideas to explore; ideas that he's turned into the short stories he shares in his new collection.

John L. French - Paradise Denied
One of the best collections you'll ever read. There isn't a single story that feels like filler. Vampires, zombies, tough cops, faeries, heroes, or superscientists, John French has got a tale for you, and it's amazing. Readers agree: this is the book you won't be able to put down.

James Roy Daley - 13 Drops Of Blood
Thirteen tales of horror, suspense, and imagination. Enter the gore-soaked exhibit, the train of terror, the graveyard of the haunted. Meet the scientist of the monsters, the woman with the thing living inside her, the living dead. Quality horror with a flair for the hardcore. Not for the squeamish.

Zombie Kong - Anthology

Zombies are bad, but ZOMBIE KONG is worse. Way worse. Big. Bad. Heavy. Hungry. This is the most original zombie anthology of all time. In the jungles, in the Arctic, in the cities, in the towns, Zombie Kong rules them all. Other zombies must bow to their god… ZOMBIE KONG!

Paul Kane - Pain Cages

Reminiscent of Stephen King's classic best-selling book Different Seasons, Paul Kane gives us an unforgettable collection of four novella-size stories. Each story is refreshingly original and delivers an emotional impact that is rarely seen in today's literature. Speculative fiction at its best.

Matt Hults - Anything Can Be Dangerous

Contains four amazing stories: Anything Can be Dangerous (the simple things in life can kill), Through the Valley of Death (a dark tale that will make you remember fear), The Finger (zombie literature has never been so extraordinary), and Feeding Frenzy (lunchtime in a place called Hell).

Bill Howard - 10 Minutes From Home

When a viral outbreak hits Toronto, Denny and Thom find themselves trapped in a town called Pontypool. As the streets begin to teem with violence, they must first find safety, and a way out of the now deadly metropolis.

Classic - Vampire Tales

Includes: J. Sheridan Lefanu / Bram Stoker / M. R. James / F. Benson / Algernon Blackwood / F. Marion Crawford / Mary E. Wilkins Freeman / James Robinson Planche / Johann Ludwig Tieck

ACKNOWLEDGEMENTS

"Burning", copyright 2010 by Rayne Hall.
Originally appeared (in a greatly different form) in the E-zine Byzarium.

"Spirits Having Flown", copyright 2003 by John Everson.
Originally published in MOTA 3: Courage, by Triple Tree Publishing.

"Digging Deep", copyright 2007 by Ramsey Campbell.
Originally appeared in Phobic, edited by Andy Murray.

Fit Camp, copyright 2010 by Shane McKenzie.
Originally appeared in Dark Recesses magazine.

CPSIA information can be obtained at www.ICGtesting.com
Printed in the USA
BVOW02s2308210415

397174BV00017B/190/P